PRAISE FOR

# THE

# TEMPS

"This boiling-pot of a novel is a vivid experiment in millennial disillusion-ment...Simultaneously a dark dystopic and a hilarious tale of bureaucratic absurdity, *The Temps* is bizarre—and unexpectedly fun."

—*Booklist* (starred review)

"A smart critique of modern life."

—*Publishers Weekly*

"DeYoung has taken a familiar end-of-the-world-as-we-know-it theme and made it something uniquely his own. Readers won't soon forget it."

—*New York Journal of Books*

"Andrew DeYoung's *The Temps* is a comic adventure for our uncertain times, a mashup of *Then We Came to the End* and *World War Z*. The result is a surprisingly funny and heartfelt satire of modern employment that should please fans of literary and speculative fiction alike."

—Adam O'Fallon Price, author of *The Hotel Neversink*

"*The Temps* is a unique take on both the corporate conspiracy plot and the zombie-apocalypse thriller. It's fast-paced, darkly funny, and full of unex-pected turns. It also holds incisive and illuminating social commentary, providing windows of insight amidst the heart-pounding action."

—Elvia Wilk, author of *Oval*

"*The Temps* is equal parts dark satire, probing character study, and fast-paced thriller. DeYoung's mesmerizing writing is by turns wry, muscular, and probing. This is an apocalyptic page-turner that asks profound ques-tions about human nature, about who we are and who we have the poten-tial to become. DeYoung's vision is both vibrant and prophetic; I couldn't put this novel down."

—Kaethe Schwehn, author of *The Rending and the Nest*

"Andrew DeYoung is a sage storyteller with the incredibly rare gift of being able to write with both poignancy and wit. *The Temps* is both terrifying and hilarious–it absolutely deserves a high-paying full-time job with excellent benefits."

—John Jodzio, author of *Knockout* and *If You Lived Here You'd Already Be Home*

"Part Great American Office Novel and part apocalyptic thriller, *The Temps* taps into the search for meaning post-college and combines it with the sharp urgency of the best dystopian fiction. With wry observations about corporate life and careful attention to the delicate intricacies of human relationships, DeYoung reminds us that the only thing worse than a meaningless temp job is a meaningless temp job during the end of the world."

—Bryan Bliss, National Book Award Longlisted author of *We'll Fly Away*

"What *The Temps* profoundly illustrates is that the most gripping science fiction doesn't emerge from the unknown, but from what we know all too well and choose to look away from. That we choose to look away at our own peril is what makes The Temps impossible to put down."

—Ben Tanzer, author of *Orphans*, *UPSTATE* and *Lost in Space*

# THE
# TEMPS

# THE
# TEMPS

## ANDREW DEYOUNG

Keylight Books
an imprint of Turner Publishing Company
Nashville, Tennessee

www.turnerpublishing.com

The Temps

Jacket design by Lauren Peters-Collaer
Book design by Susan Ramundo

Library of Congress Cataloging-in-Publication Data

Names: DeYoung, Andrew, author.
Title: The temps / by Andrew DeYoung.
Description: Nashville, Tennessee : Turner Publishing Company, [2022] |
    Identifiers: LCCN 2021026144 (print) | LCCN 2021026145 (ebook) |
    ISBN 9781684427611 (hardcover) | ISBN 9781684427604 (paperback) |
    ISBN 9781684427628 (ebook)
Subjects: LCGFT: Dystopian fiction. | Thrillers (Fiction)
Classification: LCC PS3604.E9345 T46 2022 (print) | LCC PS3604.E9345
    (ebook) | DDC 813/.6—dc23
LC record available at https://lccn.loc.gov/2021026144
LC ebook record available at https://lccn.loc.gov/2021026145

Printed in Canada

# THE
# TEMPS

# ONE

The sky on the morning of Jacob Elliott's first day at Delphi Enterprises was clear and bright, untroubled by any portent of the catastrophe that was to come.

And yet it wouldn't be accurate to say the day was cheery. Not to Jacob, driving down a busy freeway surrounded by box stores and strip malls and the vast, untamed scrubland that dominated the outskirts of the city. The slanting early light had a strange quality to it that seemed to drain everything of its color, transforming the landscape into a kind of wasteland in Jacob's squinting eyes. As his car came closer to Delphi—a huge, nondescript office complex whose reflective windows shimmered like a corporate mirage in the distance—the traffic on the highway slowed, then stopped. The emotion that rose up in Jacob's chest at that moment was one of utter desolation. He was a piece of human flotsam in a river of metal and glass, inching toward a destination made of the same dead substances.

Jacob wasn't looking forward to his new job at Delphi. The position he had taken was a temporary one in the company's mail room. The fact that he'd been reduced to this kind of work—that he *needed* the job, even if he didn't *want* it—filled him with shame. He was a college graduate, for God's sake. A star student in the department of English, the subject in which he'd majored. His senior thesis ("'The Game Is Afoot': Game Theory and Social Control in Late-Victorian Detective Fiction") had been published in an academic journal next to the work of PhD students, tenured professors, and post-docs. And he'd been waitlisted in several prestigious graduate programs (though not, a cruel voice from deep within his mind always reminded him, ultimately accepted to any of them, not even his safeties).

But that was a long time ago, three years since graduation, during which time Jacob had worked a series of low-paying and sometimes no-paying jobs: barista, clerk, intern, assistant. Over roughly the same period he'd shared an apartment in the city with a college friend. A former friend, really—their relationship had been strained by the minor stresses of living together. Dishes piled in the sink. Sharing a bathroom. The mechanics of bringing girls over. Jacob's perpetual inability to make his half of the rent. Then, four months ago, the roommate—a computer science major when they were still in school—landed an IT job with steady pay and informed Jacob that he'd be moving to a nicer place with his girlfriend. Jacob took out a Craigslist ad for a new roommate, couch-surfed for a couple weeks, then ultimately left the city and landed in his parents' basement.

Jacob once felt that he was destined for some kind of greatness, had dreamed of fame as a writer or intellectual of some sort, but the past three years had taken their toll. Now, the thing he craved most was the same thing he'd once disdained: a white-collar job as a cog in the corporatist/capitalist machine, with a salary, health benefits, and a 401k. And so, when notification of the temp listing—a job in an office, requiring no skills or experience—had buzzed on his smartphone, he applied for it at once. It may have been beneath him, may have been at a company whose business he didn't even understand (the website said something about *research*, and *intelligence*, and *analytics*), but it was at least adjacent to the kind of life he wanted: not quite fame and fortune, but not another unpaid internship or fast-food job, either.

• • •

Jacob parked in a leveled concrete structure off the freeway, then began walking toward the Delphi corporate campus. He joined a horde of other workers streaming toward the building, men and women in their twenties and thirties wearing pressed clothes in solid whites and darks, messenger bags slung over their shoulders, sipping at coffee in aluminum travel mugs. Clipped to the workers' clothes or clutched in their hands were black security badges in clear plastic casings. Mostly the crowd trudged in silence, but here and there the workers bid each other a good morning when they found themselves walking next to someone they knew. Jacob, feeling out of place in a plaid shirt and corduroys with no badge clipped to his belt loop, overheard a young man and a young woman speaking to each other.

"You coming to my status?"

"Can't, I've got a stakeholder meeting. We've got a scope-creep issue on the variable data extraction project and I need to force a decision from the exec sponsor."

"What department? Business analytics?"

"No, not analytics—intelligence. A feasibility report for the build is due to development in a week, but research needs to review it first."

Jacob tried to decipher the conversation as he walked, but try as he might, he could not force the words to bloom into anything resembling meaning.

Soon he arrived with the others at the grounds of the corporate campus. The air smelled of cut grass and rotting lilacs. Trudging down the sidewalk toward the office building, he came to a waist-high sign bearing the company's logo: "DELPHI" in sans-serif capital letters, enclosed by a swooping circle that was jagged and blotchy at the edges, as though it had been painted with a brush on a cloth canvas. This circle, in particular, was familiar to Jacob even before he'd applied to work at the company, a mark ubiquitous on stadiums and public buildings and lists of corporate sponsors for nonprofit arts organizations in the city. And yet the logo still evoked nothing specific in Jacob's mind. An empty signifier.

The building's exterior was covered entirely in opaque, reflective glass, impossible to look at without squinting in the brightness of the morning. Jacob kept his eyes down until he reached the building, then pushed through the doors, where he was startled by a puff of air whooshing through his hair as he stepped inside. He stood in a small antechamber, with another set of doors leading to the Delphi lobby. When the first door closed behind him his ears popped, as though the antechamber was pressurized and the seal was being broken and unbroken every time a new worker entered the building. Past the second set of doors, the workers tapped their black badges against the top of waist-high gates and passed through to the other side as security guards in navy blue suits looked on.

Jacob hesitated. He'd scarcely looked at the email inviting him to report for his new job at Delphi, registering only his start date. This was a pattern with Jacob, a fatal flaw: his inability to focus on the details of things he didn't care about. Student loan payment deadlines, counting out the cash drawer when he had a closing shift at Starbucks, temp jobs he needed but didn't really want. He'd simply assumed that when he arrived at Delphi, what he should do next would be clear. It wasn't.

He looked around the lobby and found a young woman—blonde, attractive—sitting behind a large transparent desk curved in the shape of a parenthesis. She looked down, absorbed in something on her computer screen. He walked toward the desk and waited for her to look up. Then, when she didn't, he said in a timid voice: "Excuse me?"

"Yes?"

"I'm Jacob Elliott. I'm working here. It's my first day."

"New hires are supposed to report to the Alpha entrance," the young woman said. "This is Epsilon."

"Oh," Jacob said. "Oh. Alpha entrance. I didn't know."

"It should've been in your hiring letter."

"Where's the Alpha entrance?"

"Hold on." She tapped at a few keys on her computer. She looked at the screen for a few seconds, then a wry smile came to her face and she looked up at Jacob again.

"What?" Jacob asked. There was something affectionate and a little condescending in the young woman's smile, as if she and Jacob knew each other and Jacob, in his confusion, was akin to a doddering but beloved old uncle. This trace of kindness in the young woman's expression, rather than alleviating Jacob's anxiety, only deepened his overwhelming feeling that he did not belong in this place, that he'd soon be found out, that he was humiliating or betraying himself in a fundamental way simply by being here in the corporate headquarters of Delphi Enterprises.

"Everything's fine," the young woman said. "It says right here in your psychometric profile that you'd probably come to the wrong entrance. All the receptionists from Alpha to Omicron have been authorized to let you into the building. I just didn't think—" She stopped herself short, shook her head, then gave a marveling laugh. "I shouldn't be surprised by now. They always know."

This mystifying monologue sent several questions bursting in Jacob's brain, but he voiced none of them.

"You probably need a security badge, yeah?"

Jacob nodded, and the young woman went for a drawer, then slid a red plastic card across the desk toward him.

"Red?" Jacob asked. "All the security badges I've seen so far are black."

"But you're a temp, right? Temp equals red badge. Black for execs, full-time employees, interns."

"Even interns get black? What color's yours?"

The wry smile again. The young woman showed Jacob her badge. Black.

"It says here you're to report to the mail room in the T-wing."

"T-wing?" Jacob could think of no system of navigation in which *T* was the first letter of a direction.

The young woman went back to the drawer, slapped a map of the building on the desktop, and made an *X* on it with a red pen.

"This is where you are," she said. "Epsilon entrance, P-wing. And this is where you're going." She put another *X* on the other side of the map. "Mail room, T-wing. It's that way."

She pointed past the security gates and down a broad concourse.

"Better hurry. It's a big building. You don't want to be late." Then she turned back to her computer screen.

Jacob sensed the conversation was over.

• • •

Jacob walked for what seemed like a long time. The Delphi building was vast, cathedral-like, with vaulting glass walls and high ceilings. The map the young woman had given him showed a building shaped like a triangle, angling sharply back on itself to enclose an interior courtyard with volley-ball courts, an outdoor picnic area, and an amphitheater. But the wide concourse Jacob was walking down gave him no view of the courtyard; the wall of windows on his left looked out to the freeway and the exurban sprawl beyond, while to his right was a solid stone wall with the occasional door and escalators leading up, and up, and up.

The concourse itself was as wide as the thoroughfare of an indoor shopping mall. At intervals Jacob passed ornate fountains, abstract sculptures, sitting areas populated by more workers tapping at laptops perched on their knees, and food courts with high-end fast-casual chains. At one food court, an aproned worker stepped from behind the counter of a Wolfgang Puck Express pushing a garbage bin on wheels. He rolled the bin to an exterior exit door, dumpsters visible through the glass beyond, and tapped his security badge to get out of the building. Jacob looked.

Red, like his. Jacob eyed his own temp-worker badge and then slipped it into his pocket. He kept walking.

The map didn't offer any scale for distance, but judging by how long Jacob walked down a single concourse before reaching a turn, each side of the triangular building was at least a half-mile long. Each side was also given a name on the map: T-wing, P-wing, and C-wing, yet another letter pointing to no clear organizational logic. Jacob walked the whole length of P-wing and arrived at T-wing after about ten minutes. Consulting the room number the young woman at reception had marked on the map, Jacob pushed through a door and stepped from the concourse into a room full of cubicles. Beyond the desks loomed ceiling-high windows, their view of the courtyard dimmed by a slight, almost imperceptible tint.

The office was surprisingly empty of workers. A few sat at their desks, but most of the cubicles were unoccupied. Instead, the Delphi workforce seemed to have moved even further inward toward the center of the triangle as Jacob had walked its perimeter. An army of Delphi employees now trudged across the grass in the central courtyard, streaming like ants from every interior exit of the three-sided building and walking to some place of convergence.

Jacob froze, wondering if he'd missed some essential instruction in the time he'd been wandering the building. Should he have been walking to the courtyard with the other employees? Near to where he stood, two male workers rose from their desks and began talking as they went together toward the door leading outside. Jacob trailed them to hear what they were talking about.

"You think Brandt is going to speak?" one asked.

"That's what I heard."

"So it's gotta be something big, then."

"Yeah, something big."

"Bad or good?"

"Good. For sure, good."

"IPO?"

"Nah, Brandt doesn't want to go public. Something major from product development, my guess."

"Which department, you think? Manufacturing?"

"Manufacturing hasn't had any real blockbusters since smart alloy. I'm guessing analytics. The chaos systems thing, probably—that's Brandt's pet project. I do lunch once a month with a coder from the department, last we talked she said she heard they were on the verge of a breakthrough."

"What, she's not even on the project?"

"No, but shit gets around."

"What's the real-world application, even? I heard Brandt has been real cagey about that. Fired a junior VP for even asking what they were working on, someone told me."

"He'll tell us today. Roll it out, reveal the application. It'll be a game changer. Bigger than smart alloy, bigger than psychometrics, bigger than Sherpa."

"Shit, man. I can't wait."

The workers reached the door and walked into the courtyard. As before, Jacob could make no sense of this conversation, and he was left wondering more than ever what Delphi's business was. Words skittered through his mind—*manufacturing, analytics, chaos systems, smart alloy, psychometrics, Sherpa.* But he couldn't make them fit together into any coherent whole. His best guess now was that Delphi was a shell company, a massive conglomerate housing disparate businesses, bits and pieces glued together by the overpowering vision of some corporate guru. Perhaps it was this mysterious Brandt, who was rumored to be speaking at whatever event was drawing the company's employees from their desks and into the sun like a homing beacon.

Jacob moved closer to the windows and squinted through the light tint of the glass, stood on the balls of his feet to crane past the bobbing heads and see where they were going. In the distance he spotted the outdoor eating areas and volleyball courts the map had promised; beyond that the ground crested in a gentle knoll and dropped off toward the far wing of the building, the opposite side of the triangle. The workers walked over the knoll, then disappeared. Jacob turned back to the map, unfolded it. They must have been walking toward the amphitheater. On the map, the amphitheater dominated almost half the courtyard, semicircular rows of seats sloping gently down toward a stage at the northernmost point of the triangle.

Jacob moved toward the exit door and pushed. It didn't open, so he dug his security badge from his pocket and tapped it on the door. The locking mechanism beeped green and he reached to open the door, but before he could, another worker—a young woman in a black pencil skirt and vertical-striped blouse—stepped in front of him.

"Sorry," she said as she pushed through to the courtyard, her high heels sinking into the grass. "All-company meeting. Black badges only."

Jacob's cheeks burned. The young woman was about his age—beautiful, tan, flush with ambition and confidence. She'd probably majored in something practical in college, business or computer science, got an entry-level job at Delphi right out of college, was taking night classes to get her MBA. Someone who knew how the world worked, knew which paths paid and which didn't. Knowledge Jacob hadn't possessed until recently—too late.

"Oh," he mumbled, backing away. "Oh. Sorry."

"Don't worry about it," she said. "You looking for something?"

The truth burst out of his mouth before he could think to stop it. "Mail room."

She pointed as the door inched closed. Jacob turned and fled.

• • •

The mail room was empty of people except for one woman sitting on a metal stool just inside the door, her arms crossed. She was older than anyone Jacob had seen at Delphi to this point. In her late fifties or sixties, the woman looked close to retirement—mousey, bespectacled, with gray hair smoothly curled at her ears, nape, and forehead.

"You're the temp," she said.

Not a question, but Jacob answered anyway. "Yes."

"You're late. Everyone's left for the all-employee meeting. I had to stay behind for you."

"I'm sorry," Jacob said. "I went to the wrong entrance. This is a big building."

The woman eased off the stool and put her feet on the ground. She was short, the crown of her head barely reaching the height of Jacob's sternum.

"I have to go," she said. "You can't come."

"I know. I've been told."

The woman gave him an apologetic look, as though she'd picked up on Jacob's defeated tone and was embarrassed to have brought up a topic that pained him. "I thought I'd train you before I left for the meeting. Give you something to do. But now . . ." She trailed off.

"It's fine," Jacob said. "I'll just . . . wait here until you get back."

The woman sighed and looked around the room, her gaze eventually settling on a wire cart on wheels with some letters and packages stacked inside.

"Well, maybe you can deliver these while I'm gone."

She grabbed the cart, wheeled it to him, then handed him a thin stack of papers bound together with a black plastic coil. Jacob flipped through the papers; together they comprised a map of the building, more detailed than the one he'd been given at reception. Each floor, each cubicle was catalogued. The woman explained to him how to match the codes on the letters and packages to the alphanumeric coding of the cubicles, ensuring that each piece of mail was delivered to the correct recipient.

"They're all first floor, but they'll take you around the whole triangle. It should keep you busy until the meeting is over. Then let's meet back here and I'll teach you how to sort the incoming mail."

Jacob nodded, surprised to find that he was relieved to have something to do, to be useful in some small way. He still felt the work was beneath him, but having a task to complete alleviated in some small part the shame of the morning's minor humiliations, the feeling of being the only person in that bustling glass hive without a place and a purpose.

"I really have to go," the woman said. "They say Tristan Brandt might be speaking."

"He's the CEO?"

The woman gaped. "You've never heard of him?"

"No," Jacob admitted.

"He's brilliant. A genius. Sort of a recluse, though. He doesn't appear to the employees very often—hardly comes out of his office, they say—so if he's speaking today it's going to be something really big."

She moved to the door, then held it for Jacob so he could wheel the cart from the mail room to the sea of cubicles.

"Hey," he called after she'd begun to walk away. "What does Delphi do, anyway?"

"Oh, heavens," she said. "What *don't* we do?"

After she'd gone, it occurred to him that he hadn't gotten her name. He told himself he'd ask for it when she returned.

• • •

Jacob pushed the cart through workspaces and conference rooms and cafeterias, supremely alone. The office space was a patchwork of walls and hallways and doors—open floorplan desk pools, cubicle farms, private offices, kitchenettes, collaborative spaces with funky couches and white-board walls. Mostly these rooms were empty, but sometimes Jacob sensed human presences nearby. The tap of computer keys or the click of a mouse from behind a chest-height partition wall. A cleared throat from inside a private work room. The shape of a rounded back, head and shoulders hunched, turned inward toward a screen. Red-badge workers like him, left behind under the buzzing light of the fluorescents while the regular employees went to their special meeting in the sun. In one room, Jacob met eyes with a girl walking to her desk with a mug of freshly steaming coffee clutched in one hand. Golden hair tumbled curling onto her shoulders, and oversized nerd-chic glasses arched from her eyebrows to below her cheekbones. She smiled awkwardly, then angled her eyes downward and kept walking.

Jacob looked at the address code on the next piece of mail, then consulted his map. The delivery was almost at the other end of the wing, near the amphitheater. Not wanting to walk such a long distance through that maze of rooms and winding cubicle lanes, he moved toward an exit door and pushed through, back to the open concourse. Above him the ceiling vaulted almost comically high, hundreds of feet over his head. He was reminded, once again, of cathedrals, of the European churches he'd once visited during a semester abroad. Jacob remembered little from these tours, couldn't remember any of the facts the tour guides had offered about the buildings' design and construction, except one: the height of a cathedral ceiling was intended to draw the eyes up, to usher supplicants from lives of bleak medieval deprivation into hallowed sanctuaries of awe. Perhaps this was the purpose of the Delphi building's design, too: to awe the corporate drones walking beneath those high ceilings, to intimidate them into states of docility and obedience.

Jacob walked almost to the top of the wing, then found a door back into the offices. At that moment a low thud drew Jacob's eyes up, past the cubicle walls to the tall windows looking onto the courtyard. The sound of thumping bass was coming from the direction of the amphitheater. They were playing music at the all-company meeting. Jacob grinned, then laughed aloud as he pictured the mail room lady (her name was probably something like *Irene* or *Carol*, he'd decided) waiting for the Delphi CEO amidst millennials and GenZers as pump-up music blared from speakers. He recalled videos he'd seen shared on Facebook and Twitter—viral at first, then ubiquitous as memes—of product rollouts at tech companies. Executives shouting into headset mics as employees screamed like tween girls at a boy-band concert, Steve Jobs accepting adulation from throngs of tech journalists, Bill Gates clapping his hands and dancing awkwardly on a stage.

Jacob walked toward the windows, then left the mail cart behind as he went right up to the glass. Abandoning work so soon, slacking his first day on the job—but he wanted to see.

The amphitheater was sunk into the ground, as Jacob had suspected. His view out the window was near the back of the amphitheater, with rows of benches leading down, concentric semicircles following the line of the building as it angled to a point at the top of the triangle. The slope of the ground sunk down below the level of the floor Jacob stood on, revealing a sub-level below his feet. From front to back the theater was at least five hundred feet long, seating thousands of employees shoulder-to-shoulder.

The back bench of the amphitheater began about twenty feet away from him, separated by a thin strip of grass. Jacob put his hand near the glass and waved, testing to see if he was visible through the windows. But nobody, not even the employees sitting closest to him, made any sign of seeing him. They kept their eyes forward, craning over the heads of the people in front of them to wait for Tristan Brandt to take the stage. The windows were all one-way glass, tinted but transparent from the inside looking out, opaque and mirrored from the outside looking in. Jacob was invisible, anonymous.

Then, below, there was a commotion—the thousands of employees standing and applauding, faces flush with sun and adulation. Jacob looked down, eyes darting to find what was creating all the excitement. Then he spotted him: a man walking to the stage, waving. Employees in the benches nearest Brandt clustered and reached toward him. He reached and grasped at their hands, accepted their touch on his back and shoulders as he made his way to the lectern.

Brandt wore blue jeans and an unbuttoned gray sport coat over a white collared shirt. Jacob couldn't quite see his face—his view was obstructed by the hordes of Delphi employees mobbing him, hoping for some contact with the CEO—but in glimpses he got the impression of a fit man in his fifties, with thinning salt-and-pepper hair. Throughout the amphitheater employees stood, clapping and whistling in a standing ovation that went on for minutes even after Brandt had leapt on the stage and taken the lectern, and that might have gone on for several more.

Might have, that is, if the poisonous yellow mist hadn't descended.

• • •

Jacob first noticed the mist when Tristan Brandt took the stage and Jacob found that he still, somehow, couldn't make out the CEO's face. A cloud of fine, yellow particulate had come between where he stood and where Brandt waited behind the podium, waving and waiting for the applause to die down. From that distance, Brandt's face was blurry, grainy. It looked almost like a poorly developed photo, and at first Jacob blinked, thinking there was something wrong with his eyes. But then the mist grew thicker, and thicker still, until he could no longer see Brandt, could no longer see any of the Delphi employees in the amphitheater, could no longer see more than an inch past the panes of glass separating him from the outside.

There came the sound of moaning. Moans of pain, voiced by thousands of people at once, loud in Jacob's ears even though the sound was muffled by the thick glass. Outside, the sound must have been deafening. Jacob felt a coldness tingle deep in his bones. He moved away from the glass, fearing to imagine what was happening in the midst of that thick shroud of yellow mist.

And then, through the murk, there came an object: a body hurling toward the glass, thumping against it. A woman, young like most of the employees of Delphi Enterprises, wearing a blouse with a skirt and matching blazer, and fashionable but sensible shoes. She hit the glass near Jacob, close enough that he could see the brown of her irises and the freckles dotting her cheeks.

"Help," she moaned. "Please, help. Please."

Then other thuds began sounding out as more bodies hit the glass up and down the length of the wing—dozens, hundreds, perhaps thousands, some thuds echoing near and others far.

But Jacob kept his eyes on the woman who'd hit the glass near him.

"Help," she croaked again, her voice growing more hoarse.

Then there was a gagging sound from deep within her throat, a *herk* as the muscles of her neck flexed tight. All over her body, blood vessels rose to visibility and burst, webbing her skin with a lattice of red.

Her muscles loosened, but she didn't go limp, didn't fall to the ground, didn't die. Instead she looked at the glass—looked, it seemed, directly at Jacob—with a new kind of expression: no longer desperate, but enraged. She bared her teeth and snarled, wolf-like, foamy spittle flying from her mouth and spattering the window. Jacob jumped back. The woman clenched her hands into fists and punched at the window so hard that Jacob could see the knuckles changing shape as they cracked against the glass. Then she put both broken hands flat against the window—the pain must have been unimaginable, but she didn't seem fazed—and began bashing her head against it, again and again. It seemed as though she was enraged at Jacob for not helping her, as though she was trying to break through the glass and kill him, except she couldn't see through the window, and Jacob knew at once who her rage was directed at: herself. Her own reflection.

She went on hitting her forehead against the window until the surface began to smear with blood, until her forehead and face were smashed, until she couldn't hit anymore and she fell unconscious—or dead—to the grass.

And then, as quickly as it had come, the mist thinned and dissipated. Jacob raised his eyes from the young woman's body slumped against the bottom of the window to the amphitheater beyond.

From one end of the amphitheater to the other, as far as he could see, was complete chaos. Fighting and death and blood as thick as a medieval battlefield. Blood running down the steps, bodies piled into mounds. The melee spilling over, spreading to the grass. Everywhere he looked, the employees of Delphi Enterprises—so well-behaved, so reverent before the mist had descended—were transformed to rage-monsters, as the woman at the window had been.

Two men bashing each other bloody with fists. A woman dragging her unconscious victim, placing his head on the edge of an amphitheater bench, and then stomping it under her flats until the skull broke open. Men garroting victims with undone neckties, leather belts, shoelaces. Women attacking with shoes, the sharp ends of high heels dripping with blood and dangling gobs of flesh, bone, and brain. Thumbs pressed deep into eye sockets until eyeballs burst. Whitened teeth ripping necks open.

Others attacked not each other but themselves, turning their rage inward. Some pounded their heads on the windows or the concrete benches of the amphitheater; others opened their wrists with their teeth. One man threw himself down the steps of the amphitheater, tumbling down to the bottom. Then, his leg broken, bent at the knee, the man began pulling himself back up the stairs with his arms to throw himself down all over again.

Jacob watched, but there was a limit to what he could see, to what he could perceive. He'd seen deaths on television, violence in movies and video games, but nothing could've prepared him for the sudden outburst of violence in the courtyard. There was no previous context, no horizon against which he could make any sense of what he was seeing. The bursting skulls. Arcing globules of blood. So he simply watched for what seemed to him like a long time but in reality was no more than five seconds—five seconds between the time when the fog lifted, giving him an unimpeded view of the horror in the courtyard, and the time when he felt his body begin to tilt back. A rush of vertigo, a loss of balance, a stumbling back—and then, suddenly, he was falling.

It wasn't until he hit the ground that he realized what had happened. He'd backed into the mail cart, gotten his legs tangled in it. He kicked loose of the cart in a sudden panic, as if it were a snake wrapped around his ankles. Then, free, he turned and ran away from the windows and toward the concourse.

In the wider space, he turned to watch the door drift closed behind him, waited until it latched. Then, hearing a similar sound further down the concourse, he turned and spotted her. The girl, the one he'd passed in the office earlier. Long hair shining gold where the light caught it, glasses, pleated skirt, flats. They caught each other's eyes, and the girl began walking cautiously toward him.

"Stay away," Jacob said. His blood surged in his veins, the animal part of his brain taking over, telling him to fight or flee.

The girl put her hands out. "I'm not—it didn't—" she stammered. "The gas. It didn't get me."

Jacob breathed out, rationality returning, the animal receding—but only partially. "Me either."

The girl's head turned. Jacob followed her gaze, looked out through the windows to the freeway and a strip mall beyond. Outside, the yellow mist was moving. Thinner, more diffuse than it had been in the courtyard, but still present, and spreading. It drifted across the freeway, where cars passed through the cloud and then swerved, went in the ditch, flipped. A semi jackknifed. Cars piled against one another in a cacophony of crashing metal. Then drivers and passengers poured out of the broken vehicles and flew at each other on the median. It wasn't until the cloud engulfed the strip mall that a siren went off. A tornado siren, or perhaps an air-raid siren, still functional from an earlier age. An alarm signifying disaster.

"There's a break room," the girl said. "With a TV. Not far from my desk. Maybe there's something on the news."

"Yeah," Jacob said. "Let's go."

He followed her.

# TWO

*Apocalypse.* From the Greek *apokalyptein*, meaning "to uncover, to unveil." Not the end of the world, as in the popular imagination, but a discovery of knowledge previously hidden. A terrible revelation that cleaves the world in two: *before* and *after*.

There had been two apocalypses in Lauren Aldiss's life, two revelations from which she could not return. Her father's death. And the things she saw after the yellow mist descended on the courtyard at Delphi Enterprises.

Now she was living in the after—she and the young man. Jacob. Sitting next to her on a couch at a more-than-respectful distance, pushed up against the far armrest, as if HR might even now be watching for any scene of impropriety between two colleagues taking a break from their work—as if such things still mattered.

Together, they watched TV.

At first there was nothing. No acknowledgment of the thing they'd seen, the thing that had happened. Only the regular daytime fare: a celebrity chef and an award-winning actress making a frittata as a studio audience looked on, *The Price Is Right* contestants bidding on a blender, the ladies of a midday talk show shouting over each other about whether a young female pop star's sexy new look was setting a bad example for girls. Even the twenty-four-hour news channels—CNN, MSNBC, Fox—stuck to their usual lineup of talking heads opining on the latest scandal emanating from the White House, heated crosstalk, cutaways to senators or spokespersons or press secretaries for reaction. This maddening delay as Lauren cycled through channels, waiting for the television to tell her what she already knew, as if she needed the press to confirm the evidence of her own eyes to know that it had been real.

A local station was the first to pick up the story, cutting in just as the celebrity chef was showing the actress how to flip the cooked frittata from the pan onto a plate.

The anchorwoman began by apologizing for interrupting regular programming, then relayed "reports of some sort of widespread incident" in the western reaches of the city. As more information came in, her description evolved. "Widespread incident" became "spontaneous rioting" became "a coordinated attack leading to massive civil unrest and looting."

It wasn't until about ten minutes into the broadcast that she finally got it right.

"A chemical event," she said, holding a finger to her ear, listening to some unseen producer feeding her new information. "That's what it's looking like right now. Officials are recommending that everyone in the tri-county area get inside if at all possible. Preferably a climate-controlled building with sealed windows and doors. Turn off all heating, cooling, and ventilation equipment. We don't have a clear picture of the effects of the gas yet, but as soon as we do we'll—"

Then another cut, a graphic accompanied by urgently thudding music, and then a different newsroom, a different anchorperson. The story had gone national. The anchorman straightened a stack of papers on the desk in front of him, then looked up to the camera and sternly reported what the local news had already discarded as incorrect: spontaneous widespread rioting and civil unrest in response to some catastrophic event.

Lauren's agitation rose. She'd seen the mist, seen its effects, with her own eyes. What good was 24/7 media if it was less instant than reality? Technology was supposed to be faster than real life, not slower. And yet here was a national newsman telling her less than she already knew—something had happened, there was unrest, yes, this was all true. But the spontaneous human chaos wasn't *in response to* some disaster, people raiding Best Buy for free flat-screens in the aftermath of a hurricane. The chaos *was* the disaster. The yellow gas turned people into monsters. To call the results of the gas "unrest" or "rioting" was too paltry a description for what she'd seen. What had happened in the Delphi courtyard was a spontaneous mass murder-suicide. A crowd turning on itself. Humans becoming animals, and those animals tearing each other apart.

"Do you have Twitter?" she asked Jacob.

He pulled a phone out of his pocket.

"There's not much," he said, flicking down the feed with his thumb. "Retweets from CNN and AP calling it 'massive civil unrest.' Some squabbling about gun control—I guess some people think it's a mass shooting. A couple people blaming ISIS. Others saying it's probably white supremacists. 'Thoughts and prayers for the victims.' No one has the real story."

"But that news lady did," Lauren said. "The local one. Before the national news cut her off."

"Yeah, but she's got local sources. Some cop who reported the gas cloud on a police scanner before getting poisoned himself. A Facebook video of the yellow mist. The national news, they're probably waiting for confirmation from FEMA or something."

Lauren swallowed back annoyance at the confidence of Jacob's tone. What did he know about it? How could he be sure? Men always thought they understood how the world worked, secure in the blithe delusion that they knew something about everything. Not thirty minutes ago Jacob had seemed more confused and scared than she was, his face pale when she first approached him, as though he feared she'd kill him where she stood. But a man was never more at ease than when explaining things to a woman, even things he only dimly understood.

Maybe he was a journalism major in school, she thought, trying to give him the benefit of the doubt. That he was alive meant he was a temp too, a red-badge like her. Someone who'd studied something impractical, couldn't find one of the few jobs in his chosen field, and was now reduced to begging for scraps from the corporate table.

"But wouldn't the national news stations get reports directly from their affiliates?" Lauren asked. "This guy should have the same information as the anchorwoman, right?"

"I don't know," Jacob said. "Maybe they have the same information but they're trying to confirm it. Or maybe they can't get any information from local reporters because everybody's—"

Jacob didn't finish his sentence. He didn't have to.

*Because everybody's dead.*

Lauren was silent, looking to the screen, hoping for evidence that Jacob was wrong. Hoping for a return to the local newsroom, the anchorwoman alive and well. But minutes kept ticking by with no cutaways to the field, no phone calls with journalists on the scene, no first-hand reports from whatever was going on. Only the anchorman vamping behind a desk, cautiously speculating from what little information came trickling into the room where he sat. The proverbial blind man, groping at an apocalyptic elephant.

"This is very preliminary," he said, "and it hasn't yet been confirmed as real, but we're going to share it with you now because it appears to contain the first real images from ground zero of this . . . this catastrophic *event* we're still struggling to get a handle on. A video uploaded to social media about an hour ago. We're going to go to it now, but first I need to warn our viewers that what you're about to see may disturb you."

The video began with movement, forms and shadows sliding across the frame, the harsh cuffing sound of some object brushing against the microphone.

"Dude," said the voice of the cameraman, "what *is* that?"

Then light, focus, the scene coming into view: a ribbon of street leading toward a city skyline. The diagonal plane of a car roof in the right of the frame, the outward jutting of an open door at the bottom, suggested that the cameraman had stepped out of his car to record the video. Cars were at a standstill in traffic along the road leading into the city, threading ant-like toward the foot of a towering skyscraper.

The tip of the building was haloed in a yellow cloud. Lauren tensed when she saw it, the shade and translucence of the mist recreating with chilling precision the physical sensations she'd experienced when watching the Delphi employees die in the courtyard. A suddenly dry mouth, slippery palms, the feeling of her innards turning to ice.

Up and down the street, other drivers climbed out of their cars and gazed up at the cloud. It billowed toward them.

"What is this?" asked someone off-camera. "A dust storm?"

"There's no wind," the cameraman said.

"Should we run?"

"Where would we go?"

The cloud engulfed the skyscraper, then the buildings lining the street, the stopped cars, the people gaping on the sidewalk. A rolling wave of gas, and of sound—the sound of screaming rising up from within the mist. Screams of pain and of rage. The silhouettes of bodies just inside the perimeter of the cloud, a stampede of people running up the street. Fleeing, or perhaps attacking—it was impossible for Lauren to tell.

"Back in the car," said the cameraman. "Now."

The cameraman climbed back in the car with his companion, slammed the doors.

"Are we going to die?" asked the cameraman's companion.

The cameraman didn't answer. Soon the car was engulfed in the yellow mist, as thick at the windows and windshield as it had been at the windows at Delphi.

"There's so much of it," Jacob said from the other side of the couch. "How could there still be so much of it?"

"There must have been another attack," Lauren said. "Another attack downtown."

*Attack.* She'd been the first to use the word, unthinking. But that was what it had to be. Not an accident, not a chemical spill or gas leak, but an attack. They were being attacked.

On TV, silhouettes were thundering past the windows of the car, hitting the doors. The screaming had grown louder. The sounds of people killing and dying just feet away from where the camera still rolled. Then one of the silhouettes landed on the car. A man who scrabbled up the hood to the windshield and began hitting at it with his fists, then with his head. Bleeping as the news covered up the sounds of panicked cursing from the men inside the car. Then more people came, fell on the hood like hail, a crush of screaming, raging bodies. The windshield cracked, then broke, and then they were inside the car, clamoring through the shards of glass to reach at the men inside. The video became, for a brief moment, a chaos of fingernails and fists and teeth, then went black.

"Jesus," said Jacob. "Jesus fucking Christ."

The screen switched back to the anchorman, who seemed to be having the same emotional response to the footage as Jacob. He probably hadn't seen it before it went live—a producer had found it, described it to the anchor over his earpiece, told him how to set it up and to warn the audience before turning to the footage. But the anchorman had first experienced the video with Lauren, with Jacob, with millions of viewers. Now he knew what Lauren and Jacob knew. Their apocalypse, their revelation, had come to him at last.

"Troubling footage," the anchorman said after a long pause. "Showing what appeared to me to be some sort of chemical event, causing widespread panic and rioting—or . . ."

Another pause. In her mind, Lauren urged him on, urged him to say what she already knew. *Come on,* she thought, *get there,* without any feeling of anger or annoyance or impatience. She felt almost tender toward the newsman now, wrested into familial affection with his image on the screen in the way that only the combination of catastrophe and television can accomplish.

"This is purely speculative of course," the newsman said, "but it looked to me almost as if that sudden rioting was an *effect* of the chemical. We'll have to keep looking into the connection between the gas and the spontaneous mass violence that seemed to follow, but as I said, it seemed to me . . . well you could see for yourself, that—"

He stopped speaking abruptly, looked down, put two fingers to his ear.

"Yes," he said, not to the camera, not to his audience, but to someone unseen, someone in the control room. Then he looked up, made eye contact again. Lauren leaned forward.

"Getting confirmation now," he said. "The Federal Emergency Management Agency has confirmed, FEMA, that this event is in fact chemical in nature, the gas cloud that we saw on that footage, it *causes* the behavior we've been seeing, this spontaneous outburst of violence, of . . . of *fury.* FEMA also notes similar events in a number of other American cities, we're getting that list for you now."

Lauren gasped as, on-screen, the anchorman looked for his tele-prompter, waiting for the list of cities to appear.

"Atlanta, Boston, Chicago, Dallas, Detroit, Los Angeles, Miami, Milwaukee, Minneapolis"—the anchorman flinched but kept his voice even as he came to the city where he was located—"New York, Phoenix, San Francisco, Seattle, and Washington, DC."

He looked down and cleared his throat, seeming to struggle with an upwelling of emotion, before looking back up to the camera and speaking again.

"No word from Homeland Security, but with incidents happening in all these cities, this increasingly looks like an attack. If you live in one of these metropolitan areas, authorities ask that you stay inside, seal all your windows and doors, and await further instruction. In fact, we're going to have a local affiliate break in a few seconds here. Please stay tuned for more information."

The picture flipped back to the local newsroom, and Lauren's stomach plunged.

"Oh my God." Her hand came up to her mouth.

The picture had gone off-kilter. The camera had fallen. A slab of gray dominated the left half of the screen where the camera lens rested against the studio floor; to the right, almost disappearing past the edge of the frame, was the hulk of the anchor's desk. Atop the desk lay the anchor-woman, her cheek resting against its smooth surface. Her eyes were glassy, and a trickle of blood ran from her nose. The camera's 90-degree perspec-tive shift made the image strange, made the slumped anchorwoman look as though she was still upright, and alive. Her dulled eyes looking directly at the camera. Off-screen, a man's voice, guttural and grunting, like a wild boar. The cameraman, perhaps, gone insane, or a producer—whichever one had breathed the gas first as it leached into the building, then killed the rest.

"It's the apocalypse," Jacob said. She glanced over and saw that he was looking at her. His voice gone hoarse. Something pleading in his eyes. "It's the end of the world."

• • •

Lauren turned down the volume after that, held the button until the anchorman's voice was nothing but a murmur. Jacob stood and walked away from the couch. Lauren glanced back and saw him tapping at the screen of his cell phone, holding it up to his ear.

"Who are you calling?" she asked. Then, when he didn't reply: "Any answer?"

Jacob was silent, waiting, then he took the phone away from his ear and shook his head.

"Nothing," he said. "The networks must be completely overloaded. I'll try again later."

Lauren tried her own phone, dialed her roommate, then her mother, but it was just as Jacob had said—three rising tones, then the recorded voice: *The number you dialed cannot be reached.* Lauren looked back up and saw that Jacob had gone to the break room refrigerator, that he had the door open and was surveying the remnants of dead workers' lunches for something to snack on. Glass dishes with colored plastic lids, foam containers with the remnants of takeout meals, names written in Sharpie on pieces of masking tape.

"Were there any other red badges in your section?" he asked. "Anyone whose food I shouldn't take?"

This was pretty cold, Lauren thought, but perhaps Jacob was trying to protect himself. A few minutes ago Jacob was almost hysterical, near to tears. Maybe getting up from the couch, trying to make his call, and looking for something to eat were all methods of avoidance, the same thing that had driven Lauren to push down the volume, to turn the apocalypse on the TV to background noise. They were pretending, for now, that it wasn't happening—that it was something that would blow over, and that things would return to normal by the end of the day.

"I was the only temp in my department," she answered. "You're the only other red badge I've ever met."

Jacob returned to the couch with two bottles of water.

"No food?" Lauren asked.

"I wasn't hungry," Jacob admitted. "I guess I just wanted to step away for a second. To get away from—"

On the screen, the anchorman murmured indistinctly. Images flashed: the burning wreckage of an airplane that had fallen from the sky, fans pouring murderous onto the field at a sporting event, a map of the continental United States with flashing red dots marking the cities where this was known to be happening.

"Yeah," said Lauren. "I get it."

Jacob turned his body away from the screen and toward her.

"So you're the only one in your department," he said. "The only temp. What's your job?"

Lauren paused a beat. There seemed to be an offer implicit in the question, and in Jacob's speaking in the present tense. Lauren took the offer, turned herself sideways on the couch until she could see the television only glancingly. She pulled her legs onto the couch and folded her knees sideways, the way she might do at her apartment late in the evening, wearing sweats and poking at a pint of ice cream with an oversized spoon, watching TV with one eye and less than half her mind.

"I write quizzes," she said.

"Quizzes?"

"Yeah, quizzes. Like, 'Which *Office* character are you?' 'What '80s sci-fi/fantasy cartoon are you?' 'Which Beatle are you?'"

"I'm sensing a pattern here."

"Yeah," Lauren said. "Mapping personality types to pop culture tropes is kind of my specialty. Plus it gets the best click rate, so my boss likes those."

Lauren heard herself following Jacob into the present tense. It felt strange, speaking this way—as if people might still take internet quizzes, as if her boss might at any moment come walking into the break room and ask her to get back to work on the "Which James Bond actor are you?" quiz, which was due by close-of-business.

"There are others too, though. 'Pick your favorite foods and we'll guess your zodiac sign.' 'What kind of hipster are you?' Stuff like that."

Jacob squinted. "What's the point?"

Lauren shook her head. "I honestly don't know. To drive clicks, I guess? Engagement? I couldn't tell you how Delphi makes money off it. They pay me for doing it. That's all I care about."

"What does Delphi *do*, anyway?"

Lauren had asked herself the same question multiple times since she started working here three months ago—but there was something aggrieved, something offended in Jacob's tone, as if the obscurity of the corporation's business was a personal affront.

Lauren's shoulders lifted, then dropped. "I have no idea," she admitted. "Anyway, it doesn't matter now."

"How old are you?"

The question was sudden, and intrusive, but these were the terms of the agreement: killing time, talking about anything but what was on the TV, avoiding the subject of friends and family and parents, all of whom were possibly (probably?) dead.

"Twenty-five. You?"

"Same," Jacob answered. "How did you get this job? What was your major?"

The two queries were delivered rapid-fire, like two halves of the same question, and hearing it Lauren understood something about Jacob, saw him snap into focus in a new way. He was the kind of person who couldn't shake college, for whom *major* was still a word carrying the most important part of his personal identity, who couldn't figure out how to function after graduation, befuddled and dismayed by the world's utter lack of regard for the things he valued. Lauren pegged him as a theater major, or maybe philosophy—self-important in school, now turned bitter.

"Double-major," Lauren said, "classics and psych." She watched Jacob's face brighten, then sour, as if she'd broken some previous agreement—more essential than their tacit agreement not to speak of the disaster taking place outside—by sullying the frivolous course of study in the humanities with something more practical. A sellout.

Which was not so different from how she felt about herself.

• • •

Lauren was in love with myth. She'd fallen for it at an early age, poring endlessly over a copy of *D'Aulaires' Book of Greek Myths* gifted to her by her grandmother for her fourth birthday. At nine, she had graduated to Edith Hamilton's *Mythology*. And then, as a teen, she'd discovered Joseph Campbell's *The Hero with a Thousand Faces*, which completely blew her mind and, she thought, justified the persistence of that childhood interest, reassuring her that it wasn't child*ish*. All this time, she hadn't merely been reading stories; with D'Aulaire, and Hamilton, and Campbell, she'd been drinking from a well of living water, with springs running deep in the earth, in the human psyche, in the cosmos itself. She'd been communing with capital-T Truth.

Her parents had been puzzled by her decision to major in classics in college. They'd known of her interest in Greek mythology—the dog-ears and cracking bindings of her three favorite books were sign enough of that—but they were of a different generation, one that didn't expect their passions to become vocations. Lauren had been a good student in high school, did well in science and math, had a head for numbers; so why not study something more practical, like engineering or accounting? After a year of this prodding Lauren caved, not dropping classics but adding a second major, one that felt adjacent, at least to her: psychology. Campbell quoted from Freud and Jung, after all; the human psyche, like mythology, was a still pond that ran deep, fed by ancient springs.

Or so Lauren reasoned, anyway.

But the psych major wasn't what she expected it to be: more numbers than art, more science than religion. Lauren was a mystic at heart, a pilgrim seeking awe. But as a psychology student she studied neurology, scientific methodology, statistics, behaviorism. The classics major had its dull moments too, mostly in language study—Latin and Greek conjugations, roots, declensions. But even there she could imagine she was a scholar studying ancient scrolls for some hidden knowledge that unlocked the world. Her psychology professors, on the other hand, seemed to her to have forgotten that in seeking to understand the human mind they were knocking at the threshold of a great mystery—if they'd ever known it at all. She'd sometimes buttonhole one of them after class to tell them of her true passions, but as soon as she started talking about the hero's journey and the monomyth their eyes would go glassy, their voices would turn vague, and they'd dismiss her with indulgent, even pitying smiles.

Still, Lauren had to admit that the psych major *did* yield more in the way of summer internships and assistantships than the classics major. She spent most summers on campus, helping one professor or another with research studies. She welcomed test subjects, administered surveys, compiled data, sent papers out for publication. She was admired in the department—a good student and a good research assistant, even if it didn't feed her soul. The work paid, if not particularly well, and so when she graduated she continued into graduate study. Her plan was to eventually get certified as a therapist and then go into private practice, work out of an apartment office like in the movies. A private sanctum where she could practice therapy her way, as a mystical quest to the holy source of the self, unhindered by the dull, unimaginative methodologies of her professors.

But there was still her thesis to think of, and it wasn't going well. She'd devised a proposal that came as close as possible to encompassing her passions while still getting the approval of her advisor: a study of the therapeutic use of myth, of the ways that individuals facing personal difficulty drafted popular stories into their struggles. Her test subjects stuttered through interview sessions, squinting with confusion as she asked leading questions about fairy tales, and folklore, and Arthurian legend. The only texts her subjects ever brought up unprompted were Harry Potter, and Star Wars, and Marvel movies. Corporate trademarks passing as myth.

Franchise storytelling had crushed humanity's cultural memory, Lauren felt. No one remembered the old stories. Talking to a cancer survivor who said his illness felt inevitable, like a battle he was predestined to fight, Lauren said she was reminded of the prophecy of Tiresias in *Oedipus Rex*, to which the chemotherapy-balded man blinked and replied, "Oedipus? Is that the one where he fucks his mom? I don't see how that applies." That night Lauren drank a whole bottle of red wine and complained to her roommate that she should've been a folklorist or an anthropologist—though even that probably wouldn't have turned out to be what she wanted, either. Ancient knowledge was passing away. There was nothing left to discover. She'd been born too late, into a time when the entire world had lost its soul—but then again, as a woman she wouldn't have wanted to be born any earlier, either. This was the cruel irony of being a young woman in the twenty-first century: the old white men were loosening their grip on the world only after they'd ruined it.

And then her father died of a heart attack.

It was Lauren's first experience of death, a thunderclap that tore her life in two. What made Thomas Aldiss's death apocalyptic for Lauren was the sudden, irrevocable knowledge that this was a thing that could happen, that someone you loved and whose existence you took for granted could simply cease to be.

The subsequent discovery that Lauren's father was not who he seemed was like a second death—the death of the man she thought she'd known. A mistress surfaced, with an adult son she claimed was fathered by Thomas. Financial complications ensued. A successful businessman when he'd been alive—the owner of a small but successful carpet installation and cleaning business—Thomas was revealed to be deep in debt, the business's books covered in red ink. (The mistress quickly disappeared after it was clear the only thing the deceased would bequeath to his survivors were bills.) Lauren's mother, Vivian Aldiss, was forced to sell their house and liquidate many of their assets in the process of setting his affairs in order.

In the end, Lauren was left not just without a father but without a key source of income. Thomas had encouraged his daughter's studies; she was the first in the family to go to college, and he believed that she'd one day make an excellent therapist. He'd demonstrated this belief with a monthly payment, delivered predictably on the first of the month to Lauren's checking account. Now, her father dead and her family's assets liquidated, Lauren was left only with her paltry graduate stipend to live on. The stipend barely paid for rent, with almost nothing left over for food and clothing. Functional poverty.

Lauren put her studies on hold, took an indefinite leave from her graduate program. Her research project was dead anyway—dead as her father, dead as her admiration for the man she thought he was. Academia was a dry well, counseling too. What she needed was a job. A decent-paying job, so she could avoid her father's fate (she'd developed a sudden fear of debt in any form). The classics degree would be no help, but there were always psychology's corporate applications to think of: consumer behaviorism, human resources management, industrial organizational psychology.

At first she couldn't find anything. Applying for jobs was like firing her résumé into space. She pressed *Send* knowing she'd never hear anything, that she may as well have been dropping her application into a black hole. Then her roommate—who was sick of Lauren's inability to make rent, but hesitant to kick her out in the midst of her bereavement—suggested that Lauren try a new smartphone app she'd heard about, something called Concierge.

"It'll help me find a job?" Lauren asked.

"It'll do way more than that," the roommate said. "Concierge is, like, a digital life coach. You answer a bunch of questions—education, experience, personality profile—and then the app just starts . . . *telling you what to do.*"

Lauren frowned. "Yuck."

The roommate shook her head fiercely. "No, it's great. I started using it just a month ago, and it's changed my life. Seriously. Concierge gives me suggestions for what to eat, when to exercise, when to go to bed, what movies and TV shows and books I might like. It talks to dating apps to match me with boys who also have a Concierge profile, point me toward the ones I'm most compatible with. Friends, too—it suggests who I should be hanging out with more, which of my friends make me happiest and can plug me into the best social networks."

A ping of anxiety went off in Lauren's stomach as she wondered what the app might already be telling others about her fitness for friendship and romance.

"Professionally, it's been a total game changer," the roommate said. "In the first week alone it told me about seventeen jobs in my field that pay better than what I was making."

"Did you apply for any of them?"

"No, because Concierge looked at how long I'd been at my company and how much I was making and suggested that it might be time to ask for a raise first. The app even gave me a script to practice with."

"And it worked?"

The roommate nodded. "Yeah. Five percent raise, an extra week of vacation time, accelerated 401k vesting. Effective last week."

"Wow," Lauren said.

She tried it. The app was free, which set off a brief alarm in Lauren's head—if the app itself wasn't a revenue stream for the company that created it, that meant the real product was *her*, her data—but she set up a profile anyway. Education, professional experience, Myers-Briggs, California Psychological Inventory, Enneagram, StrengthsFinder—the questions getting increasingly strange and intrusive.

*Did your mother breastfeed you when you were an infant?*

*How often do you masturbate?*

*What is your favorite color?*

*Do you urinate in the shower?*

*Were you bullied as a child?*

*Is there anyone in the world that you hate?*

*What do you most desire at this precise moment?*

This last question made Lauren pause. She was a bundle of wants, of aimless desires, so many that she couldn't begin to describe them or pick a single one that rose in urgency above all the others. What *did* she want? Happiness? Contentment? A snack? What she really wanted most, she realized, was simply for her life to be *different* than it was at that moment, for the world to more accurately conform to her wishes, her whims—but she couldn't tell that to Concierge, so instead she answered with the thing that had driven her to download the app in the first place: *A job*.

A graphic appeared, a whirring animated wheel, indicating that Concierge was thinking. Then it spoke to her: a female voice, subtitled with text that came briefly to the screen, then faded.

"Welcome! I'm your Concierge. Let's get started. I found a job for you."

Lauren experienced a chill of recognition when she read the company name: *Delphi*. The name of the Apollonian temple at the top of Mount

Parnassus, in Ancient Greece. The axis of the world, the home of the omphalos. The site at which the wisdom of the gods streamed down to humanity.

She applied, and got the job with little trouble.

On her first day at Delphi, Lauren discovered that the corporation's affinity for Ancient Greece ran deeper than just the company name. The building's twenty-four exterior entrances were named for the letters of the Greek alphabet. Major corporate meetings were held in an outdoor amphitheater. And the building's three wings—the sides of a massive triangle—were each named with letters corresponding, Lauren suspected, to a different Apollonian prophet: P-wing for Pythia, the Delphic oracle; T-wing for Tiresias, the blind seer featured in the works of Homer and Sophocles; and C-wing for Cassandra, the accursed prophetess whose apocalyptic predictions were not believed by those she tried to warn. All this combined to give Lauren the feeling of being drawn toward some destiny, of arriving back where she started when she first, at the age of four, picked up an illustrated children's book of myths.

But Lauren didn't understand the work, didn't understand the purpose of what she'd been hired to do. The job description had called for a degree in psychology, experience creating and administering personality surveys, and a knowledge of popular culture. She created quizzes that were psychological assessments in disguise, tricking web users to reveal their innermost selves under the guise of determining which *Star Trek* captain they were most like, which season they loved most, which flavor of pie they should eat for the rest of their lives. Delphi was harvesting user data, obviously, but for what purpose? Government spying? Targeted marketing? Something more sinister?

These questions nagged at Lauren, but she kept working at Delphi because the money was decent compared to what she'd gotten in academia. And she was good at the work.

"I'm liking the engagement numbers on your quizzes," her supervisor had told her just that morning, glancing at a spreadsheet printout. She was in her thirties, married, a hip mom of two—the kind of woman Lauren might one day aspire to be. "High click-through, above-average survey completion. You've got a feel for this. Good survey topics, good titles. The way you phrase your questions is personable, funny."

"Thank you," Lauren said, not quite sure if she should feel proud or not.

"You know, if you keep these numbers up, I might be able to talk my boss into bringing you permanent. Black badge, salary, full benefits."

"Really?"

"Think about it," the supervisor said. "We'll talk more when I get back."

And then the woman left for the all-company meeting, where she died in the mist.

# THREE

In the breakroom, Lauren told Jacob an abridged version of this story in scrambled order, beginning at both ends of the narrative with her college studies and how they related to the nature of her work at Delphi, then working her way simultaneously backward and forward to the middle of the story, her father's death—whereupon she surprised herself by immediately bursting into tears. Everything was mixed up in her head: the apocalypse of her father's death and the apocalypse taking place outside Delphi at that moment. The call from her mother, "It was a heart attack, I'm sorry, he's gone," her mind reeling, adjusting to add this to the realm of things that were possible. Then standing at the tall windows outside her cubicle and watching the violence in the amphitheater. The sudden and crushing knowledge that this, too, was a thing that could happen: the screaming, the moaning, the caved skulls, the broken bones, the blood. Civilized humans turning instantly to Furies, and tearing each other apart.

Also present in her mind was the near certainty that her father wasn't the only one who was dead, now. Her mother was dead too, and her roommate, and her friends, and thousands (or perhaps millions) of strangers—maybe even the president, the heads of government, the generals and emergency managers, everyone with the power to help and hold civilization together in the midst of this catastrophe.

And so, she cried.

Lauren felt a warmth, then looked down to see that Jacob's hand was covering her own on the couch. She looked back up and found his eyes. They were dry, but full of earnestness and urgency. Something about the moment felt uncomfortable. She and Jacob had been alone in that room for a while, with only the blunted volume of the TV to remind them that there was still a world out there—that they weren't the last two humans on earth. Lauren had seen that fierce look in a boy's eyes before. She'd seen it over candlelight and wineglasses at dinner dates, at bars with pulsing music and the din of voices, at dim apartments afterward with what was clearly a make-out mix playing in the background. Mansplaining aside, Jacob seemed sweet, and he was cute, in a nebbish sort of way—but if he was indulging some sort of repopulate-the-earth, let's-fuck-while-the-world-burns porn fantasy, Lauren was *not* okay with that.

"It's okay," he said, and gave her hand a squeeze. "It's going to be okay."

She laughed at the impotence of the cliché and pulled her hand away. "Is it? Everything's falling apart."

He looked up, eyes growing hazy. "No. The government . . . they're in a bunker, maybe, but they're still alive. I'm sure of it. The army, the National Guard, FEMA—there's someone out there holding things together. Someone has this under control."

"But everyone's dead."

"*He's* not dead," Jacob countered. Nodding toward the TV, where the anchorman soldiered on behind his desk—disheveled, but alive.

Then, there was a commotion on the screen. A blurry figure running in the background. A flitting of shadow in the studio lights. The anchorman's eyes darted, and he held his finger to his ear.

"Turn it up," Jacob said.

"I'm being told that it's time for us to move to a different location," the anchorman said. "The gas cloud has apparently drifted from New York's outer boroughs to Midtown Manhattan, where our studio is located, and . . ."

The newsman trailed off as the picture took on a yellowish tint.

"No," Jacob said at her side. "No, no, no."

The anchorman's body lurched, and he grabbed at the desk, trying to steady himself. He seemed to be gripped by a massive agony. Offscreen there was a shout and a thud. The camera rattled but held its shot, kept the anchorman in the frame as he doubled over the desk and let out a high-pitched groan, almost a wheeze. His skin turned red, then began to web with bursting blood vessels.

"Oh my God," Lauren said, covering her mouth, feeling her stomach burble hot at the back of her throat. She turned to Jacob. He was already looking away, as if he knew what was going to happen. But Lauren hadn't seen this yet, hadn't seen what the gas did to a person up close. She'd only witnessed the aftermath. And so she turned back to the screen, where the anchorman now looked up, met the camera's gaze, his eyes changing. There was a moment of stillness, and then he launched himself over the desk, wingtips clattering at the glass surface, and flew at the camera. The camera tilted, then fell amidst the sound of snarling. The screen went black—the only evidence that someone in the newsroom hadn't breathed the gas yet, that someone still had the presence of mind to flip a switch and stop the broadcast.

Lauren and Jacob sat for a minute or two without speaking, amidst the faint electronic whine of the TV's silence. Jacob stood, looking toward the door.

"Maybe," he said, "we should try to find some other survivors."

•  •  •

Jacob stepped back into the office with the uneven, slightly queasy feeling he often got when he went to a movie in the middle of the day, or spent an entire afternoon binging Netflix in his parents' basement. The feeling of lost time, of returning to a world that had spun on without him in his absence. He couldn't see the carnage in the courtyard—a wall was in the way, containing a bank of private offices and meeting rooms—but he wanted to, felt himself drawn toward it. He and Lauren had spent more than two hours in the break room, and a part of him needed to confirm that what he'd seen in the courtyard had been real, that they hadn't just dreamed it, a joint delusion experienced while sitting together on the couch.

He found a hallway and began walking in the direction of the courtyard.

"What are you doing?" Lauren asked, behind him.

He turned and looked at her. "I want to see," he said.

She shook her head. "Why?"

He couldn't explain it. "You can stay here, if you want." He kept on walking, and after a moment he heard Lauren's footsteps following behind him.

They came out of the hallway and back into an open office room, with the tall windows looking onto the courtyard beyond. As Jacob came between rows of cubicles, he saw what was on the other side of the glass.

Corpses everywhere he looked. They were draped over benches in the amphitheater, backs bent the wrong way, piled on top of each other, eyes staring at the sky. Spilling past the last row, scattered bloody over basketball courts and soccer fields. Here and there the bodies moved slightly, not quite dead, pulling themselves along the ground with the last of their strength.

"What are they doing?"

Jacob turned, surprised to find that Lauren had followed him all the way to the windows after all.

"I don't know," he said, and looked again. He spotted a still-living person near the glass. A man in short sleeves and dress pants. He pulled himself on the ground with his hands, fingers digging into the dirt. His legs appeared to be mangled, bumping loosely inside his pants like broken glass. He dragged himself in front of the window, from right to left, pulling himself away from the amphitheater toward the open space of the court-yard. The rage was still on his face, almost comical in its disconnection with the weakness of his body. Jacob tapped on the glass with his finger, then leapt back when the man snapped his eyes toward the sound.

"He must be looking for someone else who's alive," Jacob said, his stomach turning. "Someone else to fight."

His eyes on the man on the ground, Jacob leapt when something came sweeping in from the left. Jacob looked up and saw more than a dozen people, running suddenly in front of the glass where he and Lauren stood. The people were still on their feet, uninjured, their bodies almost completely unmarked by the fighting in the courtyard. Mostly men, but a few women as well. They moved close together, almost shoulder-to-shoulder, and fell on the crawling man. Their bodies made a circle so that Jacob and Lauren couldn't see what was happening to him, but it was clear enough: they were finishing him off. Killing him with their hands. Then they kept on moving. They cut a path into the center of the courtyard. There was something chilling in the way they ran so close together, like a school of fish, darting this way and that in seemingly perfect coordination.

"They're running like a pack," Lauren said, as if completing Jacob's thought. "Like a pack of wolves."

"You think they can get in?" Jacob asked.

"The doors to the courtyard are locked," Lauren said. "You have to use your security badge to get back in. You think they remember how to use their security badges, those . . . things?"

"I doubt it. The glass is strong enough to keep them out, anyway. When it happened, I saw a woman smashing her head against it—it didn't even crack."

Lauren shuddered. "I don't understand how any of them can still be alive."

"They must be the winners," Jacob said.

"Winners of what?"

"Of the battle in the courtyard," he said. "Apex predators. Top of the food chain. You saw that they were barely hurt?"

The pack fell on another victim, a woman this time. They killed her quickly, then moved on, kept running. But something had changed. Jacob squinted.

"Does it look to you like . . ." he began, then trailed off.

"Like what?"

One of the members of the pack was limping, lagging. A man, tall and broad shouldered. Favoring one of his legs. Maybe the crawling man had injured him, bitten his calf. Anyway, he was hurt.

The man fell to the back of the pack, then a pace behind, then three. When he was almost five yards behind the pack—slowing more, his limp getting worse with each stride—the person running nearest to him at the back of the pack turned. As if by telepathy the rest of the pack seemed to sense this single person's deviation from the course, and they veered at once, looped around and mobbed the limping man.

"Furies," Lauren mumbled as the man fell, then died in a hail of snarls and screams.

"What?"

"The Furies. They're deities in Greek myth. Vengeful creatures who hunt people down and kill them for their sins."

"You think that man's dying for his sins?"

Lauren shook her head. "No. I just thought of the name because those people—they seem so angry. So furious. Is that what the gas does? Amplifies a person's fury, makes it grow, until that's all that's left?"

Jacob didn't answer. He pulled the blinds closed, lines of shadow creeping across the desktop, then yanked the metal cord to flip the blinds flat.

"Come on," he said. "Let's go."

• • •

Lauren followed Jacob through the office, a patchwork maze of cubicle grids and meeting rooms leading one into the next. Sometimes their view of the courtyard was blocked, sometimes not. As they moved away from the amphitheater Lauren sensed a thinning distribution of corpses on the ground outside. But she mostly kept her eyes down, on her feet, sparing only brief glances toward the courtyard, the way one might look at an eclipse.

Jacob had insisted to Lauren that there were others close by, that he'd passed other temps at their desks while he was delivering the mail—but every time they came to a room where he thought he'd recalled the presence of one of these other people, it turned out to be empty.

"Goddammit," he muttered to himself as he led her to the entrance of yet another empty cubicle. "I swear to God there was someone here."

"Man or woman?" Lauren asked.

"Man, I think. I passed behind his back and he didn't turn, he just kept on working. But he was here. I'm sure he was."

Jacob's face was red with bafflement. He walked past Lauren and looked left and right, craning his neck over the cubicle walls as he looked for some landmark to prove to himself that this was the right room. But there was a sameness to the offices that made it impossible to know where in the building they were standing. Even Lauren, after more than two months of temping at Delphi, didn't venture too far beyond her desk and the break room where she took lunch, for fear of getting lost in that maze of identical workstations.

"I wish I still had my map," Jacob said. He turned. "Do you know any other temps?"

Lauren shook her head. "No, I told you. I was the only red badge in my department."

"I just, I can't believe that we're the only ones here. It's impossible."

Unease pricked at the surface of Lauren's skin. "There have to be more survivors. This is a big company, there must be at least a few hundred temps working in this building. They couldn't have all just disappeared." Her voice was a little shaky, and when she heard it in her own ears she realized that she was trying to convince herself that they weren't the sole survivors of a second catastrophe, a rapture that mysteriously whisked away everyone who hadn't succumbed to the gas.

"That's not what I'm worried about," Jacob said.

"What, then?"

"I'm worried they were evacuated while we were in the break room watching the news. Some emergency protocol that Delphi had in place for this kind of event. Now they're in a shelter somewhere, a bunker. That's what I'm worried about."

The prick of unease became an icy knife of panic slicing through Lauren's chest. She experienced the primal childhood fear of being left behind, of losing sight of her mother at the grocery store or shopping mall, her alarm deepened by the plausibility of what Jacob was saying. *Of course* Delphi would have some kind of procedure in place for emergencies. She should've stayed at her desk, awaited further instructions. Not holed up in a break room with some guy she'd only just met.

Except: what if all the people responsible for carrying out Delphi's emergency plan had died in the gas too?

"The concourse," Lauren said. "If there's some meeting place, some rendezvous point, it'll be in an open area."

They walked away from the courtyard, winding their way through cubicle pods, past coffee machines and water coolers, around a circular table cluttered with the detritus of a hastily-abandoned meeting, and down a dim corridor before coming out into the open air of the concourse.

Lauren looked right, then left. As far as she could tell, the concourse was empty too. Though, the space wasn't open enough to give her an unimpeded view of the whole wing. It was partitioned here and there by freestanding walls, slopes and berms and walkways, large steps, pieces of modern sculpture. It was possible that someone else could be standing in the concourse—or hiding, terrified—in a place that Lauren couldn't see.

"Which way?" Lauren asked.

Jacob pointed and they began walking.

As they walked down the concourse, Lauren glanced outside. The gas still hadn't completely dissipated. Everything was bathed in a yellow tint, subtle enough that, for a moment, Lauren wondered if she was imagining it. But no, the yellow was still there, clearly visible when she looked past the freeway to the horizon.

"Look outside," she said, and waited for Jacob's head to turn. "You think we're still in danger? Could that get inside? Like, through the ventilation system or something? Or the doors?"

They were coming up on a set of doors to the outside at that moment, and Jacob walked toward it and tugged on a handle. The door didn't move.

"Locked," he said. "Do these doors lock like the ones to the courtyard?"

Lauren shook her head. "They're not supposed to."

"Must be some kind of emergency thing."

This observation brought its own feeling of panic. Lauren didn't want the gas or the Furies to get in—but she didn't want to be trapped here either. "Try your security badge," she suggested.

Jacob fished it out of his pocket and tapped at a locking mechanism next to the door. The small light on it beeped green, and Jacob reached for the handle.

"No!" Lauren shouted, leaping forward. "Don't open it. I only wanted to see."

Jacob stepped back, and after a few seconds the light on the locking mechanism switched to red again.

"Let's keep going," Jacob said.

They kept on down the concourse, and soon spotted something in the distance that looked like it might be a person.

"Is that . . . ?" Lauren asked, craning her neck.

"I think so."

A young woman sat cross-legged at the top of an open rectangle of space that was sunk down beneath the level of the rest of the floor. On one side the rectangle abutted the windows overlooking the freeway, on the other side the concourse thinned to a narrow walkway, and at the top and bottom three steps led down to the surface, which was made of a springy, rubbery substance that sunk under Lauren's shoes when she stepped onto it.

"Hello?" she called across the space, which she now realized was an open-air yoga studio. Still the girl at the top of the rectangle said nothing, made no movement. She didn't even open her eyes. Her wrists rested limp on her knees, and her back and neck were pencil straight.

"What's wrong with her?" Jacob asked. He moved in front of Lauren and then stopped halfway to the top of the rectangle, as if suddenly struck by the girl's peacefulness and not wanting to disturb her.

Just then, from outside the building, came a percussive sound. Lauren turned away from the girl and looked at the windows, listening until the sound became recognizable. The rotors of a helicopter chopping the air.

"Do you hear that?" Lauren asked Jacob.

"I don't believe it." He too faced the window, but he glanced sideways at the girl as he spoke, checking to see if the sound of the helicopter would pull her out of her meditation. She remained still.

Lauren walked the rest of the way to the window, put her hand to the glass, and scanned the yellow sky.

"You think they're flying above the gas?"

"Maybe they're wearing masks."

At once she saw them: not one helicopter but two. A pair of dots hovering over the strip mall, growing larger as they approached the Delphi building. When they reached the freeway Lauren saw that they were army helicopters, green, with a red cross painted under the cockpit. Part of Lauren became weightless—they hadn't been left behind after all, hadn't been forgotten. Someone was coming to save them.

But then one of the helicopters banked sharply right, crashing into the other. The two helicopters spun wildly off each other, whirling through the air like maple seeds. Then they slammed down. The rotors, still spinning, chopped at the ground, shards of metal shattering and flying through the air. One helicopter fell amidst the wreckage of cars and semis on the freeway, but the other went on spinning and crashed on the grounds of Delphi, the chopping rotors sending chunks of dirt and sod flying. The helicopter slid across the lawn, riding the momentum of the crash toward the window where Lauren and Jacob were standing.

"Fuck," Lauren said, yanking her hand from the glass and stepping away. "Fuck, fuck, fuck."

The helicopter went on sliding, and for a moment Lauren was certain it would hit the building, come crashing through the glass, let the gas come creeping in—but it didn't. The helicopter slowed, then stopped some dozen yards from the windows.

For a few seconds all was still. Then people came climbing out of the wreckage. Three men wearing fatigues, two with guns strapped across their chests, one unarmed with a bag that could've been a medic's kit at his side. Each had masks, as Jacob had guessed, but the crash had jarred them loose, and Lauren watched as the now-familiar effects of the gas took place: the groaning and tightening of muscles as they were seized by what must have been an incredible pain, the bursting blood vessels—and then the rage, the fury.

The medic was the first to attack, to spring from his hands and knees on the ground and grab at one of the armed men's throats. The third man swung his automatic rifle into his hands and fired on the other two until it was clear both were dead—and then he went on firing, shredding their bodies with bullets until his clip was spent and the gun clicked on an empty chamber.

The man turned. He was the last standing, the last alive, and as he came toward the window Lauren saw that his leg had been injured by the crash. His fatigues were torn near the knee, red blood showing through the gash, and the leg seemed slightly bent at an unnatural angle. The pain of walking on it must have been intense, but the man didn't seem to notice or care. He limped toward the glass, closer, closer, and Lauren felt that he must be looking at her—except he couldn't be, the glass was opaque and reflective on the other side. He was looking at himself.

The man leveled the gun at the window and pulled the trigger. The clip was still empty, of course, and when the gun only clicked rather than fired, the cold fury on the soldier's face boiled over. He bellowed at the gun, then turned it upside-down and began bashing at the window with the butt. Lauren startled, her body giving a quake in time with the sharp crack of the gun against the window—but the glass didn't break, didn't even show any signs of developing a hairline fracture. The soldier went on bashing against the glass, hitting the butt of the gun, Lauren noted, at the level of his head, where the image of his own face must have been reflecting back to him.

When it was clear the glass wouldn't break, the soldier cast the gun aside, then grabbed at his belt, pulled a knife from a sheath. He raised the knife to his neck and swept the sharp side across his throat so quickly that Lauren's gasp came after the man's blood had already sprayed against the glass, after he'd already fallen to the ground.

This was the first time Lauren had seen a person affected by the gas turn their rage on themselves, visiting violence upon their own body. She turned, half to shield her eyes from the horror she'd already seen, half to ask Jacob why—why some of the people who breathed in the yellow gas killed others, some killed themselves, and yet others survived to band together in animal packs that hunted for new victims.

But Jacob himself had already turned away from the gruesome scene, and was facing the meditating young woman—who was no longer meditating. She'd gotten up from her yoga mat and had come a few steps toward Lauren and Jacob while their backs had been turned. She was brown-skinned, with black hair falling to her shoulders. She'd seen everything, and now she had tears in her eyes and a question on her lips.

"Why?" she demanded, as though they knew—as though it was their fault. Her voice came out shaky. "Why is this happening?"

# FOUR

All Swati Sidana had wanted was a little peace—a few moments to find her breath, to get centered, and then decide what to do next. Normally how it worked was, she'd put on some calming music, fold her legs beneath her, close her eyes, drape her wrists over her knees, and just breathe. She'd focus on the parts of her body one at a time, bring her attention inward, let go of whatever it was outside that was bothering her. After a bit of this, she could usually find some peace, could *be* peace and *bring* peace, even when the world was falling apart around her, as it seemed to be right now. But there'd be no peace today. Not after what she'd seen in the courtyard. Not after the sound of crashing helicopters, of gunfire, of blood burbling over a slit windpipe. No one could meditate through that. Not even she—who'd sat and closed her eyes and breathed through so much the past year at home, half-lotus on her bed upstairs while on the main floor her housemates argued over another of their inane "actions."

"We should lock ourselves in cages."

"Cages, what?"

"Yeah, like the cages the chickens live in. Really show those shoppers the horror of the industrialized meat system they're propping up."

"But where are we going to find person-sized chicken cages? And how will we sneak them into a grocery store?"

"Yeah, it doesn't sound practical. I think we should put duct tape over our mouths and write 'Resist' on it."

"That's really fucking stupid."

"No it's not, it's evocative. It's striking. It'll make people stop and pay attention."

"But pay attention to what? There's no context. Resist what? And what does the duct tape over our mouths mean?"

"That we're being silenced."

"That's not even the fucking point! Chickens are being tortured and killed for our food system. They don't have voices, we do. Putting duct tape over our mouths literally prevents us from communicating what we want to say. It'll confuse people."

"I agree. What we should do is something visceral. Like, dump a bunch of chicken shit on the floor. Or drink red dye and induce vomiting in the meat section. It'll look like we're puking blood."

"Um, I think that would be triggering to people with eating disorders. Besides, why are we going after grocery shoppers? Shouldn't we be targeting meat company owners, supply chains, the people with real power?"

"Change begins from the ground up, Linda . . ."

They were unserious people. White girls with dreads, boys who never wore shoes. Rich kids who got checks every month from their parents but still considered themselves political revolutionaries. Poverty tourists. She should never have agreed to live with them. But Swati hadn't realized her mistake until it was too late—until she'd already moved in. Even then, it took more than a year of living in that grungy house for Swati to admit to herself that she wanted out. That she needed to get away from Jared.

Swati had first met Jared in college. Both of them were seniors. They'd met in the usual way: at a house party. Swati was holding the stereotypical red plastic cup and scanning the crowd for a recognizable face when Jared walked up.

"I'd like to talk to you," he said. "You seem interesting."

This was not even remotely smooth, but something in the straight-forwardness of Jared's opening gambit held Swati in place. She looked at this white boy: brown hair, flannel shirt, loose jeans, leather wrist cuff. He wasn't holding a red cup like everyone else; instead he drank something brown and cloudy out of a mason jar, something he said he'd brewed himself and brought from home. They exchanged names, then got to talking about majors. Jared was women's studies. Swati confessed to majoring in business administration with a minor in exercise science. Jared frowned.

"What is it?" Swati asked.

"Capitalism is morally bankrupt," he said. His tone was that of a disappointed father, as though he was realizing he'd misjudged in thinking Swati interesting.

"Maybe," Swati said. The student body at the university was generally progressive; she'd heard arguments like this before, and she'd practiced her response. "I think it's probably amoral at worst. What makes capitalism good or bad is people. *I'm* not morally bankrupt. After graduation I want to open my own yoga and mindfulness studio. If I can learn how to work within capitalism to do something good, to bring customers a valuable service, then what's the harm?"

"That's dead-end thinking. Systems exist to propagate themselves. The logic of the system inevitably overrides the morality of the individuals working within it."

"I don't believe that. The bad examples get all the press—oil executives, chemical companies dumping arsenic in rivers, crooked bankers—but there are plenty of good, decent businesspeople who are making the world a better place."

"Yeah, and I'm sure there were a lot of good Nazis too."

"That's not a fair comparison, you can't just drop Nazis into the conversation as a trump card."

"I think the analogy is apt. You seem like a good person, Swati, but that doesn't matter. The system you're being inculcated into is inherently classist, misogynist, and racist. You really want to be part of something like that?"

In hindsight, what Swati should have said was that she probably knew a lot more about misogyny and racism than Jared did, no matter how many classes he'd taken on the topics. That she'd make her own decisions about how she'd live her life, thank you very much. But she didn't. Instead she listened as Jared held forth, spun intricate webs of critical theory and buzzy activist jargon, his thoughts winding their way into her mind and slowly displacing her own. There was a thrill in giving herself over, in succumbing. Plus listening silently gave her a chance to simply look at Jared, to admire his sinewy forearms and glistening tan skin, his beautiful brown eyes with long lashes. His voice was soft, seductive. She went home with him that night to a ramshackle house just off campus. He took her to his room on the third floor, where they had sex.

They spent more time together in the months ahead, during which Jared frequently lectured her on radical politics and gave her books to read. Sometimes they had sex, though they never, as far as Swati could tell, were really dating or in a relationship. Then, toward the end of their senior year, Jared asked her to join him and "a few awesome, politically aware people" in what he was calling "an anarchist collective."

"You can be our spiritual advisor," he said. "Our wellness guru. Practice yoga and mindfulness—but without any of the degradation of market commodification and exchange."

Swati agreed and moved into the house after graduation. It seemed like a good idea at the time—the house was old, the rent cheap, and her plan was to become a certified yoga instructor while saving up to start her business. Things were fine at first, even occasionally wonderful. In those early days Swati and her housemates ate huge communal meals made entirely of organic ingredients. They had intense political discussions late into the night, talking excitedly about the awakening of the masses and the inevitable cultural revolution that would follow. And then, sometimes, when the rest of the house was asleep, Jared would slip quietly into her bed. He'd always be gone by morning, so that Swati would be left wondering if the previous night's encounter had been nothing more than a dream.

Then negatives began compounding. Dirty dishes towered high in the sink, food was left to rot, a bathtub clog left the shower perpetually unusable. The house became infested with flies, ants, roaches, and various unidentified smells. The impotent stupidity of the collective's political actions, the frivolity of their revolutionary talk, began to grate. Swati, who'd finished a 200-hour yoga certification shortly after graduation, cobbled together a modest living teaching yoga at retirement communities, progressive church events, political action conferences—but Jared insisted that everyone forfeit all personal income to the house fund. He had principled reasons for this, having to do with the abolishment of private property and the superiority of collective decision-making as a model for community thriving, but as the months wore on the rule seemed less political than it did manipulative, even abusive.

Still, it wasn't until about a year after she'd moved in with the collective that Swati allowed herself to see that she'd made a mistake. A turning point was when she saw Jared sneaking into the room of one of the other girls, and she suddenly understood that he was sleeping with most—perhaps all—of the women in the house. After that Swati began hoarding money from yoga jobs under her mattress, and planning for an eventual escape.

· · ·

Swati couldn't quite say how she ended up with a job at Delphi Enterprises. It all happened very quickly. One moment she was scrolling her social media feeds in search of more yoga clients, the next she was looking at the Delphi temp listing, and almost immediately after that her inbox pinged with an official job offer: teaching yoga to Delphi employees two days a week, Mondays and Fridays.

Jared's face darkened with his usual disapproving frown when he heard about the job. Delphi was a soulless corporation run by one of the billionaires rigging the global economy in favor of the one percent.

But Jared couldn't seem to find anything the company had done wrong. There was nothing about Delphi on the anarchist blogs or message boards he frequented. He couldn't even determine what it was the company actually did. Still, he was certain that Delphi—and Tristan Brandt, the corporation's mysterious CEO—was crooked in some fundamental way.

"They're fucking the world over somehow, I know they are," he said. "No one participates in the capitalist system and comes out clean."

"Why can't you find anything on them, then?" Swati said. "Isn't it possible that Delphi is actually a *good* company?"

For a long time Swati had backed off her thesis that some business-people could be good, but she was beginning to find her way back to her own ideas again, to resist the lure of Jared's way of thinking. Maybe she was finally allowing herself to feel angry at him for convincing her to move in with him, for keeping all her money, for sleeping with other women without telling her. More and more, she found herself thinking of the person she might have been if she hadn't met Jared, the person she *should* have been—a yoga instructor saving her money to start her own studio, just as she'd always wanted—and felt a mournful sort of rage.

"No," Jared said. "That's impossible. There's no way Delphi's clean. I think they're probably just too deep to show up on anyone's radar."

"What the hell are you talking about?"

"You know how everything in the world is controlled by, like, five corporations, basically?"

Swati shook her head. "That's not a thing. You're just making that up."

"I'm not. You dig far enough, get past the oil companies and chemical companies and food companies and pharma companies destroying our bodies and raping the earth—behind those, like ten layers deep in the financial guts of the whole system, you get to these huge international conglomerates, these holding companies that finance everything and pull all the strings and make all the orders but then disappear as soon as indictments start to fly. It's real Illuminati shit. Maybe Delphi is one of those."

"You're losing it," Swati said. "You're getting paranoid."

"What do *you* think Delphi is, then?"

Swati rolled her eyes but didn't say anything. She thought Jared was being ridiculous, but she didn't have any alternative to offer in the face of his conspiracy theories. She'd visited Delphi's website, pored over the "About" page, but came away with no clear vision of the company's business, either.

"Maybe you could be a spy," Jared said.

"What? No."

"I'm serious. Go through the wastebaskets, figure out what they do. Then sabotage things."

"How would I do that? They hired me to teach yoga. I won't have a computer, won't have a desk."

"I'm just saying, this could be an opportunity."

"An opportunity for what?"

"To see how the system really works. From the inside. To bring the whole thing crashing down."

. . .

Swati didn't act as a spy, didn't try to sabotage Delphi's operations, only did what she'd been hired to do: she taught yoga.

She wrote down the routines at home on notepads, really worked at crafting them, at changing things up, at not repeating herself from class to class. On workdays she drove more than an hour from the city to the suburbs, where Delphi's huge glass complex lay. Inside, she'd roll out her mat at the top of the open-air yoga studio in the P-wing concourse, hook up her phone to a speaker, turn on meditation music, and wait for her students to arrive. In classes—one in the morning, one at noon, and one in the afternoon—she felt relaxed, comfortable. She led her students through a sequence of poses. She asked if she could touch them, then gently corrected their form. She told them to open their hearts, pull back their shoulders, tuck their tails. She reminded them to breathe. At the end of the class she led them in short meditations, bowed with her hands pressed together, said "namaste."

Swati liked the work. Her classes were popular, filled up quickly. And Delphi employees were so nice—young, attractive, clean, optimistic. They weren't angry all the time, weren't always looking for something to fight about. Some of them, the women, even became sort-of friends, drew her into hugs when they saw her, asked her how she was doing, called her "girl," as in: "Girl, you really kicked my ass today with that crane pose!" or "Hey girl, how's your love life?" Swati was well-liked enough in the company that the employee wellness coordinator who'd hired her was starting to talk about bringing her on full-time to teach classes every day of the week.

Then the gas cloud hit.

Swati had taught one class that morning, her 8:00 a.m. class, then dismissed her students back to their cubicles, reminded them to drink plenty of water. She took a drink of her own from a plastic water bottle with a straw, then detached her phone from the external speaker as the concourse emptied around her. She'd heard that there was an all-company meeting that day, everyone with a black badge reporting to the amphitheater. Not her, but she didn't care. After two months at Delphi, she still didn't understand any more about what the company did, and she didn't care to know. She was content just teaching yoga.

The time between classes was hers. She began by reviewing her routine in her notepad, making some adjustments for the next class. Next she sat cross-legged on her mat, closed her eyes, and did mindfulness practice. The timer on her phone was set for twenty minutes. After that, she had a book waiting for her, a domestic thriller marketed for women about dissatisfied wives and bad, possibly murderous, husbands.

She never got to the novel. Halfway through her meditation she began to hear the moaning from the courtyard. At first she ignored it, thought it might be the hum of a distant vibration in the building's HVAC system, but then the sound grew in volume and in pitch until it was no longer moaning, but screaming.

Swati opened her eyes, turned off her timer, the numbers reading 9:37. She stood and turned toward the sound of the moaning. Her skin felt cold; she drew her hands to her forearms and rubbed them up and down. Then she walked to the edge of the concourse and pushed through a door into the offices. When she came to the glass, the courtyard was bathed in the yellow gas, thick enough that she couldn't see more than a couple of feet on the other side. Then the mist lifted.

Swati stood far from the amphitheater; her view wasn't as good as Jacob's, or Lauren's. But she could still see the chaos as it spilled past the last row of the amphitheater and onto the rest of the courtyard. Delphi employees transformed by rage, falling on each other, killing each other. These people to whom she'd taught yoga. They'd seemed so nice, so well-adjusted. Smiling at one another after class, politely offering professional courtesies—thanking each other for things said in important email chains or in crucial decision-making meetings, giving congratulations for "killing it" on this project or that one, constantly assuring each other that they were "rock stars," that they were doing "such a great job." Swati had observed them and thought that the employees of Delphi Enterprises had discovered the right way to live, that it was they and not her angry, political house-mates who were the people she was meant to be surrounded by.

But now this.

Swati watched for a few minutes, strangely calm. Then her phone, which she was still holding in her hand, made a dinging noise. A woman's voice spoke to her.

*"Swati, this is your Concierge. I'm noticing your heart rate is spiking. Is everything all right?"*

"I . . . I don't know."

*"Maybe you should do some yoga?"*

"Okay."

Swati turned away from the window and went back through the office, returned to her mat. At her phone's suggestion, she did fifty sun salutations: mountain pose to forward fold, lunge, plank, cobra into down dog, then back to lunge, forward fold, reach the hands overhead, lengthen the spine, then exhale back into mountain. She did the sequences slowly, stretching them out. After she was done, the voice in her phone suggested a time of meditation. Swati obeyed, settled cross-legged on her mat, laid her wrists on her knees, palms-up, and closed her eyes.

During this time—through the sun salutations and the meditation—she heard everything that was going on around her. She heard the crashing cars on the freeway outside. Later, she thought she could sense movement nearby, perhaps from upper floors. Footsteps, echoing against the glass. She heard it all.

Meditation wasn't for escaping the world, the human consciousness jailbreaking from the prison of the present moment. It was for being more fully in the moment, and finding a freedom there. Meditation brought Swati into her physical self—which, at that moment, was precisely what she needed. Outside there was chaos, killing, death—but the violence hadn't yet defiled the sacredness of her body. This was a calming thing: that she still had the sensations of her body. Her scalp prickling. Her arms warming under the sun that still streamed through the glass. Her legs, aching pleasurably from the sun salutations. Her heart beating reliably in her chest. And the breath flowing in and out of her nostrils, bringing fresh air into her lungs, oxygen into her bloodstream.

But when she heard the sound of the helicopter crashing, heard the sound of death right outside the window, it was all too much. She opened her eyes, stood up, and demanded that the guy and the girl who'd appeared while her eyes had been closed tell her *why*, that they answer for what was happening.

But they couldn't. They were silent, just as confused and afraid as she was.

· · ·

Their names were Lauren and Jacob. Jacob didn't say much, but as soon as she'd introduced herself Lauren began asking Swati questions of her own.

"Have you seen anyone else?"

Swati shook her head. "No. But I thought I might've heard footsteps up there."

She pointed up to the elevated walkways of the upper-floor concourses, broad catwalks with metal railings looming above their heads.

"Did you call out?"

"No," Swati said.

Lauren breathed out with exasperation. "Why not?"

"I was meditating," Swati said.

"You realize we might have been left behind here?" Lauren asked. "The survivors might all be in a bunker somewhere. We can't find anyone."

Swati blinked a slow blink, breathed in and out. Lauren's panic bled off her like a physical presence, like the reek of stale sweat. At the same time, Swati was beginning to feel her own emotions again. Aside from her elevated heart rate, she hadn't yet registered the things she saw in the Delphi courtyard. She wondered when it might hit her; perhaps it was already. Retreating into yoga and meditation, leaping up with tears in her eyes when she couldn't dissociate any longer—could this be shock? Was this what reeling from the moments after a trauma felt like?

"The world's ending, you know that, right?" Lauren continued. "The thing that happened in the courtyard—it's not just here. It spread into the city. And it's happening other places too."

Swati hadn't known that—how could she? Lauren's voice was laden with disgust, as though Swati must be stupid not to know what was happening in the world outside. Swati felt her first emotion since seeing the death in the courtyard, the first one she could name, anyway: anger.

"Fuck you. Sorry I'm not exactly keeping up with the news. I did what I needed to do for myself."

"Yeah, well now what *I* need is for *you* to act like you understand the gravity of the situation we're in."

"I understand it perfectly fine. I'm not an idiot."

"Well then maybe you could tell us where you think those people you heard might've gone."

"I told you, I don't know. I didn't see them. My eyes were closed."

Lauren's eyes bulged and she looked to be on the verge of saying something else, when the guy—Jacob—stepped forward and cut in.

"This isn't helping anything."

Jacob's voice was calm, but he didn't really seem any less scared than Lauren—he was just carrying it differently, trying to be strong even though he was clearly shaken. Looking at him, Swati realized that they were *all* shocked and scared, and dealing with that feeling in different ways. It wasn't Lauren's fault that she felt the need to externalize her fear as anger in order to keep from falling apart. Swati mentally made an intention to be more compassionate with her.

"What do you suggest?" Swati asked.

Jacob looked down the concourse.

"Maybe we should find something to eat."

Swati allowed herself to laugh. The suggestion was at once blindingly stupid and obviously sensible. It seemed to have disarmed Lauren too.

"My lunch is at my desk," Lauren said, getting a cross-eyed look. She clearly didn't want to go back. Maybe her desk was close to the windows, and to retrieve her lunch she'd have to look at the courtyard again.

"I have a quinoa salad in my bag," Swati said. "It's supposed to be for me, but I could share."

"Aren't there food courts on every floor?" Jacob asked.

Lauren looked up. "What do you want to do, steal something?"

He shrugged. "Delphi can take it out of my first paycheck."

Swati laughed again. It felt good. She stood and rolled up her yoga mat, wrapped a strap around it, and then attached it to her bag.

"What are you doing?" Lauren asked.

"I'm taking my stuff with me," Swati said. "I need it, and I don't know when we'll be back."

As she slipped the strap of the bag up over her head and felt the weight of all her earthly possessions straining against her shoulder—yoga mat, water bottle, salad, Bluetooth speaker, and second set of yoga clothes to change into if she got sweaty—Swati had the feeling of embarking upon a long journey.

A quest.

# FIVE

Jacob led the way down the concourse. He didn't know his way through the Delphi building as well as Swati and Lauren did, but he'd become, for the moment, the leader of their impromptu expeditionary group. Looking for food had been his suggestion. Now he was responsible. He wondered about what restaurants they'd find at the food court, what kind of food would be available to them, whether it would be prepared or not. If there was a Starbucks, Jacob could make Swati and Lauren something, warm up a breakfast sandwich or pull shots of espresso, steam milk for cappuccinos or lattes. He'd worked at a Starbucks in a shopping mall for three months about a year ago, and he still remembered how everything worked. But he'd never been in a job where he'd had to operate a fryer or a griddle, and he didn't really know how to cook, so if Lauren or Swati wanted anything more complicated he'd be forced to admit that he didn't know how to make it.

An unpleasant realization dawned: Jacob didn't know how to survive. His head was full of the knowledge school had crammed into him—critical theory, poststructuralism and feminism and postcolonialism, the history of Western philosophy and literature, the politics of gender and race and class, how to read and deconstruct cultural texts, the basics of mathematics, biology, physics—but none of it was useful. This had been true that morning, when his degree had been useless only in getting him a good-paying corporate job that didn't make him feel ashamed; it was even truer now that the gas had descended and his education was also useless in helping him stay alive. The lie of a liberal arts education was that knowledge mattered, that the ability to be a thoughtful citizen of the world was worth a single solitary fuck. What was the point, when all it took was a yellow cloud to set civilization crumbling? What would Jacob's knowledge be worth when the gas lifted and they left the Delphi building to see what remained of the world? He couldn't hunt, couldn't fire a gun or set a trap, couldn't forage, couldn't find fresh water. All he knew how to do was warm up processed, pre-packaged foods. Tearing off plastic, turning on machines, putting flash-frozen patties or nuggets in a microwave and then bombarding them with particles.

In the midst of these thoughts, Jacob smelled something. He lifted his head, put his nose to the air of the concourse. It was the smell of cooking meat. The food court was ahead. Jacob's stomach groaned; saliva came rushing into his mouth. He hadn't eaten since that morning.

"I think someone's here," Jacob said. "You smell that?"

Swati and Lauren sniffed. Jacob began walking faster, putting distance between him and them as he rushed ahead. The food court sat in the middle of the concourse, with a square perimeter of restaurant kiosks and huts surrounding a central sitting area. The tables and chairs were empty. The restaurant signs came into view: Panda Express, Potbelly Sandwiches, Cosi, Noodles & Company, Au Bon Pain. The smell—and a sizzling sound now—seemed to be coming from a Chipotle.

"Fuck," said a voice from an unseen person in the kitchen, as a fire roared. "Fuck, fuck, fuck."

Jacob rushed around the counter and pushed through the swinging doors to find a young Black man about his age, standing at the griddle. He wore business casual clothes, pressed gray pants and a striped dress shirt unbuttoned at the collar. Sweat was on his forehead, and flames from the grill flared as high as his shoulders—the reason, no doubt, for his cursing. Frantically the young man grabbed a broad metal bowl from the countertop and used his spatula to flip the burning beef, onions, and peppers off the hot surface. Then he turned with the bowl and saw Jacob.

"Oh," the young man said. "Hey. Sorry, I didn't see you."

"It's okay," Jacob said. "I didn't say anything. I didn't want to bother you. Your hands looked a little full."

"I'm Dominic," he said.

"Jacob."

Dominic looked down at the bowl full of scorched food in one hand, the spatula in the other, with a look that suggested slight embarrassment—the look of a frantic dinner host who wasn't quite ready to receive the guests knocking at the front door with a bottle of wine. He shrugged apologetically.

"I was just making myself a burrito bowl," Dominic said. "You want me to make you something? I worked part-time at Chipotle before starting at Delphi."

Jacob eased. "Sure," he said. "If it's not too much trouble."

Dominic set the bowl on the counter. "No trouble at all."

• • •

Dominic Hill was ravenous. The hunger had hit him when he saw the catastrophe in the courtyard, when he realized what was happening outside. Suddenly it seemed very important to eat, to drink, to find all the things necessary for the survival of his body. He'd left the office and went looking for the nearest food court. Chipotle had been a second job to help pay for business school, more than a year ago. He'd left it off his résumé when he'd applied for the temp position—work at a fast-casual restaurant wasn't relevant to the Delphi business analytics department—but he was glad, now, that he'd worked there, that he knew how to fire up the griddle, knew how to cook something for himself. He'd thrown the beef on the hot surface a few minutes later, taking comfort in the sizzling sound, in the savory smell that filled the air, the heat changing the raw animal flesh into something he could put into his body, something that could sustain him. Outside, the world was falling apart, but for now he was okay. He was getting something to eat.

Now there were three others with him—Jacob, Lauren, and Swati—and he worked without talking, feeling their eyes on him. Jacob wanted a burrito, Lauren too, but Swati had said no thanks, she'd packed a lunch. After he'd cooked up another batch of marinated steak and fajita vegetables, Dominic showed Jacob and Lauren how to warm up a tortilla, fill it with rice and beans, meat and salsa, then wrap it tight without tearing. These were familiar motions, comforting rituals. They put their food on trays. Jacob and Lauren grabbed paper cups for soda from the fountain, but Dominic opened the refrigerator case and grabbed a Corona.

"Why not?" he said when he saw the others looking at him. They set their cups down and grabbed beers of their own, even Swati. Then they brought their food to the sitting area and took a rectangular table.

"So what's your story?" Dominic asked as Lauren and Jacob unpeeled the foil from their burritos and each took ravenous first bites. "Are you all in the same department?"

That couldn't be right, Dominic realized as soon as he asked; Lauren and Jacob were wearing business casual, like him, but Swati was in workout clothes, which probably made her one of Delphi's fitness contractors. She was ignoring the question, fishing in her bag for a plastic container of quinoa salad. She popped the lid, releasing the scents of lemon, cilantro, onion, and tomato. Swati poked at the contents with a fork, fluffing the quinoa before taking a bite.

Lauren chewed and swallowed. "No, we're all different departments. I'm in psychometric extraction."

Dominic had never heard of the department, didn't know what they did, but that didn't bother him—he'd gotten used to Delphi's secretiveness, its opacity. In his six months temping for business analytics he hadn't met a single person who had the whole picture of what the company did, the various businesses it maintained. Temp or permanent, most people could tell you what they did for Delphi, but few could explain the *purpose* of their job, and no one had a complete grasp of the company's operations. In place of understanding they had rumors, and lies.

"Mail room," Jacob said.

Dominic looked to Swati next. She glanced up at him and waved her fork dismissively.

"I just teach yoga," she said, as though disavowing herself of all this—Delphi, the building, the others sitting at the table, the events of the morning. "To the employees. Anyone who signs up for my class. That's it. I just, I teach yoga."

"Okay," Dominic said. "So you're from different departments. But you ended up together."

"We found each other," Lauren said. "The same way we found you."

"Have you seen any others?" Jacob asked. "Survivors?"

Dominic shook his head. "No. You're the first."

"But there have to be more, right? There's no way we're the only temps in the whole building."

"No," Dominic said. "We're not." He'd looked up the number of temps just that morning—an assignment from one of the senior analysts, who'd passed off a list of almost one hundred metrics he needed Dominic to pull from the Brain by noon, when he expected to be back from the all-company meeting. "There are 350 temps total."

"Three hundred fifty?" Lauren asked. "That's it? Ten thousand employees in this complex and only, what, three or four in a hundred are temp workers?"

"There used to be more," Dominic said, remembering the line chart he'd found in the Brain and then printed out for the senior analyst. "Almost a thousand at the high point, a year ago. But then Delphi started converting them to black badges, letting others go as projects postmortemed, and as of just this morning the number ticked up from 349 to 350 with some new hire's first day."

"It's *my* first day," Jacob said.

"I guess you're number 350, then."

"How do you know all this?" Lauren asked. "What department do you work for?"

"BA," Dominic answered. "That's business analytics. I'm a research assistant, not an actual analyst. But I still have access to a lot of the company data."

Jacob leaned forward, his burrito still gripped between his two hands. The torn end of it pointed toward Dominic like a microphone.

"Do *you* know what Delphi does?"

The way Jacob leaned on the word *you* told Dominic that it wasn't the first time Jacob had asked the question.

Dominic put the fingertips of one hand into the air as if reaching for a good answer.

"Everything," he said. "Or maybe nothing. It's hard to explain. Nobody knows the whole of it, only pieces."

"Nobody?" Jacob demanded, something aggrieved in his tone.

"Well," Dominic said, "nobody except maybe Brandt."

. . .

It was in business school that Dominic had first heard the name Tristan Brandt. Brandt wasn't exactly a celebrity CEO, the kind of household name that your average person on the street would have heard of, but he was well-known among business executives and market insiders, a revolutionary figure in the twenty-first-century global economy.

So Dominic's professor had said, anyway.

"Tristan Brandt," the professor intoned as he passed out photocopies of a profile from the *Harvard Business Review*, "is a genius. As the founder and CEO of Delphi Enterprises, he completely revolutionized complex portfolio management and value creation across multiple business sectors and growth models."

Dominic didn't really understand what this meant. The professor was a short, mole-like DBA with glasses and suspenders who did this far too often, disappeared into vague business-speak that didn't really convey anything to his night class students. The class, Dominic's last before he'd have enough credits to graduate, was called "Data Mining and Statistical Analysis for Value Creation." Dominic thought of raising his hand and asking if the professor could explain Tristan Brandt's revolutionary-whatever again in layman's terms—he guessed that most of the other night class students hadn't really understood what the professor said, either—but he thought better of it, figuring everything would become clear in the stapled HBR article coming down the row. Dominic took a glance at the title—"Tristan Brandt: The Oracle of Delphi Enterprises"—then stuffed it in his bag and went home to bed.

Dominic pulled out the article the next day over soft shells at Taco Bell, where the crew had stopped off for some lunch before their next job. His uncle Walter, eating hunched with both elbows on the table across from him, grunted and nodded his chin toward the sheaf of papers.

"What's that?"

"Reading," Dominic answered. "School."

"I don't know why you bother with that nonsense. The business is yours when I retire. I made a promise to your mother."

"I know that," Dominic said. "I know the business is coming to me. School is so I know how to run it."

"Shit," Walter said. He clicked his tongue, sucking something—a piece of lettuce, or a bit of taco meat—out of his teeth. "The roofing business isn't *that* hard. I built it from the ground without an ounce of schooling."

"Yeah, but I want to take it to the next level."

This was Dominic's line whenever Uncle Walter or his mother hassled him about his night classes—that he was learning how to grow his uncle's business into a real professional outfit. Instead of what it was: a shitty one-truck operation run out of Walter's Toyota, job quotes calculated on scraps of paper, an ad in the Yellow Pages, and a constantly rotating crew of workers. Payments in cash, no accounting system to speak of. Walter knew roofing, but no one had ever taught him how to run a business, and it showed. Dominic wanted to turn the business into a brand—give it a name and a logo, implement real job quoting and financial accounting systems, get a sales force, multiple crews, an office. That's what Dominic always said, anyway, and the line worked, put an end to their questions.

Except it was a lie. Dominic wasn't taking night classes to *improve* his uncle's business—he was taking them so he could *escape* it. Walter had pledged the business to his nephew when he was only six years old, too young to understand what was being bequeathed to him or whether he even wanted it. But that was also the year Dominic's dad had been killed by a drunk driver, and his mother wanted to see to it that her boy would be taken care of. So she went to her childless brother and wrested from him the solemn promise that the paltry roofing empire he'd built for himself would be Dominic's one day.

Dominic began working for his uncle at age eighteen, right after his high school graduation. He hated the work—hated the long, grueling days, hated waking up at first light and leaving the worksite only once the sunlight had begun to wane, hated going home with an aching back, hated getting bossed around by his uncle and treated like shit by the crew for being the owner's nephew. Most of all he hated working on rich people's homes, the way it made him feel to be doing manual labor as they walked out their front doors in suits, shouting into cell phones tucked between their shoulders and their ears as they climbed into shiny cars and cruised off to better jobs, better lives. More than anything he wanted to be one of them, one of the people who worked in an air-conditioned office, who got paid huge sums for doing next to nothing, who came home at the end of the day without a speck of dust on them.

. . .

Dominic wanted, in other words, to be someone less like his uncle and more like Tristan Brandt, whom the *HBR* article profiled with a reverence that was almost religious. Brandt was, the article said, "a prophet of the market whose ability to predict business failure and success is almost eerie" and "a wizard who has, over the course of his 30-year career, transformed seemingly worthless business assets into a multi-billion-dollar portfolio."

The son of a wealthy New York venture capitalist, Brandt studied classical philosophy at Yale before graduating and joining his father's firm. After a string of investment successes, Brandt left New York and started his own business, Delphi Enterprises. Named after the Greek temple on Mount Parnassus at which the oracle Pythia prophesied to kings and heroes, the business's key differentiator was prophetic foresight, an ability to predict with godlike accuracy which businesses could turn a profit with the right investor, and which were destined for capitalism's dustheap. Brandt's motto, and the company's, was the Delphic maxim *gnothi seauton*, which translated to "know thyself."

"Knowing yourself—knowing who you are and knowing where your strengths and weaknesses lie—is the only thing that matters," Brandt was quoted as saying in the article. "In business, in life. But nobody does. Nobody sees themselves clearly. Except us. That's our competitive advantage. We know the market, we know our competitors, and we know consumers better than they know themselves. Insight. That's how we win."

For the first fifteen years of its existence, Delphi Enterprises functioned as a typical venture capital firm. Delphi bought into small businesses on the verge of boom or bust, funded them until they grew, then divested quickly after the investment reached triple-digit return. The firm remained small in those early years, a single floor of a nondescript suburban office complex, reporting hundred-million-dollar profits every fiscal year.

Then something changed. While his investors and analysts continued doing business as usual—buying, selling, hectoring their partners on conference calls—Brandt quietly began acquiring businesses and holding on to them. Chemical companies, steel companies, product distribution centers, shipping and logistics, research firms. He bought up the marshy patch of land right next to the Delphi office, drained it, then built a new building into which he installed more than a hundred employees to manage his new holdings. (Eventually, this building would grow wing by wing into the vast Delphi triangle complex.) Virtually overnight, Delphi Enterprises had morphed from a venture capital firm to a holding company, a small but rapidly growing international conglomerate.

But it wasn't until smart alloy that Brandt's vision for Delphi began to become clear. A different company had been the one to develop the alloy, a metal compound that became structurally unstable at moderately high temperatures, then snapped back to its original form when the temperature dropped again. The company that created the alloy patented the compound but left it on the shelf, thinking it worthless—what good was a metal that started going limp at only 80 degrees Fahrenheit? But when Brandt learned of the invention from one of his research associates, he knew at once that the company had a billion-dollar idea, if only they'd possessed the insight to realize what they had. *Gnothi seauton. Know thyself.* Brandt bought the patent and handed it over to his brand-new research and development team.

The result, two years later, was Safe-T-Knife™. Dominic recognized the product name—his mother had bought a set of the knives to put next to her stove.

The design of Safe-T-Knife™ was simple but brilliant. The knives were stored in a special butcher block that plugged into the wall and kept the temperature of the blades at a consistent 55 degrees. At that temperature, the knives were strong and sharp, slicing effortlessly through cold or room-temperature foods. Because of the instability of the alloy, the knives were less effective when used on hot foods, useless for cutting cooked roast beef or carving a Thanksgiving turkey. But that was part of the design; the instability of smart alloy was what made it smart, and what made Safe-T-Knife™ safe. The blade cut through potatoes and onions and grapefruits without resistance, but turned dull as a butter knife whenever it made contact with human skin, which generally ranged in temperature from 85 to 92 degrees Fahrenheit—and inside the human body, where temperatures rose rapidly to 98.6, the alloy went as limp as a banana peel.

The number of kitchen accidents plunged almost instantly as the knife became ubiquitous in kitchens across the developed world. Emergency room visits as a result of chopping and dicing mishaps became almost nonexistent. Murder rates saw a slight decrease as incidents of rage-blinded assailants attacking family members with kitchen knives in sudden fits of passion became painful but not fatal gougings. Precise numbers were hard to come by, but it was also estimated that the Safe-T-Knife™ was responsible for foiling as many as 15 percent of suicide attempts.

Safe-T-Knife™ was a massive market success, and because Brandt had invested so heavily in manufacturing infrastructure, distribution centers, and shipping routes around the globe, Delphi reaped massive profits across the entire value chain—an estimated one billion dollars over three years from sales of the knives alone, not taking into account smart alloy's manifold other industrial applications or the revenue streams from Delphi Enterprises' increasingly significant portfolio of business holdings. Brandt's vision had been vindicated. His ongoing asset grab continued to be difficult for outside observers to comprehend—cable TV channels and internet content farms, biotech patents and military contracts, C-list social networks and virtual reality technologies, enterprise ERP and CRM software systems. Few understood the logic behind Brandt's moves, and because Delphi never went public many of these acquisitions were conducted in private. Even at the highest levels of the company, in Brandt's inner circle, no one seemed to have a firm grasp of all the company's holdings. But after smart alloy and Safe-T-Knife™, the CEO's actions were assumed by all to be not random, but rather evidence of some master plan to be unveiled at a future date.

• • •

Dominic's experience of reading this article was similar to that of discovering a sacred scroll, of communing with holy words that snapped the disparate parts of the world together. His body felt lit up from the inside, as though his skeleton were the filament of a light bulb, vibrating with energy. As he came to the last paragraph of the article—reading in his apartment, unbothered by his uncle's commentary—he stood up and began to pace around the living room in a state of mingled excitement and agitation.

This, *this*, was what he'd been looking for when he started taking business classes. Dominic flipped back to the first page of the article and looked at the picture of Tristan Brandt. The CEO had been photographed from behind in a sleek wooden chair, turned slightly to show the camera his profile, his elbow draped casually over the back. Dominic stared at the pattern of black photocopier smudges comprising the man's image and marveled that such a person could be real. Brandt had created a billion-dollar enterprise out of the detritus of the market, the worthless bits and bobs less-visionary businessmen had left lying around, and transformed them, alchemist-like, lead to gold. And yet he didn't have a mark on him, no wrinkles or sun spots on his face, no calluses or pieces of grit in his hands. No evidence of the work it had taken to create all this value.

*Value.* Dominic's professors had used the word often, dropped it casually into their lectures and PowerPoint presentations. Dominic had always taken the term to be a synonym of *money*, but at that moment it seemed to convey so much more, containing intimations not just of wealth but of virtue: goodness, justice, nobility. Tristan Brandt created value. And his company—his value-creating company—was located near to where Dominic lived.

Dominic became obsessed with the idea of working for Delphi Enterprises, obsessed with the gleaming corporate complex set at the edge of the city. He and his uncle would pass it sometimes on their way to or from a job, and Dominic would stare at the building as they drove by on the freeway. Opaque, reflective windows. An impregnable glass fortress. Dominic desperately wanted in. His uncle would whistle obliviously at the wheel as Dominic stared, and after the building passed out of sight Dominic would turn his eyes forward again, determined that Delphi would be his escape from this rattling truck and the dead-end business it carried.

After graduating from business school, Dominic haunted the "Careers" section on the Delphi website, applied for everything, the job titles and descriptions ranging from the mundane to the absurd and even silly: business analyst, research ninja, intelligence coordinator, data wizard, project manager, value alchemist, human resource architect, finance guru. Technically he wasn't qualified for any of these jobs—the descriptions always seemed to require years of experience and skills he didn't have. It was a terrible dilemma he couldn't see any way out of: he needed experience to get a job, but without a job he'd never get experience. His applications yielded nothing but dismissive auto-replies: "Thank you for applying for a career at Delphi Enterprises. Due to the large volume of applications we receive every day, we will only be contacting the candidates we are interested in interviewing." Then, nothing.

Dominic began attending job fairs, where Delphi was usually in attendance with a table full of branded swag. The dappled paint-loop logo emblazoned on tote bags, pens, water bottles. These events were depressing to Dominic, carnivals of desperation. Hotel conference spaces crowded with supplicants begging entry to the corporate temple. Dominic wandered the floor in a telescoping fisheye lens of panic, certain that everyone could see through him. With so many other people looking for jobs—people who, he was certain, were far more qualified than he was—why would any company, let alone Delphi, hire *him*?

But then at the third job fair he'd attended in a single month a recruiter pulled him aside from where he stood in line at the Delphi table, waiting to write his name on a clipboard yet again.

"I've seen you before," said the recruiter, a woman younger than him, fresh out of college. "Were you at the job fair earlier this month at the downtown convention center?"

"Yes," said Dominic. "And at one after that, at the Westin."

"You're really interested in working for Delphi, aren't you?"

Dominic nodded and called up the words he'd practiced. "I am. I find the company's approach to asset optimization across the value chain completely revolu—"

"Okay," the recruiter interrupted. "That's all great. I've seen your résumé. We'd love to bring you on. But look, I don't have many entry-level positions right now. Nothing permanent. But one of my departments is looking for an office assistant right now. It's contract, with the possibility of renewing after a year. It's a good way to get your foot in the door. Are you interested?"

Dominic's mouth closed. He understood. It wasn't what he wanted, but it was something. After a moment, he nodded and asked the recruiter to tell him more.

• • •

It still made him angry, when he thought about it. All that work, all those classes, all that debt—and for what? A temp position refilling the supply closet, making copies, scrounging data for the analysts. Still, it was better than nothing, and he had to start somewhere. Besides, he reflected now, if he'd gotten a permanent position like he wanted, he would have been outside when the gas hit. The temp job had saved his life.

"Temps," Lauren said, as if reading his mind. "We're the only ones left."

"Yeah," Dominic said. "We were the disposable ones, on our short-term contracts—but now it looks like we're the only ones in the company who survived."

Jacob leaned forward. His burrito, half-eaten and then forgotten, was in the basket next to his elbow. Rice and black beans spilled out onto the paper liner.

"You mentioned something earlier," Jacob said. "Something called the Brain. What is it?"

"I think I said I'm a research assistant for the business analysts," Dominic said. "The Brain is where I get data for them."

"It's a server?" Lauren asked.

"No," Dominic said, "a computer. A single machine with access to data from the whole company. Most departments, they get access to their own data, maybe a couple other shared servers from across the organization, but nobody sees everything. Not unless you've got access to the Brain. It's not an official name. That's just what we called it, in BA."

Business analytics was located in the P-wing of the building, in a walled office closed off from a view of the courtyard. Passing the desks of the analysts every morning on the way to his own workstation, Dominic would see them looking at colorful charts and graphs, leaning in to squint at spreadsheets full of numbers, putting their hands to their chins as they considered the metrics glowing on their screens. Dominic didn't know how they did it, plucked nuggets of insight from vast deserts of data, but it was clear to him that this was the nerve center of the company, that these men and women for whom he worked were the true oracles of Delphi.

Dominic had been the only temp in the department, which meant that all data requests came to him—and data requests, generally, sent him to the Brain. A windowless room inside the BA office, containing two computers. Inside, Dominic would go to the first computer and input his user information. This would spit out a randomly generated code, granting him a single one-hour session of access to Delphi's records. Then he'd move to the second computer—the Brain—and input the access code. Then, having gained entry to Delphi's records, he'd troll through hundreds of servers, thousands of terabytes, for the files containing the bits of data the analysts needed. Key performance indicators, portfolio burn rates, productivity metrics, earned value, planned value, top line, bottom line. Upon Dominic's exit from the Brain room, this data was subsequently fed into spreadsheets containing intricate lattices of formulae, numbers placed together in increasingly complex configurations until a droplet of insight—numbers bolded, cells highlighted in neon yellow—came spitting out at the bottom of the ledger.

"So you know everything," Jacob said. "You've seen it all. Delphi's whole business."

"No," Dominic said. "I only got to look at the Brain an hour at a time. There are millions of files, millions of data points. Most of the time, I barely understood what I was looking at."

"So the stuff you read in that article—smart alloy, Safe-T-Knife™—that's all you know. Psychometrics, Sherpa—you know anything about those?"

Dominic squinted. "I thought it was just your first day."

"I overheard a conversation," Jacob said.

"I've heard people talk about them too," Dominic said, "but I don't completely know what the projects are. Psychometrics I guess is a new psychological assessment tool. They're doing some kind of big research project."

"I was part of that," Lauren said. "That was my department. We were gathering user data from millions of people with online quizzes. I don't know why, though."

"And Sherpa?" Jacob asked.

"A software release," Dominic said. "I don't know what it does. Probably some enterprise thing for the company, or for one of the businesses in the portfolio."

Jacob sighed and looked down at the table, jabbed a finger at the remains of his burrito, as if he were angry at it. "I don't know why nobody can tell me what the fuck it is this company actually *does*. Didn't any of you people understand what you were working on? Didn't you ever ask?"

Jacob began by muttering, but by the end he was practically yelling. Dominic felt himself getting defensive, his anger rising to meet Jacob's.

"I've already told you as best I can."

"Yeah. Value creation. Analytics. Insight. Metrics. All buzzwords. You can't tell me what Delphi actually does in the world. There could be a division selling chemical weapons to terrorists and you'd call it 'supply chain logistics' or some fucking bullshit. Keep your head down and run your numbers and don't ask any questions about what's really going on."

Swati turned her head to look at Jacob. She'd remained almost entirely silent since Dominic had met her, speaking up only to tell him that she didn't want a burrito. And she was still quiet now. But Jacob's words seemed to have stirred something in her. Her face flushed, her nostrils flared.

"I don't have time for this conspiracy bullshit," Dominic said. "Brandt is a visionary. He wants to do good in the world."

"No, he wants to make a fuckton of money," Jacob said.

"That too, but he's not evil. Delphi isn't evil. Safe-T-Knife™ *saved lives*, you get that?"

"Yeah, but that's just one part of the portfolio. You admitted yourself that you don't know what all of Brandt's business holdings are."

Jacob had Dominic there. Dominic sputtered for a few seconds, then tried a different tack, changed the argument. "What do you care, anyway? Have you seen what's going on outside?"

Dominic himself hadn't, not firsthand—he'd been in the Brain room at the time, pulling data for the business analyst who'd put the request on his desk before going to the all-company: human assets, headcount liquidity, capability gaps, contractor psychometrics, numbers and data visualizations without meaning or context. But after he'd emerged from the Brain room and waited more than an hour at his desk for the analysts to return, he went looking for them and came upon the carnage in the courtyard, the yellowish tint of the air past the windows, the survivors roving like a mad pack of wolves, their clothes in tatters. He quickly figured out what had happened, his mind adjusting to add the scene before him to the realm of the possible. There was shock, fear, but also resignation and determination—this was simply another context, another situation, another set of limitations to survive within.

"Brandt is dead," Dominic said. "Everyone in the company is dead. Except for us and a few hundred other temps. What does any of it matter now?"

Jacob seemed chastened by the question; he looked down and his eyes went out of focus. When he spoke again, his voice was small.

"I like to understand things," he said. "And this—I don't understand any of this."

The referent for *any of this* was unclear—Dominic couldn't tell if Jacob was talking about Delphi's operations or the death outside. Perhaps both. Dominic felt a pang of pity for him, this white boy picking at the table with his fingernail, made small by his inability to fit recent events into his ready-made categories. Dominic knew the type: over-praised by every authority in his life, assured again and again that he was special, encouraged to follow his dreams. Angry, now, that the world wasn't what he'd been told. Whereas Dominic had never indulged in the illusion that reality was anything other than this struggle to survive. Everyone was on the take; business school had just been a way to get on the inside, become one of the ones doing the taking. Whatever shell game Delphi had been playing was over now, but there would be a new game, with new winners and losers—and Dominic was determined to be ready for it.

"Look," he said now, "the important thing is we're alive, okay? And we've found each other. Strength in numbers. And we've got food."

He stretched out his arm to draw their attention back to the food court they were sitting in: Chipotle, Panda Express, Potbelly, and the rest. A cache of frozen foods they could assemble and warm, a soda fountain to keep them hydrated.

But Lauren's eyes stayed on him. "We have to find the others. You said there were 350 temps. That means there are 346 more people in this building, alive. Where did they all go?"

Dominic paused to show that he was thinking about what Lauren was saying, even though he'd already made up his mind.

"No. You have to stop thinking like you still live in a civilization, start thinking like this is a survival situation, like you're stranded in a harsh wilderness. We have to stay close to the food. Food, and water. *Our* food, *our* water. We have to protect it."

"Protect it?" Lauren asked with a disbelieving, mirthless laugh. "What, you think someone's going to come along and fight us for it?"

"I don't know," Dominic said. "People do strange things after a disaster. We don't know what other people might do, if they're desperate enough."

Lauren looked down and blinked. She looked to Dominic as though she was struggling with the picture he was painting for her: temps fighting to the death over a cache of fast-food sandwiches, bags of chips, bottled lemonade. It *was* absurd, Dominic had to admit, but he also believed it was possible, even probable, that conditions in the Delphi complex could get just that bad. The worst would come if they were stranded long enough for food and water in the building to become scarce, for people to start feeling hungry or thirsty. That might not happen if they were rescued soon—but what if there was no one left outside to rescue them? What if the yellow gas took not days or weeks but months or years to lift?

"We stay here," Dominic insisted. "We protect the food."

"With what?" Lauren asked.

Dominic stood and walked behind the counter of the Chipotle. His backpack was nestled beneath the cash register. He reached inside and pulled out his weapon—a long curved blade.

"Jesus fuck," Jacob said as Dominic pulled it out. "Where did you get that?"

"It's the blade from one of those flat paper cutters," Dominic said. "I got it from one of the print stations, just ripped it out. We've also got knives here, mallets, boxcutters, meat tenderizers."

"You're crazy," Lauren said. "You're fucking crazy."

"I'm not saying we kill anyone," Dominic said. "Just—we need to be smart. This is *our* food. People we see, they can join us, or they can go somewhere else—but they can't take from us. If we let them take food, if we're weak, we won't make it. You see? Survival. That's the only thing that matters now."

He looked at them, at each of them, until they nodded—Jacob, then Swati, then finally Lauren.

# SIX

That night, the four of them curled up in a sitting area not far from the food court. The area was constructed in padded tiers, waist-high steps upholstered like sofas and peppered with scatter pillows. The concourse of the Delphi building had been constructed with many such spaces, where employees could go to work away from their desks. Here and there, the upholstery of the steps gave way to electrical outlets and USB ports for laptops and phones.

Swati couldn't sleep. The padding of the steps was thin, hard underneath, and the outer fabric was rough and scratchy against her skin. Outside, the lingering yellow haze made the moon glow yellow, like a weakened sun, and Swati couldn't stop thinking about what she'd seen in the courtyard. As she'd suspected, it was hitting her late—all that death. Jacob and Lauren said it was everywhere, they'd seen it on TV while she'd been meditating. The gas had spread across the whole city, and was in a dozen other cities besides. Now Dominic was saying that civilization had ended, that they might as well be living in a hostile wilderness, that the only thing now was survival. They'd become pre-modern humans. Cave people, hunter-gatherers.

Swati closed her eyes and breathed. She brought her attention to one part of her body at a time: the crown of her head, and then her face, and then her neck, and so on. Relaxing every part of her, imagining her body sinking into the cushions, gravity pulling inexorably at every atom of her body. This was another mindfulness trick, a form of self-hypnosis—*I am feeling sleepy, very sleepy*. For a moment it worked. Her eyes grew heavy, and her cheek rested leaden against the throw pillow she'd propped beneath her head.

But Swati's mind wouldn't turn off—a reminder that meditation, while occasionally useful, was decidedly unmagical. She couldn't escape her thoughts, she could only *observe* her thoughts, distance herself from them, bring her body and mind into equilibrium. But when one's thoughts were fearful, racing, despairing—what then? Tonight there would be no equilibrium, no solace. Only, at best, a deliberate cataloguing of her own anxiety, of the disaster that had, at last, overtaken her.

Swati opened her eyes and let her mind run free. She thought of her parents, who'd saved for years to send her to college, had always supported her dreams of becoming a business owner, and didn't like Jared. Unlike him, they'd never diminished or mocked her for wanting to open her own studio, never told her that her goals should be bigger or more important. After graduation, her decision to move in with Jared had caused a rift between them, her mother and father seeming to know in a way she couldn't or didn't want to that he would be a dead end for Swati, that he was no good. "You have so much promise," her father had said over the phone. "Why are you wasting your time with this boy?" Swati hadn't known what to say, so she said nothing.

They went on supporting her, sent her a few hundred dollars every month, cash, in an envelope addressed to her in her mother's unmistakable handwriting. Sometimes, a note: "Your father's psoriasis is flaring again. I lost two pounds last month. We miss you." Only later did Swati realize that her mother must have been sending the money without her father's knowledge, that he must have been angry enough about her moving in with Jared to cut her off completely. But her phone kept working, which meant that her father had at least kept her on their family's cell phone and data plan. Every time she turned on her phone and saw that she still had bars it was like a secret message: "Call if you need anything. Call when you want to come home." But she didn't, not even after she'd decided to escape the ramshackle house, to escape Jared. The prospect of admitting to her mother and father that she'd been wrong was simply too humiliating. She wanted to find her way back to them on her own terms.

They were dead, probably, now. Unless they'd managed to hole up somewhere safe, where the gas couldn't leak in—her mother at the beauty salon, her father at the hospital, where he was a neurologist. Swati suspected they were dead, hoped they were not, and she wasn't sure which was worse:

the suspecting or the hope. In any case, she didn't think she'd ever get to make that call; she'd tried her phone earlier, and though the Delphi wireless network was still working, she couldn't call anyone, the network either collapsed or overloaded. Swati would never see her parents again, she realized—because of Jared, because of her pride, because of the gas. She was filled at once with sadness, and anger, and shame, the three simultaneous emotions seeming to short-circuit something in her brain, and leaving her utterly helpless.

Almost certainly dead were her housemates, who rarely spent any time in the sort of airtight buildings that might protect them from the gas. The house had been drafty, full of holes, and if they hadn't been in the house when the gas hit then they were probably biking somewhere, to a rally or a meeting or an ill-conceived political action. The thought of their deaths came with less sadness than that of Swati's parents, but even though Swati found them annoying she didn't think they deserved to die.

Thinking of her housemates took her mind once more to Jared, who'd pulled her off the track she'd set for her life and brought her to that creaky, smelly house. Even now she couldn't believe it, couldn't say for sure what she'd been thinking in following him. And she thought, after getting the yoga instructor job at Delphi, that she was done with all that—done with the house, done with Jared. But apparently she was wrong. Because when Jacob had raged at her, Lauren, and Dominic for working at Delphi without fully understanding the company's business, it brought back all the old feelings, the familiar anger mingled with attraction. Who did he think he was, claiming some kind of purity when he was working for Delphi too? Her sudden desire to argue with Jacob was a familiar kind of arousal—Jared and Swati's arguing about capitalism and corporations had been a sort of foreplay, a prelude to the inevitable succumbing.

Even their names were similar: Jacob and Jared. These angry white boys with their tidy theories about how the world worked. Except that Jacob seemed gentler, less sure of himself. His anger at Delphi borne not of righteous anger and radical zeal, but of insecurity, uncertainty, an inability to get out of his own head. Or so Swati told herself, anyway.

Jacob was sleeping on the step below her. His body was shrouded in darkness, a faceless form, which was how she'd always liked Jared best too—as a body, warmth and weight and an earthy, not at all unpleasant smell. It was only when Jared would slip into her room at night that he'd finally shut the fuck up for once.

"Why aren't we dead?" Jacob asked now, from the darkness.

"What?"

Dominic and Lauren breathed evenly above, close enough to the food court that they'd wake up if anyone came to ransack the refrigerators.

"I said, why aren't we dead?"

Annoyance prickled beneath Swati's breastbone. "Because we're not."

"Look at the moon out there. The stars."

Swati closed her eyes. "I've seen them."

"Yellow," Jacob said. "Still yellow. The gas is still in the air—in the *atmosphere*. So why isn't it in here? Why haven't we been affected by it yet?"

"We're inside."

"But buildings have ventilation. HVAC. What's outside seeps in. Maybe it takes a while, but it gets in. We should have breathed it by now. We should be dead, like everyone else. But we're not. Why?"

Jacob waited, but Swati didn't answer. She'd learned from experience that there was little point in trying to silence a man who had something he wanted to say.

"You know what I think it is? The entrances. Have you ever noticed how when you walk in the building, there's a rush of air? That your ears pop when the door closes behind you?"

Swati *had* noticed that, now that Jacob mentioned it—but she didn't say so aloud.

"What I'm thinking is, it's a sort of decontamination chamber. Like in movies when people come from an area with radiation, before they're let in, they have to go in this room where they get a sort of, I don't know, like an air shower or something, with steam, under jets, to wash all the contamination from their clothes. I don't really know how it works, I guess, but still, the building entrance, it reminds me of that. I only used the one entrance, though—this is my first day. Are they all like that?"

By now Swati was scarcely listening. She lifted her head from the pillow and began scooting along the cushions toward the edge of the step.

"Because if they are, if every entrance is like that, purifying the outside air before people come through the second set of doors into the main building—well, why? And if the building has air purifiers in its HVAC system, purifiers that filter out every ounce of the gas before the fresh air is pumped through the vents inside—you know, same question. Because it just doesn't make sense for a normal corporate office building to have that kind of a setup, unless the people who designed the building knew this was a possibility, knew that maybe someday there'd be a chemical attack and that the company would have to hole up in here and ride out the—oh, hey, um, hello . . ."

Now Swati was lowering herself to Jacob's step, easing her body down onto the cushions. She put her cheek down next to his, close enough that she could feel the warmth of his breath on her face. She reached out and put a hand on Jacob's cheek, then slid it around to the back of his head.

"What are you—"

She pulled his head toward hers and kissed him, not quite sure why she was doing it even as it was happening. Was it to shut him up so she could go to sleep, or because she was actually attracted to him? She couldn't say—yet now their lips were pressed together, tentative at first, then parting slightly. Swati broke the kiss, then pulled back, a ripple of something she hadn't felt in a long time passing through her body.

"Jacob," she said. "Shut up."

Jacob's eyes gleamed in the darkness. He let out a rush of air. "Yeah. Okay. It's just—"

"Stop." Swati turned over and grabbed at Jacob's arm, drawing it across her middle as she nestled her backside into the softness of his abdomen. "Just don't talk anymore."

Jacob obeyed her. Swati closed her eyes and listened to the silence. There were no more words, no more thoughts. Only the blank warmth of Jacob's body next to hers, the weight of his elbow resting against her ribs, the breath ruffling the hair at the back of her neck.

And sleep, which came for Swati soon after.

• • •

Jacob and Swati's murmuring was audible from the top of the steps, where Lauren was stretched out on the cushions. She listened as they kissed, then to their hushed talking after. Long after their breathing grew slow and metronomic, emanating from their tangled forms as if from a single two-headed body, Lauren lay awake, staring up at the vaulted glass ceilings.

Her thoughts were a jumble, the events of the day—which felt like a year—writhing in her mind like a pile of snakes. She thought of the death in the courtyard, the quiz she was working on that morning, the helicopter crash, Jacob and Swati and Dominic, the news, burritos and beer in the food court. But mostly she thought of Tristan Brandt, the CEO she'd never met and hadn't spared much thought for before—he'd scarcely seemed relevant to her, a lowly temp working on silly internet quizzes. In particular she dwelled on a small detail that Dominic had shared, and which seemed of deep significance to Lauren: that Brandt had majored in classical philosophy at Yale before going into business for himself.

*Classical philosophy.* Which meant that Brandt, like Lauren, had sat at the foot of the Greeks and partaken of their ancient wisdom. Which in turn meant that she'd been right, and there was some deeper meaning to the fact that Brandt had chosen to name his company Delphi, had given the three wings of the triangular building letters corresponding to the name of a different mythic prophet. More than just a businessman picking a name he thought sounded cool.

Eventually Lauren drifted off to sleep, where the tangled skein of her thoughts became an unsettling dream. In the dream, she found herself at the top of a tall mountain—Mount Parnassus, where the temple of Delphi was located. She stood amidst marble columns, near a statue of a figure she knew to be the god Apollo. In front of her was a brass bowl on a tripod, holding a tied bouquet of herbs that burned but were not consumed, and giving off a yellow smoke. Instantly Lauren thought of the yellow gas and stepped back, but it was too late, she'd already breathed in the smoke.

She coughed. Her vision telescoped. She walked away from the bowl toward a marble balcony looking down the mountain at the world beneath.

Below, she saw a yellow cloud engulf cities, heard a cry of pain and rage rising up to reach her.

"They will all die," a voice came from beside her. "Their world will die. Even the memory of them will pass away."

Lauren looked, and saw Tristan Brandt standing next to her.

"How can I stop it?" Lauren asked.

She felt a chill at the pierce of his eyes behind his sleek rimless glasses, at the incongruity of his black business suit in the midst of the ancientness of the place they stood in.

"You must know yourself," he said. "*Gnothi seauton*."

"But I don't know *anything*," Lauren said. "I don't know anything at all."

A pitying look came to Brandt's face, and he seemed about to say something else—something that would, Lauren felt certain, make everything clear.

But then she woke up to the sound of clanging.

• • •

It was light. Morning. Lauren looked down the steps, where Jacob and Swati were coming awake as well, disentangling as though surprised to find themselves still in each other's arms. Then Lauren saw Dominic, standing above her at the edge of the food court.

"What's happening?" she said, adrenaline making her voice louder than it should have been.

Dominic waved her quiet, held a finger to his lips. The other four fingers of the same hand held the broken paper cutter blade. "Someone knocked over the bowls we stacked in one of the kitchens," he said in a quiet voice.

"Who?" she whispered.

Dominic shook his head, turning his eyes back to the food court. "I haven't seen yet."

He tightened his hand around the handle of the blade, the skin around his knuckles paling. Watching him, Lauren marveled that it had already come to this—that it hadn't even been twenty-four hours since the gas descended, yet already she might be seconds away from seeing a person killed in a fight over food.

"Don't worry," Dominic said, seeing her eyes. "I'm not going to hurt anybody. It's just a precaution. In case—"

He left the thought unfinished, which didn't reassure Lauren. She looked back down to Jacob and Swati. Swati mouthed, *What's going on?* and Lauren shook her head, motioned for them to stay where they were. Then Lauren stood up and looked with Dominic into the food court as more sounds came from inside the kitchen of Panda Express—clanking, thumping, the rustling of plastic. Then the kitchen door swung wide and a person came walking out, a guy pushing a gray cart on which he'd piled huge plastic bags of frozen food. He pushed the cart a few steps, angling it between the rows of tables and chairs, then stopped when he saw Dominic and Lauren.

"Oh, hey," he said, then glanced down at the blade in Dominic's hand and took a step back. "I—what are you . . . I don't think that's necessary."

Dominic looked down. "Just a precaution," he said. "You saw what happened outside."

There was a beat. "Yeah. I guess. That makes sense. But I'm not, I mean I wasn't—the gas didn't get me. I'm normal. I'm not going to hurt anyone."

"Good," Dominic said, but didn't let go of the blade. "Who are you?"

"I work here," the guy said.

"We all work here."

"Right," the guy said. "Right, duh. Yeah, my name's Frederick. I'm . . . well, I'm a temp. IT, help desk. I help people with—"

"Password resets and shit," Dominic finished for him. "Got it. Why are you taking our food?"

Frederick frowned. "Wasn't aware it was yours."

Dominic shrugged. "It's not, really, but that's a lot of stuff you've got there, and . . . well, we're willing to share. We just can't let you walk away with as much as you're taking. If we're going to survive in here until help comes, we'll need to be careful with the food, don't you agree?"

Frederick smiled, then laughed.

"What's funny?" Dominic asked.

"Sorry," Frederick said. "This is just a misunderstanding. I should've told you right away what I was doing. There's a big group of us on the top floor, at the cafeteria. Brent, the guy who's—well, he's our leader, kind of— he agrees with you. He thinks we should control the food supply, ration it, make sure there's enough to last until the gas lifts."

Lauren stepped up and walked toward the food court. As she passed Dominic she felt him move to stop her, but he was too slow, and she didn't look back.

"There are others?" she asked. "How many?"

"Three hundred, probably," Frederick said. "More, maybe. Brent was inside, like the rest of us, and when he saw what was going on outside, right away he sent an email to the whole company list, said anyone who's still alive should come up and meet at the top floor. I guess he figured it would be safest up there. Furthest from those . . . those crazy people who breathed in the gas, if they broke inside."

Dominic grunted. "If anyone breaks in we're all fucked. The gas would get in. High ground won't matter then."

But Lauren wasn't listening to Dominic. Something swelled in her chest, and she almost started crying from the relief. They hadn't been left behind. Jacob had been right—an emergency protocol had been initiated, albeit an informal one; she'd just missed it because she'd been in the break room watching TV rather than at her computer.

"Can we come with you?" Lauren asked.

"Of course," Frederick said.

"Lauren," came Dominic's voice from behind her shoulder.

She looked back, and he beckoned her to him with a movement of his head.

"I don't know about this," he said in a low voice when she came close. "We've got a good situation down here, by the food court—our own food supply, water, a place to sleep."

"But you said yourself—strength in numbers. Besides, this one food court has way too much food for just the four of us."

Dominic shook his head. "You don't know that. You don't know how long we'll be stuck here."

"Maybe not, but what are you going to do, kill this guy just because he wants to take some frozen potstickers and sesame chicken? You want there to be tribes, fighting each other? If there's another group of people in the building—more than three hundred of them, figuring out what to do next—I want to be part of them, not trying to survive all on my own."

Jacob and Swati, who by now had come up from their sleeping place on the lower step, stood close by and listened to Lauren and Dominic's conversation. Lauren looked at them, met their eyes. They seemed to nod.

"We're going," Lauren said. "Swati, Jacob, and me. You can stay if you want to."

The three of them went to Frederick and began walking with him. Lauren walked alongside the cart, steadying the plastic bags of food whenever one threatened to fall to the floor. After about a hundred paces she looked back at the food court and saw that Dominic was coming after them, running to catch up.

• • •

Frederick led them down the concourse, and Jacob fell to the back of the group, happy to be following again. Alone with Lauren and Swati he'd felt pressured to be a leader, to know what was going on and what should be done next to keep them safe. That was sexist, probably, but it was how he felt. Finding Dominic had taken some of that pressure off—he seemed a natural-born leader, cooking up food for himself and fashioning protective weapons out of office supplies—but in a group of only four, two guys and two girls, there was still the chance that Jacob would be called upon to do something he was unprepared to do: fight alongside Dominic to protect the group, perform a medical procedure after one of their number got injured, or sacrifice himself in some act of heroism.

But now, trudging down the concourse toward an elevator that would carry them up to the fourth level, a fortress where a group of more than three hundred survivors were waiting, Jacob could become anonymous again, his essential cowardice inconspicuous—if a coward was indeed what he was deep down. Jacob, like many privileged young men who'd never experienced real danger in their lives, often wondered how he would behave in a situation of true peril, whether he would acquit himself courageously in the face of injury or death. He had the idea, gleaned from war movies, that a man didn't really know what he was made of until he'd been in a situation requiring the use of violence. But rarely did he allow himself to believe that when the time came he'd discover unknown reserves of heroism inside himself. Rather, he suspected that he'd be the guy in the movie who pissed his pants and ran crying from the battlefront when the mortars started to fall—or, at best, an extra who'd get himself killed immediately upon charging from the trench.

In an apocalyptic scenario like the one he found himself in, he'd likewise assumed that he'd be among the first to die—vaporized by the nuclear blast, killed by the superbug created deep in a government lab. He'd seen those movies too, and he'd always felt that those who were killed quickly in the apocalypse were the lucky ones, more fortunate than the film's stars who lived to see what came after, which was often far worse than the initial catastrophe. But now, by some fluke of random luck, he found himself among just such a group of survivors, burdened with the task of staying alive in a world where every certainty had been removed. Having a confident leader to follow—Dominic, maybe, or this Brent who Frederick had told them about—would be a relief.

Following also gave Jacob the luxury of letting his mind wander to other, more pleasant thoughts. Thoughts, for instance, of Swati, and what had happened last night. The kiss. His gaze drifted to her, her messenger bag and rolled yoga mat thumping against her swaying hip as she walked close by. Then his eyes fell to the hand swinging at her waist. Should he grab it, lace his fingers in hers? Could he? Were they, like, *together* now? Or had last night's exertions been a random fluke, a chemical reaction resulting from the combination of catastrophe and physical proximity?

He decided not to take her hand—it would be too presumptuous, too prematurely romantic, and would scare her off—but at the same time resolved to put himself close to her again when they went to sleep tonight.

Frederick pushed through a door, went down a hall, and brought them to a freight elevator. He pressed a button to call the elevator to their floor.

"Have any of you been to the fourth level before?" Frederick asked as they waited.

"Not me," Jacob said. "First day."

Dominic, Lauren, and Swati all confirmed that they'd never been up that high before either.

"It's a good spot," Frederick said. "You can see pretty far from the windows up there, so we should be able to tell if there's any trouble coming."

"Or rescue?" Lauren offered.

"Right," Frederick said. "That too. Plus there's a big cafeteria—I think I mentioned that—with a lot of empty fridge and freezer space for us to store food. TVs in the dining area, in case the news comes back on."

"It's still down?" Jacob asked.

"Well, it came back for a while," Frederick said as the elevator dinged and opened. He pushed the cart onto the elevator and waited as the others climbed on with him. "Sometime yesterday the gas hit Manhattan and all the national newsrooms went down."

"I know," Jacob said. "We saw that."

"It was down for most of the day, but then it came back last night," Frederick said.

"Government?" Dominic asked.

"No," Frederick said. "Cable news. I guess the networks had bunkers somewhere, in case of an apocalypse-type situation. Anyway, they were only on about an hour before the signal went down again. Not sure why, but we figure cable and satellite systems need maintenance, right? And all the people keeping those systems going are probably dead. Or they started breaking shit when the gas got them. Either way, the TV's been dead for almost twelve hours now. No signal from any station."

Listening as the elevator rose, Jacob thought for the first time about how odd it was that they still had power, that the lights were still on and the air conditioning was still functioning as, outside, infrastructure had begun to crumble without human hands to maintain it, or perhaps as human hands began to attack it. Cable, cellular, internet, electricity. A burst of paranoia pinged in Jacob's head, similar to his thoughts the night before, when he'd wondered aloud whether the Delphi building had been built as a containment chamber, and if so, why. Could Delphi also be on a generator, with utilities and technological systems unconnected to the outside world? Why would it be, unless the person who designed the building—Brandt, he assumed—had planned for just this kind of scenario?

Jacob opened his mouth to speak some of these thoughts aloud, then stopped himself. Whenever he asked questions about Delphi, people kept getting annoyed with him. He seemed to be the only one who thought it strange that no one could say precisely what the company did. The way Lauren, Dominic, and Swati looked at him when he tried to probe what they knew about Delphi, like he had some sort of skin growth forming on his forehead, made him feel foolish and even more paranoid—even though he thought he was right. Better to keep his thoughts to himself for now, at least until the four of them had gotten settled with this new group of survivors.

"And what did the news say, before it went down?" asked Lauren. "Any idea what's going on out there?"

"It's bad," Frederick said. "The gas has spread to smaller cities, rural areas. Plus there are reports of other attacks in other cities, other countries. London, Paris, Moscow, Beijing. It's everywhere."

The elevator seemed to warp around Jacob, the walls expanding and contracting like a lung as Jacob held his own breath, trying to adjust to the information that what had happened outside Delphi Enterprises was happening everywhere, all over the world. He was still trying to steady himself when the elevator door dinged open. Jacob looked up and flinched into the sunlight. Up here they were closer to the glass ceiling that vaulted above the concourse on the ground floor, and on the other side of the panes the yellow tint to the sky was less pronounced. Past the haze the sun glowed like a star gone supernova, guts scattered across the sky. A narrow walkway overlooked the concourse, high enough that Jacob felt a little dizzy as he stepped off the elevator.

Frederick pushed the cart down the walkway and rounded a corner into a hallway, then pushed through a set of doors into a sea of cubicles. Jacob didn't see anyone, but he heard the sound of people from somewhere deep in the office, like the murmuring of a cocktail party.

"This way," said Frederick. "Other side of the wing."

• • •

Dominic couldn't say what he'd expected of the survivors' camp on the fourth floor—huts? campfires? skewered game animals turning on spits?—but it certainly wasn't the banality of what they found: a scrum of rumpled office workers standing around with their hands in their pockets and trying to make small talk, as if they'd been summoned from their desks to wish a coworker a happy birthday and were now waiting for their piece of a sheet cake. The crowd looked small, clustered loosely among a half-dozen cubicle rows squared. Three hundred plus people wasn't as many as Dominic had thought.

Dominic stayed close on Frederick's heels as the crowd parted to let the cart of frozen pan-Asian food through.

"Are you going to see Brent?" he asked.

"Yes," Frederick said. "I'll check in with him at the cafeteria, then put this food in the freezer."

"I'd like to meet him."

"Fine."

Dominic was still a little resentful about being forced to move from the food court on the bottom floor, where he'd been, if not in charge exactly, then at least in control of his own fate. Not part of this larger group, beholden with the others to the whims of someone he didn't know, or trust.

Lauren, Swati, and Jacob stayed close as they walked through the cubicles, through an open space where padded chairs had been placed in knots of four around low tables, and then to a shoulder-height partition, beyond which lay the cafeteria. There were enough tables to seat at least five hundred, mostly empty except for a few bleary-eyed survivors sitting over coffee and watery scrambled eggs, mini-muffins, toaster bagels, and mushy fruit salad. Beyond the seating area was the counter, plastic trays piled at one end of a buffet, a cash register on the other, and a swinging door to the kitchen beyond. Standing just behind the line of temps snaking through the buffet to get their food stood a young man. He was tall and broad-shouldered, prematurely bald, shiny on the top of his scalp with a pixel-scatter of black stubble on the sides and back of his head. He stood with his arms crossed, surveying the scene in the cafeteria.

"Brent," Frederick said as they got close.

The bald guy turned. He was young, like them—all of the temps were young. Dominic had scarcely seen a face in the crowd that might've been above thirty.

"What is it?"

"I've got another load of food. First floor food court. There's a lot more stuff down there."

Brent nodded. "Good. Put it in the freezer, then head back down there for the rest. Take some of the others."

"There's something else. I found more."

"Stragglers?"

Frederick angled his head toward Dominic and the others. Dominic held out his hand.

"Dominic Hill, business analytics," he said, as if it mattered—but before the gas, BA had been regarded by some as the most important department in Delphi Enterprises, the source of the company's uncanny market insight, and Dominic thought some of that authority might carry over to this moment.

Brent took his hand. "Brent Foreman." He didn't offer his department, and immediately Dominic felt foolish for having done so.

The others introduced themselves with awkward nods and first names, then Dominic cleared his throat to regain Brent's attention.

"Sorry we took so long to get up here. I guess none of us were at our computers when you sent that email. I was pulling some information from the Brain when all this happened."

Brent's eyes sharpened. "The Brain? What's that?"

Frederick was the one to answer. "It's a computer in analytics that can access all the company records. Exec office has one too, for Brandt and the VPs. I've never seen either machine, but I've worked on the servers that feed to it."

"You have access?" Brent asked, addressing Dominic.

"I do," Dominic said. "Part of my job."

"HR records?" Brent asked.

"Among other things."

"You think it's still working?"

Dominic shrugged. "I don't know. Power's still up, isn't it?"

"It is," Brent said. "There haven't even been any blips. No dimming lights, nothing like that."

"Then the Brain's probably still working. I'd have to check. Why?"

Brent turned and looked out over the cafeteria, the sitting area, the cubicles beyond. "We've got 341 people up here. Three hundred forty-five, I guess, now that you four are here. It would be nice to know if we've accounted for everyone. This is a big building, easy to get lost."

"I looked up the temp count this morning," Dominic said. "It's supposed to be 350."

"So we're missing five," Brent said. "Unless any temps ended up outside in the all-company, died in the gas. Think you could pull up a list of everyone's name? We could take a roll call, find out who's still missing."

"I could try."

"Take Frederick with you," Brent said. "He can help you if you have any issues with the network."

"I was going to go back to the food court," Frederick said. "Bring up some more supplies."

But Brent shook his head. "We've got other people who can do that. Not that many who know how to fix a server or run a system diagnostic, if he has trouble accessing the network."

"What's your plan with the food?" Dominic asked.

"For now," Brent said, "just to get control of it. I figure, between the cafeterias, food courts, vending machines, you've got maybe enough to feed all the regular employees for about a week. Ten thousand people, five business days—that's fifty thousand person-days of food. About 350 survivors, that comes out to less than a hundred days of food. Roughly. Which might be enough time for the gas to lift and for us to get out of here before people start going hungry."

Dominic put on a dubious expression. "How sure are you that your math is right?"

Brent smirked as though Dominic had said something foolish. A little rumble of embarrassment pinged in Dominic's stomach.

"Pretty sure," Brent said. "I was shift manager for the catering company that did all Delphi's food, including the food court workers. I managed the cafeteria staff, took care of shipping and sourcing. We fed the whole company. I think I can figure out how much food 350 people need."

Dominic nodded, sensing defeat. "Good to know."

"We'll be fine—but someone needs to control the food supply. Ration it."

"Right," Dominic said. "That was my thinking too."

Brent went on as though Dominic hadn't said anything. "I mean, someone gets into a food source somewhere else in the building, maybe eats too much, wastes it—or worse, lets something perishable go bad—then suddenly we've got less time. So I want to get all the food up here, inventory it, find out exactly how much we've got. And inventory the people too. Find out exactly how many survivors there are, make sure no one's unaccounted for, hiding somewhere in the building. After we know both of those things—how much food we have, how many people there are—then we'll know exactly what we're up against."

Dominic frowned, wishing he could find something lacking in Brent's plan, something to criticize or some improvement to offer.

Lauren stepped forward.

"Let us help," she said.

"What do you suggest?" Brent asked.

"Not every Delphi employee bought food from the cafeteria or the food courts," Lauren said. "Some people brown-bagged their lunches. Break rooms, kitchenettes. They all have fridges full of sandwiches, Lean Cuisines, takeout leftovers. Some of it will be perishable too. We should eat it first, or freeze it so it doesn't go bad."

"That's a good idea."

"What about desk drawers?" Swati added. "There might be snacks. Granola bars and stuff."

Brent nodded, and Dominic mentally scolded himself for not having thought of this first. He felt himself beginning to think of Brent as a boss who he wanted to impress, and despised himself for it. Brent wasn't higher in the Delphi org chart than Dominic, nor did he appear to be any older. Who was he to be barking orders, standing in the center of the cafeteria with his arms crossed like a general? All he'd done was gather the temps on the fourth floor—yet because of this, and his control over the food supply, Dominic now had to defer to Brent, pretend that he'd somehow gained some essential authority over the Delphi survivors for nothing more than sending a single all-users email.

"Do it," Brent said. "Take the bottom floor—we've already got parties scouting two, three, and four. Grab some people on the way out, if you want some help. And look for more survivors, while you're at it. Five people are still missing. I want them here."

# SEVEN

They deposited the load of food in the walk-in freezer behind the cafeteria counter, then returned to the elevator. There were more in their party now—Jacob, Lauren, Swati, Dominic, and Frederick, plus a half-dozen more temps who'd volunteered to help them as they came out through the cubicles. Their eyes were baggy, their hair frazzled, their clothes rumpled from a night of bad sleep on the floor, and they all looked relieved to have something to take them away from the group of jittery survivors clustering around the cafeteria. They shared their names, which Lauren promptly forgot almost as quickly as she heard them.

The temps rode the freight elevator down in silence, then parted at the first floor. Dominic and Frederick went down the concourse toward business analytics and the Brain. The rest headed in the other direction, toward the mail room, where Jacob had promised carts for carrying any provisions they'd find.

After they hit the mail room—the carts were plentiful, as Jacob had promised—they split into groups of two. Lauren briefly experienced the middle school fear of being picked last for sports, of being the only one in her class without a partner for a group craft project, assigned by her teacher to classmates who didn't want her—but then she felt a hand on her elbow and turned to find Swati standing just behind her.

"Will you go with me?" Swati asked, then glanced sideways at Jacob, who stood nearby with his hand on a cart and a look of abandonment on his face.

"Sure," Lauren said, watching furtively as Jacob was approached by a quiet, frizzy-haired girl in sweatpants and a long-sleeved T-shirt.

Then they split up—some to the food courts, some to the break rooms and kitchenettes, the rest to the offices and cubicle farms, where they hoped to find more food, and survivors.

• • •

Jacob picked his way through the cubicle rows like a farmhand picking crops. He tried not to think about what had just happened with Swati—he'd approached her intending to ask if she wanted to pair up with him, but when she saw him she lunged for Lauren and grabbed her by the hand. His fear was that she was already regretting last night's kiss, but maybe it was nothing. Maybe she just needed space, or maybe she simply hadn't seen him. Better not to think about it and focus on the task at hand: checking desk drawers and file cabinets for anything that might be useful.

Walking into other people's work stations felt strange, as intimate in its way as snooping through someone else's bedroom. When they were alive, the Delphi employees would've spent almost as much time in these spaces as they had at home—more, in some cases. Each cubicle contained totems of its previous occupant's personality, clues to who the dead person had been. This one had a sweet tooth, this one preferred salty snacks, another was obsessed with herbal tea. Here were pictures of the deceased's family, the spouse and kids, the dog, the vacation to Paris. Posters thumbtacked to the cubicle partitions, comic book characters, inspirational quotes. Stress balls, yo-yos, plastic figurines. Even workstations lacking personal items spoke to the individuality of the person who'd spent the majority of their waking hours there, indicating a worker who valued simplicity, minimalism, and deep concentration. One cubicle Jacob walked into contained no items at all, not even a pencil or a scrap of paper, aside from a computer with a single post-it note stuck to the screen, with the scrawled affirmation: "One thing at a time, and that done well."

Jacob opened a drawer and spotted something.

"Bag of fun-size Hersheys," Jacob called out. "You think I should take it?"

"Why not?" asked the girl, the one he'd ended up paired with.

"I don't know. It's not very nutritional."

The girl shrugged. "Calories, though."

Jacob couldn't remember the name she'd given when they all introduced themselves at the elevator. It was something gender-neutral. (Madison?) She looked out of place at Delphi, even taking into account the last twenty-four hours, which had left all the survivors looking a little frayed. But Jacob suspected that the girl (Mackenzie?) had started out frayed, beginning with her clothes. Who wore sweatpants to work?

"So, uh, Mason . . ."

"Morgan," she said.

"Shit, right, I knew that. Morgan. Sorry." (Morgan!) He was winding up to the question he'd asked multiple times since coming to Delphi, the question that seemed to irritate everyone he asked, a question that he was beginning to get sick of hearing himself—except he had to know. The drive to understand, to make sense of this place and what had happened here, was like a pressure building inside him, a physical urge he had no choice but to alleviate.

"What did you do here?" He waited, and when he heard no response over the row of cubicles separating them, he added, "For Delphi."

"I was in games," Morgan answered. "I think my technical title was 'game systems tester.'"

"What does that mean?"

"Exactly what it sounds like. I beta-tested a video game."

"Delphi was in video games?" Jacob walked into another cubicle and began opening drawers as he waited for Morgan to answer. Jackpot: a whole jar of trail mix, the kind with M&Ms sifted in with the raisins and peanuts. Jacob wondered if he could eat some, or if that would be a betrayal of the mission Brent had given them, to bring all food back to the group at the top floor for counting and rationing. He hesitated for a moment, then spun the lid off and took a handful.

"They were trying to get into games, maybe," Morgan said. "I'm a gamer; I'd have heard of Delphi if they'd released anything. But they had one game. One of those strategy-based games. You know?"

Jacob munched and swallowed before answering. "Not really."

"You're not a gamer?"

Jacob put the rest of the trail mix in his cart and pushed further down the row. "No."

"What do you do with your free time?"

"Read novels, mostly," Jacob said, which was true. He'd played video games some in high school, but in college he'd lost interest—and now, if he was honest, he was actively disdainful of adults who played video games. Jacob had become a bit of an elitist, hostile toward cultural texts that he did not regard as high art or literature. He knew this was an assholish attitude, but he didn't care, because he also thought he was right. Deep inside himself, he nursed the angry, paranoid belief that his inability to find fulfilling work was directly related to the fact that nobody read books anymore—that twenty-first-century American culture's devaluation of serious literature was somehow tied up with the entire world's rejection of *him* and what he had to offer. That Morgan was a gamer made her, in some respects, his enemy, or at least the enemy of everything he'd been educated to hold dear in life.

He chose to keep these thoughts to himself.

"Huh," Morgan said. "I read sometimes too, but—you know, games are really awesome right now. They're not like they were when we were kids. And you know, there's this whole genre of games that are basically like interactive novels, if you like reading you might really enjoy—"

"Does it matter?" Jacob interrupted. They'd come to the end of a row of cubicles, face to face once more, and Jacob saw now that talking about gaming had brought Morgan alive. Her eyes were lit up. Looking at her, Jacob could imagine her before all this happened, in the context in which she felt most comfortable, most herself: sitting in an unlit room late at night, perhaps, the flashing of a television screen lighting her face and the faces of her closest friends, beers on the coffee table and a bag of chips on the couch, shouting inside jokes into the darkness as she joyously fragged (or whatever they called kills these days) one of her opponents.

But now the smile went away from her face, and Jacob found himself wanting to apologize for reminding her that that was all over now, that her friends were dead, that the game nights she lived for (he assumed) would probably never happen again.

"I guess not," Morgan said.

"Sorry," Jacob said. "Anyway, you were saying. A strategy game."

Morgan blinked, like she'd forgotten what they were talking about. "Oh, right. Yeah, so it's one of those games where you're running a society, or pushing soldiers around on a battlefield."

Jacob nodded, continuing down the row to search more cubicles. Morgan did the same on the other side of the partition.

"Not really my kind of game," Morgan continued, "but I can appreciate them. Plus, it's not every day you find a company paying to test video games, so I didn't really complain. Anyway, the one Delphi had us testing was this science-fiction thing: you're the ruler of a distant planet, a civilization that's been around for thousands of years. And the society on the planet is totally decadent, the people are using natural resources way too fast, the planet is way overpopulated, huge wealth gap, ecosystems completely destroyed."

"Sounds fun," Jacob said sarcastically. "What's the point?"

"The point is to prevent the planet from collapsing."

"And? Was the game any good?"

"It was awful," Morgan said. "I wouldn't have bought it if they paid me."

"They did pay you," Jacob pointed out.

"Ha, right. Well, the pay sucked, and so did the game. The graphics were shit, the interface was all wonky. Plus it was impossible to win. I played four times, each game took me about a week to finish—and each time, I failed. My planet's society kept on collapsing into complete chaos, no matter what I did."

"Were there other testers?"

"Yeah. About twenty of us. They're all upstairs—we were playing the game when the gas hit."

"Huh." Jacob opened a drawer, found a six-pack of bottled water and a half-drunk fifth of Jack Daniels. He put the water in his cart, then the whiskey—after opening it, sniffing it, and taking a short pull.

"You know, it's kind of funny. I spent the last four weeks playing through all these apocalypse scenarios, and now it's almost like I'm living in the game."

"Funny?"

"Well," Morgan said. "Not funny. Helpful, maybe. You can learn a lot by playing video games. There's this other game I play . . ."

Jacob let his mind wander as Morgan blathered on about the social benefits of gaming, the problem-solving skills she'd gained over the years, her favorite recent video games, and tabletop games, which she was only *just* starting to get into. So much of being a nerd was the ability to talk obsessively about one stupid thing long after the person you were talking to had lost interest, the refusal to feel shame for the things you loved. Jacob envied Morgan, a little—he felt nothing but shame for his own loves, his own passions. So much so that he sometimes found himself hating them. They were what had rendered him useless, unemployable. Embittered.

Then, over Morgan's voice, he heard something.

"Shh!"

Morgan fell silent. Jacob listened, then heard it again.

Keyboards tapping. Mouse buttons clicking. Voices murmuring.

Jacob whispered to Morgan: "Is there anyone else in this wing? Another search party?"

"No," Morgan whispered back.

Jacob began to move toward the sound, leaving his cart behind. The noises got louder and louder, and then Jacob was walking through an entry to a larger than usual cubicle containing five desks, five chairs, five workers. Three sat staring at their screens, backs rounded as they tapped at their keyboards; near the entrance to the cubicle a girl laughed, her legs curled underneath her on her chair, as a guy leaned against her desk, evidently having just delivered a joke or a funny anecdote, coffee cup folded toward his chest. The tableau was so much like an everyday office scene that Jacob felt as though he'd wandered through a portal into an alternate dimension where nothing bad had ever happened, and Delphi Enterprises' operations proceeded as usual.

The workers looked up in unison, including the guy leaning against the desk, his smile dimming as his eyes came to Jacob.

"Can I help you?"

• • •

They were still working. Jacob couldn't believe it. The temps in the over-sized cubicle knew what was going on outside—they'd seen it the same as everyone else—but they were still working all the same.

"But why?" Jacob asked.

The guy with the coffee mug—he'd said his name was Casey—shrugged. "Got a job to do," he said.

Jacob stammered and glanced at Morgan, who'd caught up with him soon after he walked into the cubicle and now looked just as befuddled as he did.

"But it's meaningless now," Jacob finally managed. "Your job, whatever it is you were hired to do—it doesn't matter. The company, it's dead. Everything, everyone—dead."

Casey shook his head. "I don't know if that's true."

"Which part?"

"Any of it."

Jacob let a silence stretch out, looking from one face to the next. The other workers—two guys, three girls—simply looked at him, then turned back around and started working again.

"What the fuck is going on here?" Jacob asked, turning back to Casey.

Casey set down his coffee mug and angled his head, beckoning Jacob and Morgan out of the cubicle where they wouldn't disturb the workers. Jacob felt a surge of annoyance—who cared about their stupid jobs anymore?—but followed without saying anything. Outside the cubicle, Casey walked a few yards away and then leaned his shoulders against a partition, crossed his arms.

"So?" Jacob asked.

"What do you know about Delphi Enterprises? About Tristan Brandt?"

Jacob thought about what he'd learned in the last twenty-four hours. "Some," he said.

"Well," Casey said, "I know plenty. I'm part of an online rationalist-futurist community. It's a message board thing where we talk about philosophy, science, technology, innovative corporations. There's a whole sub-board about Tristan Brandt and Delphi."

"And?"

"And whatever you think you know about this place, it doesn't even begin to scratch the surface. Brandt isn't just some evolved venture capitalist, or whatever the business magazines say about him—he's actually building a utopian society for the next thousand years."

Jacob almost laughed. The carnage just outside the Delphi building was about as far from utopia as he could imagine. Even if Brandt did have plans to build an idealized society, what did it matter now?

"I don't see what that has to do with—"

"He conducts human experiments, okay?" Casey said. "Behavioral experiments, Skinner boxes, ethical predicaments. He's using the data to figure out what happens next. What human society should evolve into."

That silenced Jacob. Morgan asked, "What kind of experiments?"

"On the message board, there was this guy who'd been part of one," Casey said. "He worked at a Delphi outpost down in South America. A data processing center. One day he's at work, then people with guns come storming in, take them all hostage. Revolutionaries, guerrillas. Except instead of holding them for ransom, the guerrillas give them this weird dilemma: they're going to kill one person every hour, randomly—but any of the hostages who agree to do the killing, to hold the gun and shoot one of their coworkers in the head, they get let go and nothing bad will happen to them."

"Jesus Christ," Jacob said. "And Brandt set all that up?"

"Yeah, it was totally fake. The guerrillas were actors. Even the hostages who got shot, they were in on it—blanks in the guns, squibs for blood to make it look real. The guy who told us about it on the message board, he had no idea, he was one of the test subjects. He got scared, gave in and agreed to shoot someone. He was let go, but then the next week his bosses told him it was all a test and he'd failed. He got fired."

"And the people who passed? Who refused to kill anyone?"

"Nobody knows. They disappeared. Speculation on the message board was they got to live on Brandt's floating island, this model society he's building out in the Atlantic as a prototype for his utopia."

Jacob glanced at Morgan. She shook her head.

"I don't know," she said. "The whole thing sounds a lot like a horror movie I saw once. How do you know this guy wasn't lying to you?"

"Maybe he was," Casey said. "When it comes to Tristan Brandt, there aren't many hard facts—only rumors. But it's an awful lot of similar rumors about one guy, one company. Some of them have to be true."

"So you think this is a social experiment?" Jacob asked. "The gas, the dead people in the courtyard, the news—you think that's all fake?"

"It could be," Casey said. "Brandt has the resources to pull it off. He can hire actors, engineer a fake gas cloud, make it look like everyone's dying."

"What about the news?" Jacob asked. "I watched the news. It's happening everywhere."

"Brandt could have set up an alternate news stream," Casey said. "Paid the media to fake it, then sent the broadcast to this building only."

"Or it could be real."

Casey nodded. "Or it could be real. Either way, we've decided to behave as though Brandt is watching. If the world *is* really ending, then it's even more important to try to get to Brandt's island."

"But," Jacob said, then paused and winced. "I'm sorry to be the one to tell you this. But Brandt is dead."

Casey blinked. "What? How do you know?"

"I saw him."

"No you didn't."

"I did. I was watching through the window. Brandt came out, went to the stage, then the gas came. There's no way he could've gotten away."

Casey closed his eyes and shook his head. "No, I mean—the man you saw wasn't Brandt."

The answer startled Jacob into a brief silence. Could Casey be right? The man he'd seen take the stage could've been another Delphi leader, a senior VP. But the crowd had lost its mind when the man appeared, reaching toward him as if he was Jesus and a single brush of their fingers against his clothes could bring them healing.

"The crowd sure acted like it was Brandt."

"I'm sure they thought it was him," Casey said. "But Tristan Brandt is a recluse. They say he uses body doubles for public appearances. Some people claim they've seen him around the building—slipping into random staff meetings, wandering around the concourse, making coffee in one of the kitchens. This one guy, a black badge I knew, claimed to have pissed next to Brandt at a urinal. But no one knows. Aside from his inner circle, no one even knows what he *looks* like. The all-company was going to be his first appearance to the employees in years—but he might not've been planning on appearing at the meeting at all. Hell, he might not even be in the *building*."

"Where, then?" Morgan asked.

"His island," Casey said, then nodded toward the tall windows and the yellow sky beyond. "Riding this out. Waiting to restart things—to restart civilization—when the gas goes away."

Jacob didn't know what to say. Casey could be right—but it sounded like wishful thinking to Jacob, this idea that Brandt was hidden away somewhere, preparing to roll out a utopia, his new product, once things had settled down.

"Look," Casey said, "when we got hired, the five of us, Brandt explained the jobs to us personally. Or at least someone who said he was Brandt. I thought it was weird, the CEO giving an assignment to a bunch of temps, but one way or another, whether it was really him or just a double, he was trying to send us a message. The guy who claimed to be Brandt, he said our job was important, the most important in the whole company."

"What *is* your job?" Morgan asked.

"Data entry."

"You're fucking kidding," Jacob said.

"Hear me out," Casey said. "Brandt told us we were doing data entry for a new predictive modeling program—what he called the 'Chaos Systems Oracle.' There'd been speculation about it on the message board before I got hired, so I knew what he was talking about. Chaos systems are systems that are difficult to analyze and predict with any degree of accuracy, because they're so subject to contingency and random choice."

"So, the stock market," Morgan offered.

"Yeah, or weather. The butterfly effect, small and impossible-to-predict variables building to big outputs."

"And your role was?"

"We were inputting variables into the database that fed the Oracle," Casey said. "Thousands of them."

"What's the system?" Jacob asked. "What is the software designed to predict?"

Casey shook his head. "I don't know. All we get are numbers. Numbers, and an alphanumeric database field to plug the numbers into. Each of us can input about a thousand fields a day. We've been working at it for more than a year."

"Holy shit." No wonder they'd gone a little crazy—a year of data entry could do that to anyone. Jacob did some math in his head. A thousand variables a day, times five temps, times five business days per week, times a whole year. "That's more than a million variables."

"Yeah, 1.25 million, to be exact," Casey said. "And we've kept getting more since the gas. In fact, they've sped up in the last twenty-four hours. They come out of a printer in our cube, an old dot-matrix model, feeding from some other part of the company."

"But how do you know it's not bullshit?" Morgan asked. "What if it's just a test, to see how long you'll do a meaningless task before you quit?"

"Because I believe it's not. The Oracle is real—I've heard other people in the company talking about it. And Brandt wanted us to know that our work was important. If it *is* a test, then it's a test to determine whether or not we'll follow orders even when it means doing something boring."

Jacob was quiet. Casey's thinking had a logic to it—delusions always did.

"You've made a religion," Jacob said after a few moments.

Casey's face soured. "I don't think—"

"No, you have," Jacob said. "Brandt is your god—all-seeing, all-powerful, mysterious. He's given you a job. And if you obey—even if it doesn't make sense, *especially* if it doesn't make sense—then you think you'll be rewarded with passage to Brandt's utopia. Heaven."

Casey's eyebrows angled toward the bridge of his nose. "Fuck you. Religion is irrational. It's superstition. Everything I've told you is based entirely on facts."

"Rumors," Jacob countered. "You said so yourself."

Casey pressed his lips together, seeming to hold himself back. "Look, you can do what you want. But us—we're staying here."

"But how will you survive? What will you do for food?"

Casey set his jaw and began walking back to his desk. "Don't worry about us. We'll get by."

• • •

Lauren needed something heavy—a brick, or a hammer.

"Maybe something from the office area?" Lauren suggested. "Dominic made that . . . machete thing from a paper cutter."

"No need," Swati said. "Stay here."

Lauren waited as Swati walked from the locker room into the gym. They'd come here on Swati's suggestion. There were others looking for food, but Swati was the first to point out that they'd need extra clothes at some point, that the ones they were wearing were already grungy after twenty-four hours and a night's sleep.

Swati came back with a dumbbell.

"Heavy enough?" she asked, handing it to Lauren.

Lauren reached for one of the combination locks on the locker doors, grabbed it, yanked down. It held, but it wouldn't take much to break it open.

"Probably," she said, taking the dumbbell from Swati's hands and weighing it in her own. She glanced at the number—ten pounds—then swung it at the lock. The first couple of times she missed, put a dent in the locker door, then on the third attempt she spent more time aiming, put less into the swing in favor of accuracy. The weight of the dumbbell was enough; the thick end caught against the bulk of the lock, and it snapped open.

Lauren took the bent lock off the latch and opened the locker. She found a small duffel bag. Inside was a water bottle, athletic shoes, and workout clothes.

"Told you," Swati said.

"I guess we're all going to be dressed like we're going to the gym," Lauren said.

Swati shrugged. "It's comfortable, at least."

Lauren broke more locks, opened more lockers, found more workout clothes—and, here and there, extra pairs of business casual pants and tops, underwear, socks. She also found, in one bag, a bottle of shampoo, the same kind she used at home. She flipped it open and sniffed the familiar scent: lavender. Then she glanced up, out of the locker rooms toward the showers.

Swati followed her gaze, then looked back at Lauren.

"Why not?" Swati said.

"You think they're still working?"

"One way to find out."

Swati walked to the showers. Lauren followed a few steps behind. Swati turned a knob. The showerhead spat water onto the tile. Swati put her hand in it to test the temperature—but Lauren knew, by the steam that began to rise almost immediately, what she'd say before she said it.

"It's hot. Want to?"

Lauren nodded. They stripped and stepped into the hot spray of showers on opposite walls, their backs to each other, each giving the other privacy. Lauren closed her eyes and angled her face up into the water. She opened her mouth, let it fill, then spat a jet through pursed lips.

"God," she said. "This feels amazing. We have to tell the others."

There was no answer. Lauren listened and gradually discerned, amidst the shrieking of the showerheads, a muffled whimpering sound.

"Are you crying?"

Still Swati said nothing, and after waiting a few seconds Lauren turned and looked. The steam had turned the room hazy—Lauren thought briefly, chillingly, of the yellow gas—but through the heavy air she could see Swati at the opposite shower, forehead resting against the wall, shoulders quaking.

"You *are* crying," Lauren said. She turned off her shower and grabbed a towel from the table just outside the room, cinched it around herself under her armpits, then grabbed another for Swati. She walked to Swati, twisted the shower knob all the way to the left, then offered her the towel. "Take it," she said. "Talk to me."

Swati grabbed the towel with one hand but couldn't seem to do anything more than that. She turned, clutching the towel against her chest with one hand, then slid down the wall to the floor, sobbing now. She was sitting in standing water, the end of the towel soaking through as it touched the floor between her legs, but still Lauren followed her down, knelt on the tile and put a hand on Swati's shoulder.

"What is it?"

"All those people," Swati said. "Millions of people. Billions, even, maybe—Frederick said there were attacks in other countries. What's happening outside is happening everywhere. It's just . . . it's too much. Too big. I can't."

Lauren was stunned. There were two ways, she felt, to approach what had happened—to consider it or not to consider it, to hold it close or at arm's length. Because of the way they'd found Swati, meditating calmly while disaster reigned outside, Lauren had assumed that Swati ascribed to the second method. But now it turned out that Swati *was* considering the apocalypse outside—considering it, perhaps, even more deeply than Lauren was. Swati was mourning the deaths of millions of people she'd never even met. Whereas Lauren still hadn't even cried over what happened; every time she thought about the magnitude of the disaster, the millions and maybe billions presumed dead, the numbers overwhelmed her mind, turned it fuzzy and sucked emotion away until all that was left was a numbness. She knew about Dunbar's number, had read about it in a psychology class: 150 people that a single person could reliably know, remember, mourn over— except that Lauren, something of a social hermit, had whittled that number down to maybe a dozen. Her mom, her roommate, a few school friends, but even when she thought of them dying in the gas she still couldn't bring herself to cry. She was empty. She'd used up all her tears on her dad.

"Who did you lose?" she asked Swati now.

Swati looked at her, blinking fiercely. "My parents," she said. "My housemates—who I didn't even like that much, but still. And then I just multiply them by, like, a million, everyone who died, and . . ."

"It's a lot," Lauren said.

Swati's gaze drifted.

"It's not just them, though. It's me. There were things I wanted. Out of life. Is that selfish?"

Lauren shook her head, flinging droplets of water off the strands of her hair. "No."

"All I wanted was to open a yoga studio," Swati said. "That's it. Just a little thing—a yoga studio. A stupid dream."

"It's not," Lauren said. "It's not stupid."

"And now it'll never happen because—because what? Because someone else's dream, their whole life's fucking ambition, was to completely fuck the fucking world. Some man, probably."

"Probably." Lauren thought this was true, looking at the thing empirically. The terrorist organizations, the rogue nations, the corporations testing chemical weapons: they were all run by men. It was always a man with his finger on the button.

"I mean, what are we doing? We're gathering clothes, rummaging for food—for what? So that we can die a few days or a few weeks or a few months from now instead of today?"

"So we can survive," Lauren said, even though she scarcely believed it herself. "So we can rebuild."

"Rebuild *what*? Rebuild fucking what? Everything's gone. Even if this gas goes away and we can leave this place before we starve to death, nothing will be left."

"You don't know that. And maybe . . . I don't know, maybe you'll get to start your yoga studio after all. People will need that—they'll need to feel their bodies, to know that they're alive. In the new world."

Lauren felt foolish saying it—*the new world*. But it seemed to be a necessary idea, now.

Swati looked up, sniffed, wiped her wrist across her nose. "Yeah?"

"The world will *need* you, Swati," Lauren said, warming to her topic, beginning to believe it herself. "It'll need women. Women like you, like me—to rebuild everything the men broke. You see these guys, their first reactions to this thing—Dominic building weapons, Jacob getting paranoid, Brent trying to control everything and everyone. They'll just fuck things up again. They need us to make sure the new world isn't just as shitty as the old one."

Lauren's heart was beating fast. She felt inspired by her own speech, stirred by the call to arms she'd improvised on the spot for Swati. She felt, suddenly, that it was all true, everything she was saying. She and Swati had a mission. She was glad that they were alone, that they were naked, unclothed and vulnerable in the midst of this apocalypse. There was something daring about their nakedness, strength in the weakness of their unprotected bodies—bodies that could create life, and feed it. If the world's rebirth began anywhere, Lauren thought, it would begin here: with two women comforting each other, giving each other strength, on the floor of a shower room.

Swati had stopped crying.

"Come on," Lauren said, grabbing her by both shoulders and urging her up. "Let's get dressed."

. . .

Lauren and Swati dried off, then got dressed in workout clothes from the lockers. They dumped their dirty clothes in a laundry room adjacent to the workout room, then kept on talking as they went through the rest of the lockers and waited for the washer and dryer to finish.

"You were right," Lauren said. "These clothes are so fucking comfortable." She'd picked out a soft V-neck and loose-fitting yoga pants that swished around her ankles when she walked.

"Right?" Swati said, folding a shirt and placing it on top of her stack. "I basically live in yoga pants. Some people think it's tacky, I guess, or they don't want to see butts or whatever."

A giddy mood had come over them since the showers, like they'd toweled off not just the water but also every ounce of sadness, wrung it from their bodies as if from a damp cloth.

"Men, you mean."

"Yeah," Swati said. "Like all it takes is seeing some asscheeks in public to turn them into sex-crazed animals."

"Fuck 'em," Lauren said, swinging the dumbbell through the air to bash another lock. "It's comfortable."

"That's what I say."

"In fact, I think this should be the first law in our new world—everyone *has to* wear yoga pants all the time."

"I concur."

"How many wars you think were caused by tight collars, badly fitting pants, non-breathable fabrics?"

"Too many to count."

"Exactly. That's why it's nothing but comfortable clothes from now on. Yoga pants, sweatpants, tracksuits, pajamas. All day, every day."

Swati lifted her hand in the air, clenched, as if brandishing an imaginary scepter. "It is so decreed."

They went on piling folded garments in their carts until the stacks wobbled and threatened to topple, then left the locker room, resolving to come back for more clothes later. They pushed their carts through the locker room doors, down a hallway, and into the concourse.

"We're going to be heroes when people see these clothes," Lauren said. "There's plenty of food up there already—I think most people want a change more than they want a meal right now."

Swati pushed her cart down the concourse. "They'll be even happier when we tell them the showers are still working. There's three gyms, three shower rooms, one in every wing on the first level."

Lauren squinted. "That Brent guy will want people to go in shifts, probably," she said. "He doesn't seem to want people to wander too far."

"What are you going to do about him?"

Lauren turned, preparing to answer Swati's crack with a joke of her own, but then saw that Swati's face had gone serious. "Wait," Lauren said. "Me?"

"Yeah," Swati said. "I mean—did you mean all that stuff you said, about the new world being run by women?"

Lauren looked ahead and kept pushing her cart. Suddenly all the giddiness she'd been feeling in the locker room fled, like cockroaches skittering to the corners of a room as the light came on.

"I guess. You think I should say something to him?"

"You probably shouldn't tell him everything you told me," Swati said. "But at the very least I don't think he should be running things like . . . like some sort of *dictator*."

Lauren was silent. Swati was probably right about Brent—but why should Lauren be the one to challenge him? She'd said what she had to in the shower room to comfort Swati, and okay, maybe she had gotten a little carried away, a little caught up in what she was saying, but even if she'd ended up *believing* it—believing that the new world, if there was one, should be female—it didn't mean she thought she should be the one to *lead* it.

Lauren was embedded in these thoughts, tunneling anxiously inside herself, when Swati said, in a hoarse voice, "Oh my God," and Lauren looked up, her heart suddenly beating fast.

"What?"

Swati pointed. "Look."

And then Lauren saw her: a girl, disheveled and weeping, stumbling down the concourse toward them. She was well dressed in a cream-colored blouse, navy skirt, and sheer stockings—except that she was sweating through the blouse at the neck and armpits, and one of her stockings had fallen down and pooled around her calf. She wore no shoes, and ambled down the concourse in a zigzag pattern, like a drunk.

Lauren's first terrified thought was that the girl was one of the Furies. A survivor of the gas, of the melee in the courtyard. There was a splash of blood across her blouse, and more splattered on her face, in her hair. Lauren instinctively moved back as the girl came close, gripping at Swati's arm above the elbow.

But the girl wasn't a Fury—there was no anger in her eyes, no rage, only pleading and desperation and fear.

The girl's gaze met Lauren's, and she stumbled into her arms.

"Who are you?" Lauren asked, panic making her voice loud.

But the girl couldn't answer—she'd passed out in Lauren's arms.

# EIGHT

Dominic and Frederick came back to the cafeteria after all the other scavenging parties had already returned. They had what they'd gone for, but it had taken a long time—three access codes, three hour-long sessions on the Brain before Dominic found, deep in the HR servers, an up-to-date list of all the active temp staffers.

It was lunchtime when they returned, and walking up to the cafeteria Dominic reflected that it would have been easy to mistake the scene for a normal day in the Delphi Enterprises lunchroom. Some temps were lined up at the counter for food, others serving behind the sneezeguards in aprons and hairnets, still others smiling and chatting between bites at the tables. The consumption of food seemed to have buoyed everyone's spirits. Dominic was grudgingly impressed at Brent's ability to orchestrate the whole thing. It was only lunch, but it had still taken skills in organization and management—picking the meal, rationing it for 350 temps, recruiting and overseeing people to put it together and serve it.

"Do you have a vegan option?" Dominic heard someone ask as he and Frederick came close to the front of the line, and to his surprise the girl behind the counter nodded and placed a veggie wrap on the young man's tray in place of the turkey sandwich everyone else was getting.

Dominic got his food, then heard a shout from the cafeteria as he turned to look for a place to sit.

"Dominic!"

Jacob was sitting at a table on the other side of the cafeteria, waving his hands. Swati and Lauren weren't with him—only a frizzy-haired girl who Dominic vaguely recognized as someone from their scavenging party. Dominic went to the table and sat down.

"What is it?"

"You'll never guess what we found on our scavenging hunt."

"You actually want me to guess?" Dominic asked.

"What?" Jacob blinked. "No. Oh, this is Morgan, by the way."

Dominic gave her a nod. "Morgan. Right."

"Anyway," Jacob said, "we were searching through people's desks, looking for extra food—"

"You find anything?"

"Yeah," Jacob said, "but that's not the point of this story. The point is what we found *while* we were looking for food."

"What, then?"

"People," Jacob said. "Temps. Still working."

Dominic had peeled back the top slice of bread on his sandwich to look at what was underneath, but now he froze and glanced up at Jacob.

"You're fucking kidding me."

"No," Jacob said. "This guy Casey—he's sort of their leader, I think he's the one who convinced the rest of them to keep working. He's a conspiracy-theory guy; he thinks this whole thing is a fake put on by Tristan Brandt, a big psychological test to see how we'll react in an apocalypse scenario."

"He sounds crazy. You tell him you saw Brandt die?"

"Yeah. But he didn't believe me. He says Brandt has body doubles for public appearances. The guy I saw at the all-company might not even be Brandt."

Dominic sniffed, felt his lip curl. People like Jacob were too credulous, too eager to believe in a conspiracy, especially where corporations and rich billionaires were concerned. How strange, that those who'd had it easiest in life were the quickest to see conspiracy everywhere they looked, as if to protect themselves from their own privilege by reflexively thinking the worst of the world that had given it to them. "And you bought it?"

"Well, no. But—you studied Brandt, didn't you? He's a recluse, right?"

"Sure, he's a little private," Dominic said. "But he's not holed up in his office pissing in mason jars or anything, growing out his fingernails. I've read a lot of business articles about Brandt, and not a single one of them mentioned anything about psychological experiments on his employees. Body doubles, either."

"You've seen his picture?"

"In one of the articles, yeah," Dominic said. "The first one."

"And what did he look like?"

Dominic shrugged. In truth he didn't remember very well what Brandt had looked like in the *HBR* profile—the photocopy he'd read off of had been poor, and the photograph of Brandt had only showed the CEO's profile from the side.

"Your average bald white guy, I guess."

"Wait, did you say bald?" Jacob asked.

"Yeah."

"The guy I saw at the all-company wasn't. Full head of hair, glasses. Pretending to be Brandt. Or the real Brandt—and the guy in your article was pretending."

Thoughts tumbled through Dominic's head, his mind scrambling to adjust to this new information and come up with a reasonable explanation—a retort that could put an end to Jacob's paranoid theorizing.

"So I was thinking," Jacob continued, "you know, it all sounds crazy, but we should look into it at least."

"How?" Dominic asked.

"The Brain. You just came from it, didn't you? It's still working?"

Dominic purposefully didn't look at Jacob. He set both elbows on the table and took a bite of his sandwich, chewing slowly. The Brain *was* still working, but now that he was the only living person with user credentials that could access it, he felt possessive of it, as if the computer was a child, or a pet—something vulnerable he now had to protect from the others.

But then there was a commotion from the cubicles, and everyone turned. Plates and silverware clanking. Gasps.

"Clear a path!" Brent's voice, shouting. "Someone get her some water!"

Dominic stood, sending his chair toppling to the floor.

Between bodies, others standing and craning their necks, Dominic saw the cause of the commotion. Lauren and Swati stumbled toward the cafeteria, carrying between them the body of another girl, arms draped over their shoulders, head lolling limp on her chest with each step they took. Her clothes and hair were streaked with clotted blood.

"Holy shit," Dominic said.

"What?" Jacob said, his voice rising to a shrill register.

"They found one," Dominic said.

"One what?"

"One of the people from outside."

• • •

Actually it wasn't at all clear whether the girl had been outside or not, nor where the blood soaking her clothes and hair had come from, because even after they'd revived her, she couldn't—or wouldn't—speak.

Swati and Lauren had collapsed soon after they came into the camp, having carried the girl's limp body all the way from the first to the fourth floor. Then Brent had rushed to the girl's body, and Dominic wasn't far behind. After checking her vitals—she was breathing, her pulse was strong— Dominic suggested that maybe she'd simply fainted for lack of food.

"But what about all the fucking *blood*?" Brent had yelled, and Dominic told him to go to the kitchen to get some lemonade or juice or something with some sugar in it, calmly filing Brent's panic away for later use. After Brent was gone, Dominic looked across the girl's body and met Swati's eyes. Lauren had stepped away, her fist clenched over her mouth, her eyes red and gleaming with fearful tears. The other temps stood watching at a distance of a few yards, as if gathered for a play presented in the round. Dominic and Swati were the only ones near the body, and for a freefalling moment Dominic felt exposed. By jumping into the fray and putting himself near the unconscious girl he'd committed to a role he wasn't sure he knew how to play. He knew a bit of first aid—he'd had to learn it for his uncle's roofing business, in case one of the workers got hurt—but not enough to save a life, to prevent this girl from bleeding out in front of everybody, if that was what was going to happen.

"I need a first aid kit!" he yelled, hoping the command would make him seem authoritative and scatter some of his audience. Footsteps pounded across the floor.

"You know what you're doing?" he asked Swati in an undertone.

"A little," Swati said. "I know CPR, but—"

"But she's still breathing," Dominic said. "She's still got a heartbeat."

Swati breathed out hard and fast, like she was beginning to hyperventilate. There was a slick of sweat on her forehead, probably from the exertion of dragging the girl up to the fourth floor. But—her hair was wet. Had she showered?

"What we need to do is find where she's bleeding from," Swati said.

Dominic looked down at the girl, at the clothes covering her body. "But I don't know how—"

"Maybe let's get her some privacy," Swati said.

"Are you sure we should move her?"

Swati winced, then shrugged. "We've moved her this far already."

Together, they moved her body down the row and positioned her on the floor of a cubicle. Someone materialized at Dominic's shoulder with a first aid kit, then disappeared. He handed it to Swati.

Swati tore the kit open, riffled through it, then threw it aside. She began opening desk drawers.

"What are you looking for?" asked Dominic.

She didn't answer. She opened another drawer. Objects rattled as she fumbled around inside, then she withdrew her hand gripping at a pair of dull black scissors.

Dominic's heart leapt, imagining Swati cutting into the girl's skin with the shears. "What are you . . ." he began, and then Swati bent the jaws of the scissors wide and began hacking at the bottom of the girl's shirt. The cut slid up past the girl's navel to her breastbone. Dominic averted his eyes, giving her privacy as Swati tore the shirt the rest of the way, exposing a black bra. He grabbed at the first aid kit, readying himself with a piece of gauze and tape for when Swati found the wound.

"Where's she hurt?" Dominic asked after a moment.

"I'm not finding anything," Swati said. "I don't . . ."

"What?" Dominic demanded.

"I don't think it's her blood."

Dominic looked back at the girl's body, and discovered that her eyes had opened. They regarded him with an eerie calm. He put his hand gently on her cheek, tilted her eyes to look more directly into his. It seemed like the right thing to do.

"What happened to you?" he demanded, speaking too loudly, as though the girl might be hard of hearing. "This blood—where did it come from? Who are you?"

He fired the questions at her almost without pause between them. Her mouth didn't move, and Dominic found himself reacting to her complete silence with rising urgency, rising panic. He wanted her to speak, was desperate for it. So desperate that he didn't notice his grip getting tighter at the side of her head, didn't notice that she'd begun to whimper in pain and fear.

"Dominic," Swati said softly, then louder: "Dominic!"

He looked up. "What?"

"Let go," she said. "You're scaring her."

•   •   •

Swati looked up just as Brent came back into the cubicle with a Styrofoam cup of lemonade and an energy bar. The girl seized the cup, partially crumpling it and spilling some of the liquid as she brought it to her mouth. Then she grabbed at the energy bar, scarcely ripping off the wrapper before she tore into it, holding it close to her teeth with both hands between bites. Watching her, Swati thought of a rodent—a mouse, or a gerbil. There was something feral about the girl.

Brent began asking her questions, the same questions Dominic had been asking her seconds earlier.

"For fuck's sake," Swati said. "Can't you see the girl is in shock? She's not even wearing a shirt."

Brent didn't move right away, stood staring at the shirtless, bloodied girl for a few moments more.

"Just go!" Swati said. "Get her some more food."

Brent's face turned red and he left without a word. Dominic stood. He looked sheepish, hands rising as if he was about to thrust them in his pockets.

"You should probably go too," Swati said. She had her hand on the girl's shoulder. It felt important, just then, to be touching her. The tips of the girl's hair poked at Swati's knuckles, stiff with dried blood. She smelled like sweat, and salt, and mud.

Dominic nodded, then turned but paused at the doorway of the cubicle.

"Do you need anything?" he asked without turning back.

"Could you send Lauren in here?" Swati asked. "Tell her to bring some clothes."

Dominic's footsteps swept out of the cubicle. Swati looked at the girl's face, which stared ahead, seeming to focus on a spot in the air a few inches in front of her nose—or on some scene of horror playing out over and over in her mind. The girl closed her eyes, and her body began to quake, but she didn't make a sound. Swati began moving her hand in a slow circle on the girl's shoulder.

"It's okay," she said, "you're safe now," but she didn't know if that was really true. At that moment, *safe* felt like the farthest thing from what they were.

Soon Swati heard the sound of footsteps brushing the thin carpet at the edge of the cubicle, and she looked up to see Lauren holding some of the clothes they'd found in the first-floor locker rooms, sweatpants and a long-sleeved top.

"Can you help me with her?" Swati asked.

Lauren knelt, and together they pulled the top over her head, pushed her arms through the sleeves as though she was an infant. The dried blood in her hair and on her neck and chest smeared onto the top as they put it on her.

"We really should get her a shower before we dress her," Lauren said. "Now this one's almost as bad as the one we found her in."

"Yes," said Swati, "but it feels wrong to leave her without a shirt with all these guys around."

"What's her name?"

Swati shook her head. "I don't know. See if you can get her to talk."

Lauren bent her head down and tried to meet the girl's gaze. When she'd first woken up she'd stared directly at Dominic, then at Swati, but now that she'd been awake for a while she was no longer looking directly at people, like a shy child whose parents had told her that strangers are dangerous.

"My name is Lauren," Lauren said, patting her hand on her chest. "Lauren. That's me." Then she reached her hand toward the girl, stopping just short of touching her. "Who are you?"

The girl cowered back. Swati tried the same gambit, with the same results.

"Does she have a security badge?" Lauren asked.

Swati didn't remember seeing one, but then she glanced at the girl's skirt and there it was, a black badge encased in plastic and clipped to her waist.

"Is it okay if I look at this?" Swati asked, reaching. The girl didn't nod, but she didn't protest either—only watched Swati's hands with her eyes as she grabbed the badge. It zipped out from the clip on the girl's waistband, a cord unreeling as Swati drew it to herself and flipped it over to look at the name and photo on the other side.

"Jane," Swati read. "Her name is Jane." She let go of the badge, and it zipped back on its reel toward Jane's waist.

"You think we should bring her down to the showers now? Get all this gunk out of her hair?"

Swati noticed but didn't comment upon Lauren's avoidance of the word *blood*.

"Maybe get some more food in her first," Swati said. "The way she lunged at that energy bar makes me think she's gone this whole time without eating anything. Probably why she collapsed."

"So not . . . ?"

"No," Swati said, understanding Lauren's question and her hesitance to voice it. "She's not hurt, that I can tell. It's not hers. The blood."

Swati expected Lauren to express some relief—*thank God for that*—but instead she got quiet. "Twenty-four hours," she said after a long pause. "Since the . . . the gas."

"Yeah," Swati said. "I think so. Since the gas. Which means she was probably outside."

"So, you think this is an effect? Of the gas? You think this—turning her mute—is how it affected her?"

"I don't know," Swati said. "Maybe."

Lauren looked at Jane, who looked dolefully back at her. Swati bit her lip, seeing in that look the cruelty of their talking about her like this—as though she wasn't there and couldn't understand.

"Should we be worried? Will she turn into one of them? Attack us? Try to kill us?"

Swati closed her eyes. So many questions. Everyone had so many questions. But no answers.

"I don't know, Lauren," Swati said at last. "I just don't know."

• • •

Jane was short, petite, with straw-colored hair that ran rusty red even after fifteen minutes under the showerhead. After Swati and Lauren got her cleaned off and dressed they brought her back upstairs, coaxing her to follow them. Jane appeared to understand Swati and Lauren when they spoke. She met their eyes when they talked to her, nodded and shook her head, and obeyed every single one of their commands, albeit slowly: *lift your arms, come this way, follow me, get back on the elevator.* Jane could think, even if she couldn't talk.

A hush came over the temps when Swati, Lauren, and Jane came back toward the cubicles surrounding the cafeteria. They'd evidently been talking about Jane while she was gone, and now everyone seemed to want to get a look at her. The guys seemed especially keen to put eyes on her, this battered girl who'd come to them for shelter, rendered mute by the trauma she'd witnessed. They were probably fantasizing about her, Swati thought, writing stories in their heads in which they were the ones to bring Jane back out of her shell, to nurse her to health like a bird with a broken wing, to teach her to speak and live and love again. Swati hated them. Men were always looking to put their mark on women, to find ways of owning them. When women, usually, just wanted to be left alone.

Brent materialized out of the crowd, with Dominic close behind. They didn't say anything (perhaps they saw Swati's warning look, sensed her growing annoyance) but she could tell that they were bursting with questions. She nodded silently away from the crowd, toward a small sitting area with couches and chairs set in a wide lane between rows of cubicles. They moved toward it, and Jane sat between Swati and Lauren with her back pole-straight, as though ready to spring to her feet at the first sign of any danger. Swati felt something clamp over her arm, and she looked down to see Jane's hand gripping her hard by the elbow. On the other side, Jane had grabbed at Lauren too, pulling her closer. Lauren and Swati shared a nonplussed look. They'd become Jane's caretakers.

Dominic and Brent sat down on a couch on the other side of the sitting area, across the slim plane of a teak coffee table, and began asking their questions.

The winding conversation that followed teased out the following facts: no, Jane wasn't injured; yes, that meant the blood hadn't been hers; no, Swati and Lauren didn't know whose it was; no, Jane still hadn't started talking; no, they weren't sure what was wrong with her.

Brent thought that Jane had been outside at the all-company meeting, that her inability to speak was either an effect of the gas, an effect of the trauma of seeing the killing, or some combination of both—but Dominic wasn't convinced.

"Doesn't the gas make people kill?" Dominic said. "Doesn't it turn them into . . . what do you call them, Lauren?"

"Furies," Lauren said. "And not exactly. Some people, it turns them into Furies who kill other people—but others turn that rage inward and attack themselves. I don't know, maybe it has something to do with the pre-existing psychology of the person before they breathe the gas. Whether they have a natural tendency to externalize or internalize anger."

"Sure," Dominic said, "but Jane's not trying to kill herself. You said yourself there's not a mark on her. What kind of pre-existing psychology could turn a person mute after they breathe the gas?"

Lauren shook her head. "I don't know."

"So what are you suggesting?" Brent asked. "What do you think happened?"

Dominic hissed air through his teeth and directed his gaze upward as he thought. "I don't know. Maybe the fighting spread inside somehow. To some part of the building we don't know about. Maybe some of the Furies are already inside."

"Then how come we haven't seen them yet?" Brent asked. "No. She was outside. It's the simplest explanation, the most obvious. We've got 345 temps here on the fourth floor, Jacob and Morgan found five more down on two, then add Jane and that makes 351 total. Except you said yourself there are exactly 350 contract employees in all of Delphi. Which means that Jane has to be a full-time employee. Black badge."

Dominic turned back to Swati and Lauren. "Did you find a security badge on her?"

Swati nodded. "Black."

"Permanent employee," Dominic said.

"Unless she skipped the meeting," Lauren pointed out. "Or she was late."

"Could we try giving her something to write on?" Dominic asked. "She won't talk—but maybe she'll write."

"We tried that," Swati said. "We put a pad and a pen in her hand, but she was still so confused, it was almost like she didn't know what it was for. She didn't even make a mark. I think we just have to give her time to recover from the shock of . . . whatever happened to her."

"This is pointless," Brent said. "There's an easy way to figure out if she was outside or not. Bring her to the windows. Make her look at what's out there, in the courtyard. See how she reacts."

Jane's grip tightened around Swati's elbow, fingernails digging into Swati's skin until she had to resist the urge to cry out in pain. More evidence that Jane could understand what was being said. Swati's body clenched against both the pain of Jane's clawing and the wrongness of Brent's suggestion. The temps, all of the 350 (or the 345, at least) had been keeping their distance from the windows overlooking the courtyard. They looked frequently to the horizon for signs of life in the city, and had spread through the cubicles surrounding the cafeteria for places to sleep—but rarely did anyone step near to the windows that would give them a view of the carnage in the amphitheater or the few living Furies that still stalked there, looking for new prey. If not even the temps, who'd seen the effects of the gas from the safety of the office building behind thick corporate glass, wanted to walk to the windows, then why should they force Jane to do it? Swati found it difficult to imagine the casual cruelty, the lack of feeling, that must be hidden behind such a suggestion.

"I'm not going to let that happen," Swati said. "She's been through enough."

"Come on," Brent said, "just for a second. Don't you want to know?"

He rose from the couch and came around to their side of the coffee table, his hand outstretched to grab Jane. Jane turned, clutching now with both hands at Swati, burying her head in her neck.

"NO!" Jane shrieked in a cry so piercing that for a moment afterward Swati heard ringing in her ears. The scream was loud enough to echo throughout the wing, so that everyone on the floor must have heard it.

Swati looked up. They were all frozen. Lauren, Dominic—even Brent, standing above them with his hand still outstretched.

"There," Swati said. "You have your answer now. She was outside, okay? Now leave her alone."

# NINE

Dinner that evening was taco salad with ground beef, black beans for the vegetarians and vegans, and afterward Brent assembled all the temps together for what he was calling a "team meeting." The gathering was held in a small auditorium not far from the cafeteria, padded chairs set in tiers with writing surfaces that folded up from beside the armrest, like a college lecture hall. Brent's lackeys—a mostly male group culled from the other food service workers—handed out granola bars and bottles of water as the temps filed into the auditorium. Lauren suspected the food was intended to keep them satisfied and docile, munching like cows while Brent asserted his authority at the front of the room. *Panem et circenses.*

There were more temps than seats, and by the time the room had filled people were leaning against walls, sitting on steps, plopped cross-legged on the floor. The room was just starting to get hot when the air conditioning thudded on, and Lauren closed her eyes to briefly offer her thanks to the now-dead building engineer who had designed Delphi's self-sufficient heating, cooling, air filtration, electrical, and plumbing systems.

"Hey folks," Brent said after everyone was inside. "Thanks for being here this evening. This is a tough situation, one none of us planned on being in—I don't have to tell you that. But we're going to be okay. My people have been working really hard the past twenty-four hours to make sure of it."

Lauren felt a chill at Brent's use of "my people." It took almost no time at all, splitting humanity once again into the usual hierarchies, the stratifications and divisions: lords and subjects, rulers and ruled, bosses and employees.

"So that's the first thing I want you to know tonight: that you're in good hands. You did the right thing when you responded to my email, when you came up here and joined us on the fourth floor. Banding together was the right choice. And I'm not going to let you down. I'm going to make sure that each and every one of you survives and gets out of here. That's a promise. Frederick, lights?"

The lights in the auditorium dimmed, and a square of light appeared on a screen at the front of the room. As the projector warmed up, the light resolved into simple white words on a stark black background. Brent intoned the words as they appeared.

"*Every problem is a gift*," he quoted. "*Without problems we would not grow.*"

Brent let the words hang in the air as the source of the quotation came onto the screen.

—*Tony Robbins.*

Lauren stifled a laugh, understanding something about Brent for the first time. She pictured him at a seminar in a hotel conference room, hooting with other men in the dark as a self-help guru pumped them up from a stage. He probably lifted weights every day, drank powdered protein shakes, had personal mantras, did Toastmasters. Twenty-four hours ago Brent had been a shift manager for Delphi's catering services—now he seemed to think the gas had promoted him all the way to CEO.

Lauren looked around to see others' reactions. This was weird, right? But they just stared dully forward, the light on the projector screen reflected in their eyes.

"I collect inspiring quotes," Brent said after a long pause. "And this is one of my favorites. It's one I come back to a lot when I'm feeling depressed. When it feels like life is hell-bent on beating me down. And it's the first thing I thought of when I saw what was happening outside."

Brent had one hand up around his chest, cradling a clicker; the other was shoved deep into his pocket and jiggling nervously. He probably didn't know he was doing it, but Lauren still wished he'd stop. The motion was making it look as though Brent might be furtively masturbating, and Lauren only barely bit back another wave of giggles.

"This thing that happened to us, to all of us—it's quite a problem, isn't it? The biggest problem any of us have ever encountered. A pretty scary problem, if we're being honest."

Lauren frowned. To call the possible end of human civilization a *problem* seemed like an understatement. But murmurs of agreement sounded off from the crowd.

"But look, I don't want life to happen *to me*, I want to be the one *making* things happen. I want that for all of us. I don't want this problem to end us. I want it to make us grow. I want it to reveal who we really are. I want it to bring out the greatness in us. I want to fuckin' beat this problem into the dirt, know what I mean?"

A few male voices whooped like bros at a frat party, cheering on a friend doing a keg stand. Brent smiled, some of the nervousness seeming to bleed off his body. The hand in his pocket stopped vibrating. He lifted the remote and clicked a button. The screen changed.

*DEFINING THE PROBLEM*, the title at the top of the screen read, and as Brent kept clicking the remote there appeared bullet points detailing the direness of their situation.

• *Everyone's dead*

"Well, maybe not everyone," Brent said. "But most people, as far as we can tell. The gas hit more than a dozen major American cities. And now, smaller cities and rural areas, plus other countries around the world, according to the news. Most of the people you knew—your family, your friends—if they're not here, I'm sorry to say it, it's going to sound harsh, but it's important to look it in the face: they're probably dead."

• *No help*

"This is another thing we're not one hundred percent sure of, but it doesn't seem like there's anyone out there who's going to help us. Early on a few of us saw helicopters—but then they crashed, and for the past twenty-four hours we've been watching the skies and we haven't seen anything. No planes, no contrails. No Army or National Guard vehicles in the distance, no evidence even that the US government survived."

• *No information*

"TV is down. Cable, satellite, internet—these are all systems that require humans to maintain them, and going back to my first point," Brent pointed the remote at the screen, bringing a pinprick of red laser light to the first bullet before turning back to the audience, "if everyone's dead, then that means all those systems go down. Electric, plumbing, water treatment, food supply, all of it. Every system modern civilization depends on. If they haven't gone down already, they will soon. Which means . . ."

• *Civilization will crumble*

"There will be other survivors—but the world they inherit will be different from the one they knew before the gas. If you've ever seen a zombie movie you'll know what I'm talking about. Food and clean water will be scarce. Tools, fuel: these will all become valuable commodities. The people who remain will band together in groups that fight and kill each other. Someday it'll settle down into a new normal, but in the meantime it'll be ugly, and many of the survivors *will* come to envy the dead."

The auditorium had gone quiet. Lauren no longer felt the urge to laugh, even though every single one of Brent's thoughts sounded as though it had been taken from somewhere else: self-help gurus, inspirational posters, action movies. In spite of the clichés, Brent's description of the downfall of civilization was chilling—but even more chilling was the ease that had come over him as he spoke, the last of his nerves replaced with something approaching glee.

"Make no mistake," he said now. "Whoever's responsible for this gas cloud, they beat our asses good."

He clicked the remote.

SOLVING THE PROBLEM

"But remember what Tony Robbins says? Problems are just opportunities to grow. This problem hit us hard, but we're not dead yet. We're going to keep moving forward, we're going to punch back—and we're going to win. We're going to fucking win."

THE GOAL

"It's simple," Brent said, then clicked the remote again.

• *Survive*

"Survive," Brent repeated, "and . . ."

• *Survive*

A murmur rippled over the auditorium, the polite laughter of underlings chuckling at a boss's lame joke.

"That's it," Brent said. "Survive. Get it? It's the only plan, the only thing we have to do. We have to survive. Live long enough for the gas to go away—however long that is—then get out of here and start over. Rebuild."

*HOW WE DO IT*

"Survival is the goal," Brent said. "And here's how we pull it off."

• *Ration food*

"We have to control the food supply so that we can keep as many people fed and healthy for as long as possible. Right now, we've got enough food in the freezers to keep us all alive for three months, maybe more—and we haven't even inventoried all the food in this building yet."

• *Scavenge*

"That brings me to my next point. We have to ransack this whole building for every single thing that might be useful. That means food: a few parties started searching the food courts and desk drawers on the first floor, but we're only just getting started. We need more parties, more people scouring every corner of this place, bringing everything that's useful back up here. Not just food, but tools, knives, first aid kits. Anything that can help us, we need it. I'll organize the search parties. You want to volunteer, come talk to me after the meeting."

• *Distress signal*

"I know I said there's no one out there who can help us—but just in case, we need to figure out some kind of a way to let people outside know that we're here. I'm thinking 'HELP' spelled out in big letters on the roof, 'SOS,' something. This'll be a hard one. Whoever takes this one on will have to figure out not just how to spell it, but how to get someone out there in this gas without getting killed. Or a radio signal, if we can find the right equipment here. And last but not least . . ."

• *Weapons*

The word blipped onto the screen and then sat there, hard and cruel as an obscenity. Lauren felt Swati stir next to her and thought of their promise to each other, earlier that day, that the future would be female, not male—that if they were indeed the first generation of a new world, that they wouldn't make the same mistakes that had led to the downfall of the old one. Lauren was begrudgingly impressed by Brent's presentation.

He'd obviously put the PowerPoint together earlier that day, toiled over it, practiced his lines. But there was an undeniable masculinity to the content and style of the presentation, with its emphasis on punching back, beating asses—and, now, weapons.

"I don't know if any of you have been to the windows recently," Brent continued. "We don't like to look—it isn't pretty, what happened out there—but I've been looking. I feel like I need to. It's important to look. And a few of those . . . those *things*—"

*Furies*, thought Lauren. *They're Furies.*

"They're still alive. Still looking for prey. And if they're alive, then there are more of them, out in the city. Just wanting to get in, to attack us. I'd prefer not to ever run into one—but if I do, I want to be prepared. I want to be armed. Now, we can fashion weapons out of the things we find here in the office. Scissors come to mind. Dominic, one of the guys who joined us this morning, he made a machete out of a paper cutter. That's ingenuity, the kind of ingenuity we're going to need more of. But I think we might be able to find real weapons too. Delphi had a security team—dead now, they were in the all-company meeting—but they may have had weapons. This building was built with its own power and water systems, almost like someone knew something like this could happen someday. Someone who was planning ahead like that, there's no way they didn't stockpile some guns somewhere around here."

Brent paused to let this sink in, then turned halfway toward the screen and clicked the button one more time.

*QUESTIONS?*

Lauren felt another rustling at her elbow, and glanced to find Swati rising from her seat. Lauren's heart plunged into her stomach. Her hand darted out and grabbed at Swati's, pulling down.

"No, don't," she pled softly, anticipating with a sudden and icy certainty what had driven Swati to her feet, what she was going to say next.

Swati snatched her hand away from Lauren's.

"Excuse me," Swati said.

The people in front of them turned to look at her. Lauren sank back into her seat, cheeks burning.

"Yes?" Brent asked, his mask of confidence cracking as he tried and failed to hide his displeasure at being interrupted.

"I'm sorry, but who put you in charge, anyway?" Swati asked. "You're standing up there like you're our leader—but *I* never chose you. I came up here because I wanted to be with other people who survived this thing. Because I didn't want to be alone. Not because I wanted you to tell me what to do. I barely even know you."

Around them Lauren began to hear the rustling of people moving in their seats, soft murmurs of agreement. Swati's voice grew louder.

"I mean, before the gas came we lived in a democracy, didn't we? I didn't realize we'd woken up into a dictatorship."

Brent bent his mouth in an empty smile, a rictus of barely concealed anger. "Well, I guess it depends on how you look at it. The United States was—is—a constitutional republic, but there were plenty of other institutions before the gas that were functional dictatorships. The military, private businesses, churches. Rigid hierarchies answering to one person, with no real representation of the will of the people."

"Is that what you think this is?" Swati shot back. "The army? A church? With you as the general, the pope?"

"No. A business is what I was thinking—we're here among the remnants of a business, and I just thought it would be most effective, with the goal of group survival, if decisions fell largely to just one—"

"And you figured that one person should be you," Swati interrupted. "Without even asking. Without asking anyone if they even wanted you."

Brent was silent. The quiet stretched out in the room. Lauren held her breath.

"Your point is well-taken," Brent said at last, and the whole auditorium seemed to let out a sigh. "What do you suggest?"

Swati paused before speaking, turning slowly around to take stock of the temps surrounding her. Lauren clenched her teeth and sunk deeper into her chair, wishing herself five or ten minutes into the future, when Swati's speech would be over. But time kept on creeping forward in its regular pace, trapping Lauren in the current moment. She was in the middle of a crowded room, surrounded by bodies on every side. There was nowhere to escape to.

"Something bad happened yesterday," Swati said. "Something horrible—to all of us. We survived, but it happened to us too. The death of everything we've ever known. Of the people we loved."

Swati's voice hitched and she put her head down, pressing a knuckle to her shut lips. The sounds of sniffling and soft weeping rushed to fill the silence as people in the crowd thought about their own losses, the loved ones they'd never see again. Lauren searched inside herself but still found no tears. Then Swati lifted her eyes and kept talking.

"That world is dead now. The world of before. But all of us, sitting right here—we're the start of a new world. A different world. If we can find a way to survive, to get through this thing until the gas goes away—then we'll be the ones to rebuild it from scratch. The first generation. That's why we have to think so hard about what kind of community we make while we're stuck in here. Because whatever we make, that's what the new world will become."

Swati paused. Something seemed to ripple through the room. Swati was good at this. Lauren was impressed. Listening to Swati, Lauren almost forgot that she'd been the one to first plant these thoughts in Swati's head, that she'd inspired Swati before Swati had inspired the others. But Swati was more charismatic, more eloquent than Lauren could ever be—Lauren who loved beautiful words, classical poetry and rhetoric, but clammed up in front of crowds. She was stirred by Swati's speech, and she felt herself sitting up a little straighter.

"I'm still not hearing a concrete proposal," Brent said dismissively.

Lauren's eyes snapped toward him at the front of the room. In that moment, she could have spit on him.

"The old world was patriarchal," Swati said. "Run by old men. The new world should be led by women. That's why I think that my friend—"

Lauren's heart clenched in her chest at *my friend* and she leapt to her feet.

"I nominate Swati to lead us," she blurted out. She clamped a hand on the armrest of her chair, feeling dizzy from having stood too quickly and from the sense of everyone's eyes turning toward her at once. She steadied herself, then caught Swati's gaze. Swati was giving her a very strange look—not angry, but not exactly happy, either.

"You want Swati to replace me?" Brent asked, a sudden weakness creeping into his voice.

"No," Lauren said, looking down and blinking. Then she looked up and said again, "No. Swati said this shouldn't be a dictatorship, and I agree. There should be a . . . a *council*. A leadership council, with members elected democratically by all the survivors. And Swati should be on it."

"Why?" Brent demanded. "Why Swati? It sounded to me like she was about to suggest—"

"You all saw how she took control of the situation when Jane came to us," Lauren said. "Nobody knew what to do. *You* didn't know what to do."

She shot Brent a sharp look. He didn't say anything.

"But Swati knew what to do. She helped Jane. She was decisive, and kind. She's the kind of leader we need for the council."

Lauren whirled down to her seat, ears burning, but to her surprise as soon as she sat down there was a scattering of applause. Then, as the clapping died down, a girl's voice shouted out, "I second the motion! Swati for council!" That outburst was followed by some cheers and whoops, then a male voice—not Brent's—saying "All in favor?" and the auditorium echoed with a chorus of *ayes*. Then Brent asked, "Opposed?"

Silence.

Lauren smiled.

The motion carried.

• • •

"Keep going," Swati said breathlessly. "Don't stop."

Jacob didn't stop, he hadn't been intending to, and he didn't think he could've even if he'd wanted to—not with Swati's hand clamped hard on the back of his head, fingernails digging into his scalp. She pulled him into her, so deep that for a moment he couldn't breathe, but then he found a different angle and took a gulp of air.

Jacob hadn't forgotten his plan to put himself near Swati after the sun went down, to see if what had happened between them the night before had been more than a fluke—but it turned out to be Swati who sought *him* out, appearing at the doorway to the cubicle where he'd set up for the night as he was staring up into the darkness and trying to muster the courage to go find her.

"Hey," he'd said, propping himself up on his elbows, and she'd responded "Hey," then walked into the cubicle and fell into him, her mouth clumsily finding his. They kissed for a few seconds, and then suddenly her clothes were peeling away from her body and her hands were on his shoulders, pushing him down.

Now Jacob's head was between Swati's legs. He lapped at her doggedly—changing rhythms and varying patterns in the way that had always worked for him in the past with other women—until he heard her breathing speed up, the familiar moans and gasps. As Swati came, Jacob reached his hand up to try to silence her. There were other people nearby, sleeping in other cubicles, and Jacob didn't want them to hear. But when his fingers reached Swati's mouth, she grabbed them and bit down on the knuckle of his forefinger, hard.

"Ow!" Jacob said into the skin of Swati's thigh. "For fuck's sake."

Swati laughed, an airy sound that broke at the end as she recovered her breath.

"Don't be a baby," she said.

Jacob pulled himself up and flopped on the ground next to Swati, then massaged the bitten knuckle without saying anything in retort. Swati scared him, a little. When he and Lauren had first come upon her in the concourse, she'd seemed so peaceful, so serene. But his interactions with Swati since that initial meeting had revealed a vein of danger under her calm exterior. Swati had a rage in her. This rage didn't repel Jacob, though; on the contrary, it only attracted him more, made him think that their connection had the potential to be more than just physical, just sexual. Jacob was angry too. It was something they had in common.

"That was good," Swati said. "I'm sorry that—well, I'm not *sorry*, I just . . . I hope I didn't wake you."

"You didn't," Jacob said.

"I guess I just had all this *excess energy* in me," Swati said, as though he hadn't spoken. "From the meeting."

"Mmm," Jacob said, sensing that no response was required or even desired except one that would assure Swati he was listening, one that would give her the pretext to keep talking.

"I really didn't expect it to go like that. I mean, of course I'd been planning to get up and say something, especially after Brent was acting all . . . I don't know, just so much like a *guy*, trying to dominate everything and talking about weapons and beating asses like we can somehow go out there and just punch the gas into submission, and, well, *of course* I had to say something after that. But my point wasn't that *I* should lead, my plan was to say that Lauren—and then she said *me*, that I should be the one."

"I know," Jacob said. "I was there."

There was a beat of silence in which Jacob realized he'd said the wrong thing. Swati turned onto her side to look at him, her bare breasts brushing against his ribcage.

"You don't approve?" A trace of anger in her voice, that danger bubbling to the surface again.

"No, I think it's great," Jacob said. And he did: he was glad Swati was there to moderate Brent's authoritarian tendencies. If Jacob and Swati had any disagreement, it was only one of outlook—Swati's ascendance to leadership of the temps had made her temporarily optimistic about the future of the world, but Jacob still didn't see anything in their situation worth feeling good about.

Another silence, and Jacob looked down to see Swati gazing at him with a question in her eyes. "What?"

She broke his gaze and set her cheek on his chest. "Why did you nominate Dominic for the leadership council after I got voted in?"

Jacob set his head down and looked into the air. Above them hung a piece of modern sculpture made of wood strips planed thin as sheets of aluminum and arranged in undulating waves, the whole massive construction suspended from invisible wires so that it seemed like a cloud hanging above their heads, something that might at any moment drop and crush them both.

"I don't know," he said, shoulder blades dragging against the rough carpet as he shrugged. "He seems like a leader."

Another thing that was true, though only in part. After Swati's election, more spontaneous nominations had followed—Frederick had nominated Brent, the subsequent unanimous voice vote making his leadership official and democratic rather than self-assumed. Jacob had quickly followed by shouting Dominic's name. But now he couldn't quite say why he'd done it. Dominic seemed to want it, certainly, wanted to be counted among the temps as a person of consequence, whose opinions and preferences could become reality. And Jacob liked Dominic, as much as you could like a person who you'd only just met, and under stressful circumstances at that. But had he also, perhaps, nominated Dominic to *get him out of the way*, to keep him busy while Jacob conducted his investigations unobstructed? Not consciously, at any rate—but then after the meeting hadn't Jacob pulled Brent aside and whispered to him about the group of temps still working on the second floor? Hadn't he told Brent about his suspicions? And hadn't Brent seemed receptive, both to his paranoid theories and to his desire to investigate further, without Dominic's knowledge? In consideration of these facts, who knew what Jacob's subconscious motivations had been?

"It wasn't about you," Jacob said to Swati now. "I wasn't trying to undermine you, I promise."

And then, before she could answer, to change the subject: "What are you planning to do? In your new role."

"I don't know," Swati said at first, which Jacob felt sure was a lie. She'd been thinking about it, probably, lying awake and turning it over in her mind, unable to sleep—that was what had driven her to his cubicle in the first place.

"I keep thinking," she continued after a long pause, "that what I need to do here, what I'm *supposed* to do, is the same thing I've been training for. The thing I've always wanted to do."

"So, yoga," Jacob said.

"Yes," Swati said. "And mindfulness. Brent only wants us to survive, to live—but survive for what? Live how? That's what I want to think about, to help other people think about. How to live better, more at peace, even in the midst of . . ." She trailed off and took a different tack. "Before, every-thing was so out of balance. The world, people. All these negative energies flaring. Disequilibrium. But maybe we have a new chance now, like I was saying in the meeting. A chance to make a new world."

"You think?" Jacob asked.

Swati sighed. "I just want to help people live more fully in the moment—in their bodies, in their minds. Everything at rest."

Jacob didn't say anything. *Rest* sounded nice, but he couldn't think of anything worse than living more fully in his mind. His biggest problem was his tendency to get lost in his own head, sucked into a swirling vortex of obsessive, negative thoughts. He thought deeply about things that other people had the tendency to gloss over. In college, this quality had been a source of pride, the thing that made him excel at digging into literary texts and finding embedded messages, hidden meanings and significances that others couldn't see. But now his analytical mind was a source of almost-constant psychological pain. His life had become a text to obsessively pore over, yielding no satisfactory interpretations. This had been the case not just since the gas, but even earlier, before graduation. In fact, if Jacob really thought about it, he could pinpoint the exact day it began: the day during senior year when he'd gone to his campus mailbox and found three letters from different graduate schools—one Ivy League and two state universities with well-regarded English PhD programs. Small envelopes, all of them, all with some variant of the same message, which he couldn't bear to read in its entirety: "We regret to inform you that . . ." The moment of crushing disappointment now tied up in his mind with the later moment, when he stood at the windows to the courtyard and saw the beginning of the end of the world. Both were an apocalypse of a kind—one personal, one global. Except that the latter apocalypse felt personal too; as he'd looked in on the Delphi Enterprises all-company meeting and seen the crowd turn on itself, the violence had seemed to be an attack directed at him, a horror show staged for his benefit, so that the subsequent crumbling of the world had felt like nothing more than an intensification of his pre-existing predica-ment. His future, his assumptions about the world, his very identity had all been obliterated, leaving only uncertainty. Before the gas and after, he no longer knew how or who to be, what to want or to hope for—or if *hope* was even warranted anymore.

How could he explain any of this to Swati? How could she understand it? She couldn't.

But then, to his surprise, he heard her say exactly what he was thinking, albeit with an optimistic rather than despairing undertone:

"I just feel like anything's possible. Don't you?"

"Yeah," he responded, adding mentally: *That's exactly the problem. That's exactly what's so terrifying.*

*Anything's possible.*

# INTERLUDE

. . .

Time passes for the temps both slowly and quickly, the moments seeming at once brief and infinite in their duration. This strange dilation owing in large part to the obliteration of the temps' former routines, the rituals they once used to parcel out their days—morning hygienic practices, bus commutes, post-work happy hours, grocery shopping, the binge watching of streaming TV. Without these customs, time stretches out vast and desolate like a desert, until new patterns, new habits gradually grow to take their place. New ways of marking time. And so, when the temps think back to the horrible morning of the gas, it sometimes seems to them that months or even years have elapsed, sometimes that it's only been a week or two. To know for certain how long they've been marooned inside the headquarters of Delphi Enterprises, they must consult the white board in the cafeteria that used to hold the day's specials—chicken and wild rice soup, tempeh reubens, fajita salad with cilantro-lime dressing—but which Brent now uses to track the days. Six vertical lines and a diagonal slash to mark the passage of every week. Here, they count, their eyes brushing over the place at day twelve where Brent switched from red to blue when his dry-erase marker ran out of ink.

Days, then weeks, then a month, then more.

The temps split up into search parties and fan out across the building. First they look for food, empty the restaurant freezers and break room refrigerators of everything edible. Plastic bags of shredded iceberg lettuce, frozen reconstituted veggie patties, Lean Cuisines, granola bars, beef jerky, salted sunflower seeds. Bulk-sized containers of salsa, ranch dressing, sour cream. Giant jars of dill pickle spears.

Then, having collected every edible morsel, they go back for more. The purpose of returning is unclear, but the temps have nothing better to do, and so they keep coming, wave after wave of scavenging trips. Their eyes passing once more over surfaces they've already searched, reconsidering the utility of objects they formerly passed over. The temps ransack every cubicle, every drawer, every file cabinet and supply closet. They strip the office bare, like locusts ravaging a field of crops. And then, at the end of the day, they return to the fourth floor with their items, things they grabbed because they thought they might be useful, or—later, when most of the good stuff has already been taken—because they simply want them. The objects becoming stranger by the day.

Scotch tape. Scissors. Staplers. Pet rocks. Stress balls. Stuffed animals. Empty Pez dispensers with cartoon heads—Tweety Bird, Homer Simpson, Wolverine. Knitted blankets. Ironic needlepoints, posters with funny phrases. "Take a Number." "Don't Mansplain Me, Bro!" "YOLO Bitches!"

The temps spread out through the top floor, each picking a cubicle to call their own. A place to store the items they find on other floors, a desk to sleep under. Most call their cubicles "apartments," though some think privately that the ten-by-ten living spaces are more like cells. The temps furnish their apartments with items recovered in scavenging parties. Pillows and cushions taken from break rooms are used to make beds, and enough of the permanent employees had blankets at their cubicles for each temp to get at least one. In the desk drawers they put changes of clothes from the locker rooms, again enough so that each of them has at least two outfits, sometimes three or more, including the clothes they wore to work on the day of the gas. Another drawer for toiletries—deodorant, shampoo, toothpaste, even makeup, for the women who find it and still care enough to apply it every morning. Not all the employees of Delphi Enterprises brought such items to work, kept them at their desk or at a locker in the employee health club—but in a company of ten thousand, a large enough percentage did to supply a mere 350 temps.

They decorate their apartments, adorn the desktops and walls with objects speaking to their personalities. Posters with phrases either inspirational or sarcastic. Movie stills. Plastic figurines. Collectible shot glasses from cities now turned to postapocalyptic wastelands: New Orleans, Miami, San Francisco. They write their names at the entrance to their cubicles, officially marking each space as their own. These labels vary in complexity. Some people simply scrawl their names on a piece of computer paper with black Sharpie, then pin the paper to the entrance with a thumb tack. Others turn the task into a craft project, embellishing their names with intricate, colorful designs, adding glitter or folded paper constructions, then framing their creations or cracking open the plastic nameplates and sliding their new labels inside. Some set out bowls of candy, Skittles or mini Butterfingers, to entice temps from neighboring cubicles to visit them during the day. Others crave their privacy, hanging blankets or pieces of cloth across the cubicle entrance to discourage anyone from disturbing them.

Nothing comes of Brent's hope for a distress call. The temps can't figure out how to rig a radio signal, they don't have the right equipment, and nobody dares to venture outside to etch an SOS on the roof or in the grass of the courtyard. They never find weapons, either. Either Delphi's security workers didn't have guns, or they hid them well, in a part of the building the temps can't reach. It doesn't matter; the threat of the Furies dissipates soon enough, the pack in the courtyard falling one by one as they collapse from dehydration or exhaustion. Soon, every one of the roving predators is dead, and the temps no longer have any reason to need weapons.

After the first few weeks, a sense of abundance creeps up among them, at odds with Brent's dire apocalyptic warnings, his careful protection of the food supply, his daily rationing. The building is so large, so full of the leavings of dead employees, the detritus of their hours spent at work, that the resources available to the temps feel infinite. They recover more food than Brent had guessed, enough for four months rather than the initially estimated three. And surely, they think, *surely* that will be enough to keep them fed until the gas lifts, at which point they'll have the abundance of a crumbled American civilization at the height of its affluence to sustain them. Grocery stores full of canned beans, Cheetos, Twinkies, everything loaded with enough preservatives to keep for decades.

Some of the temps can even, on a good day, forget the basic facts of their situation, the predicament they're in. These temps simply choose not to remember that the world ended, that they survived a catastrophe, that they're stranded in the office building of a corporation that paid them shitty hourly wages to do humiliating jobs that weren't even supposed to last, that they are at best a few months away from a hunger sharper and more painful than any of them have ever known. Among these temps—the ones who can forget—their situation feels less like a survival scenario than it does an extended co-ed campout, a spring break trip, maybe even a party. Sure, there's plenty of crying, plenty of despairing, especially the first few days: temps who simply leak from the eyes for 48 or 72 hours at a stretch, audible weeping at night when others are trying to sleep, the more sensitive among them entering long periods of mourning for the death of loved ones and for the world they knew. And sometimes, too, a group of the temps will walk to the concourse and look to the horizon, watching the city for signs of life. Occasionally they'll hear explosions in the distance, see plumes of smoke rising into the air, and they'll wonder what's happening. This passes soon enough—the wondering, watching, and weeping—and within the second week the majority of the temps have turned their eyes and minds inward, to the community, the civilization, the culture they're creating for themselves in the wreckage of Delphi Enterprises.

At first the hours pass aimless and empty, but gradually the temps begin to fill their days with scheduled activities. Swati institutes a morning yoga session on the first floor, in the sun of the concourse. The first day, ten temps come. The next day, the number of yogis doubles, and attendance grows from there until Swati has to add a second class, a third, a fourth— and now she's as busy teaching yoga and dreaming up new class routines as she was before the gas. Busier, even.

Other temps hold events of their own. Ice cream socials, mixers, afternoon happy hours, Ping-Pong round-robins. The gatherings informal at first, but then a group forms, comprised of temps who'd missed previous callings as event planners or cruise directors. The temps call the group the "party-planning committee," a joking reference to a long-running network sitcom several of them used to watch religiously. The members of the planning group don't appreciate the joke, though; they call themselves the "community team."

Each team member has different strengths. Becky, formerly of accounts payable, specializes in food-centered events: Taco Tuesday, baked potato bar, build-your-own sundaes, an Oktoberfest with beer and pretzels. Spencer, from marketing, likes activities, events that require attendees to do or make something: around-the-office mini-golf, office chair races, a talent show with singing and skits and even a standup routine. Rosa, from human resources, seems most concerned about the mental health of the survivors, organizing poorly attended events in which the temps can process their complicated emotions and get to know each other on a deeper level. At a survivor support group, she arranges folding chairs in a circle and invites everyone to talk about their feelings, their dead loved ones, everything they'll miss about the old world. She passes around a box of tissues when people start to cry. James, the fourth and final member of the community team, just wants to party. He filches some stereo equipment from the media department, where he worked before the gas, then sets up a DJ table in a huge meeting room on the third floor and blares house music for the hundred or so temps who come, nightly, to dance.

The community team is surprisingly organized: each of their events is advertised around the office with a four-color poster designed by Spencer, who has InDesign experience, and most of the events are catered. At first Brent and Dominic are hesitant to give up food from the communal supply for their events, but the team develops a requisition form in which they list the supplies they're requesting, then estimate the approximate attendance to justify the consumption of resources. They develop yet another form so that temps not on the committee can propose their own ideas for events, and before long there's not a day that goes by without at least one thing happening: running club, scavenger hunts, game nights, speed dating. Most events have alcohol; Delphi Enterprises was a cool workplace catering to millennials, with fridges full of beer and wine in almost every department.

Jacob and Swati are the first couple, but they're not the last. Temps pair off quickly, some going on "dates" to one of the planned events, then walking the halls of Delphi Enterprises and talking long into the night. Others skip dating and go straight to sex. The far side of the fourth floor becomes the place to go for nighttime assignations, a place for sexual partners to be alone without disturbing others who simply want to sleep. Before long, a peaceful nighttime walk along the P-wing is liable to be disturbed by moans of pleasure rising from the cubicles like the chirping of crickets from a dark wood.

Birth control is surprisingly easy to come by. Some wonder: *Who brings condoms to work?* But there they are, a few stowed deep in some dead employee's desk drawer, next to the staples and correction tape. Sometimes a whole box of Trojans. These go in a glass bowl, in turn placed on a table in the cafeteria, where guys pass and grab a handful when they're feeling hopeful. The bowl frequently gets low, but somehow in the morning it is always replenished with more shiny square packets.

With romance comes gossip—who is sleeping with whom, but also who is cheating on whom with whom, who's straight and who's gay and who's bi, who might be in an open relationship, who's exclusive, who's just playing the field. For a week, the temps are aflutter after a rumor starts that Jacob and Swati have stopped using protection, are trying to have a baby. The temps' eyes light up—a baby! The firstborn of a new world! The rumor not salacious but full of wonderment and awe. The thought of a child, of parenthood, shifts everything the temps are doing into a new and more serious register. They are, after all, the only survivors of the gas that they know of. When the yellow cloud lifts, the world will be theirs. They're adults—not *girls and guys* (the terms they persisted in using for themselves and their peers long after college was over) but *women and men.*

At the end of the week Jacob and Swati dispel the rumor. They're not trying to have a baby. But some don't believe them, and for others the rumor has brought about a fundamental change, and *they* stop using protection when they meet their partners at night in P-wing. No confirmed pregnancies yet, but surely it won't be long.

Every so often the temps' attention turns back to the gas. They watch the sky, wait for it to turn from yellow to blue again. They sometimes wonder what happened, who did this, and why. Theories range from the mundane to the outlandish: terrorists, a rogue state, aliens preparing for an invasion, environmentalists who wanted to kill all humans and let animals inherit the earth, Illuminati. Some of them can't let go of these thoughts, but most of them glance outside, shake their heads, and then turn back to the new lives they've made for themselves inside this building. They eat, they fuck, they play—and wait, and wait, and wait. None knows precisely what it is they're waiting for, but everyone knows deep down that they're waiting for *something*. Something new to happen.

Then, one day, it does.

• • •

# TEN

That morning Swati woke to find that Jacob was gone. His pillow still dented from the weight of his head, but cold to the touch.

She wasn't alarmed; this had been happening more and more over the past few weeks. Jacob was an early riser, but in the early days, when they'd just started sleeping together, he'd stay in bed until Swati woke up with the harsh buttery light of dawn.

"Good morning," he'd say, then roll over and tangle himself up with her. Sometimes they'd have sex, sometimes not—but either way, it was nice.

But now he was often gone when Swati opened her eyes, awoken early by some restlessness, some vague agitation.

Swati got up and stuffed a bag full of everything she'd need for the day: yoga mat, smartphone, speaker, water bottle. Then she went to the cafeteria for a toasted English muffin with butter and jam from packets, her tradition. From there she went to the elevator, munching, and pressed the button for the first floor. Then she turned down the concourse, thinking about Jacob as she walked.

He was such a strange guy: sweet, gentle—but troubled too. Sometimes they'd be lying in her cubicle, talking about something or other, when his eyes would turn vague and she'd know she lost him again. Getting him back from such a state was like waking a sleepwalker. Looking at him, at his glazed-over eyes, she was reminded of clients she'd worked with whose bodies had become deformed after trauma, muscles and bones reforming, hunching to protect a remembered pain. Jacob's mind was like that, she thought, bent around some psychic wound like a tree trunk knotting around an iron railing.

Now she wondered again if she'd made a mistake, if in hooking up with Jacob she'd once again chosen a guy who, like Jared, was driven by dark obsessions, hidden angers, vague grievances. She began walking a little faster, worried that Jacob wouldn't be in their usual spot—gone not just from the bed they shared but from her life permanently. But then she saw him in the distance: a green-aproned figure moving around behind the counter of the Starbucks in the food court. She breathed out.

"Hey," Jacob said when she came close. "Good morning."

"You got up early again," Swati said.

"Sorry," he said, and leaned over the counter to give her a peck. "I woke up at four and couldn't get back to sleep."

"What did you do?"

"Walked," Jacob said, releasing some espresso grounds from the grinder and then tamping them down in the portafilter basket. "Just walked. And thought."

This was always his answer—the same answer he gave at the end of the day, when Swati was done with her yoga classes and they met back at the cafeteria. All Jacob ever did was walk, and think. Swati figured he was probably up to more than that, though. She suspected he might be working on a project of some kind. Writing something, maybe, a novel, or a memoir of surviving the gas. Swati knew that writing a book was an aspiration of his; he'd talked about it enough. But then Cristina from legal said she once saw Jacob rooting through a file cabinet on the second floor, and Swati didn't know what to say, what to think. Was Jacob still entertaining paranoid fantasies about Delphi Enterprises? Pursuing his conspiracy theories? They didn't talk about it—and Swati didn't ask.

Jacob notched the filter into the espresso machine and looked up at her. "Mocha?"

Swati shook her head. "What's the one with honey?"

"Miel," Jacob said.

"That."

Jacob nodded and got to work. Swati waited.

This daily trek to the coffee kiosk had become a morning tradition for them both. The restaurants surrounding the Starbucks had all been stripped of their provisions long ago, but for some reason the caffeine outpost had been spared, perhaps owing to the fact that the fourth-floor cafeteria had no espresso machine. And so the temps just left the coffeeshop alone, until one day when someone observed that it was the first official day of fall. Swati's gaze had drifted toward the window as she said longingly, practically to herself, "God, I'd kill for a Pumpkin Spice Latte."

"I could make you one of those," Jacob had said.

"Really?"

"Of course," he'd said, and offered to make her one the following morning, before her first yoga class of the day. It wasn't quite the same— weeks ago Brent had frozen all the milk to keep it from spoiling, and it never tasted quite right after it thawed, but the pumpkin syrup was still good, and coffee was still coffee. The nostalgia of the familiar flavors as they coated her tongue warmed Swati all over. Then her morning students had seen her Starbucks cup, smelled the PSL, and asked her where she'd gotten it. The next day, a few dozen people showed up at the Starbucks after Jacob and Swati, asking for lattes, and Frappucinos, and caramel macchiatos of their own—and thus a tradition was born.

And here they came now, drifting down the hallway in their workout clothes, rolled yoga mats propped under their arms.

"Swati!" Jacob called out from the pickup counter, then winked as he passed the cup to her and turned back to the espresso machine to start making drinks for the others.

Swati glanced at the cup and laughed; Jacob had written her name in Sharpie, dotting the *i* with a heart. He *could* be sweet, sometimes.

But by the time he'd finished making drinks for everyone he'd already started to float away from her, the look in his eyes growing distant, as it always did.

"You want to join us?" Swati asked as Jacob took off his apron and folded it over the swinging door that led behind the counter. "We're working on breath practices today."

She always offered. She was desperate to get him in a class, to fix what- ever was wrong with him. The way to the mind was through the body. But he always declined.

"Nah," he said. "I'm good. You have fun though."

He gave her a peck on the cheek and began walking away. Everyone else began to drift in the opposite direction, toward the yoga space where

Swati had always done her classes, before and after the gas—but she didn't follow, not at first. Something kept her where she was, watching Jacob as he receded down the concourse, then found a door into the offices. She held on to this image of him, the last image, before he slipped through the door.

Then Swati turned away and joined the others.

• • •

Jacob took a looping route through the fields of cubicles, turning right and left at random, doubling back, veering blind into darkened hallways. Alternating between walking and running. Pausing often to check behind him. To listen.

He had no real reason to suspect he was being followed—but he felt paranoid nonetheless, and he'd become increasingly more so in the past few weeks.

Ever since getting access to the Brain.

Frederick had been the one to get him into the system, at Brent's request, and without Dominic's knowledge. First Frederick had tried to guess at Dominic's user password, but after a few failed attempts he gave up and tried a different approach. Ultimately he ended up using his own user credentials from the IT department, where he'd worked before the gas, to create a clone of Dominic's user profile, with its own secret username and password. Jacob didn't completely understand what Frederick had done, if he was honest; all he knew was that the new credentials Frederick gave him granted him the access he wanted.

So perhaps his paranoia had to do with Dominic—his friend, if only nominally. Dominic hadn't wanted to give up his sole access to Delphi's company records, and he'd be angry if he knew what Jacob was doing.

Or maybe it was about something more than that. Jacob's daylong sessions at the Brain—punctuated by expeditions deep into the guts of Delphi Enterprises to dig through the company's paper records—had begun to feel like his library time back in college, researching papers for his lit classes, hot on the trail of an exciting thesis, something new to say about a bit of Shakespeare, or Eliot, or Woolf. A cup of coffee in his carrel, the paper cup nested in his empties, stacked sometimes three or even four lips high. He'd be shaky with caffeine as he hunched over at least four types of text simultaneously: a primary source, the text he was attempting to explicate in a fresh way; a bit of critical theory, something by Foucault or Kristeva or Said; an article or four printed from JSTOR, written by people who'd also dealt with the core text; and, ideally, a bit of historical/cultural flotsam, something the author might've read as they were penning their great work—a political pamphlet, say, a nugget of outmoded philosophy, a piece of social journalism, or a document of medical investigative ephemera, the weirder and more anachronistic the better. He'd hop between texts, striking them together in his mind like pieces of flint, hoping for a spark of meaning that could turn into an interpretive fire. When he found it, the spark, he'd pursue it through the texts in a quivery state that probably had to do with the fact that he was usually, by then, on his fifth or sixth cup of coffee—but which he attributed always to the ecstasy of meaning-making, of tying the disparate parts of the world together, of discovering messages hidden in the interstices.

And wasn't that what paranoia was? Wasn't it really, when you came down to it, nothing more than a form of that interpretive ecstasy? A state in which everything throbbed with potential significance, serving as evidence for some grand design? Just because you were paranoid didn't mean they weren't out to get you, the saying went—and ultimately paranoia wasn't that dissimilar from religion, or ideology: they were all systems of belief in which the world *meant* something, in which the chaos actually made sense. Somewhere along the line, order had become a bad thing; people saw you fitting things together, adding things up, and they said you were delusional, superstitious, or just plain stupid. When in Jacob's mind, the world making sense was a *good* thing, not a bad one—evidence of uncanny perception, not of paranoia.

And that was what he was seeking, Jacob reflected as he came through the empty desks of the business analytics department and opened the door to the room where the Brain of Delphi Enterprises was housed: the spark of meaning that would set everything alight. A blaze that would bring the whole place to the ground, burn it to ashes.

Jacob hunched without sitting at the security screen, the terminal that would yield up a security code for an hour of access to the Brain. He typed in the user information from Dominic's cloned account and received a string of letters and numbers, which he copied down onto a piece of paper with the stub of pencil that was always on the desktop. Then he turned to the Brain and typed in the code.

"Access Denied."

Jacob frowned, turned back to the piece of paper and typed the code again, more carefully this time, paying close attention to capital letters, to the difference between *O*'s and zeros, lowercase *L*'s and ones.

Success. The access screen blipped away and was replaced by a file explorer, a list of servers that grew as connections were established: first 1, then 20, then 50, then the whole list, 74 separate departmental servers, each with hundreds of subfolders, thousands of files, billions upon billions of bits of data. Far too much for a single person to read, much less to interpret—except that that was exactly what Jacob was here to do, and as he moved the mouse to hover over the list of servers, searching for one he hadn't been in already, it seemed to him that the screen was a veil, the pixels vibrating with something just out of reach, and *surely*, he thought, *surely some revelation is at hand.*

• • •

Not that Jacob's investigations had begun so promisingly. For a long time, in the early days, nothing Jacob encountered in the guts of Delphi's databases seemed to mean anything at all. Patent applications, letters of intent, profit and loss statements—cascades of numbers, and technical jargon, and legalese. Jacob could understand none of it, couldn't interpret it, because he hadn't been taught how to. The keys to these obscure documents had been handed out in other classes, other disciplines, other courses of study: engineering, biosciences, accounting, law. Had he encountered a sonnet on the Brain, or the draft of a novel, he might've known what to do. But in a sea of business files he was unmoored, adrift. He'd open a file—a text document, spreadsheet, or scan—glance at it with glossy eyes, then close it and move on to the next.

Ultimately it was a conversation with Lauren that first gave him a way into the data, a spike to drive into the rock edifice of raw information. He'd noted, in his research, that several of the servers and sub-folders contained the term *psychometrics* in various configurations: *Psychometric research, Psychometric development, Psychometric extraction, Psychometric analysis.* He'd heard the word before, eavesdropped on a pre-gas conversation in which two regular employees had used the term, and he recalled that Lauren had done some work with psychometrics.

He asked her about it that evening, over chicken-and-rice casserole and steamed broccoli in the cafeteria.

"Psychometrics are exactly what they sound like," Lauren said. "You're a words guy, aren't you? Didn't you ever study Greek and Latin roots?"

Jacob frowned and poked at his food with his fork. It glistened under the fluorescent lighting, not looking very appetizing.

"*Psych*," Jacob said, "having to do with the human mind. *Metric*—a system of measurement. So . . . a psychological system of classification and measurement?"

"Right," Lauren said. "Any tool that uses scoring to classify human psychology. Myers-Briggs, that's a psychometric. But Delphi had their own system—a proprietary one, acquired and patented. The human psyche measured across 57 vectors, each ranked on a scale of one to five."

"And it was used for?"

"I was never clear on that," Lauren said. "I was in psychometric extraction—our job was just to get the measurements. That's what my quizzes were for. After I wrote them, they'd get shared on social media; anyone clicking the link got taken to one of Delphi's content mill sites, where the company would harvest their user data and then associate their quiz answers with their consumer profile. Then my department would hand over the psychometrics to the company."

"Any guesses?"

Lauren shrugged. "Targeted advertising, probably. Market research. Why?"

"No reason," Jacob said.

It wasn't much—the definition of a single term—but it turned out to be the thread Jacob needed to get to the center of Delphi's labyrinth. There were still entire swaths of the company data Jacob couldn't understand (the whole of the manufacturing division was still completely impenetrable), but psychometrics proved to have been a major part of Delphi's operations in the years since smart alloy and Safe-T-Knife™. Enough of the documents in the Brain were related to psychometrics either directly or tangentially that Jacob began to suspect that the psychological profiling method could have been central to Delphi's emerging strategy, and had even perhaps been a component of the new initiative Tristan Brandt was planning to unveil at the all-company meeting.

The psychometrics servers yielded vast mountains of information: a database of consumer records with names and birthdates matched to the promised 57 numeric scores of Delphi's proprietary psychometric measurement tool, plus a deep cache of ancillary documentation that sliced and diced the core data pool. Market research reports, sociological analyses, PowerPoint presentations laden with charts and graphs, actuarial tables and complex statistical instruments extrapolating what percentage of the world population was lonely, sexually frustrated, unhappy at work; how many had daddy issues, addictive personalities; which psychometric subsets might soon develop drinking problems, cheat on their spouses, or be in the market for a new refrigerator/freezer.

There was so much data Jacob started to become bored again, looking at it all—until he found, deep in the Psychometric Extraction server, a one-page charter for a project the company was calling "Sherpa."

Jacob recognized the name—it had been another thing he'd overheard, on the day of the gas. He could still remember snippets of the conversation, in which two of the regular employees had been speculating about the subject of the all-company meeting.

*It'll be a game changer*, one of them had said. *Bigger than smart alloy, bigger than psychometrics, bigger than Sherpa.*

Which to Jacob suggested a progression: smart alloy (and, by association, Safe-T-Knife™) had flooded the company with enough working capital to expand into psychometrics, psychometrics had somehow led to Sherpa—and Sherpa might have led to whatever was next, whatever Brandt was going to unveil on the day of the gas.

Jacob opened the file.

But Sherpa turned out to be nothing more than the beta of a mobile app—the project charter called it an "all-in-one digital assistant" that would "leverage consumer behavioral data to guide app users toward the products, experiences, people, and life choices most suited to their unique psychometric profile." A little creepy, maybe, but nothing too shocking. Jacob figured most of his mobile apps spied on him on some level. The social media platforms he used had been suggesting products to him for years. And there was no guarantee that this particular app had even made it past beta to be offered on the open market. Except that those Delphi employees had said it was "big," so it must have gone somewhere. Then Jacob looked down the document and found, spilling over the lined edges of a field labeled "Executive Sponsor," the confident, jagged scribble of a signature.

Tristan Brandt.

"Whoa," Jacob said aloud, mentally calculating how many projects must have been active at any given time at a place like Delphi, and how busy Brandt must have been, to come up with the vanishingly small percentage of company initiatives that were important enough for him to personally oversee.

Jacob looked more closely at the document and discovered that Psychometric Extraction, Lauren's department, hadn't even spearheaded the Sherpa project; they'd only been key stakeholders, along with the Strategic Partnerships, Product Optimization, and Innovention teams. Whereas the lead for the project was a director from something called the "Futures" department.

There was no other Sherpa documentation housed in the Psychometric Extraction server, and the charter was only a copy, a scan of a paper document. Jacob exited Psychometric Extraction and moused his cursor over the Futures department folder.

The server's contents were sparser than those of any other server he'd perused—and stranger too. Folders labeled *Nostradamus*, *Prophecies*, *Psychics*, *Game Theory*, *Oracles*, *Science Fiction*, *Chaos Models*, *Eschaton*. Jacob scrolled past all of them to find what he was looking for: *Sherpa*. He opened the project folder and began poking around inside.

What he found was mostly the typical detritus (he assumed) of an app development project: Gantt charts and weekly status updates, burn rate calculations and resource allocation analyses, user flows, information architecture, wireframes, design rounds, bug fix logs, A/B user testing reports. And, deep in an innocuous sub-folder labeled *Rollout*, the minutes from a meeting about brand naming.

Jacob opened the file and skimmed it. The minutes reported that Sherpa was moving out of beta testing and nearing public rollout—and now marketing was requesting a new name for the app, fearing "Sherpa" would be interpreted by the public as being culturally insensitive to people of Tibetan and Nepalese descent. The project team agreed—Sherpa had only ever been intended as an internal project name—and undertook a product branding session, with the most-favored possibilities listed right in the minutes: *Personal Assistant, Digital Secretary, Life Coach.*

And, at the bottom of the list, another name, one Jacob knew—the recognition arcing fast and hot through his brain, like lightning against a stormy night sky.

*Concierge.*

• • •

*Of course. Concierge.*

Jacob knew the app, he'd had it on his phone before the gas—probably *still* had it on his phone, in fact. (He hadn't used the device in weeks.)

His mother had been the one to tell him about Concierge and to suggest that he might benefit by downloading it. She'd heard about it from a friend of hers, someone with whom she did weekly Pilates, occasionally going out for drinks at the wine bar around the corner after class. The friend was another mother of a recent college graduate, who told Jacob's mother over flatbreads and Chardonnay that the app had, in the course of a single month of use, matched her wayward daughter with a good entry-level job in her field, an affordable apartment, and a boyfriend who was actually *nice* for a change.

"Just try it," his mother had said when she came home, slightly buzzed. "What do you have to lose?"

Nothing, Jacob had reflected—except his pride, his dignity, his intellectual integrity. Jacob had serious concerns about the growing hegemony of technocapitalist ideology, which in his opinion had turned everyone in the world into lab rats, tapping at tiny screens for a pellet of food and a jolt to their pleasure centers. Technology had made everyone shallow; now people spent all day photographing their food and texting, no time appreciating the things that really mattered: literature, and philosophy, and art. (Never mind that Jacob was as addicted to his phone as anyone he knew, that he spent more of his leisure time interacting and arguing with friends and strangers on social media than he did reading or writing, the things he professed to love.) To trust an *app*, this Concierge, to somehow provide what he most wanted in life felt too much like making technology his god, the entity to whom he looked to supply all good things.

But Jacob was also desperate—desperate for a job, desperate for a girlfriend. And though he suspected his mother was suggesting Concierge to get rid of him, to get him out of her basement, he was desperate for *that* too. So he tried the app.

The first thing Concierge had Jacob do was set up a user profile, linking to every social media account he'd ever had. Then the app began asking him questions. Strange questions, invasive ones.

*Are you comfortable defecating in public bathrooms?*

*Do you pray?*

*Have you ever entertained sexual fantasies about a teacher or other authority figure?*

*Do you seek out or avoid crowds?*

*What superpower would you prefer: invisibility or flight?*

Jacob answered them all, and then the app simply began . . . telling him what to do. Its soothing, feminine voice breaking into his everyday routines to suggest what to eat, what to wear. Concierge notified him of short cuts through heavy traffic, new bus routes that took him more quickly to his destinations. It told him what books to read, what movies and TV shows to watch. Knowing Jacob had a passion for literature—or that he claimed to, at least—Concierge made him aware of a series of local literary events at bars, with free admission. Occasionally the app suggested a calming breathing exercise, seeming to sense precisely when he was feeling angry, frustrated, or overwhelmed. Jacob knew, on some level, that the app was spying on him—listening to his conversations, tracking his movements, somehow even reading his biometrics, his heart rate and blood pressure—but for the most part he simply didn't care. Concierge was making his life better in a thousand small ways; privacy seemed a small price to pay.

Concierge didn't get around to finding him a new place to live, or a girl-friend (although, given some more time, it might have come close; Jacob ended up meeting several willowy young literary women who were exactly his type at the bar readings the app sent him to)—but it did get him a job. Specifically, it connected him with the temp mail room job at Delphi.

A fact that seemed suddenly significant and even suspicious, now that it turned out Delphi Enterprises had owned the app itself.

The discovery sent Jacob back to the temps, gently probing to learn whether they, too, had come to Delphi via Concierge.

Lauren had used the app. So had Swati. Not Dominic. Morgan had heard about the game testing job through Concierge. Brent hadn't used the app, but Frederick was another Concierge user, as were Casey and the other four data-entry workers, who were still soldiering away in their oversized cubicle on the second floor, tapping numbers into an ever-growing data-base. Jacob didn't talk to everyone, but based on his sampling he estimated that almost ninety percent of the temps had been recruited to their jobs through the Concierge app.

And that had to be significant, didn't it? If Delphi's own technology had drawn most of the temps to the company, there had to be some purpose, some significance in their all being there. Perhaps Jacob—and all the others—had been chosen.

But chosen for what?

The question sat hard in Jacob's brain, like a pebble in a shoe—immov-able, impossible to kick loose. Theories: the gas was fake, and they'd been selected for a massive psychological experiment. Or it was real, and they'd been chosen to . . . what? Repopulate the earth?

. . .

More revelations followed, more documents. Jacob performed searches on "Concierge" and "Sherpa" and found, also in the *Futures* department folder, a presentation titled *ConciergeMktPenDataLev.pptx*. The slides showed the app to have achieved a stunning level of market penetration a year and a half after its release: more than 50 percent of all smartphone users were estimated to have downloaded the app, and among the coveted 18- to 34-year-old demographic, that number rose to 84 percent active users—"active" defined as people who interacted with Concierge once or more every day.

This ubiquity had allowed Delphi to reap massive revenues. Concierge pushed users toward goods and services that were part of Delphi's business portfolio; other companies paid hefty sponsorship fees for the app to do the same with their products.

But Concierge's profitability barely took up two slides; apparently revenue wasn't the company's main aim in developing the app. The rest of the presentation focused on what could be done with the psychometric data mined from the app, which was far richer and more accurate than the data the company had gleaned from its other methods of psychometric extraction, which included personality quizzes, software that tracked consumer behavior online, or the outright purchase of customer information from research firms. Concierge was to these primitive methods, the presentation held, as the internal combustion engine was to the horse and buggy. The dataset they'd gleaned from the app was vast, deep, with far more potential analytical value than anything the company had gathered prior to Concierge's productization.

A flowchart showed how the Concierge data would be migrated and leveraged. The path began at the upper-left corner of the slide with a black clip-art figure with a window in his head, the ruffled outline of a brain sitting inside. An arrow pointed from the figure's head toward a black box labeled "Concierge." From there the data flowed through a forking maze of servers and databases and software platforms before the tributaries began merging again and the information spit out the other side into its destination: another black box, labeled "CSO/Apoc."

"CSO," Jacob guessed, was the "Chaos Systems Oracle," the predictive modeling software into which Casey and his coworkers were still, weeks later, inputting variables. But "Apoc"? Following a hunch, Jacob pulled Morgan aside one night after dark.

"The video game you were testing," Jacob said. "The one where you were trying to keep a planet from collapsing into chaos. Did it have a name?"

"It did," Morgan said. "Just a test name. They'd have changed it before release."

"What was it?"

"Apocalypse," she said.

So the Chaos Systems Oracle was real, and so was the game. They weren't bullshit experiments, even if neither system was what the temps working on it—Morgan's group or Casey's—had been told it was. Apocalypse was not a video game, but a predictive model—and a model not just of the stock market or weather patterns but of the whole of human civilization.

"So what did Tristan Brandt want? What was he doing?" That was the key question—the one Jacob had asked Casey a few days ago, after volunteering to Brent to be the one to bring the five temps their daily share of food from the cafeteria.

"Simple," Casey had said. "Brandt wants to save the world. To help human society transition to a fully post-scarcity economy, before we eat ourselves alive."

Jacob squinted and shook his head, befuddled once more by Casey's switch in tenses—*Brandt wants* when he was dead and could no longer want anything, *before we eat ourselves alive* when human civilization had already self-cannibalized in the yellow mist. So Casey was sticking to his illusions: Brandt was alive, and the apocalypse was a fake.

"I don't believe it," Jacob said. "There had to be something more to it than that. There are no Bruce Waynes in real life—billionaires don't care about the world. They only care about themselves. Their own wealth, their own power. Brandt was evil, somehow. I know he was."

Casey gave him a look of surprise that blended immediately to pity, as though it was Jacob and not Casey who was the delusional one.

"Maybe," Casey said gently, with the tone of an adult trying to calm a tantruming child, "the more important question is, why is this so important to you? What are you looking for?"

The question irked Jacob, lodged in him like a pin bone in the back of his throat as he returned to the Brain and kept digging deeper and deeper into Delphi's servers. What *was* he looking for? He'd found plenty already, enough to tell a compelling story about what the company had been up to before the gas. Hints of malevolence, perhaps even a conspiracy. So what was he waiting for? Brent had been asking him, more and more, if he'd found anything interesting yet, and there was no reason for Jacob not to give him everything he had. But something held him back.

"Not yet," he told Brent, always. "Give me a few more days."

The problem, Jacob realized, was that he still hadn't found the one thing he was looking for, the thing he had been seeking out from the beginning, since the gas cloud rose up yellow into the sky . . . or earlier, even: the day he'd graduated from college and emerged into a world that wasn't at all what he'd expected.

Which was—what, exactly? Proof of something, even if he didn't quite know what. Proof that they'd been lied to, perhaps, all of them, by everybody—beginning with every parent and teacher who'd told them that they were special, that they could do anything, that if they worked hard and followed their hearts the world would give them everything they'd ever dreamed of. Proof that Tristan Brandt and Delphi had lied to them too, even if he didn't yet understand how, or why. Proof that the older generation had completely fucked the world before handing it over to them. Proof that there was some meaning in this chaos—even if that meaning was only that there was someone to blame.

• • •

And so, now, as Jacob moused the cursor down to the server he'd been exploring for the past couple of days, he held his breath for the briefest of moments before clicking. The server was titled *Eschaton*, and it had proven to be another source of surprising revelations, a constellation of meaning equal to, if so far unconnected from, the fountain of interpretations that had resulted from the cluster of Sherpa/Concierge and Oracle/Apocalypse. If anything, the files in *Eschaton* (a word he only dimly recognized; he'd been meaning to ask Lauren what it meant) were even more surprising, more shocking than anything he'd found so far, a progression of cryptic executive memos, political and philosophical manifestos, futuristic product proposals, and utopian thought experiments.

The server opened and Jacob scrolled down to the folder he'd been working through the day before, one titled *Solutions*. A dull name, but he'd learned over the weeks that the folders and documents with the most boring titles often held the most shocking information.

The folder contained nineteen text documents. *Solution1.docx*, *Solution2.docx*, *Solution3.docx*, and on like that until *Solution19.docx*. Jacob had read through the first eighteen the day before—outlandish solutions to a problem that was not clearly stated in the documentation. Now, he opened Solution 19, and read.

"Holy shit," Jacob muttered as his eyes scanned the screen. "Holy fucking shit."

Here it was. The final piece, the information he'd been looking for from the beginning. All this time, it had been waiting for him.

Jacob hit "Print," then got up and left the room. He made for the printer on the other side of the office, which hummed and whirred and then spat out a single sheet of paper just as Jacob reached it. He grabbed the paper, held it in his hand, then looked up to see someone approaching him. A familiar face.

"Hey," he said. "What are you doing here?"

It was, in spite of everything, such a banal, everyday scene—coworkers meeting at the printer, exchanging pleasantries—and because of this fact Jacob's mind couldn't quite make sense of the dark object that was in the person's hand, nor the sound that came from it. Everything was so out of context that he could only catalog his sensations: the acrid tang of smoke, a sharp pinprick pain in his chest, the feeling of falling.

And the rustle of the printer paper as it was snatched from his fingers.

# ELEVEN

Lauren had started with Heraclitus. "All is flux, nothing stays still." Everything that came after seemed extraneous, dubious embellishments of the basic fact: everything changed, all the time. Which may have made her whole project foolish. Lauren didn't care. It was something for her to hold on to.

She'd started two weeks after the gas, when the novelty of living this way—eating and sleeping and bathing in an office complex together with some three hundred others roughly her age—had begun to wear off. One day, bored, she'd gone to a supply closet and found a nice notebook, stuck a blank mailing label to the front, and wrote, with an ultra-fine black Sharpie: "The Book of Knowledge."

Inside she wrote down everything she knew, everything she remembered, everything she didn't want to forget. Heraclitus and the pre-Socratic philosophers, beloved lines of Herodotus, Aristotle's golden mean, the invocation of the Muse from *The Iliad*, a few lines of Ovid and Virgil. Each quote in its original language, paired with Lauren's own translation to English—and then, because writing it all down had begun to make her feel nostalgic, she flipped the page and conjugated *amare*, "to love," the Latin infinitive that was every classics student's first lesson—the *a-b-c, 1-2-3, do-re-mi* of the discipline. *Amo, Amas, Amat . . .*

She moved on to Campbell, the link between her love of the classics and her later study of psychology.

*The standard path of the mythological adventure of the hero is a magnification of the formula represented in the rites of passage: separation—initiation—return: which might be named the nuclear unit of the monomyth.*

Rites of passage. Was that what this was? A passage into adulthood, a hero's journey? Perhaps the act of growing up was always a succession of apocalypses, a series of world-ending cataclysms. Leave it to them to be the generation to make the metaphor literal.

Lauren passed the book to others, asking them to inscribe it with knowledge of their own, the things they'd learned that they wished never to be forgotten. The results were always surprising. Brent returned the book to her with a few quotations from Adam Smith's *Wealth of Nations*, the writings of Milton Friedman, and Beatles lyrics. Swati wrote down Patanjali's *ashtanga*, the eight limbs of yoga, plus a few things she'd retained from her business classes (the three Ps of marketing, the basic structure of a balance sheet, the difference between liquid and illiquid assets), and then, unattributed, "Education is a system of imposed ignorance." (When Lauren asked her about this last quotation, Swati shrugged and said it was from something her ex-boyfriend had made her read.) Dominic, meanwhile, turned out to be a passionate reader of pop science and theoretical physics, writing down Newton's laws, a few key formulas, and a summary of the theory of natural selection.

Now Lauren paged through the sheets that had been covered by Morgan, a math major in college, who'd filled the pages all the way to their margins with proofs and theorems. The formulas progressed by a logic Lauren couldn't follow, the proof identifiable only by its familiar final result: the Pythagorean theorem, the quadratic equation, $\pi r^2$. (Lauren felt a pang as she thought of her father, a dumb joke he told sometimes: "Pi r squared? I thought pie are round!")

She flipped more pages until she came to the ones that had just been filled by Jacob. She'd given him the book a few days before with instructions to return it when he'd finished, and this morning she'd woken up to find the book waiting for her on the desk of the cubicle she slept in.

As expected, Jacob had written down famous quotations from literary masterpieces. She saw all the usual suspects: *Whan that Aprille with shoures soote, Tomorrow and tomorrow and tomorrow, It is a truth universally acknowledged . . .* The George Eliot quote about hidden lives and unhistoric acts, the one by T.S. Eliot about the world ending with a whimper, not a bang.

The book, Lauren realized, didn't just preserve knowledge; it preserved their past selves, captured them in amber. But their identities weren't set in stone. They were changing whether they wanted to or not, just as the world outside had changed.

Which brought her back to the beginning of the book—back to Heraclitus, back to movement and flux. She read the quotation again. It filled her with an absurd sense of hope. There was no such thing as extinction; only transformation. For Heraclitus, the death of one thing was always the birth of another, the cosmos an ever-roiling fire, rekindling as it burned up.

Lauren wondered again what was being revealed in the aftermath of the gas—what new worlds and new selves were emerging from the crucible of Delphi Enterprises.

Then Lauren heard footsteps at the door of her cubicle. She looked up, expecting Jane, who hadn't strayed too far from Lauren's side in the six weeks since they'd found her—but it wasn't Jane. It was Swati.

"What's going on?" Lauren asked, seeing the look of barely contained distress on Swati's face.

"It's Jacob," Swati said. "I can't find him anywhere. We usually meet here for lunch, but he didn't show."

"I don't know where he is," Lauren said. "Where did you see him last?"

"Starbucks," Swati said. "Before my first yoga class. And then he left to do . . . whatever he does all day."

This interested Lauren. She'd noted Jacob's long, unexplained absences, but she figured that if anyone knew what he was up to, it was probably Swati. Apparently not.

"Let's ask Brent," she said. "I see them talking sometimes at the end of the day."

Swati nodded, holding her lips together. Lauren wasn't worried about Jacob—he was late to lunch, so what?—but she could tell that Swati was, that her friend was in fact barely holding back panic. In the reaction Lauren saw how far Swati had fallen for Jacob; you only made up catastrophic stories in your head for the absence of people you really cared about, for spouses or your own kids. That Swati seemed to be entertaining such morbid fantasies about Jacob was evidence that she was not, as she often told Lauren, "just having fun" with Jacob. It had become more serious.

And so, as they walked out of the cubicle, Lauren put a hand on Swati's shoulder. Swati let out a breath and leaned slightly into Lauren as they walked. No words passed between them; they didn't need to speak. Lauren paused at the next cubicle over, Jane's. The mute girl sat inside on the desk chair, looking at the burlap covering of her empty pinboard wall. Jane did this sometimes, just sat and stared, and whenever she did Lauren felt a pain knife through her gut as she imagined what Jane might be seeing: the trauma that had turned her silent. Lauren tried to distract her from these reveries, kept her busy and talked to her for as many of their waking hours as possible—but there was only so much one-sided conversation a person could stand.

"Jane," Lauren said now, "Swati and I are going to talk to Brent. Do you want to come with us?"

Jane turned, blinked, then nodded.

The three women came into the cafeteria and saw Dominic and Brent sitting at a far table, against the windows. The lunch hour was ending, people filtering from the cafeteria back into the office as the temps up in the rotation for kitchen duty hefted steam trays and stacks of plates to the dishwashers in back.

Dominic and Brent raised their eyes as Lauren and the others came close.

"Hey," Brent said, looking past Lauren to address Swati, his fellow councilmember. "We were just going over the food sup—"

"Jacob's gone," Swati said, anguish coming through in her voice.

Brent blanched, tensed. "What happened to him?"

Lauren held out her hands. "Hold on a second. We don't know that Jacob's *gone*—Swati just can't find him. This is a big place; he's probably just out wandering around somewhere. I was just hoping maybe you might know where."

Dominic shook his head. "Not a clue."

Lauren looked to Brent. He didn't say anything, didn't meet her gaze.

"Brent," Lauren said. "Come on. I know you know something. I see you talking to Jacob sometimes at the end of the day, whispering like you don't want anyone to hear what you're saying. What have you and Jacob been up to?"

There was a silence. "Brent?" Dominic asked, breaking it.

Brent looked up—at Lauren, not Dominic.

"He's at the Brain," Brent said. "Digging through Delphi's company records."

Dominic didn't say anything, but Lauren noted his jaw muscle bulge, his back straighten, his eyes go hard.

"Why?" Swati asked. "What could Jacob possibly want in the company records? What could *you*?"

Brent paused before answering, as if he knew he'd only upset Swati more by saying anything.

"Brent, come on," Lauren said. "Can't you see Swati's worried about him?"

Brent sighed. "Jacob had a theory," he said. "Something about the gas being fake, a psychological experiment—or not fake, but that Delphi was responsible for it, and maybe Brandt was still alive somewhere. I don't know. It sounded crazy to me, but . . . but Jacob really sounded like he thought there might be something there, and I thought, what's the harm."

"How did he get in?" Dominic asked. "I'm the only one with a business analytics user login."

Brent angled his gaze into the empty space between him and Dominic but didn't meet his eyes. "I had Frederick clone your account."

Dominic breathed slowly through his nose. "Fuck's sake," he said, then got up and stalked away.

After he'd gone, Swati slapped Brent across the face. Lauren held her breath at the sound of it, the hard crack of skin against skin.

"You're a real asshole, you know that?" Swati said. "Jacob didn't need that. You know he didn't. It's not good for him. He could've been doing anything with his time. *Anything.* And you gave him this."

Lauren reached out her hand and put it in the crook of Swati's arm, held her and pulled back.

"Swati," she said. "Just leave him."

Swati looked back.

"Let's go," Lauren said. "I know where business analytics is. I can show you."

Swati relented, began to move in the direction Lauren was pulling her—but not before turning back once more to say something else to Brent.

"You should have known better."

• • •

Or perhaps she was the one who should have known better, Swati thought to herself as she went with Lauren and Jane to the elevator, then to the first floor. She felt colossally stupid. She'd done it again: fallen for a guy whose mind was elsewhere, whose obsessions led him away from her and into dark, circling dead ends where she couldn't follow.

It wasn't that she thought Jacob was *wrong* to be paranoid—just that it seemed like a waste of time. *Of course* Delphi had been up to some fucked-up shit; *of course* there was someone out there who was to blame for the gas. These things were self-evident, as obvious and undeniable as the pile of corpses out the windows in the courtyard, the thousands of bodies rotting in the sun. But who gave a shit? She'd heard all of Jacob's grievances, knew them well: his student loan debt, his impractical college major, his grad school rejections, his complete lack of job prospects. The overall sense of his having been lied to, which had only been deepened by the gas. But what did it matter, now? Everyone who gave a shit about his student loans was probably dead, which meant his debt was effectively forgiven and he'd gone to college for free. As for jobs, once they got out of Delphi (*if* they ever got out of Delphi, a voice deep inside her corrected), the new economy would be theirs for the taking, opportunities aplenty now that the world had been depopulated.

Everything was possible now, that was the point, the thing Jacob couldn't seem to grasp. The world before had been so crowded, so full of history. Everything worth having had already been claimed by previous generations, tagged and priced and gentrified beyond the reach of everyone her age, everyone who was just trying to start out. But now the world was blank again, a canvas upon which they could paint their hopes and dreams. That's what Swati was doing. She'd wanted to teach yoga—and now she was doing it, without any of the trouble of getting investors, applying for loans, pleading with white men in suits for permission to pursue her life's work. The gas was terrible, many people had died, yet this was the silver lining: that they no longer had to ask for permission. And wasn't this what guys like Jacob *wanted*? A return to manifest destiny, to the pioneer days, with frontiers to explore and kingdoms to conquer? Yet now that it was here, he still found reasons to pout, to brood, to wallow in angst.

As they walked down the concourse toward business analytics, Swati was practicing all this in her head, an angry speech that was intended to be like the slap she'd given Brent: something to snap Jacob out of his funk, call him back to her. *You fucking asshole what is the point of this all I wanted was to teach yoga that's all I wanted so why can't you be content with what you have too*, except in her mind the face she imagined hurling these words at was Jared's, and try as she might she could not summon Jacob's visage to her mind—as though, in her anger, she'd completely forgotten what he looked like.

But it turned out she needn't have practiced any speech at all—because when they arrived at the Brain Jacob was nowhere to be found. On the desk was a half-empty Starbucks cup, its sides greasy-brown with coffee residue, a nub of pencil and a pad of paper with cryptic words and drawings (an arrow connected the words "Sherpa" and "Apocalypse/Oracle"; a list labeled "Possibilities" included entries for "Human experimentation" and "World civilization reboot"). But no Jacob.

Next to the pad of paper Lauren found a manila folder with multiple printed pages inside. She fluttered through the pages, and Swati saw a flip-book of memos, spreadsheets, infographics. The folder tab labeled, in fine-point black marker, "Research."

"Maybe he's at the printer?" Swati said, her annoyance once more dimmed by worry, by the inability to find Jacob.

"I think it's at the other side of the department," Lauren said.

They went back out into the business analytics office and walked to the other side of the room. Swati pictured Jacob standing at the printer with his fists propped against his hip bones, waiting for the machine to spit out a piece of paper. He'd look up as they approached, befuddled. Apologize when they told him they'd been looking for him. *I lost track of time*, he'd say as he squeezed Swati around the waist, gave her a penitent peck on the cheek. The reunion scented with the odor of fresh toner. Surely that was how it would happen, Swati thought.

But when they came in view of the printer alcove he wasn't there, and Swati's stomach dropped again.

"Goddamn it," she said. "Where the fuck is he?"

Then Lauren said: "Is that blood?"

Swati looked. And yes, there it was: a small splotch on the floor just in front of the printer, an actor's stage mark right where Jacob should have been standing. Too light to be black ink, too dark and rust-colored for magenta; too small to be truly alarming, yet too large to be from something as innocuous as a nosebleed.

Swati looked back up at Lauren's eyes, stricken—certain, now, that something horrible had happened to Jacob, that the bloodstain belonged to him.

*Save me from this feeling*, she wanted to say to Lauren, her friend, *save me from caring about this boy, this stupid boy—save me from having to mourn yet another death.*

But before she could say anything, all the lights in the room went out. With the sudden darkness there descended something equally terrifying: a perfect silence that was the absence of all the sounds Swati hadn't known, until then, that she'd been hearing all along. The vents, the fans, the filters and purifiers.

Every system that had been keeping them alive these past six weeks. Gone.

• • •

Dominic was in his cubicle when the power went out. Stewing. Thinking about how Brent and Jacob had conspired to betray him.

He'd come to like Brent over the past six weeks, more than he'd expected to when he'd first joined the council. Back then, he'd viewed Brent as a threat—someone who was grasping at power, desperate for it as a way to make himself feel big, but undeserving of it. Foolish, hot-headed. The time since then hadn't dispelled this notion, exactly—if anything, Dominic was more certain than ever that Brent just *wasn't very smart*—but it had added other layers to Dominic's growing mental portrait of his and Swati's co-leader. Because sometimes Brent talked about his life before the gas, and the picture he painted was small, almost pathetic. As if Brent was trying to cut himself down rather than build himself up in Dominic's eyes, boasting about how pitiable he'd been before all this. A college dropout unable to find decent work, living in his mom's basement. Watching movies, playing video games. Wasting away. Their generation was the subject of much discussion in society at large—culture writers held them to be lazy, aimless, and sad, killing (as if they were murderers) such august American institutions as home ownership, marriage, entrepreneurship, brunch. It wasn't true, Dominic felt; his peers weren't like that. But Brent seemed to be the prototype about which all the think pieces had been written. The embodiment of every pathetic stereotype.

It was almost enough to make Dominic feel for the guy. Who *wouldn't* try to be important, a leader, after years of frustration and disappointment? He and Brent weren't so different, after all—they'd both been fucked by the world in different ways, and even if their circumstances weren't the same (Brent was still a white dude, after all) the feeling was maybe some version of the same thing.

But then Brent went behind his back, sent Jacob to the Brain without asking his permission first, and the whole thing reminded Dominic of what would have happened if the gas hadn't descended and wiped everything away: Brent would have passed him by. Leapt from his shit temp job as a cafeteria shift manager to some position in corporate leadership, promoted far past the point of his incompetence. Getting twice as far working half as hard.

And Jacob too—another pathetic white boy living in his parents' basement, a temporary failure to launch who'd still have ended up ahead of

Dominic in life in spite of all Dominic's hard work. Jacob was his friend, Dominic had thought, except then he'd conspired with Brent to undermine him, the way all white men did when the chips were down. Coming together to maintain their advantage, their privilege. Barely knowing that they were doing it, perhaps, hiding it even from themselves so that they could deny it if confronted, act offended that anyone could ever think them racist. All Jacob would have had to do was ask him, and Dominic would have given him his credentials, full access to the system—maybe not without some discussion, some questions (*Why?* came to Dominic's mind even now), but he'd have relented eventually. But instead, what did Jacob do? Went to Brent, his rival, his enemy. Who didn't care about what was in the Delphi records any more than Dominic did—honestly, who gave a shit, now?—but would use Jacob's paranoia, his wild, delusional theorizing, to send Dominic a message. Show him who was really boss.

And so Dominic sat, thinking, pondering what to do next. What he could do to get back at Brent, gain the upper hand. Should he pretend it didn't matter to him, let it roll off his back? Or make a maneuver somehow, outflank Brent, make a power play? Would Swati help? Lauren? Even Jacob? Perhaps Jacob *had* found something in the records—maybe something that really *mattered*, something about Brent, a performance review, maybe, something that could be used to humiliate him in front of the other temps, push him off the council.

Maybe.

But then the lights went out, and the fans, the vents, the air purifiers. The sound of voices rose up from the cubicles and rows around him, the other temps crying out in confusion and alarm and fear. And Dominic thought of the freezers, keeping their food supply from rotting. He stood up and moved into the row.

Morgan, his neighbor a few doors down, had come to the entrance of her cubicle. She met his eyes as he passed.

"Dominic," she said. "What's happening?"

"I don't know," he said. "Stay here. Keep the others calm, would you? We've got it."

"But—"

"We've got it!" he said again, more forcefully, closing off further discussion, then ran down the row toward the cafeteria.

He found Brent in the kitchen (he used it as his *de facto* office—another power move, staying closest to the food supply). He was checking the food, the freezer door open. As Dominic walked in, Brent backed up and let the door swing shut. A gust of cold air buffeted Dominic's face.

"Dead?" he asked.

Brent nodded. "It's off. We have maybe four hours before it starts to thaw."

"But what about the vents? The purifiers?"

"I don't know," Brent said. "How long does it take outside air to get in through the ventilation system?"

"Hell if I know. An hour? Maybe two?" It was just a guess, a wild one, but the price of being too cautious seemed worse than the price of underestimating the danger they were in. To have survived this long only to die not from starvation or infighting but from the gas, the thing they'd escaped to begin with, was so absurd as to be infuriating. It couldn't happen.

"The sky is almost back to normal by now," Brent said. "Maybe we'll be fine."

"You honestly want to risk it? We need to get the power back on."

Brent nodded. "Of course."

"You still have those schematics? The ones they found down in facilities management?" The "they" in this statement was a group of temps who'd come back from a scavenging run a few weeks back with some blueprints among an assortment of other bits and bobs, useless shit from people's desks. Dominic didn't know their names, and they'd been allowed to keep everything they'd found for their cubicles, their apartments—except for the blueprints, which had become the property of the council.

Brent moved to the table in the center of the kitchen and started rooting through his papers—printouts calculating daily food and water inventories, projected rates of consumption, leadership council meeting minutes, approved or rejected requisition forms for party supplies. He pulled the schematics from the bottom of the stack, a sheaf of oversized papers with blue and black printing on them. He swept the other sheets off the table and onto the floor, then set the schematics flat on top.

"Have you looked at these yet?" Dominic asked, joining him at the table.

"A little," Brent said. "I don't really know what I'm looking at. You worked construction, didn't you?"

"Yeah," Dominic said. "Roofing. I'm not exactly an expert on electrical, HVAC, plumbing, or anything like that."

"But you know how to read a blueprint, right?"

Dominic looked down at the sheets, which Brent had slid across the table toward him. Perhaps this was how he could get back at Brent and Jacob: by quietly, effortlessly being better than them. He flipped the schematics around and looked at them.

"It looks to me like the building gets its power from a grid a few miles north of here. A wind farm, maybe. The electricity comes here in underground cables, then gets plugged into the Delphi systems through this transformer station, here."

He pointed. Brent came over to his side of the table and looked.

"Is that . . . ?" Brent began.

"Yeah," Dominic said. "Outside. In the courtyard."

"Shit."

Dominic stared at the gray rectangle of the transformer station—an island surrounded by gas, by death. Underground power lines spidered out from the station to the corners of the building, powering the systems they needed to stay alive. But then, parallel to the blue lines of the electrical current, Dominic saw another set of double lines.

"Hold on a second," he said.

"What?"

"I think . . ." he began, then trailed off.

"Spit it out, man!" Brent yelled.

"I think these might be tunnels."

• • •

Swati barreled up the steps two at a time, barely fazed by the power outage or the resulting darkness of the stairwell. All she could think about was Jacob, his disappearance, the blotch of rust-colored blood on the carpet where she thought she'd find him. About getting to the top, to the cafeteria, where she could ask the others if they'd seen him, maybe gather a search party if no one knew where he was.

Lauren, meanwhile, seemed to be thinking about the blackout enough for the both of them—huffing and puffing a flight behind, pleading with Swati to slow down, complaining about the darkness.

"I can't see a thing in this dark," she said. "Would you wait up?"

Swati stood at the top of a flight and waited until she could see two dim outlines—Lauren and Jane—bobbing up the steps after her.

"Do you smell that?" Lauren asked.

In the dark, Swati rolled her eyes. "Smell what?"

"I don't know," Lauren said. "Something. Sort of metallic. But a little bit earthy too. You don't smell it?"

"No," Swati said, though now that she paused to sniff she had to admit that there was something in the air, something new—if only the natural smell of the stairwell, of cinderblock walls and metal railings, pipes and wiring, the guts of the building. Or the gas. It was impossible to be sure; Swati had never smelled it before. None of them had. The only people who had were dead now.

Swati chose not to share any of these thoughts with Lauren; it would only slow them down more. Better to stick to her denial that there was anything amiss. Even if the gas was leaching into the building, there was nothing they could do about it.

"Come on," Swati said when Lauren and Jane reached her. "We're almost there."

When they got to the top floor, everyone had flooded into the cafeteria and clustered around the kitchen, chattering fearfully. Past the crowd was Dominic, standing on the buffet with his arms outstretched, trying to silence them.

"People!" he shouted. "People! The power's out—we know, and we have a plan."

The crowd began to quiet down, but just as Dominic opened his mouth to speak again Swati found herself shouting into the brief silence: "Jacob's gone!"

Heads turned, pivoting away from Dominic and toward her. Heat rose to her cheeks as the eyes of more than three hundred temps came on her at once. Dominic's brow knotted and he called, over the heads of the crowd, "What?"

"Jacob's gone," Swati said, quieter now. "We went to the Brain to look for him, he was supposed to be there, we found signs that he'd been there just today . . . but he was gone. And there was a bloodstain on the carpet. I think—I have a feeling the blood was his."

Dominic blinked and didn't respond right away. Then he lifted his hand. "One thing at a time. First we have to take care of this power outage."

Swati tensed but didn't argue. Dominic was right.

"Brent and I have been looking at some blueprints of the building. It looks like there's a power transformer in a little building out in the court-yard, not far from the basketball courts. We can't get to it because of the gas. But it looks to me like there's a tunnel from the main building to the transformer. So we need a volunteer—anyone whose job took them into the tunnels, who knows how to get us in."

Swati sensed movement at her back. She glanced and saw Jane opening her mouth as if to speak. She made a high, pinched sound.

"What is it?" Lauren whispered. "Do you know anything about the tunnels?"

Swati stepped toward Jane and grabbed her by the elbow, a little too hard. "If you know something you should speak up."

"Swati," Lauren said, softly but firmly. "Stop. You're scaring her."

Swati snapped her eyes up to Lauren, anger rising—but just then there was another voice at the front of the crowd, male. She looked ahead and saw a hand in the air.

"I've been in the tunnels," the voice said. "I can get you in."

"Great," Dominic said. He paused to confer with Brent, who stood on the floor behind him. Then Dominic turned his eyes to the crowd again. "The three of us are going to take the tunnels, see if we can get the power back. The rest of you, just hang tight. We'll get it fixed."

"What about Jacob?" Swati asked.

Dominic nodded. "Anyone who wants to help look for Jacob, check in with Swati."

There was a moment of quiet where everything seemed to be held at bay, an energy about to burst forth into the building. The polarities of the molecules in the air shifting, lining up in a single direction.

Dominic broke the silence. "All right," he said, then clapped his hands together. "Let's go."

# TWELVE

The guy who'd volunteered to take Dominic and Brent into the tunnels was named Anton. He led them down the stairwell, below the first floor, to a locked door with a keypad next to it. Then he keyed in his access code. Dominic watched Anton's forefinger, memorizing the order of the numbers. The lock beeped, then Anton shouldered it open. Inside, everything was dark.

"Flashlights on," Anton said. They all clicked their lights and swung the beams up into the darkness. A long cinderblock hallway stretched far into the distance, beyond the reach of the lights.

"You know where you're going?" Dominic asked.

Anton shook his head. "No. I'd only worked here a week when the thing happened. You're the one with the map."

Dominic sighed. His skin tingled. A cold air seemed to blow up from the tunnel. What if there was a part of the tunnel open to the outside air, the gas?

"All right," he said, sensing that the other two were waiting for him to do something. "Let's do it."

Dominic plunged inside, then heard the footsteps of the others following him.

"So you were facilities?" he asked Anton. "I didn't know they hired temps for that department."

"A bunch of the other facilities guys got called to another job, some special project that ran a few weeks. Needed temps to backfill their regular work."

"What did you do?"

"Changed light bulbs, mostly."

"That's it?"

"Big building," Anton said. "Lot of light bulbs."

"Hey," Brent said. "How many corporate CEOs does it take to—"

"Don't fucking start," Anton said. "It was a job. Just a job."

"And you had a code to get down here because?" Dominic asked.

"Supplies. Light bulbs. Cleaning products."

"You scavenge down here?" Dominic asked. "Bring anything up for the group?"

"No," Anton said. "Too fucking creepy."

He was right about that, Dominic thought. The walls were close on either side of them, but their footsteps echoed like the space was much larger than a simple hallway, like there were cavernous expanses waiting just beyond the reach of their flashlights, or around a corner somewhere. At intervals they passed intersections, turns, stairs going up or down, but Dominic shined his light on the map and kept them going straight. A couple of times, the sound of their walking bounced off distant walls and echoed back to their ears, so that Dominic thought they were being followed. Once, he swung his flashlight around, pointed it backward, where they'd come from.

"What is it?" Brent asked.

"Nothing," Dominic said. "I just thought I heard—nothing."

"Sound's weird down here," Anton said. "And the darkness. Plays tricks."

"Yeah," Dominic said, then moved the beam of his flashlight forward again, to another intersection. He bent the light up, to the ceiling. Above their heads, black power cables thick as tree limbs curved to the left.

"I think it's this way."

"Lead on," Brent said. "We're following you."

Dominic peered around the corner. His flashlight found the end of a short corridor, a door with a small square window at head-height.

"This is it," he said.

They walked down the corridor—fifty yards, perhaps a hundred—and as they did Dominic's feeling of being followed returned. The sound of a fourth set of footsteps, out of sync with theirs. But he chalked it up to the echo and kept going until he reached the door. Locked.

"Shit," he said. "Another keypad. Try your code again?"

Anton keyed it in and the lock blinked green. "After you."

Dominic pushed through, then Brent. Inside, Dominic found a small concrete room, thirty feet square. Metal stairs leading up, a soft glow of sunlight above. At the top of the stairs he glimpsed transformer boxes, wiring, buttons and switches on a wall panel.

"We're here," Dominic said.

But instead of responding Brent said, "What are you doing?" Dominic turned back.

Brent faced the door, his flashlight beam pointed into the hallway, where Anton still stood about ten paces from the door. He looked back as well, his flashlight pointed toward the intersection where they'd turned. Still facing away, he shook his head.

"I thought I heard something," Anton said. "Footsteps."

Brent laughed. "Dominic's got you hearing things," he said. "Come on."

Anton turned, and just then there came three loud bangs from the hallway behind him, echoing huge and deafening against the cement walls. With the sounds came flashes of bright white light, blinding. Anton slumped to his knees, then to the ground. His falling body revealing a black silhouette in the darkness far behind him, face invisible.

Dominic and Brent just stood for a moment, looking from Anton's body on the ground to the silhouette on the other side of the corridor, too stunned to say anything. Then the silhouette raised its arm and fired again. There was a metal clang, a spray of stone shards hitting Dominic's cheek, and he threw himself down to the floor.

"Close the door!" he yelled.

Brent, also on the floor, kicked the door closed, then threw himself against it. On the other side, Dominic heard footsteps getting closer, the keypad on the other side beginning to beep.

"Shit," Dominic said, then skittered toward the door and placed his back against it. "He's trying to get in. We have to hold it."

Together they pressed against the door as hard as they could as the beeping continued, more buttons than just the four Anton had pushed to get them in the tunnels or into this room. From his place on the floor, still straining hard with his shoulders to keep the door closed, Dominic looked up to the keypad on his side of the door, the keypad they'd use to get out. A red light blinked five times, then held solid. The footsteps began to run away.

"The fuck?" Dominic muttered, pushing himself to his feet and peering carefully out the tiny window at the top of the door. He looked just in time to see the silhouette disappear around the corner. Then he looked down to the keypad, a realization thudding hard in his stomach.

He reached out his hand and tried the code he'd seen Anton type in. *3857.* The keypad beeped red. He tried it again. *3857.* Still red.

"Shit," he said. "Shit shit shit shit shit fuck shit."

"What is it?" Brent asked, standing up.

"He wasn't trying to get in. He was changing the key code."

"You mean?"

Dominic looked at Brent, shined the flashlight in his face. Brent flinched, grimaced.

"I mean we're trapped."

•　•　•

"You know he's dead, right?"

"How do you figure?"

"You think it's a coincidence Jacob goes missing the same time as the power goes out? Someone's fucking with us. Someone from the company."

Swati froze on the other side of the cubicle partition wall. They were looking for Jacob, about thirty of them fanning out through the floors, shouting his name into the offices like searchers looking for a lost child in the woods. Swati had come into this room to see how one of the search parties was doing, if they'd found anything—but she walked in on this conversation instead. Two guys casually discussing her boyfriend's death, as if searching for him—a job they'd volunteered for—was pointless.

"Who?" the second guy asked. "Who do you think's doing it?"

"I don't know. A survivor. Someone who wasn't at the all-company. A VP, maybe, or Brandt. You know, there are some people who say that wasn't really him at the meeting."

"But why would they want to kill the power? Why would they want to kill Jacob?"

"Because he got too close. He found something, in the Brain, and they had to get rid of him before he shared it. Then they cut the power to get rid of the rest of us."

"A saboteur."

"Right."

"What if it's Jacob?"

Swati crept down the row, staying close enough that she could hear what was being said on the other side. Setting her feet soft and soundless on the carpet as she eavesdropped.

"What do you mean?"

"The saboteur. Maybe it's Jacob, and that's why he disappeared. Maybe he found something on the Brain that . . . that *turned* him, put him on the company's side. Found the survivors, the VPs or whatever, and agreed to get rid of us for them."

The voices were almost to the end of the row. Swati stood up straight and walked around the last cubicle, stomping hard to announce her presence, and came face-to-face with the guys, whose faces she dimly recognized.

"Interesting theory," she said. "What stopped you from sharing it with me when I asked you to help find Jacob?"

"Swati . . ." sputtered one of the guys. By his voice Swati figured he was the one who'd started this theorizing. "I'm sorry. We were just . . . trying to figure out what may have happened to him. Going through possibilities. I don't really think he's—"

"Save it," Swati said. "I take it you didn't find anything here?"

The other guy shook his head. "No."

"This is pointless."

"We should head back to the cafeteria," the first guy said. "He's probably there by now. He'd have gone back after the power got cut, right?"

"I thought you said he was dead," Swati shot back. Then, looking to the other one, "Or that he was the one who cut the power."

"I don't *think* anything," said the second guy. "I was just . . . speculating."

Swati stared at both of them, her jaw working. She should have shouted, put a scare into them—she was on the leadership council, after all. A person of some importance around here. But she couldn't muster the strength. She breathed out. Perhaps they *should* go back to the cafeteria. Jacob wasn't a lost puppy; he could find his way back. Better to be in the place where Jacob would expect her to be than to be wandering through the building in the half-dark, increasing the likelihood that someone else would get lost—or *taken*, if these guys were right and they were being targeted by a saboteur. Plus Lauren had stayed at the cafeteria, holed up in her cubicle with the stack of papers from the Brain. Maybe, she'd said, the documents contained some clue to what Jacob had found, where he'd gone, what had happened. Suddenly Swati wanted to go back to see if Jacob had appeared while she was gone—or if not, if Lauren had found anything interesting, anything that could help.

"Forget it," Swati said. "Yeah, head back. I'll try to gather the others."

Before any of them could turn away, one of the guys turned his head to the ceiling.

"You hear that?" he asked.

"What?" Swati said.

"White noise. Fans, I think. The air filtration's back on."

Now that he mentioned it, Swati *did* hear something—and just as she was about to say so, all the lights came on overhead, a wave of low thuds as the circuits reestablished themselves across the building, followed by the low buzz of the fluorescents slowly brightening.

Dominic and Brent had done it.

• • •

It had turned out to be nothing more than a broken connection, a master switch thrown from *On* to *Off*. No more difficult than resetting the breakers on a house. Dominic had never trained in electrical, didn't know shit about major grids and transfer systems like what they had at Delphi—but he knew how to pull a lever and push buttons.

"Someone *did* this," Dominic said. "It's not a system failure. Someone came down here and threw the switch."

*Boom, boom, boom.*

"Are you listening to me?"

Brent wasn't. He was down below, beating at the door to get back in the tunnels. His pounding echoing low and solid, the sound of an object that wasn't going to move, no matter how hard Brent slammed his body against it.

*Boom, boom, boom.*

"Fuck," he said. "My shoulder is killing me."

"Don't bother. It's reinforced steel. You'll break your bones before you get through that thing."

"Well, what do you suggest?" Brent said, coming up the stairs. "We're trapped in here. You want to just wait until we starve?"

"Of course not," Dominic said. "Don't be stupid."

"What, then?" Brent demanded. "The others will notice we're missing— but they can't get to us if that . . . that *guy* changed all the key codes." Brent looked down, blinking hard. "Unless—you think we could guess the code? It's only four numbers, how many combinations you think there could be? A few thousand? It'll take us a day, maybe two, but we could do it."

Dominic shook his head. "No. You hear how many buttons that guy was pushing? It sounded to me like he was changing the digits in the code to ten, maybe more. That brings the number of combinations from thousands to . . ." He paused, trying to add it all up.

"Millions?" Brent offered. "Billions?"

"A lot," Dominic said.

"Fuck. That's it. We're dead."

"No," Dominic said. Brent looked up, and Dominic gestured with his head toward a door on the other side of the room. The door was steel, like the one down the stairs, with another small window—that's where the sunlight was coming from. The sky still yellowish beyond, even though just that morning Dominic had looked outside and thought to himself that the gas might have been lifting.

"Nuh-uh," said Brent, shaking his head. "No."

"You have any better ideas?"

"But the gas," Brent said. "We'll die."

Dominic put the blueprints atop a transformer box, unfurled them. "Look at this." He pointed. "The transfer station we're stuck in, it's not that far from the T-wing. See? Probably a hundred yards to the nearest entrance. If we run we could get to it in seconds."

"The outside entrances are locked, aren't they?"

Dominic dug in his pocket and came out with the red rectangle in its plastic casing. "I've got my pass. I came prepared."

"So what, we should just . . . hold our breath?"

Dominic walked to the door. He looked through the window. The ground was littered with corpses, the shapes of the bodies beginning to bubble and cave as they decomposed, clothes gone dusty and faded under the sun—but past the slumped dead Dominic saw a door in the glass edifice of the Delphi complex, behind which the fans and purifiers were undoubtedly back on, cleansing the air as he and Brent wasted time in their stone bunker.

"I'm going," Dominic said, pulling back from the window. He flipped the deadbolt, twisted the lock on the knob. "You can close the door behind me if you want."

"Fuck," Brent muttered to himself, looking down and beginning to pace. He stopped and squared up to Dominic. "All right. I'm coming with you."

"Ready?"

Brent nodded but then said, "Wait, no. Not yet." He breathed a few more times, then nodded again. "Okay. Now."

Dominic took a deep breath, then opened the door and ran.

After more than a month of being indoors, the feeling of the outside air was like plunging into ice water. The air was cold—it was late October—but above all it was the sense of space that disoriented Dominic, the feeling of no ceiling above his head, the emptiness extending past the atmosphere and into space, all the way to the edge of the universe. His eyes ached, and he thought it was probably the sun, but then wondered about the gas. Could that be the thing that was pricking at his eyes? He began to panic—what if the gas could get into his body somehow even though he was holding his breath?—but then forced himself to focus.

He ran quickly but carefully, watching his feet, dodging the bodies, trying to make sure his feet landed on solid ground. It was like an obstacle course, he thought, like running through the tires in a boot camp. Once he accidentally ran into a dead end of bodies and couldn't help but step on them to fight his way out. His feet wobbled as he stomped over them, the corpses breaking down underfoot as the soles of his shoes made contact with them. Feeling this, the way the bodies had begun to liquefy, turn gelatinous, Dominic's stomach heaved and he felt vomit burble up his throat. He choked it down, forced himself to keep running.

It couldn't have been long—twenty seconds, maybe thirty—but it felt like forever, that running. But eventually Dominic reached the glass door. He pounded his keycard on the lock, heard it beep, then put his shoulder to the door.

It didn't move.

Dominic's panic rose again, and he almost opened his mouth. It took every ounce of concentration he had not to breathe. His lungs ached.

He looked down. The security pad had a green light on it—the door was unlocked. He pounded again, still nothing. Then he saw, next to the security pad: a handle, not a bar.

Pull, not push.

Dominic almost laughed.

He pulled on the door handle. It flew open into the courtyard. Dominic stumbled inside, ran a dozen feet away from the door, and gasped.

"Holy shit," he said, falling to the ground, more thankful than he'd ever been to be breathing, for the feeling of relief that was flooding his lungs, spreading from his chest to the tips of his fingers and toes. It was a second or two before he'd regained enough awareness of his surroundings to recognize that there were no sounds of footsteps around him, no other relieved breaths.

"Brent," he said, then looked back, through the wall of windows.

He was still outside. On the ground, his foot hooked in the leg of a corpse.

"No," Dominic said, coming to his feet and rushing to the glass. He put his fingers on the door, which had drifted closed. "Get up."

Brent kicked free of the corpse and scrabbled away on hands and knees, pushed himself to his feet, and kept on running. When he reached the door, Dominic held his breath again and pushed it open. Brent came into the building and fell at once to his hands and knees, coughing. As the door closed once again, Dominic found himself backing away from Brent.

"Did you breathe it?" Dominic asked.

Brent went on coughing. Dominic kept backing away, sure that any second now, Brent would turn into one of those *things*—into a Fury.

"Brent. Talk to me. Did you breathe out there?"

Still nothing. Dominic glanced around; his eyes fell on a pair of scissors on a nearby desktop. He grabbed them, held them at his side.

"Brent!" he yelled.

"I'm fine," Brent said, his voice hoarse, thinned by all the coughing, but otherwise normal. "Okay? I'm fine."

"You didn't breathe?"

"I did," Brent admitted. "A little bit. When I fell. But I'm—I'm fine. Maybe . . ."

He stopped talking, back hunching as another wave of coughs gripped him by the spine and abdomen. Dominic clenched his fist around the scissors, began to lift it up, the tip angling downward.

"Maybe what?"

The coughing passed, and Brent looked up at him. Dominic let the hand holding the scissors fall.

"Maybe the gas has thinned enough," Brent said. "Maybe it's safe to go outside."

· · ·

But Brent *wasn't* fine—a fact that became clearer and clearer to Dominic as they made their way back to the fourth floor, to the cafeteria. Dominic walked behind Brent, his hand still on the scissors, which he'd furtively slipped into his pocket. Brent's own walking was more like a stumble, like he was dizzy and could barely keep his feet. In the elevator, Dominic got a good look at his face: sweaty at the hairline and temples, eyes darting, panicky. Dominic let Brent walk off the elevator first, then kept a wide berth as they approached the cafeteria.

Lauren came out of a cubicle, stacks of paper in her hand.

"Dominic," she said. "You have to look at this."

He glanced up at her and gave her a warning look, a subtle shake of the head. A brief confusion came to Lauren's eyes, but then her gaze fell on Brent, and she pressed herself up against the cubicle wall to let him by, the papers falling to the floor.

"What's with him?" she asked Dominic after Brent had passed.

More temps were coming out now, coming to greet Dominic and Brent on their triumphant return. Dominic rushed forward and waved them away from Brent.

"Give him some space, everybody," he said.

Then an alarm blared. A white light strobed from some uncertain origin.

"What's that?" Lauren asked, her voice rising.

Brent answered in a croak. "The fire alarm." He looked up. "No."

Brent ran past the gathering temps and into the cafeteria. Dominic looked up, his eyes following, and saw the source of the alarm.

Smoke, pouring from the cafeteria. From the kitchen.

"No," Dominic said, already running.

The smoke grew thick at the edge of the cafeteria, almost overpowering at the buffet—and at the entrance to the kitchen Dominic felt the heat. Brent emerged, the sweat on his forehead and his frenzied eyes now seeming appropriate rather than alarming. He held a red fire extinguisher in his hands.

"Get another one!" he shouted, pointing back into the seating area, then plunged back in. Dominic ran past tables to another extinguisher cabinet on the wall, broke the glass. Then, sprinting back to the kitchen, he felt another presence just behind him, and glanced back to see Frederick at his heels, also carrying a fire extinguisher.

Inside the kitchen, everything was ablaze. The flames coming off the tile floor as though someone had spilled gas and dropped a match. At the far wall, the dry supplies blazed—the breakfast cereal and granola bars, dry sauce mixes, flour, and spices. Brent fought his way to the shelves, spraying a path with the extinguisher, but Dominic didn't think he'd make it in time; the supplies would be a total loss. On the other side of the room, flames billowed out through the open door of the freezer as well.

"The food!" Dominic yelled to Frederick over the roar of the fire, then angled his head toward the freezer. Frederick nodded, and they began spraying together at the flames, trying to clear a path toward the freezer.

Eventually they beat back the flames, poured extinguisher spray into the freezer until the only thing that came out was smoke. Dominic waved his hands in front of his face and backed away from the door, coughing. It was impossible to see inside the freezer. They'd have to wait for the smoke to clear before they could know how bad the damage was, how much food they'd lost. Dominic's guess was most of it. The sudden sense of scarcity, of not having enough, was familiar to Dominic—an old enemy, or perhaps a friend. The feeling of welcoming it back was almost affectionate. Dominic always knew it would come to this: survivors fighting over scraps, struggling to survive. This was why he hadn't wanted to join the temps on the fourth floor to begin with. Better to hoard supplies, protect them, fight off anyone who came for them. But Lauren had convinced him that there was strength in numbers. A sour vindication swelled in his chest.

"I knew it," he muttered. "I fucking knew it."

Behind him, Brent raged.

"Fuck!" he yelled. "Fuck fuck fuck goddammit fuck fuck!"

"Brent," Frederick murmured. "Calm down. It's going to be okay. We're going to figure it out."

But Brent wasn't paying attention, by the sound of him—he'd stopped cursing and had started to groan. A sound more guttural and anguished than any Dominic had heard from any human before. Dominic turned around and saw that Brent was doubled over on the floor by the shelves of burned supplies. Frederick crept up behind him, put a hand on his shoulder.

"Frederick, don't," Dominic said. But it was too late.

Brent whirled around just as Frederick touched him, his arms flying like those of a ragdoll. The back of his fist caught Frederick across the face, and he went sprawling. Then Brent launched on top of him, pressed his thumbs into Frederick's eyes. Brent's skin had gone webbed with burst blood vessels, and his groan had turned into an animal growl.

Frederick screamed, grabbing at Brent's arms.

Dominic moved. He ran a couple steps, then launched himself at Brent. He'd played defensive back in high school, and still remembered his coach's advice for how to make a tackle: *shoulders low, arms wide, wrap him up, drive through.* There was a slow-motion feeling to it, always, a feeling that returned now as Dominic gathered Brent up in his arms and felt his weight shift, began to move with him, a kind of violent intimacy in the embrace. On the floor their bodies came apart again, sprawling in different directions. Dominic's skull juddered across the tile like a bouncing glass marble. He groaned, rolled onto his back, tried to get up. But before he could, Brent was on top of him.

Brent's hands went immediately for Dominic's throat, and for a split second Dominic felt panic as Brent's thumbs pressed hard against his windpipe. Then, in a move that surprised even Dominic with its gracefulness, more instinctive than conscious, Dominic swept both arms in circles, bringing his hands up over his sternum and parting Brent's fingers from his throat. He locked Brent's elbows at his sides.

Brent snarled. His eyes bulged with rage. Up close, Dominic could see that the burst blood vessels had spread even to the whites of Brent's eyeballs. The pupils dilated wide, swallowing the color of the iris. Brent's breath hot on Dominic's face, spittle wetting his cheeks. He opened his mouth wide and lunged toward Dominic, snapping, trying to bite a chunk of him: the meat of his cheek, or his throat. The teeth closing only on air for now—but he was strong, so strong, and Dominic's angle, straining Brent's arms close to his torso, gave Dominic poor leverage.

Then there was a flash of gray, a glint of light, a sonorous clang, as though someone had just hit a gong. Brent's head bent sideways on his neck, then came back to center. The shape of his skull had changed, a sphere gone partially oblong—but still he strained toward Dominic, the muscles in his neck bulging as he tried to tear out his windpipe. Dominic looked past Brent's face, his eyes focusing on the figure beyond. Frederick, standing over them. A stainless-steel frying pan in his hands.

"Again," Dominic said, and Frederick swung.

And again. And again. Each time Brent held his grip on Dominic's body, far longer than it seemed he should have been able to—but with each blow from the frying pan Brent's grip got a little weaker, and finally he slumped to the ground.

Dominic scrabbled away from him and stood next to Frederick. On the ground, Brent writhed. He blinked. Then his eyes found them again, and he turned himself over. Began crawling toward them. Murder still in his animal eyes.

"How is this possible?" Dominic asked, inching back while thinking of horror movie villains: Jason, Michael Myers, Jigsaw, still alive when they should have been dead. Brent's head was a bloody mangle. "How can he still be coming at us?"

Dominic looked at Frederick. He was crying.

"I can't," he said. "I can't finish him."

Dominic reached into his pocket. The scissors were still there. He bent down and lifted them high, plunged them into Brent's back. Put all his arm into it, driving the scissors deep and high, where he thought the heart would be.

Brent slumped dead.

# THIRTEEN

Lauren filed to the auditorium with the other temps. Silence hung in the air as they trudged to the door, as if they were walking to a funeral, or an execution. Under her arms Lauren held the manila folder with Jacob's papers—a secret waiting to be revealed.

The line slowed, then stopped at the door. Lauren stepped out of the line and looked. Frederick and Dominic stood at the entrance to the auditorium with security wands, asking everyone to raise their arms. A knife in Frederick's other hand, the paper-cutter blade in Dominic's. Lauren chilled to see the blades. Dominic's weapon had scarcely made an appearance in six and a half weeks, since the first day they'd met each other; Lauren thought he'd thrown it away. Hoped it, perhaps. Yet here it was again, the weapon brought back into commission now that one person had disappeared, and two others were dead.

"Lift your arms," Dominic said when Lauren got to the front of the line.

"Is this really necessary?"

"Lauren."

"You *know* I didn't shoot Anton."

"I have to search everyone. No exceptions. Come on. Just make this easy for me."

Lauren sighed and lifted her arms. The manila folder in one hand.

Dominic ran the wand over her arms, then up and down her torso. "What's that?" he asked, nodding upward at the folder.

"Research," Lauren said. "Jacob's."

Dominic's eyebrows lifted. "Oh yeah? Anything interesting?"

Lauren made no sign. "A few things."

Dominic waved with the wand into the auditorium. "Come on. You're clean. We'll talk about it later."

In the auditorium, Lauren purposely took a seat near the front, on an aisle. At the head of the room stood Swati. She didn't hold any weapons, but the look on her face was sharp, surveying the swelling crowd as if she suspected any one of them, or all of them at once, of abducting Jacob.

After everyone was inside Dominic strode to the front. He set his security wand and the blade on the tabletop, then looked at Swati and nodded. Swati turned her eyes up.

"Everyone," she said. "Thanks for being here."

No one made a sound, but Lauren thought that she could feel the room bristle. After everything that had happened, they had no choice but to be here. Anyone who didn't show up for Dominic and Swati's emergency meeting would be suspected as the saboteur. Dominic's blade and Frederick's knife couldn't control all of them; if they rose up now and stormed the exit, Frederick wouldn't be able to hold them back. But the threat represented by the visibility of the weapons was enough to keep them in line—that, and the quickly spreading story of what had happened to Anton, the honest fear that any of them could be next if they didn't find the killer.

"I have a feeling that most of you know what happened by now," Swati said. "But in case you haven't heard yet, or in case you *have* heard something but you're not sure what to believe, I'll tell you. This morning, Jacob Elliot went missing. The power went out. And then . . ."

She trailed off and looked to Dominic.

"Brent, Anton, and I went into the tunnels to get to the building's power station," Dominic said. "Anton was shot dead by someone in the tunnels. Brent and I got away, but we discovered that the power failure was the result of someone purposely flipping the switch. We suspect the same person who killed Anton. And then—"

Dominic's throat cleared with a grunt that seemed to take him by surprise. He shook his head and looked down.

"On our way back," he continued, "Brent breathed the gas. For a while we thought he was okay, that the gas was too weak to have any effect—but then when we got back here he turned into a Fury. Frederick and I had to . . . well, we had to kill him. And there's one more thing. The saboteur—or *saboteurs*, we don't know—burned our food supply. Totally torched it.

Swati and I just got done with an inventory. There's enough salvageable food to last us two weeks. Maybe less."

Dominic stared into the crowd. There was complete silence.

"Our situation has fundamentally changed," Dominic said. "For the past six weeks we had more than we needed. It was easy. Fun, even. Maybe some of us got lulled into a false sense of security—me included. It seemed like it would never end. But now it has. The reality of what happened out there," Dominic pointed through the wall, then brought his finger down, pointed at the spot of floor he stood on, "it's here now. It's inside. We're going to have to make some hard choices in the days ahead. Fun time is over—the word from here on out is *survival.*"

Lauren listened with growing restlessness, running her fingers along the edges of the manila folder, tempting a paper cut. Everything Dominic was saying was true, but he seemed to be enjoying saying it too much, relishing the grimness of it. Or, perhaps, relishing the fact that now he was the one saying it, not Brent. He'd been waiting for this, Lauren felt— waiting to lead, waiting for their artificial abundance to end and the direness of their situation to reassert itself. This was what he'd been prophesying since the beginning: survivors watching each other suspiciously, fighting for the few resources that remained, killing in order to live. Now that it was here, Lauren couldn't deny that she was glad Dominic was in charge, keeping people in line with his air of authority and makeshift blade—but she also found herself hating him for seeing it so clearly, for being right all along.

"There's another thing," Swati said, moving forward as Dominic inched back, the crowd's attention shifting effortlessly from one to the other. They must have choreographed, planned. "The saboteur. We have to find him."

"Or her," Dominic said.

"Or her," Swati acknowledged. "Or them. We have to stretch out our remaining supplies as long as we can, make them last until the gas lifts completely. We can't do that with a saboteur running around. Cutting power, killing people, going after the food supply. That's why we're going to have to question everybody. Whereabouts for the last twenty-four hours, alibis—every one of you. And nobody leaves this room until we're done."

The room erupted with shouts of protest. Lauren looked behind her, up the steps to the exit. Frederick stood holding his knife—not brandishing it, not threatening anyone with it, but making sure everyone saw it.

"We'll try to make it as quick as we can," Dominic said. "Pass out food if the questioning goes past dinner. But it's the only way. And nobody gets out of this room unless you get past Frederick. And anyone who *does* try to leave—you've just jumped to the top of our suspect list. Got it?"

Lauren stood. This had gone on long enough. Dominic and Swati were her friends, but they weren't thinking clearly. Swati had lost Jacob, Dominic had seen two survivors die; the events had clearly made them afraid, and now their fear was making them act irrationally. Perhaps anyone who'd seen what they'd seen would react the same—but Lauren had information that could change everything. She'd only been sitting on it for the last hour or so, since she realized what she had. But that was more than enough; too long, in fact. It was time to share what she knew.

Lauren cleared her throat. Dominic and Swati's eyes swung toward her simultaneously.

"Yes?" Swati asked.

"I'm sorry to interrupt, but I think I have something here that could shed some light on this whole situation." Lauren held up the folder.

"What is it?" Swati asked. "Is that . . . ?"

"Jacob's," Lauren said. "Yes. The papers he printed off the Brain. This is what he was working on when he disappeared."

Murmurs of interest rose up from the crowd, but Dominic walked forward with his hand out, trying to silence them.

"Not now. I told you—we can talk about that later."

Swati looked at him. "But I want to hear this."

"When we interview her. We can start with Lauren."

"No," Lauren said firmly. "Everyone should hear this. The information that's in this file, what Jacob found—there've been enough secrets. This affects us all."

She looked hard at Dominic, and he looked back. A long, brittle moment. Then Dominic's body eased almost imperceptibly, the barest relenting.

"Fine," he said, moving to the side. "You have the floor."

Lauren stepped into the aisle and walked down to the stage, feeling everyone's eyes on her back. But she took her time, breathed, laid out Jacob's papers on the lectern, stacked them in piles. One pile for Concierge. One for Apocalypse. The Brandt memo by itself. Then, finally, Eschaton.

"Okay," she said, turning around and facing her audience. "Where shall we begin?"

• • •

Lauren herself had begun with Eschaton—an irony, since in the Greek *eschatos* meant "last." But the Eschaton files were on top of the pile. She could have flipped the stack, read the documents in the order in which Jacob had most likely discovered and printed them. But she didn't suppose the order would make much difference. And so, as Dominic and Brent searched for a way to restore the power, and still later, as Dominic and Swati inventoried the salvageable food, she sat in her cubicle and read carefully through Jacob's documents, in reverse chronological order.

It was difficult at first to tell what Eschaton *was*. The files' common subject seemed to be the ultimate destiny of human civilization on earth—but what business did a for-profit corporation have in utopianism? What profit motive could there be? She went through the Eschaton files once, then doubled back and read them a second time, trying to find a productization plan, a revenue stream, commodification. But there was nothing. Only sociopolitical analyses, global population projections, covert human behavioral studies. Prototype plans for underground cities, geodomes, manmade floating continents. Wildest of all were the *Solutions* documents, eighteen of them, proposing potential methods by which Delphi could sweep away the current world order and usher in a global utopia. Bizarre, outlandish stuff. An international espionage and assassination network empowered to topple regimes, kill intransigent leaders, install puppet rulers. Coups, militias, revolutions. Benevolent corporate takeovers of key world governments. A revolutionized form of corporate lobbying. A new political party and subsequent realignment of American politics. Shadow regimes. Space exploration. Mars colonization.

And then, at the end of the Eschaton documentation, midway down Jacob's stack of papers, Lauren found the source of all this corporate activity, this bureaucratic flailing: a memo, addressed from Tristan Brandt to "Delphi Enterprises Leadership Group." The subject was "Our New Purpose."

.  .  .

*There is a fatal weakness in human civilization. The world stands at the precipice of massive global catastrophe, but democracy and capitalism—the dominant structural modes of the human social organism—are incapable of coordinating the capabilities of individuals and societies to solve the problems that they themselves have created. Utopia is within our reach. But in its current configuration, civilization will be unable to grasp it. The global cataclysms we face in a few decades', years', or even months' time force us to reevaluate notions that have been the foundation of liberal democracy and global capitalism for the past century. Among the concepts that must be done away with are: the social contract, representative government, and the very presumption of the individual as a free and rational economic actor possessing certain inalienable human rights.*

*I have come to see that history is a series of repetitions, a swirling and accelerating succession of epochs both peaceful and chaotic. The last period of chaos was the early twentieth century, when two world wars brought death and destruction around the globe. The period immediately following these wars was one of relative peace and prosperity. Capitalism created huge amounts of wealth and security for billions of people. Democracies thrived. Crop yields exploded; advances in medicine, sanitation, and food preservation extended life expectancy. Human populations grew at astonishing rates not seen by any other species in the history of the planet.*

*This period of stability is nearly at an end. Our prosperity was not the result of capitalism alone, but of an excess of resources—of land, of crops, of fossil fuels and useful metals—that led to an excess of capital and opportunity for the global population. As long as this abundance persisted, it seemed that there might be no end to capitalism's growth, to the tired and poor and huddled masses who might one day benefit from the riches of the global economy. But this material abundance could not last forever. Indeed, it will not. We are about to enter a period of scarcity, in which the bonds that tie individuals together in civil society will be frayed by a struggle of all against all—first for privilege and societal advantage, then for capital, finally for the necessities of life: food, shelter, and water.*

*I can already hear the question, the rejoinder: But Tristan, what about technology—not least* our *technologies, the ones we've developed together here at Delphi Enterprises? Yes, technology could save us—but it is my increasing belief that the advancements needed to usher human civilization into a future techno-utopia may come too late . . . and that even if they don't, the human social organism isn't intelligent or adaptive enough to make the necessary societal adjustments to adopt these technologies. (I call this societal adaptation "The Turn"; the difficulty of the Turn is the wicked problem that stands between us and our ultimate goal.)*

*In the absence of adequate human leadership, it falls to Delphi Enterprises to lead civilization into the future. I envision a global political order beyond democracy, beyond even capitalism (perhaps it's an advanced capitalism, a pure capitalism): a state of affairs I have termed "neo-feudalism." In a neo-feudal system, global power will reside in the hands of billionaires, the winners of the capitalist competition, and corporations will be their fiefdoms—meritocratic totalitarian collectives in which power and influence reside in the hands of an exceptional few, vassal-VPs to their CEO-lords, and in which the many (i.e. the workers) live in a state of happy serfdom, fed and clothed and entertained but unburdened by any expectation of human rights, self-determination, personal achievement, or self-actualization.*

*This state of affairs is the Eschaton—the end of human history, "end" in this usage meaning both "a final endpoint" and "an ultimate realization of purpose." And it is this Eschaton that we, the leaders of Delphi Enterprises, must now work to make manifest.*

. . .

Lauren felt dizzy as she read, felt as though she was rushing through space—like her chair was tilting back, and back, and back into a yawning black void, but never tipping all the way over. Alice, tumbling through the rabbit hole.

There was something familiar about the memo. Perhaps it was Brandt's way of writing, of presenting ideas. She could see the classical training in his background, the study of Greek philosophy. That overly formal, Victorian way of speaking people fell into when they'd spent enough time in ancient texts, musty tomes. She also recognized the *ideas*—recognized them because she'd thought some of them herself, lying awake at night and worrying over all the ways that humanity was just *doomed*.

But then the memo rushed to its end and suddenly Lauren's stomach turned, nauseated to realize that her thoughts, moving in synch with Brandt's, could bring her to this hideous destination: neo-feudalism, the death of democracy, the abolition of self-determination and universal human rights. So *this* was the origin of Delphi's Eschaton initiative, this reasonable-sounding but deep-down-insane memo. No wonder the project's results had been so unsettling, so wild.

Lauren looked closer at the memo, noticed the blotchiness of the print. Had Jacob photocopied it? Or—more likely, she realized—the file he'd printed from was itself a copy, a scan, not the original email or text document. As if the file's existence was itself illicit, put on the Eschaton server not by Brandt or one of the memo's original recipients, but by some underling who'd seen it one day on the printer tray, or stolen it from his boss's desk when he went in to get approval on something unrelated. Maybe the senior VPs who'd gotten the memo would've rather ignored it. Lauren could imagine their muttering now, *There goes Brandt again with his crazy ideas, maybe if we don't say anything it'll blow over.* But it didn't blow over. One way or another, the memo had gotten out, where it had caused ripples: corporate upheaval, bureaucratic scrambling.

Working even further back in Jacob's documents, Lauren began to see a logic in their progression. Everything centered around the memo: Eschaton flowed away from it, but Concierge and Apocalypse flowed toward it. Concierge, Delphi's data mining app, feeding into Apocalypse, the human civilization modeling program. Had the results of the modeling been bad enough to make Brandt fire off the memo in a fit of despair? If Morgan and her fellow gamers had found a way to win Apocalypse, to steer human civilization toward utopia rather than ruin, could all of this have been avoided?

. . .

Now, in the auditorium, Lauren summarized Jacob's files in what she thought was probably the correct order—first Concierge, then Apocalypse, then the Brandt memo, then Eschaton last. There were no interruptions. Only one pause, when Lauren asked the temps how many had been Concierge users before the gas—almost all raised their hands, Lauren guessed more than ninety percent.

"So," she said when she'd finished, after letting a long pause draw out, "I said I thought this was relevant to what we're going through right now. And this is what I think's going on: I think the saboteur, or saboteurs, whoever they are—they're not from us. They're from the outside, from the company. Delphi. Messing with us. I think Brandt is alive, I think he's here somewhere, and I think that we're part of his experiment. He recruited us with Concierge, used the app to get us on the payroll. Hand-picked us for our unique psychometrics. I think the experiment has something to do with Apocalypse, something with Eschaton—picking people to be part of his utopia, maybe."

"And the gas?"

Lauren looked to the side. The question had come from Dominic, who was leaning against the wall with his arms crossed.

"Maybe it's a fake," Lauren said. "If anyone could do it, it's Brandt."

Dominic sniffed. "Some fake. I killed Brent with my own hands."

Lauren bent her head and let her eyes close, then open again. "Or maybe it's not a fake. Maybe it's real. Probably it's real. Either way, I think the company is behind it somehow."

"But you've got no proof."

"No," Lauren said. "Only a hunch."

Then a sound came from the crowd. A chair creaking, the seat thudding up on its hinge. Lauren looked. A guy was standing, making his way down the row, muttering apologies as he squeezed past people's knees. Lauren moved around to the side of the stage to see his face. It was Casey. The temp who'd kept working after the gas, pressed on doing data entry with four others.

"Where are you going?" Lauren asked.

He reached the aisle and looked at her. "Back to work."

The statement, delivered so bluntly, put Lauren off-balance. She searched for something to say, but after an awkward, sputtering pause all she could manage was, "Why?"

"You said maybe Brandt was picking people for his utopia," Casey said. "For Eschaton. Well, from that memo you read it sounded to me like he's looking for serfs, people who can follow orders. The last order Brandt gave me—the last order he gave *any* of us—was to do our jobs for Delphi. So that's what I'm going to do. Maybe if Brandt is watching he'll take us away from here before the food runs out." He turned back to the row of auditorium seats. "Come on, guys."

Four others stood and followed him. At the aisle, they made their way up the steps to the exit. Frederick stepped in front of them, knife held out. Casey looked down at the blade, then back up at Frederick. The crowd, heads turned to see what would happen next, seemed to hold their breath.

"You sure you want to do that?" Casey asked. "Or would you rather come with us?"

The question seemed to unsettle Frederick, but he kept the knife out.

"Let them go," Dominic said. There was exhaustion, defeat in his voice. "Just let them all go."

Frederick stood aside and let them pass. After the doors clicked closed behind them, others stood from their seats and trudged to the exit—then still others, until the auditorium was all but empty. Frederick was the last to go—glancing down at the knife in his hand, blinking at it as though he'd been sleepwalking and woke up with it. Then he dropped it to the floor and went through the door. Only Lauren, Dominic, Swati, and Jane (sitting in the front row, silent as always) were left. It felt to Lauren as though something had died, that an epoch had come to an end. A minor apocalypse, a small but devastating revelation. They were living, once more, in the after.

"Well," Dominic said. "What do we do now?"

# FOURTEEN

"This is crazy," Lauren said.

"Yeah," Swati said, even though she thought it was more complicated than that. Lauren was partly right: what had happened in the temps' minds since learning everything that was in Jacob's files *was* crazy. But it also made perfect sense. Maybe the most dangerous ideas were crazy and sane at the same time.

Swati, Lauren, and Jane stood together at the edge of a large office space on the second floor. Watching. In the center of the space the cubicles buzzed with activity: the murmur of voices, the slurp of hot coffee sipped gingerly from mugs, muted laughter as two coworkers shared a joke, the ubiquitous clacking of fingertips on keyboards. There was nothing to distinguish the scene from a real, functioning office—nothing except the fact that no real work was taking place. At best, the temps were playacting.

This was the result of the meeting in the auditorium, of Lauren's impromptu presentation. A few of the temps were still on the fourth floor, maybe ten or twenty of them, lying in their cubicles all day, staring at the same spot of carpet or wall. Accepting their deaths. Others—a few dozen—had decided to party until the food ran out. James, the DJ from the party-planning committee, had turned his occasional meeting-room raves into a 24-7 affair, participants dancing and drinking and grinding to house music until they quite literally dropped to the floor from exhaustion. Swati poked her head in once and heard, amidst the thumping bass, moans of pleasure, or pain. The room smelling of stale beer, sweat, and semen. She hadn't gone back.

But the rest of the temps—those not giving themselves over to despair or hedonism—had all come here, to the second floor. Clustering around Casey and the data-entry workers, claiming cubicles, working with Frederick from IT to get their computers set up for some near approximation of what their jobs had been before the gas. For the past three days, from 8:30 to 5, with coffee and lunch breaks between, they'd all been typing, sending each other emails, chatting at the printers, calling meetings, complaining about how busy they were.

"Hey, working hard?" Swati heard a guy say now, swinging by a friend's cubicle and setting his shoulder against the door. "Or hardly working?"

"Ha ha," the other guy said. "Wanna hit happy hour after this?"

From the other side of the office, a girl exited one of the cubicles and came toward them. "If I made another pot of coffee, would you have any? I know it's a little late, but I need a caffeine hit if I'm going to get through all these expense reports."

"Oh, for fuck's sake," Lauren muttered, and the girl flinched.

Swati gave Lauren a look, then smiled at the girl. "None for me, thanks," she said. "But I'm sure people wouldn't mind if you made another pot."

"Thanks," the girl said. "You're right. Lot of people working late tonight, seems like. Big deadline coming up."

Swati winced but kept her smile; *deadline* had become a sort of code among the working temps for the day the food was gone and they ran out of time to be rescued by Tristan Brandt, gathered up into his Eschaton. The girl turned and walked away to the kitchenette at the end of the hall.

"This is not what I'd intended," Lauren said after the girl left.

Swati shrugged. "But it sort of makes sense, doesn't it?"

"No," Lauren said. "It doesn't. At all."

"Oh, come on. Isn't this basically what people have been doing for hundreds of years, with religion? Some absent, all-seeing god is watching—and if you do certain things, do them exactly the right way, that god will rescue you, bring you into paradise."

"I guess," Lauren said. "This is sort of like that."

*Sort of* like that? Swati thought it was *exactly* like that. That there were no supervisors, no company to work for, transformed the temps' pointless typing, emailing, and copying into ritual. The language they used—remembered phrases like "I'll have that to you by end of day" or "Let's take that question offline" or "It seems like we're having some version control issues"—now seemed like incantations, wards against death and despair. They even had a new theory about what had happened to Jacob: he wasn't dead, wasn't kidnapped, wasn't even the saboteur. Rather, he'd been saved by Brandt, the first to be whisked away to Eschaton as a reward for discovering the truth in the Brain. Swati thought there was some illogic in this theory's purported connection to the temps' current behavior—Jacob had been mail room, not analytics, and he'd been following no order from the company in going to the Brain. But in the broad strokes, the myth bolstered their new worldview, their belief that their salvation would come, if it came at all, by working. Sitting at a desk. Staring at a screen. Waiting to die.

"You know," Swati said, "*I* kept working after the gas. I kept teaching yoga. In fact, I'm still teaching it now. Morning, noon, and five, for anyone who wants to come."

"That's different," Lauren said. "Yoga is your calling. It's your bliss."

Swati rolled her eyes. "Don't Joseph-Campbell me."

"Sorry."

"Anyway, Miss Follow-Your-Bliss," Swati said, "what are you going to do? Are you going to join the workers? Start writing personality quizzes again? Join the rave-orgy, maybe? Or lie down on four and wait to die?"

"I don't know," Lauren said. "None of them sound very appealing, to be honest."

"How about a hero's journey instead?"

Lauren turned to her, eyebrows raised. "What?"

"I said how about—"

"I heard you," Lauren said, raising a hand in interruption. "What I meant was—what do you have in mind?"

"I want to find Brandt."

• • •

Dominic grabbed at the printer display panel and batted it lightly with the fingers of one hand. "Piece of shit," he muttered, hitting harder. "Why won't you print? It's right fucking there."

He stabbed at buttons, trying to bring the machine to life, but nothing happened—only a high-pitched beeping, like a protest. Dominic let out a bellow of frustration, giving the printer a kick as he pushed himself away from it. He made so much noise that he didn't hear the footsteps until they were almost upon him. The sudden sound sent a burst of fear coursing through his veins. He was, after all, standing in the precise location of Jacob's last known whereabouts, perhaps even doing the exact thing Jacob had been doing when he was taken, and as he looked up to see who it was he instinctively darted his eyes to the countertop where he'd set his blade, in case he'd need to defend himself.

His heart thudded loud, then slowed in the very next beat, creating a dizzying head rush of relief.

It was only Lauren, Swati, and Jane.

"Shit," he said. "You scared me."

"Sorry," Swati said. "But we need to talk. Thought we might find you here."

"Yeah," Dominic said, casting his gaze over the cubicles. They stood in the business analytics department. He could see his old desk from where he now stood, and beyond it, the door to the Brain. He'd worked hard to get into the company, and the workstations had been his reward. He'd spent enough time at both of them before the gas that he began to think of them as a second home—a home he'd now returned to, like an old man asking to see his old bedroom before he dies. "I guess I didn't know what else to do."

"So, you too?" Swati asked.

"Me too what?"

"You're working," Swati said. "Like the others. Doing your old job."

Dominic thought before speaking. "I don't know what I'm doing," he admitted. "I mean, yeah, my old job was here. But I was always doing work for the business analysts, and they're all dead now. Maybe I could pretend, like the others are doing. I tried, for about half a day. But it felt pointless. Tristan Brandt, if he *is* alive, testing us somehow—he doesn't care about us doing pointless shit. That's not how we're going to get him to save us."

Swati seemed to consider this. Behind her, Lauren simply watched with Jane, quiet. Lauren had always seemed so confident, so self-possessed—but the recent events had undone her too.

"What *are* you doing, then?" Swati asked.

Dominic shrugged. "Covering my bases? Hanging out? Just . . . *being* here?"

Swati shot him a dubious look. "Pretty minor stuff to be swearing at the printer over."

Dominic sighed. "Fine. Investigating, I guess. Seeing for myself. Trying to figure out what there is in Delphi's data that's so big Jacob could get disappeared over it."

"And?"

Dominic shook his head. "Nothing. Except this file in the printer log, the last one that came through from the Brain."

He pointed at the display. Swati looked at it, then Lauren. Lauren's head snapped up, a sudden frenzy in her eyes.

"Solution 19," she said.

"That mean something to you?" Dominic asked.

"There were solutions documents in Jacob's files. They were part of the Eschaton project, a bunch of weird ideas for transitioning the world from the current state to Brandt's new world order." Lauren paused. "The ones I saw were numbered 1 to 18."

"This is it," Swati said, the excitement palpable in her voice. "Solution 19. That has to be the reason Jacob disappeared."

"To keep him from sharing the document?" Lauren asked. "Or as a reward for his finding it? Is it a cover-up, or a game?"

"I don't know," Swati said, squinting. She snapped her head up at Dominic. "What's in the file?"

Dominic shook his head. "Wish I knew. I can't get it to print. It's listed in the log, but it doesn't seem like the printer caches anything more than the name."

"Well, could you do a filename search on the Brain?"

"Did it already," Dominic said. "There's nothing."

"How's that possible?" Lauren asked. "If Jacob printed it, the file has to be on there somewhere."

"There's a server missing," Dominic said. "It's on the list, but the Brain just can't access it anymore."

"Which server?"

"It's called *Futures*," Dominic said. "That must be where Jacob found most of his information. Because I can't find much of anything on Concierge, Apocalypse, or Eschaton. There are references to the projects in other servers, but all the files and file paths they point to are just dead. I had Frederick take a look—but he says it seems like someone disconnected the server, changed the credentials."

Lauren looked down again at the printer display. Something of what Dominic had been feeling minutes earlier showed on her face as she gripped the sides of the screen, knuckles whitening as if she could simply squeeze the file from the machine, like juice from a lemon.

"Solution 19," she said. "You guys, what if—"

"What?" Dominic asked.

She looked up. Her face gone pale. "What if Solution 19 was the gas? Save the world by killing it and starting over?"

"I don't believe that," Dominic said, looking down and trying to blink away the thought—Tristan Brandt and Delphi as the architects of a global genocide. "I can't believe that could be true. I studied Brandt in school. He was good. Filthy rich, okay—but he was still one of the good guys. That's why I wanted to come work for the company. I wouldn't have bothered otherwise."

It was more complicated than that and Dominic knew it—but he let the half-truth stand for now. The other half of the truth was that Dominic envied Brandt his power, his alpha dominance of the whole world. There was something seductive about a winner, an attraction that was almost sexual; Dominic had felt himself drawn to Delphi, like a pigeon to a homing signal, to be close to that power. To emulate it, if he could. Now, to think that he'd been sucked in by a villain, a world-destroyer, would say something about himself that Dominic couldn't quite bring himself to countenance—not yet.

"We don't know anything yet," Swati said. "That's why I think we should find him."

"Who? Brandt?"

"He's the one person who can tell us what's really going on. Whether the gas came from the company. Why he brought us here. If there's really an Eschaton. And what happened to Jacob."

"But how?" Dominic said. "We've been over every inch of this building. The Delphi executives' offices are in a completely different building—Parnassus Tower."

"It's on the grounds, isn't it?" Swati asked.

"Yeah," Dominic said. "More than five hundred yards away. We'd never make it without breathing the gas."

"The tunnels," Swati said.

Dominic shook his head. "No. There's a tunnel from here to Parnassus, but I've tried all the entrances, and Anton's code doesn't work anymore. Either the codes have all been changed, or Anton never had a code for the tunnel to Parnassus. Even if Brandt *is* here—if he's not dead, which still seems pretty crazy to me—we'll never be able to get to him."

"I know how to get there," Swati said. "Someone can take us."

"Who?"

Swati pointed, and Dominic looked. Jane. The mute girl looked up, her face slack with surprise, fear—but also resignation and relief. The expression of someone who'd finally been found out. Who'd just been unburdened of a secret she'd wanted to speak aloud, but couldn't.

"Her," said Swati.

• • •

Swati still didn't like going into the cubicle. The one she'd shared, for a time, with Jacob. The blankets, rumpled on the floor, still smelled of him. She hadn't touched them since he disappeared, hadn't even looked at them. She couldn't abide their reminder of the way Jacob had slipped out of bed early that morning, the morning he'd vanished. Instead, she'd been sleeping down on the first floor near the open-air yoga studio, using as a mattress four foam yoga mats unfurled. Returning to the cubicle—*their* cubicle, their apartment—only when she needed something, not looking down, grabbing what she'd come for and leaving as quickly as she could.

It was during one such trip—she'd needed to retrieve her notebook, the one with her yoga routines in it—that she'd found herself exiting the cubicle with some paper printouts also in her hand. Jacob had shown them to her about a week before, a few days before his disappearance.

"I'm not going to tell you what they are," Jacob had said. "I just want you to look at them, no context, and tell me if you think the guy in the pictures is the same person."

"Okay," Swati had said cautiously, drawing out the word and flipping her voice up at the end, a question: *what do you want now?* It was a test, she knew—the greater Jacob's nonchalance, the closer he was observing, the more he cared about her response. He wanted a certain answer, probably; if he didn't get it, this casual quiz might turn into an argument. Or worse, a few days of sullenness as Jacob disappeared even further into his restlessness, his vague resentments.

Luckily, Swati managed to give Jacob the answer he wanted. The photographs he gave her were of a business executive in a series of meetings. Wearing a well-tailored suit with tie, fingers splayed in urgent gestural communication as he held forth in a meeting, others listening in rapt attention, chins resting on knuckles. In another shot, the executive had shed his suit coat and rolled up his shirtsleeves to sketch an idea—presumably something brilliantly disruptive and value-additive—on a whiteboard. In a third, he was dressed more casually in a zip-up knit with a tall collar, sitting on a couch with a female underling and explaining something to her on a piece of paper.

The pictures all appeared to be of the same person—a thin man with glasses and a receding gray hairline—until she looked a little closer and realized that there were small differences between the three. One had a slightly more pronounced jawline; this one had smaller ears; the third was less wrinkled than the other two. Not the same person so much as they were versions of the same person, paid impersonators—like a parade of Elvises on the Vegas strip.

"No," she'd said after looking the photos over one more time. "They're not the same. They look a lot alike, but they're different people."

"Right!" Jacob said, clearly excited that she'd said what he wanted her to. "But they're *supposed* to be of the same person, is the thing. They're all supposed to be pictures of Brandt."

"Where did you get these?" Swati had asked.

"Around," Jacob said dismissively. "Casey says he thinks Delphi had body doubles for Brandt."

"That's dumb. Why would a company do that?"

"I don't know. Delphi's not a normal company, though, is it?"

• • •

No, Delphi wasn't a normal company—that much was clear now. And Swati now knew where Jacob had gotten the photographs: the Brain. Some PR server, maybe, with stock shots in case the business press ever needed a picture of Brandt looking like a master of the universe.

But the pictures contained something Swati hadn't noticed when Jacob first shared them with her, so focused had she been on his question, whether the men in the pictures were the same person. She noticed it days later, after Jacob was gone and she came out of their cubicle with the photographs unexpectedly in her hand, tucked under the notebook she'd come for.

Jane was in the pictures. All three of them. In the photograph of Brandt (or someone pretending to be Brandt) speaking at a meeting, she sat a little behind him, legs demurely crossed, scribbling something on a pad of paper. She looked on as another Brandt, bare-armed, sketched some capitalist brilliance on the dry-erase board. And she was the female underling to whom the third Brandt patiently mansplained on the couch.

Swati came out of the cubicle now and handed the photographs to Dominic. He looked at them, then handed them to Lauren.

"Holy shit," Lauren said.

"Yeah," Swati said. "I think she might've been Brandt's executive assistant."

Lauren turned to Jane. "Is that right?"

Jane, tight-lipped, nodded.

"Do you know if Brandt is alive?"

She shook her head.

"But you can get us to Parnassus?"

Jane nodded again.

"When do you want to go?" Swati asked the others.

Dominic and Lauren looked at each other.

"Why not now?" Dominic asked.

"Okay," Swati said. "Lauren?"

Lauren nodded. "Yeah. Let's go. There's just one thing I need to do before we leave."

• • •

Lauren went to her cubicle and shoved some things in a bag. A change of clothes, toothpaste, deodorant. She paused at the manila folder still holding Jacob's files, then slid them in the bag as well and slung it over her shoulder. She shouldn't have needed to pack; if the Parnassus Tower was really only a half-mile away by tunnel, and if Jane could indeed get them in, then the quest to find Tristan Brandt wouldn't be a very long hero's journey. More of a hero's saunter, a hero's stroll. But the saboteur was still out there, the Minotaur of this particular labyrinth. If he shot one of them, or stranded them in the tunnels like he had Brent and Dominic, then Lauren might be glad to have the supplies—the ability to brush her teeth and change her clothes before she died in darkness.

She went to the kitchen and grabbed some food from the paltry remaining supplies. A can of peaches, a jar of olives, a single granola bar, and a bottle of water with a partially melted cap where it had only just kissed the flames.

"You said you wanted to stop somewhere?" Swati asked at the elevators.

"Third floor," Lauren said. "The gamers."

Swati nodded, then Dominic, then Jane, none of them seeming to wonder what she wanted, what she was looking for. They were all seeking something now—that was the point of this quest, wasn't it, the journey to get answers from the Oracle of Delphi Enterprises? Lauren couldn't say precisely what it was Dominic and Swati wanted, but she assumed it was some form of the thing she desired: an answer to the riddle of her own life's upending by the thing that had happened to the world, a reconciliation of inner and outer realities, the deepest desires of her heart against the horrible contingencies of history, and economy, and catastrophe. A way to make sense of it all.

That's what she wanted from Tristan Brandt—but first: the gamers. They were clustered in a few rows of workstations on the third floor. They hunched over their screens, faces lit by the glow, clicking and tapping and mousing to try to beat Apocalypse—as if by winning the game and preventing a simulated human civilization from descending to chaos they could reveal the actual apocalypse to have been a fake all along, and bring an end to this ruse.

Lauren walked the rows, Dominic and Swati and Jane close behind her. Then she found who she was looking for.

"Morgan," she said.

Morgan turned in her chair. "Lauren. Hey."

"So you're working too?"

Morgan flinched, like she found it a little embarrassing, knew how absurd it must look to an outside observer. "I don't know. I guess. It seemed about as good as any of the alternatives."

"I get it," Lauren said. She nodded to Morgan's screen. "So, any progress? Has anyone won that thing yet?"

Morgan shook her head. "No. It's, like, an unbeatable game. I guess humanity really was screwed, one way or another."

Lauren moved into Morgan's cubicle, came around behind her chair. "Can you show me how it works?"

Morgan explained the game as the others looked on. In a strip along the right side of the screen were almost a dozen data readouts for global population, birth and death rates, food supplies, fossil fuels, average global temperatures, worldwide sea levels. Occupying the rest of the screen was a map of the earth, color-coded for areas of democracy and dictatorship, anarchy, sociopolitical strife, and civil war.

"How do you change things?" Lauren asked.

"That's what makes the game so hard," Morgan said. "The only way you can influence the course of events is through what the game calls 'influence nodes.'"

She zoomed in on a part of the map until avatars of actual people were visible, walking around the simulated landscape like ants. Many of them had their heads down, looking at something in their hands.

"Are those . . . ?"

"They look like phones, don't they?" Morgan said. "When I first started playing the game I thought it was a sort of speculative sci-fi thing, like a theoretical mind-control technology—but now I know the game's actually a simulation I don't know. Maybe the influence nodes are actually—"

"Concierge," said Lauren.

"Yeah," Morgan said. "You can use the influence nodes to change people's behavior—like, you could try to get them to adopt more sustainable technologies, elect environmentalist politicians, move out of single-family housing into apartments and arcologies. And you can increase your influence over the population by distributing more influence nodes, getting them into more countries and into more people's hands—but it's sort of a balancing act. The more time you spend pushing influence nodes on the population, the more influence you get but the less time you spend actually influencing people, and vice versa. Meanwhile the point of complete civilization collapse keeps getting closer and closer."

"How far are you?"

"I just started a new game," Morgan said. "This is baseline."

"Are you open to trying something?"

"Sure," Morgan said. "Anything."

"Can you make an apocalypse event happen?" Lauren asked. "Like the thing that happened outside?"

Morgan gave Lauren a strange look, but answered the question. "Sure. Nuclear war, terrorist attack, even alien invasion. I've never tried it before. I figure, the point of the game is to *avoid* apocalypse, right?"

"Right," Lauren said. "But I just want you to try it. See what happens."

"All right," Morgan said, turning back to the keyboard. "What do you want me to try?"

She brought up a disaster menu with a few commands. Lauren pointed.

"How about terrorist attack?"

"What kind?"

Lauren looked at the options. "Chemical attack."

"Location?"

"Worldwide. Coordinated."

"Death rate?"

"What do you guys think?" Lauren asked, turning back to the others. They'd all gone pale, but Dominic met Lauren's eyes and answered without wavering.

"Seventy-five percent at least."

Lauren nodded. "Do it."

Morgan keyed it in, then let the simulation go. As expected, the map lit up red, and the global population indicator plunged.

"How fast is this?" Lauren asked.

"About one simulated week elapsing every second."

"Can you speed it up?"

"Sure," Morgan said. "How fast are you thinking?"

"How about a decade every second?"

Morgan sped up the simulation. The global population numbers immediately stabilized, stayed flat for a few seconds, then began to inch up again. The red on the map began to fade. As the seconds ticked by, there were flares of red and orange indicating sudden outbursts of violence and war across the globe, but after about a minute most of the map had turned green, indicating peace and relative stability. Meanwhile, on the right, the average global temperature climbed at first, then plateaued before beginning to go down again. Sea levels fell, revealing patches of land that had been underwater for centuries. Graphical outbursts indicated catastrophic storms, persistent drought, fires, and famines—but with increasingly lesser frequency as time went by. Meanwhile, colorful dotted and solid lines extended across the map.

"Holy shit," Morgan breathed. "Holy fucking shit."

"What?" Lauren said. "What are those?"

"Supply lines. Food, water, electricity, natural resources. Plus growing political stability, low rates of violence and war, and recovering population numbers." Morgan stared at the screen a few seconds more, then snapped her head up to Lauren. "I think you just beat Apocalypse."

"Really?"

Morgan looked back to the game, breathing audibly through her open mouth, as though she had to check to make sure it was real.

"More than five hundred years have elapsed," Morgan said. "Whenever I've played before—whenever *any* of us have played—the human population has been extinct by now."

Lauren looked to Dominic, Swati, and Jane. "Solution 19," she said.

"What?" Morgan asked. "What's Solution 19?"

Lauren shook her head. "Nothing. Thanks for your time," she said, then walked out of the cubicle. Dominic and Swati parted to let her pass. "Let's go."

# FIFTEEN

"So Brandt was trying to do good," Dominic said. "He was trying to save the world."

"You're kidding, right?" Lauren said. "Save the world by destroying it?"

"I know, but—the model. You saw. An apocalypse now saves the human race in the long run. The ends justify—"

"Don't," Lauren said. "I can't believe you're defending this. We're talking about the deaths of billions of people."

"I'm not defending anything. I'm just thinking. Besides, we still don't *know* that Delphi even did it."

"I think we know."

"But we don't. There's no direct evidence."

"No direct evidence!" Lauren shouted.

"Stop talking," Swati snapped. "Both of you."

They were in the tunnels. As expected, Jane had been able to get them into the Parnassus tunnel, which started at the place where the T- and P-wings joined. She'd tapped a code into the keypad, then the door came open with a sigh. Inside, Dominic and Lauren had argued the whole way, their voices echoing up and down the corridor. It had only been a few minutes, but their constant talk had already given Swati a headache—besides which she kept imagining someone else in the corridor with them. Listening, lying in wait.

"What is it?" Lauren asked.

"Can we just cool it on the speculation?" Swati asked. "We're doing this to get answers, right? So let's go get them."

Lauren and Dominic nodded and they walked on in silence, which was precisely what Swati wanted. Silence. The ability to be in this moment—standing on the threshold, she hoped, of a revelation that would explain everything they'd been through, everything they'd lost, and what they should do next. If she'd been alone, Swati would have sat down in the middle of the long corridor, crossed her legs and closed her eyes; instead she breathed deliberately as she walked, trying to open a peaceful space inside herself. Preparing herself to meet whatever might lie on the other side of the corridor.

They came to a place where the corridor widened. Large vertical pipes ran from floor to ceiling along the left side. On the right was a concrete ledge with ladders going down. Another pipe below, large enough for a person to stand in without crouching, portholes at intervals along the top.

They were about halfway through the space when Dominic spoke.

"Hold on."

"What now?" Swati asked.

"Do you hear that?" Dominic turned. In his right hand he held the blade, his knuckles paling as his grip tightened around it—and just as he turned back to face the dark corridor from which they'd come, there was a crack of gunfire.

Dominic's shoulder snapped back as if yanked by an invisible hand. Blood misted warm on Swati's face, then went immediately cold in the underground air. Swati looked down. Dominic was on the ground.

"Run!" he shouted.

She looked up. Down the corridor, in an area of darkness between the overhead lights, a figure came toward them, arm outstretched. There was a flash of white, another loud crack. Swati dove to the ground, pushed herself against the wall into the space between two pipes. Then she looked back to the center of the corridor and saw that Dominic had disappeared too. His blade left behind on the floor, in a puddle of red. She snatched the blade and brought it back into her hiding place.

Lauren, too, was nowhere to be found—but Jane stood in the center of the corridor between the vertical pipes and the concrete ledge.

"*Jane*," Swati hissed. "*Jane, you have to hide.*"

But the girl didn't move—paralysis temporarily added to her muteness. Footsteps tapped closer, but there were no more gunshots.

"Jane," a voice said.

It was Casey.

"It *is* Jane, isn't it? Brandt told me about you."

Jane didn't say anything.

"I'm not going to kill you," Casey said. "Brandt told me not to. He wants you to come back. He wants you with him. But I need to find the others. Jane. Look at me. Where are they?"

Jane's eyes darted down to the place where Swati hid, then back up to Casey—a movement so quick Swati couldn't be sure if she was about to give her up or not.

"Just point," Casey said. "All you have to do is point. I'll do the rest."

Jane turned around and pointed to the other end of the large space, past the pipes.

"Okay," Casey said. "Okay."

Now there came the sound of shuffling footsteps. Jane turned, stepped aside, meeting Swati's eyes once more as she put her heels to the ledge. Swati nodded, gripped the blade, brought it up above her shoulder.

She saw the gun first, the tip of the barrel, peeking out from around the pipe. Then Casey's hand, then his arm, then all of him, advancing forward, quivering, intent on the other side of the corridor.

Swati leapt forward and swung the blade down at Casey's arm.

Maybe she'd watched too many movies. She'd half-thought that the blade would take Casey's arm clean off, amputate it with a single swipe. But it was a dull blade, designed for cutting paper, and it only lodged in Casey's forearm, sunk a half-inch into his flesh with a wet thud that vibrated sickeningly up Swati's arm. Casey grunted, screamed. His arm bent. The blade clattered to the ground. Swati looked down at it, then back up at Casey.

"You fucking bitch!" he yelled, turning toward her with the gun.

Swati's stomach bubbled to the back of her throat.

He hadn't even dropped the gun.

Swati closed her eyes and waited for the gunshot, wondered momentarily if she'd feel anything, any pain, before death turned everything black.

But the gunshot didn't come—only another grunt, a fall, and she opened her eyes to see Casey sprawled on the ground. Behind him, gripping at his ankle, was Dominic, reaching up from below the concrete ledge to yank Casey's feet out from under him. His head poked just above the ledge; she met his eyes.

"The gun!" he yelled.

Stunned, seemingly unable to move, she looked down. The gun was at her feet. Casey reached, strained against Dominic's grip to snatch for it. Just as Swati saw it, just as her brain was beginning to catch up to what had happened while her eyes had been closed, and sending, finally, a message to her body to move, to grab at the gun before Casey's fingers could touch it, another hand stole into her field of vision and clutched the gun.

Swati looked up. Jane.

Jane met Swati's eyes, then looked at the gun in her hand.

"Point it at him," Swati suggested.

Jane stepped back and straightened her arm, pointed the gun down at Casey's head. He kept on struggling, kicking against Dominic's grip on his foot, trying to lunge toward Swati and Jane.

Swati gave him a kick in the torso—soft, not as hard as she could have kicked, but enough to send a message. Casey went still.

"Enough," Swati said. "It's over."

· · ·

They got Casey propped up against a wall. He cradled his arm, the one Swati had gouged, but Dominic had it worse—blood was streaming from his shoulder, soaking through his shirt. He hissed every time he moved.

"You okay?" Swati asked.

"I'll be fine," Dominic said, and nodded at Casey. "Focus on him."

Swati looked back down. Casey's eyes were on Jane, who held the gun pointed toward him. He looked like he might have been wondering if Jane knew how to work the gun, and whether he had the guts to risk it.

"Hey," Swati said, and snapped her fingers. "Look at me."

Every ounce of grace had left her body, everything she practiced yoga and mindfulness to cultivate simply gone in a sudden flood of rage. She wished the blade had been sharper, that she *had* simply chopped Casey's arm off.

"What did you do with Jacob?"

Casey winced, cradled his arm. "I killed him," he said. Trying to make it sound nonchalant, like he didn't care, but it didn't come off.

"Why?" Swati asked, her heart squeezing as she forced herself to stay focused.

"Brandt told me to."

"Brandt," Swati said. "You've spoken with him?"

Casey was silent. Staring at her with a challenge in his eyes, to make sure she knew the silence was deliberate.

Swati lifted her foot and put it on Casey's arm, the bad one. She pressed down. Casey groaned.

"Swati," Lauren said from somewhere at her back, but Swati could scarcely hear her. She was imagining Casey killing Jacob, imagining looking him in his dumb doe eyes and shooting him. Her foot pressed down harder. Casey's groan rose in pitch to a desperate whine.

"There's no point in this," Swati said. "We've got a gun, and a blade. You killed for Brandt; you want to die for him too?"

"Fine," Casey grunted. "You win."

Swati took her foot away. Casey gasped, breathed out.

"Okay," she said. "So, you were saying. You communicated with Brandt."

"He emailed me," Casey said. "About a week ago."

"And?"

"And I thought it was a joke at first. Someone playing a prank on me. People knew we were working because we thought Brandt was still alive—I thought someone was having some fun. One of the other temps. But then he gave me a code to get into the tunnel, invited me to come see him. And it worked."

Dominic stepped forward. "So he really is alive? You actually saw him?"

"I did," Casey said. "I've been up Parnassus Tower and saw him with my own eyes."

"What did he say? Did he tell you the meaning of all of this?"

*All of this.* Swati heard herself say it. She'd begun to talk like the others, expecting Brandt to hold the answers not just to Delphi Enterprises or the gas but to everything—the very meaning of life.

"No," Casey said. "He only said that there was someone digging through Delphi's data warehouse, and he wanted me to stop him before he got too deep."

"He told you to kill Jacob."

"Not in so many words," Casey said. "He didn't use Jacob's name, only told me when and where to find him. And he didn't tell me to kill him, either. But he did give me the gun."

"And the power?" Lauren asked. "The food? He told you to do all that too?"

"Yes," Casey said.

"So he wanted you to kill everyone," Swati said. "Not just Jacob."

Casey shook his head. "That's not—I don't think that's what he wanted. I thought he was probably trying to . . ." He drifted off, staring forward.

"What?" Swati asked, trying to resist the anger surging inside her, the overpowering urge to step on his wound again. "Trying to what?"

"I thought he was just trying to introduce some new variables," Casey said. "Speed up the experiment. Bring it to an end."

"He told you that?" Lauren asked. "He said it was an experiment?"

"I didn't ask," Casey said. "I only did what he told me to."

A grunt of annoyance rattled in Dominic's throat. "He doesn't know anything. This is pointless." He turned to Jane, took the gun out of her hand, then gave it to Swati.

Swati looked at the gun, turned it over. "What's this for?"

"He killed Jacob," Dominic said. "You should be the one."

She swallowed. "Is the safety . . . ?"

"It's off," Dominic said. "How do you think he shot me?"

"Wait," Casey said, pushing himself up straighter against the wall. "Hang on a second. You said that if I talked—"

Swati pointed the gun at his head, and his arms shot up.

"Swati, please. Let's talk about this. You don't have to—"

"Shut up," Swati said, silencing him. "You shut the fuck up. If you talk one more time I swear to God I'm going to shoot you through the fucking head."

Casey closed his eyes. His eyelids sheared away two tears onto his cheeks. His arms, still upheld, began to quiver.

Swati put her finger against the trigger, felt the pressure of it. She took a couple steps forward, put the barrel of the gun directly on Casey's forehead.

"Swati." Lauren's voice. "Swati, you don't want to do this."

Swati tried to summon the anger she'd felt just moments earlier—the overpowering rage that had led her to step on Casey's wound. But she couldn't find it. The feeling that rose up in its stead was one of utter revulsion. To kill Casey, all she'd have to do was put some pressure on the trigger with her finger. But should couldn't do it. Not without vomiting all over the floor.

She stepped back and let her arm fall.

"I can't," she said, looking at Dominic. "I'm sorry. I just can't."

Casey's eyes snapped open. He began to cry with relief.

Dominic sighed. "Well, we can't have him following us."

Swati handed him the gun. "You do it then."

Dominic stepped toward Casey and cracked him across the face with the butt of the gun. He slumped to the ground, unconscious.

"There," Dominic said. "Let's keep going."

• • •

Dominic moved out ahead of the group as they walked through the final stretch of the tunnel. His shoulder throbbed with every heartbeat but otherwise felt numb. That was probably a bad sign; the lack of feeling could mean nerve damage, shock, or even that he was about to pass out from blood loss. But Dominic didn't stop, didn't even slow when the tunnel grew brighter, the lights stronger and more frequent as they came to the foot of Parnassus Tower. The only thing that mattered was getting to Brandt.

They came to a reinforced door. Dominic tried the knob. Locked.

"Code," he said. "Enter it."

Jane stepped forward and entered the numbers, giving him a concerned look out of the corner of her eye. The others were quiet. Dominic knew he was worrying them, scaring them even, knew he'd begun to act frenzied and crazy since talking with Casey. The circumstances seemed to call for it. He kept his eyes on the keypad. When it turned green, he seized the doorknob again. This time, it turned.

They came into a basement room, well-lit, with dark concrete walls and television screens from floor to ceiling. The screens were on, cycling through security feeds of the Delphi complex. Most of the screens showed empty rooms, unoccupied workstations, but now and then a screen would blink to a shot of the temps milling around the cafeteria, doing their made-up work in their cubicles on the second floor, or slumped exhausted on the floor of the party room in various states of undress, a strobe still blinking in time with inaudible EDM.

Dominic moved through the room as the others lingered by the door. He looked at the screens, glanced at a coffee mug on a table, then found a webbed steel locker in a corner. He nudged the door; it drifted open, unlatched.

Inside were weapons—handguns identical to the one they'd taken off Casey.

"Security room," he said. "This must be how Brandt was keeping tabs on us. How he knew Jacob had gotten into the Brain."

Lauren came into the room and pointed at a screen. "Look."

Dominic turned his head. The screen Lauren was pointing at showed an image of the tunnel, the pipes running up the wall and beneath the concrete ledge. Dominic moved closer, squinting. Just visible past one of the pipes were Casey's feet, his heels on the ground and his toes pointing straight up at the ceiling. Then the image flipped, showed an empty kitch-enette and eating area.

"If anyone was watching . . ." Lauren started to say.

"I know," Dominic said.

They went down a dark cinderblock hall, the air cool and dank, then up a staircase to an unlocked door. They came out into a glass lobby. Dominic blinked as the sinking sun pierced his eyes. A reception desk loomed at the end of the lobby. Above the desk, a shiny metal sculpture of the Delphi logo was mounted on a stone wall.

Dominic stopped. Lauren drew up even with him. He felt her eyes on him.

"Dominic?" she asked. "You okay?"

He looked at her. "We're here."

She nodded. "I know."

But she didn't, not really—didn't know what it meant to him, anyway. This had been what he wanted since the beginning, ever since he read about Tristan Brandt for business school: he wanted to gain entry to Delphi Enterprises, work his way up through the corporate bureaucracy, climb the org chart, then eventually ascend the heights of Parnassus Tower, meet the great man himself. He'd felt he was destined for it, and it turned out he'd been right—but he'd never thought it would be like this, storming the holy of holies rather than being invited in, holding a gun in his hand. Was he pausing at the threshold because he was overcome by achieving his dream—or because he knew that as soon as he climbed into those elevators his dream would be dead forever?

Dominic stayed planted to the floor long enough that eventually the women walked ahead of him, and he found himself having to hustle to keep up. They passed the empty reception desk and clicked down a shiny marble floor past a bank of elevators. Lauren hit the button, and one of the elevators dinged immediately, the up arrow lit red. Inside, Dominic hit the button for 50—the top floor. The elevator zoomed up.

"Here we go," he said as the doors opened.

They stepped off the elevator into another large reception area. The room was the shape of a large oval, the walls covered in light wooden paneling. Sleek couches, chairs, and tables in a Scandinavian style: hard lines, low-slung. The oval shape of the room was cut in half by a solid wall in darker wood, reddish-brown, with a double door set in the middle of it. Opposite the double-door was a stone slab of a desk, another oval. Jane moved toward the desk and ran her hands over the surface. She seemed to let out a hard breath. Then, after a moment, she moved around the desk and sat. She set her head against the webbed back of the chair and closed her eyes. Dominic watched her and understood that the chair, and the desk, had been hers once, before all this.

Then her head snapped up at a sound. Dominic followed her gaze to a place alongside the desk, where a gap between the wall and the tall windows on the other side of the room suggested a corridor leading to more rooms. Footsteps shuffled down the hall, growing louder—and then a man walked into the room. He wore a white button-up shirt, gone yellow around the neck, over a similarly stained undershirt. He wore no pants, the bulge of a pair of briefs just visible beneath the hanging tails of the unbuttoned shirt. Argyle socks on his feet, yanked high on his calves.

The man was looking down as he padded into the room, poking with a spoon at an opened jar. As he came around the desk he took the spoon out of the jar and put it in his mouth—then he looked up and froze when he saw them.

There came a voice from the hall. "Did you fucking steal my peanut butter again?" Another man came into the room, wearing blue jeans and a polo shirt. His face looked similar to the first man—both were white, both slightly bald and gray, both middle-aged, fit, and beginning to wrinkle.

The first man, button-up, pulled the spoon out of his mouth and pointed at Jane. "Look who it is," he said, his voice muffled by the glob of peanut butter in his mouth.

"Holy shit," said polo shirt. "Jane. We thought you were dead."

Dominic stepped forward. "Which one of you is Brandt?"

The men looked at him. "Neither of us," said polo shirt.

Button-up shook his head. "Nope." He smacked his lips, swallowed. "I'm Brandt 1. This is Brandt 2."

"Doubles?" Dominic asked.

Button-up, Brandt 1, nodded.

"So the real Brandt—was that him in the amphitheater? Is he dead?"

"No," said polo shirt, Brandt 2. "That was Brandt 3."

"Glen," said Brandt 1. "Poor bastard."

"Where's the real Tristan Brandt?" Dominic asked.

Brandt 1 and 2 pointed in unison at the double doors.

"That's his office," said Brandt 1.

Dominic lifted his gun and pointed it at the Brandts. Both lifted their arms in the air. Brandt 1's spoon and jar of peanut butter fell to the floor.

"We're going to go talk to him," said Dominic. "You two better not pull anything while we're in there."

Brandt 2 shook his head. "We're just actors," he said. "That's all. Tristan calls the shots."

Dominic held the gun on them and looked at the others. Swati shrugged. Lauren had already started to move toward the double doors.

"Come on," Swati said. "Put the gun down. I don't think you'll need it."

Dominic lowered the gun, but he didn't drop it.

They went through the double doors into a cramped space, walls and ceiling lined in the same dark wood. Then through another set of doors into Brandt's office.

The room was bigger than the reception area, more apartment than office. There was a desk on one side of the room, the surface done in opaque black glass, but two-thirds of the room was given over to what looked like a living space. A sitting area was furnished with chairs and couches. Free weights, medicine balls, and a freestanding punching bag stood in a workout space. A rectangular table with place settings and a hanging chandelier served as the dining room. A flat-screen TV hung on one wall. And a partition wall cordoned off an area that Dominic guessed Brandt used for bathing, changing his clothes, and sleeping. Beyond it all, at the far end of the room from where they'd entered, marble steps led up to a landing, glass doors leading to a balcony beyond.

On the landing, facing the glass, was a single leather chair; in the chair, framed against the sun setting in a blaze of yellow and red, was the outline of shoulders, a head. A glass of something—bourbon or brandy—sitting on a low table next to the chair.

The figure stood, tossed back the drink, then set it back on the table. He turned and walked down the steps. As he came closer, the glare of the sunset subsided, and Dominic saw a man wearing a perfectly tailored gray suit, tie hanging and coming to a point right at his belt line. As the man walked down the steps he buttoned his suit jacket, then shoved a hand into his pocket as his wingtips tapped on the bottom step, bringing him level with Dominic, Lauren, Swati, and Jane.

The man regarded them from across the room.

"Hello," he said. "My name is Tristan Brandt. I've been waiting for you."

. . .

It was exactly as Lauren had expected it to be—exactly as she'd dreamed it. Standing there at the top floor of Parnassus Tower, her feet planted on a platform far above the ground, she thought of the temple at the peak of Mount Parnassus. The home of Pythia, the Delphic oracle. The oracle's supplicants—philosophers, heroes, and kings—reported seeing a prophet on a tripod throne, steam emanating from a fissure in the mountain beneath her. Sitting on this throne, breathing this mystical vapor, the oracle would intone riddles unlocking the mysteries of her visitors' lives, their fates, their destinies. Was Brandt now that oracle? Was he really so powerful that he'd managed to shift the world's axis to the place where they now stood?

There was a long silence where they all waited for someone else to be the first to speak.

"You have questions," Brandt said at last. "You've come here for answers."

"Yes," Lauren said, stepping forward.

Brandt bowed his head and closed his eyes, then opened them as his head lifted again. An invitation.

"Is it real?" Lauren asked.

"Which part?"

"The gas. Did the world really end?"

"The gas is real," Brandt said. "Billions are dead. But the world didn't end. It still hasn't."

The answer seemed designed to push her to other questions—Eschaton, maybe, or Brandt's reasons in choosing them, the temps, to survive. She'd get there.

"Is Delphi responsible for the gas?"

Brandt was silent for a few seconds. Lauren thought maybe he was angry, offended by the question. But when he spoke, his voice was calm.

"Yes and no," Brandt said. "For now let's just say I knew it was going to happen and didn't stop it. I couldn't. These things get their own momentum. At a certain point the only viable option is not prevention, but mitigation. Leveraging, even."

Lauren squinted down and gave her head a shake. *Mitigation. Leveraging.* "I don't understand," Lauren said. "Are you talking about Solution 19?"

"In part," he said.

"What *is* Solution 19?"

"Solution 19," said Brandt, "was a backup plan. Our modeling showed us that an apocalypse event was inevitable within a few years' time. Species-ending, once all the post-event contingencies played out. We didn't think we could stop the event—but some in the company thought we could at least prevent it from leading to the extinction of *Homo sapiens.*"

"And use it to make the Turn," Lauren offered.

Brandt smiled. His teeth flashed white in the center of his darkened silhouette. The sunset blazed at his shoulders.

"You've read my memo."

"It read more like a manifesto."

Brandt bowed his head again, assenting to the correction. "In any case, if you've read it, then you know."

"Know what?"

"Our intent was never to destroy. Only to save."

Lauren breathed out in frustration. They'd come for answers, and Brandt claimed to be willing to give them—but already she felt like she understood less than she had when she walked into his office. Lauren glanced at Swati and Dominic. They nodded her on. She turned back to Brandt and took a few steps closer.

"You saved *us*," she said. "Why? Was it an accident, or did you choose us?"

"You survived," Brandt said, "because a computer algorithm selected your psychometric profiles out of millions as potential candidates for a society that I am designing, prototyping, and developing as a replacement to this one. This chaotic society that died in the gas."

Lauren was about to ask her next question when Swati cut in.

"If all this is true," Swati asked, "then why the cover-up? Why did you kill Jacob?"

Brandt looked past Lauren to Swati and blinked, seemingly surprised at the question. "There's no cover-up. Jacob's fine."

"But Casey said—"

"Exactly what I told him to. Everything you've been through—everything since the gas—has been a test designed, by me, to determine which of you are worthy."

"Worthy," Lauren repeated.

"Of moving to the next step of the experiment."

"Jacob's alive?" Swati asked, her voice gone thin and airy, like she might suddenly be struggling to breathe. She put a hand on her chest, clutching invisible pearls. "Can I see him?"

"Soon," Brandt said.

Lauren studied him, looked at his face, weighed his expression. "There's really an Eschaton?"

He met her eyes. "Eschaton is real," he said. "It's waiting for you. Waiting for all of—"

Brandt stopped talking. Everything in him seemed suddenly to break—his voice cracking, the lines of his face tearing and wrinkling like crumpled wax paper, his back jerking to a hunch. A keening sound escaped him, his hand came up to visor his eyes, and his mouth stretched into a shape that looked at once like a smile and a grimace. It was a few seconds before Lauren realized he'd started crying.

"Oh God," he wept. "I can't do this. I can't fucking do this."

He dropped his hand. Tears were pouring out of his eyes. He shuddered, then broke into a run. Lauren stepped back as Brandt barreled headlong toward her, thinking he'd lost his mind and was about to attack her—but then just before he collided with her, he veered. Lauren spun around to watch as he flew past Swati and Dominic, then slid to his knees in front of Jane. He grabbed Jane around the waist and buried his head in her stomach.

"Jane, I'm sorry," he sobbed, clutching at her, the sound of his voice muffled in her shirt. "It wasn't supposed to be like this."

Jane's arms were held out, not touching him, and the look on her face was so peculiar: a mixture of absence and discomfort, the face a person makes when their body is being used for something they don't enjoy, a blood draw or pelvic exam. But her expression also bore a trace of annoyance, of exasperation, as if Brandt were a child, she a mother too frazzled to deal with his latest tantrum. As if this wasn't the first time Brandt had forced her to adopt this posture, to put up with this humiliation.

As if, Lauren thought, this had happened to Jane before.

# SIXTEEN

Jane had never been much of a talker. As a child, her first word didn't come until the age of two; in school, she never raised her hand and stammered when called upon. She was a puzzlement to her father, a talker by trade—a trial lawyer, rhetorician, and raconteur. He was rarely out of the office, except to drink martinis by the quart at his favorite bar, but in the thin strips of time he did spend at home, his preferred method of bonding with his children was verbal sparring. At the dinner table he'd arrange debates between her older brothers, preside like a judge over their arguing and scold them for lazy thinking, fallacies in logic. "Spit it out, girl!" he'd boom to Jane when he turned to her for an opinion on the topic of the day—if superior smarts or strength were more valuable in dealing with bullies on the playground, the relative merits of an earned versus freely given allowance, whether or not their mother was trying to choke them all with this dry fucking roast. His breath hot and foul with gin and olive brine. All Jane could manage, inevitably, was a stutter.

Her parents brought her to speech therapists periodically throughout her childhood, but each of the experts said the same thing: there was nothing wrong with her. She was capable of speaking, and in fact she did quite well in some contexts—speaking cogently one-on-one, voluminously to herself, to dolls or imaginary friends—but when she had an audience of more than one or two, her words simply dried up, turned to sand in her mouth.

Jane couldn't explain it, even to herself. She knew she had poetry in her—beautiful language, moving speeches. She was smarter than her stupid brothers, who teased and tormented her when her mother wasn't around to scold them. The problem came in bringing what was inside out. Somewhere between her mind and her mouth, the signal got garbled, and that inner poetry became stumbling, mumbling, stuttering. It was painful, this inability to express what was inside her. And so, most often, she simply chose not to speak.

She did fine in school, managed As and Bs. She worked hard, was good at math and writing. Class speeches and presentations were painful, her knees quaking visibly, her breath coming fast and panicked between every word. Her classmates looking down, coughing awkwardly, even the mean kids embarrassed for her. After she graduated from high school she decided not to go on to college. Instead, she took online courses to become an executive assistant.

She practiced obsessively for her Delphi interview, delivering a speech to the mirror—then, after the HR lady began asking questions, she went back to direct quotations from the speech: *I am organized. I am smart. I am proactive. I am conscientious.*

"You don't talk much, do you?" a man interjected, his presence in the interview unexplained. Jane would later learn that this man was Tristan Brandt.

Jane turned to him, trying to formulate a response, fearing the usual physiological responses: sweaty palms, shaking voice, shortness of breath. But there was something strangely calming in the man's face. She focused on his eyes, anchored herself there, and delivered her one extemporaneous answer—to this day, one of the proudest moments of her life:

"As I understand it, my job isn't to talk. It's to listen to you talk."

He laughed, and offered her the job on the spot.

• • •

Tristan Brandt reminded Jane of her father. Brandt's profession, like her father's, seemed to be talking—talking in meetings, talking in presentations, talking to the press. He was always polished, always eloquent; when he spoke, others went silent, leaning forward with expressions of intense concentration. Jane imagined this was how her father was at work, though she'd never witnessed him in the office, or in court. But by the way he behaved at home Jane simply assumed he was the kind of man who dominated his audience with words, opening his mouth and letting perfectly formed sentences and crystalline thoughts just fall out.

There was one crucial difference between the two men: Brandt was kind. He could push others around when he wanted to, browbeat and belittle—Jane had seen him do it in meetings, to underlings who weren't performing to his liking. But Brandt always spoke gently to her. He thanked her constantly, told her she was doing a good job. "If only all of my employees were as good as you," he'd say aloud in others' hearing when Jane materialized at his shoulder with something he wanted before he'd even asked for it—a pen, a handkerchief, a printed document containing the exact information he needed right that second. At the end of a particularly productive day, before sending her home, he'd look her in the eye and say, "Jane, I don't know what I'd do without you." His hand brushing her arm as she blushed and turned away, mumbling her thanks.

She'd do anything for him—she felt this intensely, felt the danger in it, but also the rightness. She was his assistant. Doing what he said was her job. In his presence she felt ushered into peacefulness for the first time in her life. Surrounded by his brilliant words, his ever-flowing business talk, it was impossible to be angry anymore about her own inability to speak, to adequately express her own thoughts. Orbiting in the gravitational pull of his charisma, she felt completely at rest, exactly where she was meant to be. What could she give him in exchange—except everything?

This sense of wanting to give herself over to him was amplified by her parallel sense that Brandt was deeply unhappy, lacking in some fundamental way in spite of his brilliance, his company, his money. He was married, but she knew (because he told her) that his marriage was an unhappy one. His wife didn't understand him, didn't even love him, he suspected, spending all her time and affection instead on their son.

"I shouldn't be burdening you like this," Brandt would say to Jane at the end of these confessions. "But you're the only one I can talk to."

He worked longer and longer hours, until Jane began to suspect that he was no longer going home. He was already in his office when she arrived at seven in the morning, there still when she went home at six in the evening. Once, arriving even earlier than usual to transcribe some meeting notes, she poked her head in his office and heard, from behind the partition wall, the sound of Brandt brushing his teeth at an unseen sink, rinsing and spitting. Arranging for Brandt's dry cleaning, she began to have his garments picked up and delivered to his office rather than his house.

Gradually, there were other worrying signs as well, red flags not just of strife at home, but of stress at work. Once tireless and energetic in the office, Brandt began to sigh with exhaustion between one task and another, clutching his glasses between his fingers and driving the heels of his hands into his eyes. The lines of his face began to deepen, his skin took on a grayish hue, and he began to lose weight. He stopped going to meetings, sending one of his proxies instead, the doubles hired to be Brandt's eyes and ears in a company grown too large to be managed by one person. Increasingly, the documents Jane brought him from other departments—reports, recommendations, and project progress summaries for his review and approval—seemed to be bringing him grief. The stacks of paper were labeled with obscure project names like *Apocalypse*, *Oracle*, and *Eschaton*. Brandt thanked Jane for bringing them to him, thanked her again for taking them away, but the data contained in these documents made him sad more than anything. Jane wondered privately if perhaps the company wasn't doing so well, if after a run of successes with Safe-T-Knife™ and Concierge Brandt had made some miscalculation and now the company was posting losses for the first time in years. She almost asked him, then thought better of it—her job was not to speak, to offer ideas of her own, but only to enable Brandt's innate greatness to issue into the world unencumbered.

Sometimes she glanced at the documents she brought in to Brandt's office, but lacking any context, she rarely understood what she read. Once, she brought in a manila folder labeled *Eschaton Solutions*. Brandt reviewed the documents for an hour, then called her back in to transcribe his notes and send them back to the junior VP who'd sent the recommendations. Brandt's responses were scrawled in pen on the documents themselves, labeled 1 through 19. Most of the recommendations Brandt had simply dismissed out of hand: "Impractical," he wrote on Solution 1, "Think bigger" on Solution 5, "Low impact" on Solution 8, "Too many contingencies" on

Solution 11. The only sheet that had garnered a remotely positive response had been Solution 19.

"Interesting thought work," Brandt had written. "Keep pushing."

• • •

A week later, Jane brought in another dossier, the tab on the folder reading *Apocalypse Model Predictions*. She walked the files into Brandt's office around four, then went to her desk to finish some final tasks. She went back into Brandt's office two hours later to see if there was anything else he needed from her before she left for the day.

She found him sitting on a couch, hunched over the papers splayed on the teak coffee table before him. He was crying—the pinched sort of crying men do, quaking silently at the shoulders, leaking from the eyes and nose, muffled sobs only just barely escaping from pressed lips.

"I'm sorry," he said, looking up as Jane rushed to him. "You shouldn't see me like this."

"Mr. Brandt," she said breathlessly, sitting next to him. She was intently aware of her hands—should she touch him? Put a hand on his shoulder? He'd touched her so many times before, brushing her upper arm or the small of her back in brief expressions of gratitude, but she'd never dared to touch him; it would've been like touching a shaman, a wizard, a god. She decided to keep her hands in her lap.

"Can I get you anything?" she asked.

Brandt covered his face. "A bourbon," he said into his hands. "Neat."

Jane got up and crossed the room to the decanter. When she came back she saw that there was another glass already on the coffee table, empty. That was another similarity between Brandt and her father—both were drinkers, though Brandt liked whiskey while her father was partial to gin. As she came to the couch he turned, as though he'd been watching and waiting for her to approach. He stole his arms around her waist, buried his head in her stomach.

Jane froze. Brandt's face was warm against her skin, the heat of it burning through the thin silk blouse she was wearing. He made a muffled sobbing sound, and she felt a wetness bleed through the fabric.

"I don't know how much longer I can do this," he said. "I can't take it anymore."

Jane still held the whiskey in her hand. She glanced at the glass, then at the table; there was no way she could reach far enough to set it down, not in this position. She put her other hand in Brandt's thinning hair, curled her fingers in it.

"There, there," she said, a useless consolation, but it was what her mother always said to her when her brothers or her father had driven her to tears. "It's going to be all right."

Brandt stood up and put his mouth on hers. His breath was hot with whiskey—he was already drunk. Then she felt his hand curl around her breast, and it surprised her so much that she dropped the glass. It shattered on the marble floor. The sound parted them.

"Oh," she said, putting her hand to her mouth as if the mistake were hers, as if she was the one who'd overstepped a boundary.

"It's okay," he said, waving dismissively at the mess. "The maid will get it. It's okay."

He wobbled on his feet, closed and opened his eyes in a slow blink. Jane took advantage of the moment to shift the balance and become his assistant again, pretend the preceding advance had never happened. She grasped him by the shoulders and helped lower him to the couch.

"Mr. Brandt," she said, "I think you should lie down."

"I'm fine," he slurred, his back lowering to the cushions. "I'm going to be fine."

She propped a pillow under his head, then cleaned up the mess. The glass had shattered clean into seven large shards; she palmed them to the garbage, then mopped up the spilled whiskey with a cloth. Then she turned back to the couch.

Brandt was asleep.

. . .

Jane gathered up the papers from the coffee table and fled the room. At the door, she gave a single glance back. Brandt snored, his mouth wide open.

Jane took the papers to her desk, then began scanning Brandt's notes to send back to the person who'd submitted them for review, an associate project manager for the Eschaton initiative. She gave the sheets a glance as they passed through the scanner—charts and graphs, a rectangular map of the world with alarming red color blooms pockmarked here and there, like mushroom clouds seen from space. Each report ended with a list of code outputs she didn't know how to read, culminating with the same message every time: *Comp Sys Fail.* Brandt's scribbled notes on these pages ran a spectrum from befuddled to aggrieved to angry, the handwriting getting progressively messier as Jane got to the bottom of the stack.

*How is this possible?*

*Double-check accuracy of modeling software*

*Need more variables*

*There must be some way to improve these outcomes*

*Completely unacceptable*

*How are we not having ANY impact?!*

*For fuck's sake*

Then, scrawled across the last page in thick black pen, the jagged letters barely legible: *Exterminate them all.*

Jane chilled at this last note—what did it mean? Exterminate who, or what? What were these reports? It wasn't for her to ask these questions. She dutifully scanned the pages, then attached the scans to an email to the associate project manager and hit *Send.* The computer made a whooshing sound as the file left her computer and rushed through the ether to its destination somewhere in the Delphi organization.

The door creaked; Jane looked up. Brandt came into the reception room, squinting against the overhead lights. Outside, night had fallen.

"Mr. Brandt," Jane said. "Do you need anything?"

He blinked hard, using all the muscles in his face. His headache must have been tremendous. Jane wondered what he remembered—if he'd later be able to recall making a pass at her, or even the notes he'd scribbled on the reports. For a moment, she regretted sending them; maybe Brandt had never intended his jottings to be shared, only writing them in a moment of anger, frustration, and drunken weakness.

"I want to show you something," Brandt said.

Jane looked away, wincing. After what had happened in Brandt's office, she didn't want to stay—not while he was drunk and in this state of emotional instability. He didn't seem upset any more, no longer on the edge of tears, but now there had come an icy calm beneath his drunkenness that made her worried. For a moment, she toyed with saying no; maybe her insubordination would be another thing he forgot, once he sobered up. But he was her boss. She couldn't refuse.

"Okay," she said.

Brandt went back into his office, then returned with an object in his hand. When he came closer, Jane saw it was a syringe.

"Roll up your sleeve," he said, grasping her hand.

She felt her heart beat in her throat. "Hang on . . . I don't really want—"

But it was too late; Brandt had already jammed the needle into her upper arm, piercing right through her blouse.

"There," Brandt said. "Now you're immune."

"Immune to what?"

"You'll see."

They took the elevator down, past the first floor, past even the tunnel level, and into a subbasement.

"You ever been down here?" Brandt asked.

Jane shook her head and followed Brandt down some corridors, then into a dark room. Brandt hit a switch and the lights came on.

The room was large as a gymnasium, with concrete walls and ceilings. On the floor, lined in neat rows and columns, were dozens of upright metal cylinders. Jane glanced at Brandt. He looked over the cylinders with a strange look on his face, like that of a father gazing upon a failed child, a family embarrassment. She'd seen that look before—it was the expression her own father had turned on her whenever she stammered at the dinner table.

"What is this?" Jane asked.

"A mistake," Brandt said. "Early on, after the success of Safe-T-Knife™, I got cocky. It had saved so many lives, I started to get excited about the idea of consumer products saving the world. So I acquired a pharma company that was working on an experimental drug—the ultimate antidepressant, they called it. They didn't even know what they had."

The slur in Brandt's voice had diminished, as though his fervency was sweeping away the effects of the alcohol on his brain.

"I saw the patents—the company had come up with a chemical mechanism to target the brain's centers of negative emotion. Evolutionary impulses to dominance, anger, hatred, fear. They'd pitched it as an antidepressant, but I knew it was more than that. It was a solution to the problem of human pain, of violence. I envisioned selling it over the counter in an inhalable form, pricing it cheap, adding something to make it a little habit-forming, maybe. Can you imagine it?" He glanced toward her, a small smile on his face, Brandt the persuasive leader, the guru CEO, momentarily restored. "Millions of people, billions, walking around with the drug, inhaling it through nebulizers, cigarettes, pipes, vape pens, taking hits of it throughout the day. Constantly depressing their impulses to violence, to cruelty. Experiencing joy. True joy."

He glanced back to the cylinders, walked toward one, ran his palm up its smooth metal casing. There was something sexual in the movement, something masturbatory—and Jane took a step away from him, thinking again of what had happened in the office, and of what strange sexual fantasies he might be entertaining now. Something had broken between them in the last two hours; Jane could see now that Brandt was like her father in all the bad ways too.

Brandt let his hand drop. "But it didn't work. As soon as we acquired the company and all the patents, the trials started going bad. The drug targeted all the right brain centers, but it did the opposite of what it was supposed to. Small doses of the drug resulted in a higher incidence of anger and violence issues, suicidal ideation, depression. Large doses turned test subjects into . . . I don't know—*animals*. People became possessed by all the evolutionary impulses we were trying to suppress."

"What went wrong?"

"I thought for a while that the company falsified their reporting to make the drug more appealing to potential buyers," Brandt said. "Or that the problems started when we went from lab rats to humans. But now, I'm starting to think my mistake was not a scientific one, but a philosophical one."

"Philosophical?"

Brandt turned and looked at her. "I thought there was something to the human person aside from fear and anger. Something deeper, something better. I was wrong. There's nothing. Negative feeling—evil, for lack of a better term—is the fundamental ground of humanity."

Jane looked away and cast her eyes over the room, the cylinders standing straight like totems, altars to some unknown god.

"So you're just . . . abandoning it down here?"

"No," Brandt said. "Repackaging it. As a chemical weapon. We're looking for buyers now."

Suddenly Jane felt very cold, and she knew what the cylinders reminded her of.

Missiles. They looked like missiles.

• • •

A month passed without event. Brandt recovered, stopped crying, stopped drinking. Jane went to work on time, left on time. She waited to walk into Brandt's office until she knew there were others meeting with him already, placed documents on his desk and slid them across rather than walking around to hand them to him directly. Only belatedly did she realize what she was doing: trying to keep from being alone with him, staying out of his arms' reach.

It wasn't difficult. After the night he made a pass at her and then took her into the sublevel to show her the chemical weapons cache, he threw himself into preparations for an upcoming meeting, to be held with all regular employees in Delphi's amphitheater. Brandt didn't tell her the purpose of this meeting, didn't involve her in his speechwriting (he seemed to be keeping his distance from her too), but she sensed that it must be something big. He took visitors all day, sitting down with a rotation of junior and senior vice presidents, departments heads, portfolio directors.

On the morning of the all-company meeting, Jane could scarcely concentrate. The whole company seemed to be holding its breath, employees talking to each other in hushed voices as she passed through the Parnassus building on her way to her desk. The sunshine at the top of the tower was brilliant, eye-blindingly white as it flared through the ceiling-high windows encircling her desk. A yellow envelope waited on her keyboard. Jane sat down and picked it up. It was an interoffice mail envelope, addressed to Brandt. She picked it up and unlooped the string tying it closed, nudged the papers out onto her desk.

"S19 prep complete," read a sticky note at the top of the stack, "ready at your go." Underneath were shipping forms, customs reports, bills of lading for freight sent to Delphi property holdings in New York, Los Angeles, London, Tokyo, Moscow. Shipments scattered like dandelion seeds across the globe. "Hazardous Materials," the freight descriptions read, "very volatile."

Jane stood up and walked the papers into Brandt's office.

"Mr. Brandt?" she called into the space, but there was no answer. He was gone.

She went back to her desk with the papers and stared at her blank screen. She hadn't even turned her computer on yet. After a few minutes she stood and went back to the elevator, took it down past the first floor to the second sublevel. She took the same corridors she'd taken with Brandt a month earlier, but when she came to the metal door, her security badge wouldn't let her in. She peeked through the square window. All the cylinders were gone.

She stepped back, breathing heavy. Her back hit the opposite wall. Then she heard something—footsteps, hushed voices, creaking, and the trundling of wheels.

"Hello?" she called into the dark hall. There was no answer. The sounds continued, got more distant, and she moved toward them.

She speedwalked blind through corridors she'd never been in before, stopped at turns to listen and pick a direction. The corridors grew darker, then brighter; she ran up a concrete ramp to a set of double doors and pushed through.

Jane blinked at the blinding sunlight. The world blazed white, then dimmed, the landscape taking shape around her as her eyes readjusted. She stood at the foot of the Parnassus Building, at a shipping entrance; a long strip of sidewalk ribboned its way across the green grass toward the main Delphi complex. A pair of figures were halfway down the sidewalk, pushing something.

"Hey!" she yelled, and the figures turned. She ran toward them, trying not to lose her balance on her high heels. As she came closer she saw that the figures were both men in their thirties: one wore a shirt and tie, the other wore the gray uniform of a Delphi facilities worker. The latter pushed a cart to which a gray metallic cylinder had been strapped, lying horizontal.

"What are you doing?" Jane asked, breathless from running. She'd lost her shoes on the path, and now approached the two men in bare feet.

"Just moving something," the man in the tie said.

"Do you know who I am?" Jane asked.

"Should I?"

"I'm Tristan Brandt's personal assistant. Tell me what you're doing with that." She pointed to the cylinder. The missile.

"I'm not supposed to talk about it," the man said. He wasn't blinking, and there was a quaver in his voice, as if he wasn't quite sure that what he was doing was right, now that he'd been found out. "My boss told me—he said the order came from Brandt."

"Then why don't I know about it?" This was false bluster—plenty of Brandt's directives trickled down into the organization without passing through Jane first.

The man licked his lips with a dart of his tongue. "What's his announcement today?"

"What?"

"The all-company. Brandt is speaking. What's it about?"

Jane shook her head. "You know I can't tell you that." A half-truth: she couldn't tell him because she didn't know.

The man stepped closer to her. "It's Eschaton, isn't it? That's the rumor."

Jane felt off-balance. The man was standing too close to her. Her heels wobbled on the edge of the sidewalk; she stepped backward, the grass prickling up between her toes.

"Eschaton," she said. "I keep seeing that word. What is it?"

The man's eyes bulged. "The new world." The muscles in his face eased, a new confidence settling there. He shook his head and turned away. "Come on," he said to the facilities worker. "Let's keep going. She doesn't know anything. No authority."

The facilities man hesitated. "Maybe we should wait," he said. "Get confirmation before we do this."

The man in the tie joined him at the back of the cart and began pushing, leaning forward against the weight of the cylinder, his tendons straining beneath his dress socks.

"It's a secret project," he assured the facilities man. "Secret orders. Trust me. Brandt will reward you for this, when the Eschaton comes."

"Stop," Jane pled, running around to the front of the cart. She tried to push it the other way, but only managed to divert its momentum down the sidewalk. The corner wheel thudded off the concrete and into the grass. The facilities man fell to his knees. The cart juddered. Then one of the straps snapped, and the cylinder rolled off the cart.

"Fuck," the facilities man said as the cylinder clanged on the ground. For a moment it lay inert, and all three of them were frozen.

Then a puff of yellow gas plumed out of a seam in the metal, and Jane couldn't see anything.

. . .

She must have gone unconscious for a moment or two, because she awoke on the grass, surrounded by a yellow fog so thick she could scarcely see her own hands when she held them in front of her face. Her lungs ached, and as she lay there the ache spread from her lungs throughout her body. Soon—it was hard to say how soon—her entire body felt like it was on fire. The pain obliterated her thoughts. Perhaps she screamed, perhaps she convulsed; it was hard to say in that blinding white agony, which seemed to have dissolved her limbs.

And then, just as quickly, the pain passed. Jane sensed somehow that something had been rearranged, the paths in her mind disconnected, scrambled, and rerouted. Brandt had given her the antidote, he'd told her she was immune—but perhaps in blocking the chemical agent from targeting her brain's centers for rage, and aggression, and fear, it had diverted the gas into other neurological hubs, rewiring her brain in other ways.

She sat up and put a hand to her head, which ached as though from a night of drinking. Then she heard something. Animal, guttural. Snarling. She tried to call out—*hello?*—but somehow the word only echoed in her head without coming out of her mouth. Strange, but she didn't think about it. She didn't have time.

Through the haze, off to her left, she spotted a dark figure. Shoulders hunched, stumbling, something gorilla-like in its gait. The figure turned toward her, its head snapping suddenly in her direction as though it smelled her, and with a sudden rush of animal adrenaline Jane realized she was being hunted. Her body went completely still, by some instinct. But it didn't matter. He (the facilities man? the man with the tie?) had spotted her, and she had no camouflage, no natural markings, with which to blend into her environment. The figure lumbered toward her.

And then, suddenly, another object hurtled through the air toward the first figure, flying out of Jane's blind spot. Both figures went to the ground, and through the haze Jane could see one figure close its jaws around the other's neck and snap its head back, ripping the throat from the spine. There came the sound of gurgling. One man lay dead on the grass, the other balanced on his haunches.

Then he turned to Jane.

Panic flooded her veins. She found the ability to move, scrabbling back like a crab. She screamed when she hit an object—the cart. She flipped over, pushed herself to her feet, and sprinted blindly. She heard the snarling behind her and imagined the man morphing into a wolf, literally snapping at her heels. Then something came up out of the fog and bit her foot—or maybe it only seemed to be a bite and was really only a hard, sudden grab. Either way, she fell.

Jane's hands went hard to the grass and closed around something, a smooth and angular object. Her fingers clamored over it: a spike, a strap—one of her high heels. Just as the man's weight launched onto her she flipped onto her back and swung the shoe hard at his head. The heel connected with the side of his head and glanced off; she swung again, and now the heel lodged in his skull, two inches deep.

Blood gushed from his head like sugar pouring from a torn paper sack, splashing hot and viscous over her face, her neck, her clothes. So much blood. The head was full of capillaries, thousands of tiny blood vessels; she'd learned that somewhere. High school health class, maybe. The man's eyes dimmed and he slumped on her. The dead weight of him made it impossible for her to move.

Jane went unconscious once more.

• • •

When Jane woke up again it was dark, with the barest hint of light on the horizon. Evening, or perhaps morning—she couldn't be sure which, because she'd completely lost her sense of direction. The hazy dark had stripped the world of its landmarks. Jane couldn't see Parnassus, couldn't see Delphi. Only the sidewalk, a few feet away from her, was visible.

The man's dead body was still on top of her. Her own body ached with the weight. Her muscles felt weak, inert, but somehow she managed to wriggle out from under him. Then she limped to the sidewalk and followed it to Parnassus, circled around to the front entrance. She tapped her badge on the double doors, but the security pad beeped red, and when she pulled on the handle the door rattled but didn't open.

She tried again and again, pressing her badge against the black security pad and then yanking on the handle. A knot of panic rose up in her throat as the door stayed shut. Had someone changed the security settings? Or was it some emergency protocol, a lockdown mechanism deployed in case of disaster?

Jane leaned against the glass, cupped her hands around her eyes, and looked inside. She didn't see anyone, but she pounded on the glass anyway, and shouted.

Or tried to shout. Because when she opened her mouth to yell *Help*, she was shocked to discover that she couldn't manage anything more than an inchoate bellow. The sound she made didn't even resemble a word. Stunned, she stepped back from the door, looking down at her toenails, and tried to say it again: *help*. But she couldn't. Try as she might, she couldn't convince her lips, her tongue, and her larynx to work together to make the correct sounds. The inability felt like a version of what she'd always struggled with—a disconnect between her brain and her mouth, between her thoughts and her speech. But now it was heightened, no longer a mere disconnect, a garbled signal, but an actual dead end. A gaping chasm had opened up somewhere in her central nervous system. Some mainframe had been hacked, critical wires slashed.

The gas? She'd seen what it had done to those other two men. Was this what it did to her?

Disoriented and light-headed, she circled back around the building and made her way down the sidewalk again. Her limbs had begun to feel rubbery, and her walk was more of a stumble. She shambled along the path for what seemed like a long time. In the distance, the light had gotten brighter—it was morning, then; she'd passed out for most of a day and through the night. When she finally reached the Delphi building she fully expected her badge not to work on that door either, but to her surprise the security pad blinked green. She used the last of her strength to lean the door open. Then she collapsed inside and began to weep. It was a long time before she pulled herself up again—exhausted, mute, hair and skin tight with clotting blood—to look for other survivors.

• • •

Now Jane was back—back in Parnassus, back in Brandt's office, back, even, in the exact physical position she'd been in before Brandt drunkenly threw himself at her: standing, Brandt crying, his face pressed wetly against the soft flesh of her stomach. She looked down at him and wondered: What did he know? Had it been his fault, all along? Or had it been a rogue group within Delphi who'd set the groundwork for the gas, a team of deranged org chart climbers who'd divined some genocidal marching orders from Brandt's more cryptic communications: the memo, the encouraging notes on Solution 19, and *Exterminate them all?*

"Forgive me," Brandt blubbered at her waist. "Jane, please. Forgive me."

But forgive him for what? For kissing her, groping her? For destroying the world? Maybe he didn't even know what he wanted to be absolved of.

"I don't understand. What's going on here?"

Jane looked up. It was Dominic. Jane grabbed Brandt's shoulders and pushed herself away from him, leaving him alone on the floor. Kneeling, listing a little to the left. Jane snapped her fingers at him, then pointed at Dominic. *Answer him.*

"It's all bullshit," Brandt said. "It's all a lie."

Dominic licked his lips, looking like he was thinking. In the long pause, Lauren was the one to take up the questioning next.

"So Eschaton isn't real?"

"It's real," said Brandt. "But it's—it's nothing. Just a tiny little island out in the Caribbean. A garden, generators, some living quarters."

"I thought it was supposed to be a whole new society," Lauren said. "A new world."

"We were only in the prototype phase," said Brandt, sniffling. "That's what I was going to announce at the meeting. A recruitment program. One hundred people, Delphi employees, selected to be part of the first Eschaton prototype society. A two-year pilot program to test and learn, work out the kinks before we rolled it out on a larger scale."

"A prototype," Lauren repeated. "But you never announced the program. You didn't even go to the meeting."

Brandt winced and began blubbering again. "I got scared," he said, hanging his head. "There was some communication flying around the morning of the meeting, and I started to get an idea that something might be happening."

Dominic's neck bulged. "And you didn't try to stop it?"

"It was too late!" Brandt screamed, ropes of spittle flying from his lips to the floor. "It already had too much momentum by then. And the groups responsible—they thought I'd ordered it. I couldn't stop it. Not without—"

"Losing face?" Dominic interrupted. "The whole fucking world died, you asshole. You fucking killed it."

Brandt shook his head, first slow, then faster and faster. "No. I didn't do anything. You don't understand how . . . how *hard* it is, running an organization with as much complexity as Delphi Enterprises. The scale of it, the magnitude. There's no way for one person to manage it all—but they all expect me to, they look to me. And so I pretend, and they hang on my every word like . . . like *children*. I talk in meetings and they jot down everything I say, they take it into their corners and they pore over it, they puzzle over it like it's holy scripture. They turn it into assignments, into projects; they give it to their underlings and say, 'Here, this is what Brandt wants, make it happen,' and the rats scurry into their corners and make their monstrosities, whittle away at the fabric of everything that's good because they think someone told them to. They're all just trying to please their bosses, who are trying to please *their* bosses, who are trying to please *their* bosses, all the way up to me—but I'm not in control, don't you see? The whole thing is a machine, but I'm not the one running the machine, no; I'm just another cog in the machine. It's . . . it's an *artificial intelligence*, is what it is. You want someone to blame, blame that. Blame *it*."

Dominic turned away. His hand was flexing around the gun. Jane could tell he wanted to use it.

Lauren's chin turned slightly up. "So we're not special," she said softly. "You didn't choose us. You didn't save us. And there's no utopia waiting for us. Is there?"

Brandt looked down again. "No," he said.

"And Jacob," Swati added. "He *is* dead."

Brandt nodded, head still hanging. "Yes."

There was a long silence. Jane made a decision. She walked to Dominic and put her fingers on the gun. Dominic glanced up and met her eyes. She tried to communicate something with her gaze—perhaps she'd never talk again, never be able to communicate what had happened to her or what she'd seen, but she had to try, and she had to try now. If someone was going to kill Brandt, she wanted to be the one to do it. Perhaps she couldn't communicate everything that was inside her with only her eyes, but hopefully she could communicate enough. It worked: Dominic nodded, then let go of the gun.

Jane walked back to Brandt and pointed the gun at his forehead. His eyes bulged with sudden fear, then he closed them.

"Yes," he said, calming. "Yes, please. Please Jane, yes."

He put his hands on the barrel, pulled it hard against his skull.

"Do it," he said. "Come on. Just do it. Fucking do it."

But she couldn't. Not now. Her resolve had been firm when she'd first taken the gun from Dominic—she'd never shot a gun, never wanted to, and certainly never wanted to kill anyone, but if she was ever going to do it, now would be the time: staring down the man who'd sexually harassed her, then murdered billions of people across the world and blamed it all on the company he'd created. But then he started asking for it, and now she couldn't do it. He'd ruined it. She clenched her teeth and tried to gather her resolve once more. She began to tighten her finger around the trigger.

Then, noises: the chop of a helicopter rotor, thundering footsteps on the roof, crashing glass, and a dozen male voices shouting at once.

"Drop the gun!"

# SEVENTEEN

They poured into the room, black-clad, rifles out. A SWAT team, or maybe military, special forces—Lauren didn't know. She should have put her hands up, probably, but she was so disoriented by everything that had happened in the last ten minutes that now she couldn't move at all, not even when one of them rushed up and pointed his rifle at her. The man's face looked like that of a giant beetle, with huge black eyes and a segmented polyhedron mesh of mouth and nose that Lauren only belatedly recognized as the breathing apparatus of a gas mask. All the figures wore them, a dozen or more.

"Clear!" the man standing in front of her shouted, his voice reverberating inside his mask, and Lauren jumped—what could this outburst mean? That he was about to shoot?

But it turned out he wasn't yelling at her; he was shouting back to some rear guard, perhaps through a walkie-talkie embedded in the mask. He lowered his gun, then the others lowered theirs, all but the figure standing before Jane, who was still holding the gun at her side.

"Jane," Lauren hissed across the room. "Put it down."

Jane looked at her hand as though she'd forgotten the gun was there, then set it on the floor. The figure in front of her lowered his gun.

There was a click. They all turned. The office door came open, then another man came walking in. He had the same mask on his face, but he held no weapon, wore no body armor. He carried himself with the bearing of an officer, a man accustomed to seeing his orders followed. There were decorations on his chest, his shoulders. The men parted to let him through as he strode across the room, boots clomping heavy on the tile.

He walked up to Brandt, who was still kneeling. Then the man lifted his hand and grabbed his mask by the breathing apparatus, pulled it off his face. He was a stern old military man, his cheeks deeply lined, his hair close-shorn.

"Tristan Brandt?" he asked.

"Yes," Brandt said.

"Sir, I need you to come with me."

Five seconds of silence ticked by, then Brandt stood. His clothes had gone rumpled in all his sniveling and pleading, his shirt come untucked, the tails visible underneath the hem of his suit jacket. He shoved his shirt back into his pants, ran his hand flat around the inside of his belt line, pulling the wrinkles smooth. His back straightened. He adjusted his tie, tugged at his cuffs—and just like that, he was back: Tristan Brandt the CEO, Tristan Brandt the billionaire, Tristan Brandt the master of the universe.

"Where are you taking me?" he asked.

Lauren waited for the answer—to prison, to justice, to court, to some international tribunal where wise judges would reckon publicly with the thing that had happened to the world, and with Brandt's part in it.

But the officer didn't say any of that.

"The government is reforming," the officer said. "Rebuilding. We need your help."

"There's still a government?"

The officer nodded. "A remnant. Enough to take back control. Enough to keep things from sliding into chaos."

"What's the death rate?"

"Our analysts estimate at least seventy-five percent globally," the officer said. "Ninety in some places, where the gas was heaviest. Major cities got the worst of the attacks, but some smaller cities and outlying areas escaped mostly unscathed. Our real problem now is the chaos that followed the gas. Infrastructure, supply lines, governance, policing—it's all gone. All it took was a little nudge to topple the global order. That's why I was sent to find you. We understand that you've done some work on this sort of thing."

"You want to rebuild," Brandt said. "You want to start from scratch."

"Yes," the officer said. "There's a council. You're wanted on it."

Brandt nodded. "Of course. I'd be honored."

Lauren was unable to speak. It seemed like an absurdist play—the words barely made sense. Only now, at the end, did she process what was happening: Brandt was not being punished for what he'd done, but rewarded.

"But what about the gas?" she asked.

Both men looked at her.

"What about it?" the officer asked.

"It came from *here*," Lauren said. "The end of the world started *here*. At Delphi."

Brandt shook his head and turned back to the officer, mouth open, about to deny it, but the military man nodded. Brandt's mouth clicked closed.

"We know," the officer said. "We know about the weapon. It was a government contract. Delphi was developing it for the military. Some intel analysts looked at this whole thing a few weeks ago, concluded that some fanatics must have infiltrated the company and stolen the chemical to mount their attack. I saw the report." The officer looked to Brandt. "You were cleared of any wrongdoing."

"But that's not right!" Lauren cried. "He knew! He could've stopped it, but—"

"I WANT HER TO COME WITH ME!" Brandt bellowed suddenly, interrupting her.

"What?" Lauren asked.

"She needs to come with me, this young woman," Brandt said. "And her friends. All four of them. I want them all on the council with me."

The officer paused, then nodded. "That's fine."

"I don't understand," Lauren said.

Brandt turned and walked toward her. "Come with me," he whispered. "Please. We can rebuild it together."

Lauren pulled back. Brandt was ugly, up close. Not at all like she'd expected him to be. Visible black pores on his nose, a scalp glistening with sweat, his skin like a wax sculpture. He looked dead, preserved. His bottom teeth were yellowing, and under the tailored suit he smelled of panic and body odor. Maybe this was what Jacob had learned, the discovery he'd died for—that Brandt was evil, empty at the core.

"I thought you were an oracle," Lauren said, her voice low, so the officer couldn't hear. "I thought you knew the secret to everything."

"That's just branding," Brandt said. "I'm a businessman. Just a businessman."

All at once she understood. It was a contract, a bargain, a trade. Silence for power, a seat at the table. They'd keep quiet about what they knew, what they understood—and in exchange they'd have a voice, a say in the shape of the world to come.

"Lauren." She turned. It was Swati.

"Our new world," Swati said. "Maybe this is how we make it."

Lauren shook her head. "It can't be. It can't be the way."

She looked to Dominic. Surely he'd have a plan, some way to fight back against this insanity. But she saw in his eyes that he too was on his way to surrendering, to accepting this terrible bargain.

"You too?"

He shrugged a helpless shrug. "They gave us the jobs they didn't want and asked us to thank them for it. They killed everything good in the world and expected us to be grateful. You think they'd just let us take it, after all that?"

Lauren turned her eyes to Jane, wondering for the millionth time what knowledge lay behind those eyes. What she'd seen. What Brandt had done to her. Perhaps she'd speak again one day, tell them everything. For now, she nodded. Even Jane. Lauren sighed.

And maybe this was simply the way things were always done. Every new generation swore to themselves that they would be different, different from the hacks and the sellouts who had preceded them—yet hadn't the temps simply recreated the same corporate hierarchies and political power structures in the wreckage of Delphi Enterprises? Hadn't they spoken the same empty words, carried out the same workaday rituals? Hadn't they even created religions for themselves? Weren't they turning into their parents, their bosses, even now? The trick was not to avoid this transformation; the trick was to let yourself be co-opted—to morph into your mom, your supervisor, your CEO—while still preserving something pure and good inside. To flatter the old man slowly handing over the keys, never forgetting your own plans for what you'll do with that power once you've got it in your hand. *Yes sir. Thank you sir. You're absolutely right sir.* Maybe this was the price, the cost of inheriting the world. Was she willing to pay it?

Lauren turned back to Brandt and the officer. "There are others," she said. "In the main building. They're running out of food."

"We'll send another party," the officer said. "We're evacuating the whole city. Your friends will be fine."

Lauren took a deep breath, pausing in the moment, the before. Once she said it, then it would be real, and there'd be no turning back.

"Okay then. We'll come with you."

The officer nodded, then whistled through his teeth and twirled his fingers in the air above his head. His men retreated from the room.

To Brandt, Lauren added, in a whisper: "Don't forget what we know." A warning, in case he ever forgot who was really in charge.

"I won't," he said.

And then the soldiers were back in the room, putting gas masks on their faces, hustling them out, rushing them upstairs to the roof, where helicopters sat waiting for them, rotors pulsing.

Brandt and the body doubles went with the officer to a smaller helicopter, but the others were escorted to the large helicopter with the other soldiers. The soldier running alongside Lauren put a hand between her shoulders and pressed her into a crouch as they came under the rotors. Lauren's hair whipped around her ears. She clambered into the helicopter, then sat in a seat just opposite the door. The soldier strapped her in, then moved to the back of the chopper, toward the tail.

The rotors sped up, and the helicopter lifted off the ground. The sunset blazed in shades of red and orange through the open rectangle in the side of the chopper's hull. Lauren closed her eyes. The sun's orb was implanted on her eyelids, a flaring afterimage.

Up and up they went, then the helicopter pitched forward and they were streaking through the air. After a few minutes they banked right, the tilt giving Lauren a view through the door toward the ground as they veered over the city. The straps strained against her shoulders. Her hair hung past her cheeks, like vines curling into her field of vision.

Below was the wreckage of the city. Some buildings blackened, others razed. Cars piled on top of each other on the freeway. And, everywhere, bodies: bodies decomposing and bodies newly dead, bodies sprinkled over the ground in their clothes, bodies being picked at by birds and squirrels and raccoons. A city overrun with the dead.

Then the helicopter straightened, and the sunset came into Lauren's vision again.

"We're clear!" a voice shouted from the cockpit.

The air outside the helicopter began to clear, to drain of its yellow hues. The soldiers began to take off their masks. They worked their jaws, dragged fingernails through their hair, then leaned together and muttered things Lauren couldn't hear over the hacking of the rotors.

Lauren undid her own mask, then looked next to herself, where Dominic and Jane and Swati were strapped in. Swati sat closest to her, her eyes glistening. Lauren ran a hand over her own face and realized that she, too, was crying.

"Swati," she said, and her friend turned. "What are we doing?"

"We're making it new," Swati said.

It was nothing she hadn't already heard, what Swati was saying, nothing they hadn't talked about together many times before—but Lauren heard it now and felt a sudden panic. They were impostors, here on a lie. Surely they'd be found out.

"But are we qualified?" Lauren asked.

Swati laughed. "No. But I don't care. *He* didn't. He just made the world what he wanted, made it in his own image. Now it's our turn."

Lauren felt Swati's hand curl around hers and give it a squeeze.

Yes. Swati was right. Something in Lauren's chest began to lift, to rise. It was hard to see, from here, how they could ever rebuild what had been destroyed, how they could replace it with something better than what had come before—but maybe that had always been true, since the dawn of time. The future was always unimaginable, and the world was always ending. New worlds were born perpetually from the ashes of the old, and every moment was a fresh apocalypse—an end and a beginning wrapped in one.

Lauren smiled and squeezed back.

"Okay," she said, and turned her eyes once more to the sunset, which blurred through her tears like an ever-burning fire. "Okay."

• • •

# ACKNOWLEDGMENTS

I'm incredibly grateful to Stephanie Beard for seeing something worthwhile in this book long after I'd given up on it. Her enthusiasm for the story has been instrumental in making *The Temps* what it is and bringing it into the world.

Additional thanks are due to the excellent team at Turner Publishing and Keylight Books, most especially to Todd Bottorff, Lauren Ash, and Ezra Fitz, each of whom went above and beyond in their support throughout the process.

My friends Christian Dahlager, Bryan Bliss, and Leigh Finke all read early versions of this manuscript, sometimes more than one version of it, and encouraged me not to give up on it. I'm grateful to each of them for insisting to me that there was something here worth sticking with.

I'm beyond fortunate to be able to depend on the constant love and support of my family—particularly that of my wife Sarah, my first and best reader, my sharpest critic and my biggest fan. Thank you, Sarah, for all the joy and meaning you bring to my story, every single day.

# ABOUT THE AUTHOR

**Andrew DeYoung** is an author and editor living in St. Paul with his wife and two children. His debut novel, *The Exo Project*, was the winner of a Minnesota Book Award.